A TASTE OF PASSION

Lyric plucked a velvety golden peach from a bright blue bowl. Cocking her head, she rubbed the soft fuzzed skin to her cheek. Looking directly into David's eyes, she took a large bite, her lips trailing over the torn flesh. The overripe fruit's juice burst out and ran down her slender wrist.

With one gentle move, David cradled her wrist in his palm and brought it to his mouth. Slowly as a cat enjoying cream, he licked away the nectar. He kissed the faint blue thread of fluttering life just below the thin skin of her wrist. David pulled her nearer and took a great, slow bite from her ripe fruit, then released Lyric's wrist.

"Would you like one of your own?" she asked innocently, gesturing toward the blushing golden peaches.

David leaned on one elbow to recline regally, like an emperor on his couch. "Actually, I want yours," he said with a flashing smile.

LOVE SPELL NEW YORK CITY

LOVE SPELL®

February 1996

Published by

Dorchester Publishing Co., Inc.
276 Fifth Avenue
New York, NY 10001

Printed in the United States of America.

To Vincent, who took the greatest challenge of his lifetime with the words "I do." Thank you. I still "do," sweetheart, now and always.

—Lark

To John: He always believed I could—and made me believe it, too.

—Sandra

And especially for Nolan: till we meet again.

ACKNOWLEDGMENTS

- Joanna Cagan, our editor, for her kindness and wise advice.
- Natasha Kern, our agent, for making us tough.
- Robin Givens, for truly knowing and loving the real me. Darlin!
- Kim Cannon, for having the courage to stand by me through thick and thin...and an unforgettable night with Anne Rice and Courtney Love.
- Gloria Callihan, for reminding me to rise above it, like a true Southern lady.
- Helen Wusso, for drying many tears and being my oasis.
- Nora Roberts, for her genuine kindness.
- Firemen of Germantown Station #3, Shift A, for letting us play with their equipment.
- Rita Madole, for her painstaking critique, brilliant suggestions and so much more.
- Kathryn Falk, for opening the door to romance.
- Shirley Hailstock, for her enthusiam and help with our career.
- Barbara Christopher, for taking the chance to be friends.
- Allison Ferguson, for being my cheerleader.
- Libby Afflerbach, for her years of faithful support and encouragement. We've been around the outside course together more than once.
- Letty Parks, a sister in pursuit of the art of words who always has kind words for me.
- Cherrie, Pat, Kathleen, and Robin, for welcoming me in a strange place.
- Annie and Nolan, for their unconditional furry love.

Flames of Rapture

Prologue

Salem, Massachusetts—1692

"To the burning post!"

A woman's shrill voice pierced Sarah's consciousness. "Send her to Satan. We'll have no witch in our midst."

They led her to the outskirts of town, bound like a hobbled beast. A stabbing pain shot through her, radiating from below her navel. She stumbled to the hard cold earth. Two men gripped her beneath each arm and jerked her back to her feet. Sarah felt a warm trickle from her womb as the fragile soul of Dante's child tore away and seeped from her body.

She drew near the execution post and realized it had been erected in front of Capt. Wolfton's home. She would die there, steps from his front door, for his morbid satisfaction. Sarah could see her own meager belongings were to be the kindling used to fuel the fire for her death. Her precious loom and spinning wheel had been broken and tossed into the heap of dry wood piled at the base of the central pine column. The resinous pine would blaze like a tall candle.

The frenzied crowd gathered. Vicious taunts were hurled like stones, bruising her soul. Here and there excited men carried blazing torches, swinging them to make them roar and flare smoke into the still air.

She heard a disembodied voice read the proclamation: "Seamstress Sarah Morgan, the village of Salem will tolerate no witchcraft in our dominion. Your sin of consorting with the Devil and conspiring to commit treason with your husband, the traitor Dante Huels, has been exposed."

Her eyes closed in grief for the infant she would never hold close to her heart. A baby Dante would never know.

A man lashed her quickly to the wooden post. "Mistress Morgan . . . I'm sorry," he whispered, his lips scarcely moving. "Forgive me, 'tis all I can do." His eyes met hers as he slipped a small pouch around her slender neck.

At least someone had compassion. The pouch contained gunpowder. The explosion, though fierce, would spare her the crowd-pleasing slower agony of death in the flames.

Storm clouds boiled above the bleak house. The air was charged with supernatural energy that did not approve of what was about to take place.

The crowd quieted as attention swung to the balcony above the front entrance of the house. The shuttered doors swung open with a crash. A squat man with small gleaming eyes strutted out. Sarah saw him pause and survey the restive crowd, as if basking in the victory of the moment.

She would be a public sinner, sent to her reward by his decree. Her example would serve to warn any that had been tempted by her beauty and manner. He was powerful and he was righteous. And only he, in his heart, and Sarah herself, would know why she was dying for his pleasure today.

Capt. Quinton Harrel Wolfton posed above Sarah, leering at her in triumph, gripping something tightly. He raised his arm slowly, dramatically revealing his prize. From behind her snarled curtain of hair, through the mist of restrained tears, she saw Dante's red coat held high as a trophy.

Dante was dead. Dead.

There was no pain, only loss and anger. Uncontrolled rage churned deep inside her brain. Suddenly the power from within surged forth, projecting its life and energy as each word Sarah uttered met and merged with the undulating angry clouds.

"Darksome night and shining moon,
Hearken to this witch's rune.
East then south, west then north,
Hear! Come! I call thee forth!"

Sarah's eyes met and locked with Wolfton's. She spoke clearly and commandingly. "What you hold is not yours to own. A spell of justice I do empower. My wrath you will beg never to have stirred." Her voice vibrated with otherworldly potency as the crowd recoiled in terror.

"Capt. Quinton Wolfton, I curse your soul with entrapment and bind it in the house you stand." Deafening thunder rolled, and the now silent crowd cringed.

"Possession of that garment binds your soul never to leave this land.
Dust you were and dust you shall be.
By all the powers of land and sea,
As I do will, so mote it be!"

A brilliant chain of lightning wildly lit the sky to seal her last covenant.

"Open the gates of hell." Wolfton's gloating words mocked her. "Light her bed of fire."

Chapter One

New York City, the present

Through a filmy drizzle, Lyric Solei watched the taillights of the New York City coroner's van disappear into the cloak of night. She stood numbly within the area marked off by the yellow tape emblazoned with the words CRIME SCENE.

Shining yellow, the same color as the ribbons in the little girl's hair. Ribbons that Lyric had first seen in her vision over a week ago. Yellow, the color of vitality, now represented death in its most gruesome form: the sadistic murder of a child.

Television and tabloid reporters alike clamored and shouted urgent questions from behind the police barriers, calling into the dilapidated old autobody shop. Each was jockeying for position to get the first story involving the new police chief who was nowhere to be found at the moment.

Their search for the police chief momentarily unsuccessful, someone in the mob spotted Lyric.

"It's Lyric Solei, the psychic investigator. Ms. Solei, Ms. Solei." The Channel Five reporter's voice rang out above the rest, breaking Lyric's daze. "You've worked successfully on so many previous murder investigations with past Chief Harrison, how does it feel to be ignored on this case?"

"Please." Lyric shielded her face and turned away from the cameras. "No comment." Escaping from the press and drawing close to where the body was discovered, she wove her way through what seemed to be every policeman, detective, and paramedic in the state. Not all of them knew she had been banned from this investigation, and those who did were turning a sympathetic blind eye tonight.

Jennifer Lee had been imprisoned in the mechanic's pit of an abandoned garage. It had been covered with sheets of rusty tin roofing and weighted with tire rims. No one heard the weak cries of a sweet three-year-old girl. She had just learned to ride her tricycle. The bright pink trike, the last gift her doting parents gave her, now lay motionless nearby. She had spent the final three weeks of her life in this macabre cement dungeon.

A fireman, smeared with ancient grease, ascended the steps, emerging from the opening in the tomblike pit. He cradled the innocent moppet gently in his arms, her messily braided pigtails flopping over his canvas jacket sleeves. Pigtails caught in bright yellow ribbons. She was limp.

They had missed saving her by only hours. Lyric tasted bile at the back of her throat and swallowed hard to keep from retching. Her hands trembled. The combined odors of human waste and fetid air made her gasp for breath. At the bottom of the oil-slick black pit, white chalk outlined a bizarre hop-scotch pattern where the body had lain.

She felt weak, powerless, guilty. With her psychic intuition, Lyric had helped to recover many dead bodies, even those of other children, but this was different. She stepped into the weary fireman's path and gazed into Jennifer Lee's face.

"I'm so sorry." Lyric spoke tenderly. She reached out and closed the girl's glazed eyes, breaking her frozen stare. Lyric stroked Jennifer Lee's cold cheek with the back of her fingers. Smudges of oil clung. "Blessed be, little one," she whispered.

As the fire fighter pushed past, one of the ribbons caught on a button of Lyric's jacket and slipped from the toddler's hair. Lyric grasped the greasy woven silk tightly. This tiny fragment was what she had needed. She pressed it to her lips. With this she could have found the lost lamb herself. But the police had refused to grant her a single clue, a touch of anything of Jennifer's. They had forbidden her parents to give Lyric anything, even to speak to her.

Now the ribbon carried a fading message for Lyric from the tiny soul. "Don't stop your work. . . . It's not your fault. . . . Remember me." Too late for help.

She tore her thoughts away from the ribbon and scanned the scene where firemen and detectives continued to mill about the cement tomb. Lyric had always thought of firemen as the heroes, but here they were just another link in the chain of unbelieving civil servants.

The killer had told Jennifer Lee it was a secret playhouse filled with beautiful dolls made especially for her. He had told the police he'd been inspired by the fairy tale Hansel and Gretel, only the "gingerbread house" was underground. It was easy to lure a three-year-old. So trusting. There was a copy of the Grimms' storybook buried with the youngster to keep her company while he was away from her.

She had finally died of heat exhaustion and lack of water. Her kidnapper was apprehended and held without bail for suspicion of murder. He spent three days in jail before he tried to cut a deal by telling where his victim was. Jennifer Lee had been saved from a more grisly death, but death was not kind, and it came nonetheless.

Lyric continued to search through the crowd for the specific man she held accountable for Jennifer Lee's prolonged torture. It didn't surprise her he had the nerve to walk right past her without so much as a glance. She knew there would be no apology. He was making his way through the myriad of emergency vehicles back to the safety of his black luxury car. It was obvious he wasn't man enough to admit he was wrong; more than likely he had never considered the possibility that he might have been mistaken. Lyric didn't fit in his equation at all, one way or the other. In the name of his pride and ignorance, someone had died.

"You just don't get it, do you?" Her voice was sharp with anger. It cut like a whip crack through the din of voices and traffic, sirens and city hum.

Police Chief Palmer Whitney Timmons stopped in his tracks. His khaki raincoat swirled in the New York mist like a sinister cape as he turned to face Lyric. Cigarette smoke escaped his lips and trailed behind him as he took three menacing strides toward her, fists rigidly balled by his sides.

"I told you I could have found her for you over a week ago. You could have found her alive then." Although furious, Lyric kept her voice low. "You should have let me try."

With another pull of the filterless cigarette, Chief

Timmons's mouth made a harsh straight line. A tiny muscle in his jaw worked with rapid tension. It wouldn't do for the reporters to see a spat between me and the psychic nutso, he thought. I'm Mr. Straight Arrow. And I'm staying that way. He flicked a glance toward the press corps, milling near the grease pit, camera lights glaring. Controlling himself, he let the smoke trickle out of his nostrils slowly. Behind him, a car turned, flashing its lights and throwing his shadow before him. The grimy haze and mist surrounded him with an illuminated aura, spreading for a moment like blackened wings.

"Look, psychic lady, or whatever you call yourself. *You* just don't get it." He stepped very close and jabbed at her shoulder sharply with his rigid index finger to drive home his point. He held the lit cigarette scissored tightly between stained fingers. "My job . . . *my job* . . . is to find people. Bad people, good people. Solve crimes. We are the police. We use facts. Hard tangible facts, not some sort of . . . inspired vision or memory flash you conjure up from something you hold in your hand . . . or the spicy food you had the night before." He punctuated this speech with several more jabs, cigarette ash spilling down Lyric's blouse.

"Your services will no longer be required by the Metro Police Department. Not that they ever were." Timmons took another deep drag on the stump of his Camel and blew the smoke slowly and deliberately into her face. He flicked the butt to the ground and snuffed the dying spark with his sole.

Lyric narrowed her eyes and opened her mouth to refute him. She was stopped by Timmons placing his forefinger to his lips briefly in a patronizing gesture, reiterating his own authority.

"I told you before and I'll tell you this one last

time." He wagged his finger at her, then pulled his pack of cigarettes out of his tailored shirt pocket. He paused to light another Camel, then stared directly into her eyes. "If you don't get out of my face with the psychic bullshit and out of my jurisdiction, I'll arrest you for obstructing justice, not to mention fraud and wasting my time. Do I make myself clear?"

First one newscaster and then another noticed the clash of wills. They charged toward the hostile pair, cameras aimed and microphones pointed like bayonets.

"This case is closed." Timmons turned his back to Lyric. He gave a confident wave to the press as the lights from the squad cars and paramedic units bathed him in a red glow.

Salem, Massachusetts, three weeks later

Steam rose, thickening the air as water plunged at full force into the deep claw-footed tub. Lyric Solei pulled her cosmetic kit and toiletries from her suitcase. She needed a soothing bath, a cleansing of the body and of the spirit to help her make the annual transition from hectic city to serene hometown.

Summer, sweet summer in her own house, filled with memories and treasures. As she did every year, she resolved to make the summer her own time, a time to forget the frustrations and abrasions of life in New York. Once she had welcomed the anonymity of the city, but now it only intensified her feelings of alienation.

Her work in the field of restoration and preservation of antique clothing had brought her material rewards. Her second line of work, as a discreet psychic locator of lost items, and sometimes people, had lately brought her only pain.

But this was summer, her carefree time. She would put away her severe work suits and bring out the graceful vintage clothes she loved. As a diversion she chose to make a project of discovering the history of the old house on Stage Road. There always seemed to be something haunting, yet beckoning, about that ever-vacant house. Perhaps this summer would be the time to discover why she'd felt drawn to peek into the tightly closed windows as a girl, and drive by the neglected gardens as an adult.

No better time to start than now.

She had brought several of her personal preparations of bath salts and other herbal compounds for her annual summer stay. There were plenty of shops in Salem offering all the necessary accessories and supplies, both for the tourist or the true Wiccan, but she preferred to use her own potions.

An exquisite hand-blown bottle held an evocatively fragrant bath mixture. As she drew out the wide gold-tinted stopper she smiled, remembering the day she bought the bottle in Cairo: a dusty hot Egyptian day.

Geranium for protection. The heavy, almost feline smell of the dry, dark red petals melded with the clean pine fragrance of the rosemary. Rosemary for remembrance. Over all, the Oriental topnote of the frankincense lent a mysterious accent. It was the persistent subtle aroma that hung in cathedrals and churches for centuries. Frankincense, for otherworldly vision.

Sprinkling a handful of salts and petals into the inviting water, Lyric said a quick prayer addressing the living spirit of the water. With her face tilted reverently upward, she spoke softly, entreating the

Goddess. "I feel there is karma for me in that house, but how? What is my lesson to be learned?" She looked down to watch the force from the faucet swirl the herbs and empower the fluid the great porcelain cauldron contained.

She was naked, adorned only with a unique gold medallion dangling from an intricately linked thin chain. The chain was long enough to allow the disk to rest just between her breasts. If moved to the left, the medallion would poise directly over her heart. The ornament was pure gold, about the size of a 50 cent piece, and quite heavy. She rubbed her thumb over the edge of the disk where tiny runes were deeply scribed, as if they were dancing a magic circle dance. The metallic texture was satiny from years of gentle abrasion against warm skin.

Twenty years ago, when she was six, her father had given her the heirloom pendant. He tied a special knot in the chain to allow it to hang properly on her thin young neck. As she grew, she had untied the knot and let the chain out, so always it had hung near her heart, her life's blood. It had been her mother's, and her mother's mother's, and so on, handed solemnly down the line of believers for generations.

Her father had kept it safe around his own neck after her mother's death, until the time was right for Lyric to own this part of her history. Lyric understood its power and mystery from the first moment she had felt it swing heavy against her skin, reminding her of her lineage. For these 20 years, it had stayed warm from her body's own heat, and alive. It had always protected and inspired her. It was her most precious possession.

From her first conscious thoughts, she understood that she had very special and important talents. As she matured, it became more and more natural for her to know the history of an article simply by holding it in her hands. Like an open book, images and impressions of the owner and uses of an item would reveal themselves. It was the gift that had shaped the choice of her life's work.

To hold a gown of yellowed silk, and see the weaver at the loom, then the seamstress at her task, and finally the bride dancing at her wedding, the garment's hem swirling in time to the music, was the wonder and delight of her calling. To handle a tattered shirt and know the agony of the owner's body beneath the browned dry slashes from a sword was the pain and distress of her skill.

Lyric stepped into the tub. The hot water engulfed her. Her pale skin quickly glowed pink from the warmth. Stretching out, she allowed the infused water to swirl over and around her breasts, her shoulders, every inch of her petite frame. She visualized her body, spirit, and soul becoming cleansed and purified. As she submerged herself completely, the water flushed through her auburn hair and rippled across her face.

She surfaced from the total immersion and leaned against the sloping back of the tub. As her mind became clear and calm, she began to focus on the steam rising from the water. She watched the energy change and soon a vision began to form. As the steam rose she began to perceive a hazy scene.

Look closer, her inner voice murmured. *Here is the first key to what you seek.*

The steam became mist. A shadowy figure of a man knelt at the foot of a massive oak.

Look deeper still, the voice instructed.

The lean figure wore a soiled red coat. Underneath the woolen outer garment, a sweat-stained tunic clung to his body. His shoulder-length hair hung in wet dark strings about his face as he bowed his head in apparent exhaustion. He appeared to have stumbled. He was bound with a leather strip that had worked a raw sticky channel around his wrists. Suddenly the man was prodded cruelly with a musket, knocking him flat into the trodden mud.

"Back on your feet, you filthy Colonial traitor. You'll not die yet," an armed man barked in a thick Yorkshire accent. Two soldiers hauled the captive roughly to his feet, putting in a few more cuffs and blows in the process.

The enlisted men drew back slightly in respect as a pale man in a rumpled but elaborate uniform stepped before the prisoner. "Nor nearly so pleasantly, eh, Huels?" The arrogant officer flipped open the prisoner's jacket with his riding crop and pulled a small packet of letters from the inside pocket. He tapped the folded paper on his palm and smiled unpleasantly before tucking the documents into his waistcoat.

He snatched a rifle from one of the nearby troopers, and shoved the end of the barrel under Huels's chin to pry his face upward. "You thought to prove treason, did you not, Huels? Well, indeed you have," the officer said with a sneer. His scalp shone through thin hair the color of faded pages. "Your treason. You and your whore-witch Sarah Morgan shall mock me no longer." He panted, his every breath labored with unwholesome excitement.

"Such sweet victory to see you both die at my command." His wide froglike mouth twisted into a sadistic grimace as his voice whistled and lisped through gapped pegs of brown teeth.

Huels slowly, painfully brought himself to his full height, towering over his captors. He threw back his head and a haunting face was revealed. Hooded, brooding eyes filled with sorrow and sadness, a sadness that did not appear to be for himself. A large slash on his left cheek oozed droplets of blood. His nose was swollen from a recent break. His lips were full, but cracked by thirst.

The parched sensation in Huels's throat was replicated in Lyric's own. She could feel his agony in all its intensity.

Suddenly she felt rough scratches at her left temple. The vision dissolved. She turned to confront the odd sensation and bumped noses with Nolan. The big black-and-white cat was sitting on the edge of the tub. He had licked a droplet of water from her temple as a loving reminder he was watching over her.

Lyric sat up and splashed the now-tepid water on her face and swished little waves over her body. She said a quiet thanks for the unusual message. Its urgency was clear to her but not its meaning.

"Oh, Nolan. What could all this mean? What could this have to do with that house?" She pulled out the plug and visualized all the negativity that had surrounded her spiraling down and draining away with the herbal water.

Lyric stood slowly and stepped out of the tub to dry herself with a soft towel. Her skin retained the alabaster glow from the water's early warmth, but she noticed her fingertips and toes had shriveled and pruned. Her bath had seemed like only minutes.

Absently regarding herself in the bathroom's old-fashioned pier mirror, she was still in the groggy limbo between this world and a higher level of consciousness. Lyric smoothed over a small crescent-shaped birthmark on her inner left thigh. It was a most intimate tiny brand. In older times this little mark would have surely cost her her life for having been thought the signature of something black and fiendish, the touch of the Devil himself. She knew it was simply a reminder of her enchanted heritage.

Lyric reached for her gown. She had purchased a new nightgown to celebrate her summer freedom. The emerald green silk reminded her of the gowns Celtic queens wore when women ruled with their wild strong consorts by their side. The fabric wasn't appropriate for that period but this was her fantasy, not a history lesson. Green, the color of life, hope, and new beginnings. The color made a striking contrast to the thick rust mane tumbling down her back.

Relaxed and ready for a good night's rest, she lifted her cat and draped him across her shoulder like the leopard skins of an ancient Egyptian priestess. Nolan was a great source of comfort and love.

As she stroked Nolan, she turned the haunting vision of the bound man's face over in her mind. Why was she given this sight as a clue to the country house's identity?

She crossed the room to the great carved bed that had been hers all of her life. It waited for her untiringly, through the years when she had traveled all over the world, and still waited when she lived in New York and yearned for its comfort. The graceful necks and heads of swans stretched up toward garlands of grapes and roses carved into the dark walnut posts. The wings and bodies of the swans spread down into the headboard, and frisking foxes played across the length of polished wood. Puffy down pillows lay in a drift, full of the buoyancy of fresh sunshine. The crisp white linens were turned back invitingly, and the fresh evening breeze already brought scents of night-blooming flowers into the room. Nolan slid down Lyric's back like water and disappeared into the next room intent on his own nocturnal pursuits.

Tomorrow, she thought sleepily, my discoveries start tomorrow.

Chapter Two

With one final hard stroke of fulfillment, the task was complete. David Langston rocked back on his haunches. Sweat trickled from each temple and glistened on his neck. He was spent.

"You're beautiful," his throaty voice whispered. The flats of his palms caressed and stroked the object of his affection.

The old door was finally sanded smooth.

The sun dappled spots of shade and light around the backyard of the old house on Stage Road. A stray sunbeam shot a glint off the chrome trim of David's big red-and-black Harley-Davidson parked under a spreading oak. A neat row of paint cans, stripper, and brushes sat on a makeshift bench nearby.

David stood and wiped across his breastbone, through a small tangle of dark hair, and over to his right shoulder. Leftover sawdust made a gritty mixture with his own perspiration. David winced as he accidentally grazed a tender patch of flesh.

He looked down at the emerald and plum scales texturing the serpent tattoo that rippled with every flex of his right shoulder. Coiled in a figure eight around a medieval sword, the snake devoured its tail while keeping a menacing jewel red eye on any observers. The self-inflicted wound was still tender and raw. The sharp pain of the grit made David hope the inner pain would heal soon as well.

His grimace was only temporary as he reflected on his decision to make an outward statement to himself.

The serpent had chosen him, leaping at him through the haze of butterflies and skulls. David remembered the night he'd made his decision to start a new life. He had found himself at Skin and Bones, the local tattoo parlor. Numbed to the eyeballs on grief and not quite a dozen beers, he felt no physical pain as the sharp needles sewed a symbol of new beginnings into his flesh. The last bit of itchy brown scab sloughed off just this week, leaving new, delicately tinted skin. Like a butterfly freed from its grotesquely decaying cocoon, David was pleased with both the tattoo and the changes in his life.

It was Thursday, and he had the morning for his own before tonight's duty at the fire station in town. He was intent on pouring every spare minute he had into reviving the structure that someday would be his home. The house would be the symbol of rebuilding his life after grieving so long for his loss. He had spent the whole 28 years of his life in and around Atlanta, Georgia, and had never before given thought to putting roots down elsewhere. But now he had a reason to transplant himself and no reason to stay in Atlanta, so here he was. The more energy he exerted, the more he began to connect with his new surroundings.

The structure of the house was basically sound. David wondered why no one else had ever been compelled to look beyond the neglect. He smiled, secretly glad no one had. He'd always enjoyed creating something beautiful from a thing others ignored. A lovingly restored old car absorbed his attention as a teenager. Later it had been battered furniture, stripped and sanded into useful and admired antiques. This would be the biggest project yet, but he felt confident. He was patient.

As he stood with his hands on his hips, a welcome sea breeze sent fingers of coolness over his fatigued muscles. David surveyed the back walls of the scaly gray monster of a house he meant to resuscitate.

David walked through the house, seeing the rooms the way he imagined them when he would be finished. The kitchen, now gloomy and smoke stained, would be sunny, with pale yellow walls and a fire in the fireplace. A long trestle table would stand in the center of the room. He knew just how he would build it, and rub the pine with oil and wax to make it smooth as butter.

The walls of the entry hall had once been painted with hunting scenes, tiny riders and horses, little green trees and white fences. This would be a restoration beyond his skills; perhaps he could read about it and learn how it was done. David touched one of the little mounted figures carefully, but a dry flake of paint came away at his touch.

He frowned and brushed his fingers on the leg of his jeans. He looked up the wide stairs that led to the bedrooms on the second floor. The rooms to the rear had sweeping ocean views.

The room that ran the entire length of the front

of the house had a vista extending across the front yard, taking in the carriage drive and circle, and down the long shady drive that led to the county road. He had spread his old sleeping bag there, and claimed it as his.

"Little by little," he said softly to the dusty empty rooms. "Then they'll all know you have a history to be reckoned with." He turned and went back through the kitchen to the backyard to continue his work.

W. Hayton Weems leaned back at his desk. The overloaded chair made a small tired shriek of straining metal and wood. Weems picked up the newly signed check and waved it absently as he stared out the grimy window of his real estate office.

Finally sold the old house. On the books for years. In fact it would be a real trick to find just who to send the check to. Probably the county would get the profit for back taxes. After he took his commission, of course.

A good thing that mushy-talking Southern boy had wandered in, looking for a "fixer-upper." Well, he sure had one now. Nothing like a newcomer in the community to get the real estate values hopping. Weems grunted out a chuckle.

Real estate had always been in his blood, but as long as Weems or anyone in his family could remember, that house had been vacant. None of the locals would have it as a gift, even if they were all too young to remember the reason why. Some just had a feeling about the tattered old hulk. Two stories of creaky floors, age-splintered banisters, rats, and overgrown vines.

Every wavy hand-poured glass windowpane was intact in the ancient chestnut frames. Generations of local mischief-makers hadn't dared to throw a rock at the malevolent window eyes. Shutters carefully planed to fit over the precious panes now sagged loosely. Last year's big storm had ripped off roofs all over the town, but not a single shutter of the mansion had been dislodged despite their apparent fragility.

A once-graceful carriage drive had circled up to the front door, but the gravel was lost in rank weeds. Strangling foliage grew everywhere, in fact, except at the very center of the old turnaround. The earth in the center remained stubbornly, totally barren there, as if acid had been poured to sterilize the soil of any precious energy.

An involuntary shiver touched Weems despite the summer day's heat, and he rubbed his hands up his arms as if something coldly repulsive had touched him there. He was glad he hadn't had to take the young man over and show him the house. He remembered his grandmother's stories about the colony of bats that still swarmed out of the old garret door near the roof.

Weems waved the check gently near a fly that had landed on the lip of the dirty soda bottle on his desk. The fly hesitated, then stepped closer to the enticing opening. With a quick downward clap of his palm, Weems propelled the hapless fly to the bottom of the bottle. The fly struggled vainly in the sticky residue. Fourteen. Weems smiled thinly and set the bottle on the windowsill.

Grandmother once mentioned the house had been in his family, but she never would tell him any more about it. She mumbled about a curse on the house, or something like that, and shut up tight. Hell, these old houses in New England were all cursed, he reflected. Cursed with bad plumbing, leaky roofs, bats in the attic, and nosy neighbors.

He guessed the Southern gentleman would find all that out. Kind of closemouthed, the stranger was, but he had written a check in the amount that Weems had asked, at a 1953 price, too. He wished he had updated the asking price on the house, but there hadn't been any interest in the wreck since he had been working here at Salem Real Estate, OUR MOTTO: HOUSES THAT WILL CAST A SPELL ON YOU.

Well, he had gotten rid of the white elephant. And it was paid in full . . . written out right here to him, *Pay to the order of Wolfton Hayton Weems.*

They were near. The dust stirred across the floor in tiny eddies unrelated to the still stale air trapped inside the dead rooms for so long.

Near, yes, so near. I need the energy of the tall man and the wily woman with the flaming hair. Even now she has the ember hair that drew me so, once long ago.

Near. The moisture of the blood will bring power, strength and power. And pleasure. Yes, pleasure. Because these two are special, so very special. They were the ones who trapped me here. Here in the dust, the ashes of age.

Once he had hunted and drawn strength from the ones of little blood, little warm things that brought the warm moisture. But he had lost his power, taking this little blood of little things.

Yes, she was the one who drew me to the end, to this shameful end of skulking in the dust, until I am the dust, drinking the blood of the little ones that squeak and squeal softly in the night, and rustle and fly out when the moon comes up.

But he couldn't leave. Not to leave and ride and whip and see the wonderful blood, the blood of life.

He was bound in the dust, in the house, to this tiny plot of land where once he ruled, where blood once flowed for his pleasure, at his command. This bondage was painful, so painful. The dryness, the powerlessness. He suffered, and while he suffered, he planned.

At last. I knew they would come. I can wait forever, but now I know the end is near. The end. They will bring me their blood, and their power, and I can escape. I will escape, have my revenge, and leave them to be the dust.

The ashy dust, the dust that laid so thick in Wolfton House, moved and formed.

Where the dust is, I am, and I am everywhere.

Chapter Three

Lyric decided to make a morning expedition to the house that she had termed her summer project. She dressed in soft old jeans and a sea green brushed silk shirt and picked up her car keys for the trip out to Stage Road.

Alerted by the jingle of the keys, Nolan dashed outside and sat expectantly by the car door. Lyric opened the door for him and he hopped in majestically. She rolled down the window for his sniffing satisfaction as he curled his paws under him and assumed his traveling pose for the trip to the country.

The pleasant drive out of town took her past tidy houses with summer gardens full of the season's vegetables and bright flowers. Lyric kept the car windows open to enjoy the sights and smells of the morning-fresh country scenes, so different from her surroundings in the pollution-dulled city.

As she drove, Lyric thought about the old house, so secluded and beguiling, that had captured her imagination on her childhood rambles into the countryside. She still hadn't really made up her mind if she would enter the forbidding door or just peek into the windows. Why did the place unnerve her so? What could the vision of the tormented bound man mean in relation to this decaying old house?

She knew she needed to resolve the menacing vibrations she'd always felt from the house and understand what, if any, was her deeper connection.

Maybe more could be learned simply by looking up its records at the county courthouse. Yes, perhaps that would be a good step. Perhaps she should visit the town tax office first and talk to some of the old-timers there and gather what tidbits of history she could.

At last she reached the narrow turnoff that wound into the Wolfton property, marked by a crumbled stone column on either side. The piles of rubble seemed to be held together only by the efforts of the tangled vines that swarmed over the fractured mossy stones.

Her father had told her that once the area on both sides of the drive had been a lush English-style country garden, with sculpted hedges and tumbling rose arbors. It had fallen into disuse and decay long before he or even his grandfather had driven past the low fieldstone walls. Now the slightest outlines were barely discernible in the absence of a gardener's discipline.

The drive was almost invisible under a lush growth of lazily leaning wildflowers, grasses, and runner vines. Swaying tree limbs reached close overhead to form a tunnel of leafy darkness diminishing into the distance.

Practically no one ever drove out here. The seclusion of the house appealed to her, but also made her uneasy. It was almost eight miles from the nearest highway. The town had grown away from this area, perhaps blocked by the apparent reluctance of any of the citizens to buy Wolfton land.

She thought again of her plan to visit the security of the town tax office rather than the unusual house itself. Then the haunted face of the man in the red coat rose before her eyes. He was no coward. Would she be one?

A faded Salem Real Estate sign leaned drunkenly in the dusty roadside grass, but a fresh, bravely yellow SOLD! sticker had been hastily slapped over the almost unreadable paint.

Sold? Who would be willing to put in the love, time, and effort for something of the past like the timeworn dwelling hidden at the end of the tunnel? Perhaps someone else had found the allure of the building as compelling as she. The sign was the motivation for her decision. It would have to be now, before a new owner changed the spirit of the house to his own.

Lyric turned into the old lane, driving as carefully as possible, leaning slightly forward in the seat and gripping the steering wheel with both hands. She forced the small car slowly down the drive, grimacing involuntarily as she heard the wild plants rake and scrape along the car's dark blue paint with strong vegetable fingers. She hoped there were no big rocks hidden, lying in wait for an unwary oil pan or transmission. A single faint trail of crushed grass led down the weed-carpeted driveway.

Lyric stopped her car on what was once the gracious circular drive for the original owner's carriage. She imagined lacquered black wooden carriage wheels and horses' dancing hooves crushing the same stones. Now sullen tough weeds wrestled with the pebbles for dominance.

There it stood, as forbidding and tantalizing as she remembered it. Weathered shutters and grayed board siding covered secrets that yearned toward her like sad, sick children. Although often imagining another life within the once grand walls, Lyric had never dared to violate the seal and step through to confirm her fantasies and fears.

Lyric got out of her car and closed the door softly. She could hear the gentle moaning of the wind in the tall pines nearby. She slid up and sat on the car fender for a moment and took in her surroundings. The boom of the waves on the nearby cliffs was muted, but the salt tang of the air was sharp and fresh. Somehow the sounds of wind and waves only made the silence deeper. The house still looked empty; the new owner evidently had not claimed it.

All houses had a soul and this one seemed to breathe with a melancholy sadness that spoke to Lyric's heart. Then again, there was always a feeling of sinister secretiveness whenever she approached it.

Nolan put his forepaws on the car windowsill, meowed, and sniffed the summer breeze. His whiskers twitched as he spotted a tiny movement under a brown shrub by the door. Suddenly he leapt out the car window and raced down the crumbling brick path. His field mouse quarry made a hurried escape through the narrowly open door with the cat fast behind him, scattering leaves in his enthusiastic pursuit. Nolan's hunter instinct forced the issue and made a decision for Lyric. She couldn't leave her beloved familiar; entering the house was now unavoidable.

Lyric gingerly made her way down the front path, trying to avoid the thorns and burrs standing guard, reaching their sharp spears toward her jeans and bare ankles. She avoided the turned and missing bricks on the steps and hesitated before opening the door. Clasping her hands together, she looked around the facade one last time, taking in the dead vines, the weathered gray wood. Taking a deep breath, she unlaced her fingers and reached for the smooth brass handle. A sudden gust of wind swept the door from her grasp, as if someone had jerked the door open in a rude welcome.

For a second, Lyric stood on the sunlit step, apprehensive about confronting the darkness that lay inside. The door hung open before her, the wind calm once more. What did her senses tell her? There was life here. She felt a presence permeating the house.

She stepped inside, unconsciously treading as silently as possible. "Nolan," she called in a hoarse stage whisper. The sound of her voice did not comfort her. She found herself as quiet as the mouse being hunted. Far inside the rooms she heard a small rustle; then all was silent.

To her left was a large drawing room with an imposing fireplace. The carvings on the white marble mantel gleamed dully through their shrouds of cobwebs and dust. She was surprised the house had not been pillaged long ago. None of the usual signs of invasion, the wanton destruction of anything beautiful, was to be seen. Only the decay of time.

The wooden floors were carpeted by drifts of ashy dust and even a few leaves, but seemed in almost perfect condition. Here and there she could see the trail the new owner had made as disturbances in the deep dust, big footprints next to the small marks of the field mouse trails that laced like ghostly ribbons across the broad floor planks.

At the right a staircase led to the second floor. Ah, there . . . Nolan's fresh paw prints led clearly up the stairs.

"Nolan!" she whispered as loudly as she dared. A faint meow came from far upstairs.

Lyric started slowly up the steps, feeling more and more like a trespasser. She could feel an aura of disapproval radiating from the walls around her. One step, then two. She reached out to the banister, but quickly withdrew her hand when the thick dust coated her fingers like soot. Nervously she wiped her fingers across her thigh, and left a charcoal black streak. The third step gave a loud squeak that sent her hopping up the next two steps in startled reaction. She paused on the next step to let her heart stop pounding.

Get a grip, she scolded herself. It's only the same old house you've seen all your life. Calm down. Tune in if you're so scared. Her guardian angel voices had been silent so far, although her common sense was telling her to find her cat and scram.

She steadfastly took the bull by the horns and strode more briskly up the remaining steps. Six, seven, SQUEAK! . . . nineteneleventwelve and thirteen on the landing.

The upstairs seemed lighter, and the spacious landing opened into a wide hall leading right and left past other rooms. Lyric called "Nolan!" again as loudly as she dared, then saw a faint pattern of cat tracks in the dust. She followed them into the first room in front of her and walked in softly.

These windows were unshuttered, and Lyric was

struck immediately by the dramatic view of the ocean from the large many-paned windows. The elevation gave a panorama of miles of empty blue-gray ocean, the horizon stretching away into silvery infinity. A ship passing into the town's harbor would go on parade past the eyes in the ever-watching house. Black wet boulders of the steep coastal cliff tumbled into the sea right below the house itself.

There were a few articles of furniture left in the room, obviously not those of the new owner. Here was a large leather-bound chest with the lid thrown open. The rock-hard leather bindings were scarred by sharp mouse teeth. Near the chest, a faded wing chair sat, directed in such an angle for an occupant to take in the unending passion of the waves crashing on the unyielding stones below.

The contents of the chest had been pulled out haphazardly, spilling onto the floor. Muted colors and frayed laces mingled in fragile disarray. A tangle of clothing tossed on the chair lay as if they were lovers' discards. An air of stolen intimacy hung in the empty room like old smoke.

At the bottom of the pile something peeked out, mutely begging to be picked up. Lyric touched a homespun red sleeve trimmed in narrow black-and-white braid. Momentarily forgetting her earlier apprehensions—and her missing cat—Lyric rummaged gently through the garments. She pushed aside a dusty heap of faded green-striped brocade and yellowed linen so frail as to be practically transparent. She suppressed a sneeze as a small cloud of dust puffed out of the folds. Tugging carefully, she freed the rest of the article. A man's coat.

She felt a tingle of excitement begin when she realized the age of the garment was within the period of the house's early construction. It had to be well over 200 years old, probably more like 300. Discovery of the history of garments like these was her career. Years of study in Europe had fine-tuned her skills to identify any type of fabric and garment, even to recognize the dyes and technique of weaving. But what made her the best in her field was that amazing inner talent, her ability of psychometry, the capacity to touch an object and know the maker, use, and owners. What would this mellow old coat say to her?

She flexed the fabric gently between her fingers and held it to the light to closely examine the weaving pattern and technique. The fabric was amazingly firm and undamaged. The woman who had spun the wool and woven the cloth plainly was an artist in her craft.

Lyric held the coat up before her. It had been made for a man of good size in that era of small men, she mused. Held suspended by both shoulders, it almost dragged the floor. It would fit a tall man today, one with broad shoulders. The styling was military. It reminded her of something; last night's vision, the bound man under the tree had worn such a coat.

Brass buttons had been firmly attached long ago. The buttons were tarnished green by the sea air. She held the coat to her face and inhaled deeply, and caught a smell of smoke, and an underlying tang of musky sweat. The sweat of fear or of love?

She held the coat to her face, and the first tendrils of the vision of its past leapt toward her. Urgent tremors of communication swept into her head. First a great swell of love, but that was quickly smothered by fear, waves of fear, and desperation. *Danger, her life was in danger, but so was the life of someone she loved.* The adrenaline from 300 years past began to pound through her veins as she clutched the coat closely to her chest.

Rusty dry hinges squealed, followed by a crash. The door downstairs slammed shut, shattering her concentration. Heavy boots clattered in the echoing entryway. The sound ripped into her vision of the past, scattering it like the sea foam on the rocks below. Footsteps started up the stairs. The third step gave a shriek of warning, and the footsteps paused.

Lyric froze guiltily; the coat slipped from her grip. An unreasoning panic knotted her stomach. She glanced around the room frantically. No place to hide. No closets in the room. All the horrid tales of assault in isolated places rushed into her head.

Between the choice of assault and the embarrassment of being caught trespassing, she preferred recovery from the latter.

Only a few steps before her intrusion was discovered. The footsteps began again. The eighth step groaned. Desperately she searched for a means of escape. With a rush of relief, it came to her. The windows. Lyric fumbled to open the nearest window. No luck; it was sealed shut by decades of grime. The dirt of the backyard seemed to be a mile below her.

The door was her only hope. She dashed across the room and pressed her slender body against the wall behind the door, forcing herself not to breathe. Her pulse pounded in her ears. Fear wadded in her throat and begged for release.

The door swung open. Her fate stood filling the doorway.

Lyric stood rigid, collecting energy to flee as a mouse gathers energy to make a desperate sprint. The man was close enough to smell. It was almost familiar, a clean scent mingled with the earthiness of exertion. An irrational attraction tugged and intrigued her. Sex and danger must have the same odor. She was held captive by her own fear, mesmerized by his erotic aura.

She peeked cautiously through the crack between door and frame. The man was at least six foot three, wearing tight jeans and a baggy faded-to-gray sweatshirt with the sleeves ripped out. When he turned slightly, Lyric read ATLANTA FIRE DEPARTMENT lettered across his chest. Crimson droplets spattered across the lettering, and there were brilliant red smudges wiped on his jeans, arms, and face. He held a pointed stake coated in the same red liquid. Residue of the thick, sticky substance was beginning to congeal at the point. Lyric had always had a romantic place in her heart for vampires but dying like one now didn't appeal to her. She held her breath.

He surveyed the room briefly, then turned. Lyric saw a flash of the same hauntingly intense dark eyes that had stared at her through the steamy vision the night before.

Lyric's senses were engorged and overwhelmed. Her thoughts collided. She strained to hear as the man's footsteps diminished. She counted as her heart beat 100 times—the longest minute of her life. That was it, all she could stand. She would come back later to find Nolan.

She slipped cautiously from behind the door and tiptoed back to the landing. She crept down the stairs, mindful to skip steps eight and three. Out the front door, almost free. In her haste, she stumbled over a loose brick from the steps and skidded over the gravel. The jagged pebbles ripped through her jeans and shredded the flesh on her left knee. Searing pain shot through her leg as she scrambled to her feet and limped the rest of the way to the car. Blood soaked the denim around the gash.

Lyric groped to find her car keys. She fumbled to slip the serrated metal into the slot and start the engine as quickly as possible, eyes focused on her escape.

"Is this what you're looking for?"

With a gasp, Lyric whirled to see the mysterious man at her window. Nolan's chubby body was cradled placidly in the man's powerful arms. The cat's white patches were smudged with the sticky red stuff that spattered the man's shirt and jeans.

Panic began to strangle her. *Composure, composure,* her mind was shouting. "Yes, he's mine." Her voice squeaked. "I'm sorry for the intrusion; he just leapt out." She hoped he couldn't recognize the quaver still in her throat.

"Are you lost?" The man squatted next to the car door, so close Lyric could see the jet stubble piercing his skin. It shadowed and defined the strong lines of his jaw, intensifying dimples which served as quotation marks to set off a slight smile.

As she looked at the stubble of his beard, an illogical fantasy popped into her head; him in nothing but the full foam of shaving lather, white against tan. The edge of the straight razor would scrape across his jaw with a faint rough sound. The cold blade would cut a swath across his taut skin and skim his plump ripe lips, clean and sharp. The lather would smell like mint. He would turn sideways to her, away from the fogged mirror, and smile slowly. She could feel the ivory handle in her own hand.

His eyes smoldered seductively beneath suspicious brows. He peered so intently at her she knew he was watching her thin silk blouse leap with every galvanizing beat of her heart.

"I thought the house was empty," she said, eyeing the cat now asleep and strangely comfortable in this mysterious man's arms. The steering wheel felt slippery and warm beneath her nervously sweaty palms. "I've always been curious about this place. Guess I never thought anyone else felt the same connection." Anxiety was making her insides hum and her words run out too quickly.

"Well, you know what they say . . . curiosity killed the cat." The man dropped his smile. "Guess you want him back."

He stood up and slipped the drowsy feline into the backseat, lightly brushing the length of his forearm against the back of her neck. The touch seemed to go on forever. The strong woody odor of turpentine struck her and she realized sheepishly the red smudges were paint, not blood.

Lyric was startled at how her skin tingled under the warmth of his touch. She had a brief image of how Nolan must feel cradled in those powerful arms. As he pulled his arm back gently, there was a light trail of gritty residue left on her skin. The simple gesture stirred an acutely sensual emotion within her. The thought of this man coaxing a purr from her flashed through her mind, causing her feminine muscles to twinge.

"Anyway, this house is my destiny now. If I can ever scrape away all the layers, I'm sure there's something rewarding just beneath the surface." He spoke with assurance, standing with his thumbs hooked into his belt loops, looking across the peeling facade.

Lyric's breath was not stolen by fear, but rather the powerful pull of alarmingly confident sexuality. "Thank you for finding my cat. I'm sorry to have bothered you." She spoke abruptly in the tension of the moment and hastily released the emergency brake. "Good-bye." As she accelerated out the drive, she caught a glimpse of him standing alone in the driveway, his figure spotlighted in the glaring noonday sun. Had she seen that form, that handsome body, before?

Chapter Four

"Langston! Quick, come look at this." David's friend Ben called to him from the rec room at the fire station. "Man, you gotta see this. Carwell Winston is at it again. This time he's got one of our local celebrities under the gun. He's gonna grill her about witchcraft and psychic stuff." Ben motioned for his friend to come out of the kitchen to join him. "She's a pretty hot-looking redhead."

"How can you watch that awful 'Invasive Eye' program? Can you believe it's nationally syndicated?" David punched the ON button on the dishwasher and came out of the kitchen, his cleaning duties finished. Everyone but Ben and he had already scattered for the evening. David gestured toward the TV with his full Coke can. "Besides, I'm not into all that hocus-pocus."

"Well, neither am I, but check out the guest. She lives here in the summer. Has an old family house around somewhere. I don't think I've ever seen her, though. I know I would have remembered that face . . . angel eyes and fantastic hair, from what I saw of the opening clips. Body that would stop a freight train, too." Ben took a piece of popcorn from the bowl and threw it at David. David was wearing his favorite T-shirt emblazoned with bright red lettering: HUG A FIREMAN; FEEL WARM ALL OVER.

Ben adjusted the volume and shook more salt onto the popcorn. "After all, expiring minds want to know." He popped the tab on his can of Coke as a punctuation to his statement.

"How can people believe in this bizarre psychic stuff? It's hard enough to trust the things you can see, much less things you can't." David jammed a hand into his side pocket. With his right hand, he waved the Coke can derisively at the television screen.

"Lighten up, Langston. Just tune out the sound and watch the pretty pictures. I guarantee this woman's worth watching."

The friends settled down in the comfortably furnished rec room for a little evening entertainment. A long blue couch stretched across one wall, faced by a large-screen color TV. A wooden coffee table and battered hassock stood in front of the couch. A large basket of magazines and newspapers overflowed next to a nearby recliner chair.

The walls were cluttered with framed awards and citations earned by their unit of fire fighters. One frame featured a newspaper article picturing Ben in his turnout uniform, smiling broadly, holding a bedraggled kitten at the base of his fire truck's extension ladder.

David slouched on one end of the couch and stretched his long legs. "I guess this can't rot my brains any worse than the paint thinner out at the house." Scooping up a handful of Ben's popcorn, he munched as the opening credits to the show rolled. He propped his boots on the battered hassock.

"Good evening and welcome to 'The Invasive Eye.' " A short, pompous man in a shiny white polyester suit spoke smugly to the camera. His steel gray hair was carefully coiffed into a blow-dried swelling and sprayed to rigidity for maximum sheen.

"Didn't he used to sell used cars in Philadelphia? Went up on fraud charges or something?" David asked. "Turned his car dealership into some kind of religion and had old ladies sending in their pension checks." He licked the popcorn butter from his fingers, and reached for another fistful.

"He's a real weasel. Those stupid yuppie suspenders and those goofy blue glasses . . . He thinks he's so superior to all his guests. Mr. Suave." Ben provided the color commentary. "You know his hair transplant didn't take," he gloated, ruffling his own thick brown hair. "It's a rug. That's why they never show a side shot. I hate him. Everybody does. It's part of his appeal."

"Why are you watching this?" David flipped a piece of popcorn into the air and caught it in his mouth. It was a skill he had perfected as a teenager and continued to polish carefully.

"This woman tonight is supposed to have some sort of special talent for finding lost people, especially children. She's not your basic beachfront gypsy fortune-teller. I hope she really gives him hell. Plus she's a real knockout." Ben winked at David and turned his attention back to the screen just as the announcer was coming back from the commercial break.

"Tonight we would like to welcome Ms. Lyric Solei, museum curator and free-lance psychic detective for the New York Metropolitan Police. I'm your host"—he paused breathlessly and rolled his eyes for maximum effect—"Carwell Winston."

Winston turned and addressed his guest in his best professionally greasy tone. "Ms. Solei—or would you prefer to be called Madam Solei?" The smarmy interviewer laid out his first shot of condescension. He glanced over his glasses into the camera lens to include the viewer in his confidence.

"Ms. Solei will do, thank you." Lyric's firm voice broke in before he could continue. She kept her composure, obviously aware of the barrage of questions about to besiege her.

"Good, good. Don't let that self-righteous bastard get the upper hand." Ben leaned forward and coached the TV screen enthusiastically.

David sat hypnotized, his popcorn forgotten. This was the woman who had watched him this morning in his house. Her elegance was stunning. David thought her voice resonated as clear and pure as a crystal goblet struck with a silver spoon. Her voice seemed to carry all the colors of the rainbow in its tone. It took his breath away. Or perhaps it made him breathe faster; he wasn't sure. Her grace and unpretentiousness were a sharp contrast to Winston's slick attitude and appearance. David felt his palms start to tingle as she spoke.

A tailored peach-colored silk suit showed her delicate features to the nation. The color was perfect for her creamy skin. The quality and refinement of the understated style and fabric spoke for her taste and attitude just as Winston's flashy artificial diamond pinky ring did for his.

A white chiffon blouse peeked from beneath the jacket's collar. A gold medallion gleamed at the vee of the neckline, and Lyric reached up and dropped it behind the blouse fabric in a smooth motion. The suit jacket was modest and almost puritanically plain, but hugged and caressed her full breasts. There was no hiding the woman within. David noticed her beautiful legs, long and shapely, the kind of legs short skirts were made for.

David didn't see any damage to her knee. Probably this show was taped. *Hey, right!* He had found her cat's tag. He had a reason to talk to her, to see her again. He rubbed his thumb over the small bump in his watch pocket. What would Ben say if he knew that little tag was in his pocket right now?

"Is this taped?" David took a sip of his drink and acted casual. Suddenly the cola didn't seem very cold.

"Yeah, I think it's a week delayed."

Her hair was braided and coiled very high on top of her head, in one of those ageless classic designs. Perhaps this was her method of appearing a little taller, since she was quite delicate. Her hair was a spectacular red color, and proved unmistakably that she was his guilty trespasser this morning. It emphasized the slenderness of her neck, the fragile ivory nape exposed. David wished he could see that beautiful braid undone and wound around his fingers, spread over his pillow. . . . He stuck the cold can between his legs and crossed his ankles on the hassock.

A snapshot of a smiling three-year-old flashed on the screen. Her bright blue eyes sparkling with mischief, she had her arms flung around a tolerant mutt dog. David felt a familiar sadness wrench in his gut, for the woman and the child.

"Recently you were involved in the search for this abducted little girl, Jennifer Lee Jenkins. Over the last two months practically everyone in America has come to know this sweet, innocent face. She was eventually found dead in a sealed concrete tomb. The police had spent weeks using scientifically proven methods of investigation. They are trained to know what to look for and yet they found nothing. What made you think you could reveal any missing clues to find this child?" Winston made his first tactical move; a reasonable-sounding question.

"I have helped to find several missing children in the past, quite successfully with the aid of my psychic guides," Lyric said with composure. "Usually there is no—"

"So this isn't the first time you've wasted the taxpayers' money and the police's time." Winston cut into her explanation. "How do you feel about profiting from these poor parents' misery?" He put on his best pious manner and paused to inhale for his next onslaught. Her answer really didn't matter to him.

Lyric took advantage of the pause. "First, I would like to make it clear that I am not a paid employee of any police department." She could obviously play this game as well as Winston. "I offer my services without charge to anyone. In regard to wasting their time, in my opinion the police wasted the last critical moments of Jennifer Lee's life by not acting more quickly on my intuition. My heart goes out to the Jenkins family. The death of a child is devastating, no matter what the situation. No one has profited here."

Winston ignored her intelligent answer as if nothing had been said. He plowed into his next innuendo-laden question. "You say you heed the voices of your spirit guides. Just how do you go about that? Do you hear voices from beyond the grave? Oh, I guess if they were from beyond the grave they would be too late." Winston grinned and goggled at the camera in a close-up as if he thought he'd scored a hit. Snickers went up from the audience, probably screened to support his viewpoint. "How about a crystal ball? Get good reception on that?" More snickers.

"My psychic guides are what you might call my guardian angels, Mr. Winston. They watch over me and protect me. Sometimes they help me to protect and help others." The camera swept to her face. Her emerald green eyes looked calm, but David thought he saw dangerously combative glints deep inside. Her eyes were the thing that had struck him this morning when he first saw her. Big and alight with intelligence, sparkling expressive eyes in that lovely face.

Ben shifted and took a long swig of his drink. "This is just a game to ol' Winny-boy to see how quickly he can strike his victim down into submission." He was still rooting for tonight's beautiful target to put Winston in his place. "It's just a matter of time."

"She seems to be the one in control so far," David answered. Would she be the wily, elegant mongoose, letting the snake tire itself by futile strikes, until she could sink her fangs into the serpent's neck and dispatch him with one well-placed crunch? He hoped so.

Winston added another of his witty comments. "Most people who hear voices from their angels also carry their clothes around the streets in a bag. You don't look like you got that suit out of a dumpster, Madam . . . I mean *Ms.* Solei." His eyes wandered lasciviously over her body.

David thought Winston's leer would leave a slimy

track like that of a garden slug. His sympathy for her grew. He hoped he hadn't looked at her like that. She was beautiful enough to inspire a stare from any male.

"By using your self-professed psychic powers to detect her location, you still couldn't save her from such a horrific death. Would you say this is your biggest failure to date?" Winston oozed another venomous question in his most unctuous tones.

Ben bounced back on the couch, popcorn flying. "Yeah! He's going in for blood now! Give him what for, pretty lady!" Ben cheered on his favorite. The program had been fairly tame up to now.

"I would say this is one of the greatest preventable losses I've ever felt. The failure, sir, to save this child was not on my part. Perhaps you should interview Police Capt. Timmons. He could verify that I had pinpointed the location of the child four days before he decided to act on my suggestion.

"Jennifer Lee could have certainly been rescued in time if the attitudes and beliefs of people reached beyond what they can only see, feel, taste, and touch. Sometimes you must have faith in a power higher than yourself."

David saw Lyric had not shifted in her posture. Her hands remained folded placidly in her lap. Her quiet body radiated complete self-possession. Why was a woman who could sit completely still so sexy?

Ben took up the cause of his heroine, although she didn't seem to need any help from him or anyone. "Is she cool or what? She's an ice cube. Most people cave in after the first couple of minutes. I've never seen anyone make him sweat like that."

Winston cleared his throat and sipped water nervously from his glass. He dabbed at his forehead delicately with a pristine white handkerchief. He applied his virtuous face, the one that he had practiced by studying hours of tapes of popular television evangelists.

"I understand you practice a religion called Wicca. Doesn't that mean witch? Are you practicing witchcraft? Have you been a deviant all your life?" Winston bombarded her with relentless, and not necessarily relevant, questions.

Lyric did not seem discomfited. "I was raised in the Wiccan tradition. Our beliefs are ancient. Wicca means 'wise one' and is also called the Old Religion."

David saw Winston shift and open his mouth to butt in. He gaped like a fish, opening and closing his mouth, trying to slip another double-edged question into the interview. He was plainly losing control. The camera seemed to prefer to linger on Lyric's cleavage instead of Winston's increasingly sweaty face. David empathized with the cameraman. Any shot of Lyric Solei was infinitely better than one of Carwell.

Lyric continued her explanation. "It is the worship and recognition of nature, the seasons and what they represent, the elements and the strengths they provide. It is respect for the world and universe in which we live. Wicca draws on all the senses in order to attain psychic and spiritual awareness to better yourself and help others. I believe you must be grateful, thankful for what you receive, and in turn give back to replace the energies you have taken. You may do what you will as long as it harms none."

The camera panned over the audience in a standard audience-reaction shot. David saw many faces that were previously hostile now softening, heads nodding in agreement. The demeanor of this woman gave the seal of truth to her statement.

Winston shuffled his question cards quickly, skipping to the more sensational ones he really liked. He was grappling to keep the audience on his side. "So do you sacrifice cats and drink their blood only on the full moon or just whenever you need the power?"

Lyric still held her self-possession, exercising incredible self-restraint, but David thought he saw a real flash of anger in her brilliant eyes.

"I bet she'd like to drink *his* blood right now," David joked. "I'd have probably decked him after the bag lady crack. What a pompous arrogant ass. Selectively deaf, isn't he? She just told him her beliefs were to harm none." He crushed his can and dropped it in the nearby trash bin.

"Jerk," Ben agreed, and tipped out the last of the popcorn bowl. "She's doing OK, though."

"We do not kill senselessly. Blood rituals are not a part of my beliefs or practice. As I said previously, harm none."

"Oh, so you're a vegetarian, too." Winston seized on the word *kill* and made what he thought was a splendid extemporaneous comment. There was no audience support, and he continued rapidly, "What does it matter if you kill anything if you have this reincarnation thing to fall back on?"

David and Ben groaned in unison. The man had no brain whatsoever.

"Reincarnation has nothing to do with killing. Reincarnation is the belief most Wiccans hold that we have lived before, and that we will probably exist again. As we pass though our incarnations, our lives, we try to perfect ourselves by lessons and experiences learned from previous lifetimes."

David listened intently and stored that information away for later examination.

Winston blundered on his way, hardly noticing that his interview was in shambles, himself a clear loser. "Since this last mistake disproves your theory, where do you intend to go from here? How could you continue to believe in something that has been proved false?"

For the first time, Lyric leaned forward slightly in her chair as if to give emphasis to her words. "I made no mistake here, Mr. Winston. My psychic ability is a divine gift. It is a gift that is in us all. In order to benefit from it, we must acknowledge it and embrace one another with support and love. You cannot have this challenging hatred of the unknown and all that you do not understand.

"This child could have been saved if there had been cooperation. One person cannot save the world from all the pain and hatred; it takes cooperation. Nothing has disproved my beliefs."

"Yeah! That's telling ol' ferret face!" Ben cheered for their beautiful champion. "Kick him again while he's down."

It was time to wrap up the program, usually a time when the guest was blithering in helpless rage. Since this was clearly not happening, Winston tried for a parting shot. "Well then, Ms. Solei, maybe you could give a sample of what you can do. Tell me something about my future." Winston sat back confidently as if he had regained his footing.

"Uh oh, you're in trouble now, slimeball," Ben crowed in delight. "Let's just hope she doesn't dial up his past or it will be Dealing for Dollars down at the car lot again."

The barest suggestion of a smile crossed Lyric's lips. "I'd be happy to let you in on your fate, Billy Ray. But I'd like to hold your hand while I do it."

She extended her small, perfectly manicured hand. "That is, if you don't mind holding hands with a . . . witch."

David saw Winston's eyes flicker at the use of the unusual name. Winston squirmed, but thrust out his right palm for inspection.

"I thought his name was Carwell." David flexed his hand and visualized her small fingers surrounded by his strength. His large hands could protect her from vultures like Carwell Winston. His hands could touch that beautiful hair, pull the pins out, spread it like auburn silk over her rounded breasts. . . . He blinked hard and tried to force his concentration on the screen.

Ben was absorbed in the final scenes of the show. "I bet he changed his name when he started doing this TV watchdog type of business. Guess he thought it made him sound more respectable. Still sounds like a used car salesman to me. Shoot, she'll probably see something really disgusting and won't be able to tell it on TV."

Lyric glanced at Winston's thick palm. The camera zoomed in closely enough to see trickles of sweaty moisture in the grooves. Lyric placed her fingers over Winston's palm and looked up into his face. David saw the slightest trace of a smile cross her lips again. She was gazing directly into Winston's eyes, a position he evidently felt hard to hold. He shifted his rodentlike gaze rapidly from her hands to her face and back down again.

"She's got him now. Those beady eyes are rolling!" Ben exclaimed. David could see Ben was plainly satisfied with the outcome of the battle. It was true; she was an extraordinary woman.

"Take care, Mr. Winston, of those you taunt. Someone is inquiring into your house as we speak and perhaps there are secrets inside you do not want public."

David thought he could see a glint of humor in her eyes.

"Perhaps we should discuss what is in your . . . closet?" Lyric asked in a mild tone, but her dancing eyes seemed to be saying something else altogether.

"Er, um, tell me what's in store for my future. I know what's in my house." Beads of sweat rolled from Winston's hairline. His eyes started to water as his mascara began to melt.

David grinned mischievously and said, "I bet he's going to kill whatever producer set this up as a piece-of-cake interview."

"Aww, why's he trying to change the subject? I bet he's got the biggest, slimiest secrets of all." Ben protested the change of subject.

This time Lyric's smile was more discernible.

"What? What is it?" Winston sat up tensely and tried unsuccessfully to disguise the nervousness in his voice.

"Divine justice can never be cheated. I see numbers, and large amounts of money, green and gold. Yes, it's very clear; I see you surrounded by accounts, ledgers, and balance sheets."

Carwell Winston's eyes glazed. "So I'm going to be rich, am I? Guess that's what you tell all the people."

"No, that's not what I'm saying. It appears to me that you will be audited shortly. I do hope your books are in order this time." Lyric sat back with a serene expression.

"Yes!" David and Ben howled with laughter. They pummeled each other and rolled about on the couch. What a hit!

Carwell Winston snatched his hand free and balled his fist by his side, rolling his eyes like a scared horse. He gabbled out the closing set lines of the program. "That's all for this edition of 'The Invasive Eye.' Join us next week for the Incredible Suck-a-Raisin Diet, and does it really suck. . . . Arggh! *Work!*"

The credits began to roll jerkily as the camera faithfully recorded a shot of Carwell hurriedly leaving the set and retreating in disarray, his notes spilling to the floor. Usually the show ended with glowingly heroic, carefully backlit depictions of Carwell as a white-suited crime-fighting crusader. Tonight the show ended with a single figure, seated tranquilly at center stage: Lyric Solei, clear winner.

Ben picked up the remote control and started flicking through the channels. "Man, she was great. Really kicked him in the gutter where he belongs. What a woman."

David nodded in agreement. She was more than great; she was extraordinary. She ate Winston for lunch and never broke a sweat. What a woman, indeed. Too bad she was a charlatan. She couldn't really believe in all that magic business. But knowing all that didn't seem to stop the turmoil she had started in his hormones.

David rose and stretched elaborately. "Night, Ben."

Ben settled back for the late-evening news broadcast and glanced good-naturedly up at David. "Yeah, good night . . . sweet dreams, since I can tell who you'll be dreaming about." Ben popped another can. "Me, too, I bet."

David left Ben to the rest of the night's TV and went upstairs for a shower, still thinking of the satiny feel of that delectable neck, the one he had brushed ever so lightly this morning.

* * *

Across town Lyric switched her TV off with a smash to the remote button. "That's it! What an absolute idiot." She slammed the pillow she had been holding on her lap into her chair. Several tiny wisps of down floated to the floor. Still furious, she picked the cushion up and squeezed it the way she would like to squeeze Carwell Winston's pudgy, self-righteous neck. She threw the hapless pillow back into the chair as hard as she could.

"Why did I ever agree to go on that stupid program?" In her heart she knew exactly why she had agreed: to help the public understand that psychics, Wiccans, and pagans in general were people, too. They were usually people who had a desire to help people with their talents, as misunderstood and mysterious as they might seem to be.

She picked up the pillow again and squashed it unmercifully. "I'm so tired of dealing with people who make fun of what they don't understand. I'm only trying to help." She huffed and stormed about her bedroom. "Why do I have to lay my heart and soul out on the line for their inspection? For what? They don't even appreciate what I'm trying to do."

Nolan, her audience, yawned an enormous cat yawn and clicked his fangs shut. He seemed colossally uninterested.

Lyric jerked the lace curtains to one side and glared out the window. Fireflies winked in the flowers below her window. Such a peaceful scene in the faint moonlight. She didn't feel peaceful. The new police captain had scoffed at her offer of help and practically laughed in her face. He had shrugged and coldly informed her that the case was closed.

Yes, that was how she felt. Closed. She would close herself away from all the disbelief and taunting. She was home now and did not have to deal with those sort of people in her own hometown. Ending her relationship with the police department was right.

Lyric touched her forehead to the cool windowpane and squeezed her eyes shut, trying to force the image of the little girl's dead eyes out of her mind. How could Capt. Timmons be so stubborn, so close-minded when a life was at stake? What difference did it make what methods saved her? Of course, it would cost his pride to act on her visions—obviously too high a price to pay for such a small, young life. The heavy face of the police chief flashed behind her lids. Her eyes flew open, dissolving his condescending smile.

Timmons seemed to take some perverse pleasure in setting her up. He didn't care what it had cost. The child was simply a pawn in a sick game he was playing with her, trying to prove she was wrong. He would prove that by-the-book was his way and the only way.

She had always believed that the men in uniforms were the good guys. Not anymore. One sight of a blue shirt and a badge and she was out of there. Any trust of a man in uniform was completely gone.

"I'm fed up with the police. The whole bureaucratic, civil servant lot of them." Lyric spun away from the window and drop-kicked the pillow over the bed and into the far wall.

It was right to end with the police for the same reason it had been right to end her relationship with Dr. James Patrick last year. She had met him at the art museum. He was a fellow historian, delightfully mussed and academic as he wandered about the crates and boxes while the complicated French Masters' exhibition was being mounted. There was an endearing smudge of dirt on his cheek. She brushed it off and he invited her to dinner.

She had gone against her inner voices, and stubbornly allowed the initial friendship to develop into intimacy. Her guides had finally sat back and let her take her lumps when she ignored their repeated warnings. No teacher like experience.

After two years, he had continued to indulge her as if she were a fantasizing child whenever she had mentioned her religion. And as for relying on her psychic talents for anything as large as finding a lost set of car keys, that was out around him.

When he finally started pressuring her to start seeing a psychiatrist, it was time to cut the losses. He was plainly not the one for her. Never mind flashing ice blue eyes, a fabulous tan, and a 32-foot sailboat. Lyric sighed. She certainly did like to sail.

"No more, Nolan. I just don't have the heart to do it anymore. If they know so much, let them take care of the lost ones themselves." Lyric scooped up the cat from the bed and sat down in the big rocker. She cuddled and stroked him, the way she wished she could be stroked. She began to rock and hum an ancient Gaelic lullaby. Her father would sing it to her when she was a child and feeling lonely after her mother's death.

Lyric rocked and sang, letting herself relax. Gradually the rocking slowed to a calmer pace. She caressed Nolan's round body and rubbed under his chin. "Nolan! Where's your tag?" Wolfton House; the tag must have been lost there.

Wolfton House . . . and its new owner. She remembered the fright and then the attraction. Pleasant emotions were disturbingly yet welcomely awakened by the memory of this afternoon. A confusion of feelings was triggered by the memory of this intriguing, distracting man.

His warm brown eyes, so alert and wary, like the eyes of a beautiful buck deer. His thick black eyelashes, long enough to cast a shadow on his cheeks. When she first saw his eyes through the crack in the door, it was like an arrow piercing her heart. She smiled and let her breath out slowly when that thought passed through her mind; just like a Valentine card, a heart and an arrow. She had felt it so strongly.

How silly of her to hide like that, to think the paint was blood. But in the hollow old house, things did not always seem to be what they were. Strange house, strange man.

Lyric rocked and absently fondled Nolan's soft fur. As she recalled the man's soft dark hair, ruffled by the wind, her strokes turned more gentle and tender. She would like to touch his hair, to brush it back and let it cascade and ruffle over her fingers; see it falling around his face, over her face, toward her. She imagined his hair damp after a bath and how it would feel rubbed playfully over her breasts, her stomach. Tickling her thighs . . .

The cat looked up as the rhythm of the caresses changed. He blinked wisely and stretched out his forelegs, stretching his white toes and basking in the attention.

Surely the man would return the tag. Her phone number and address were on it. She had felt an air of confused tension hanging around them at Wolfton House. Perhaps when they met again she would be more herself. And the dark stranger who made her heart jump? What would he be like?

Chapter Five

I bet she's more trouble than she's worth. David lay on his narrow bed at the fire station. He reached for the tiny red medal he'd found on his drive that afternoon. The tag was engraved NOLAN, and under the name, an address and a phone number. Dangling the tag from his hand, he pondered what contact he should have with this unusual woman who intruded in strangers' houses.

Tonight on the television program she had handled herself with grace and self-assurance, appearing to be in her element. At his house, she had seemed like a frightened child caught trespassing.

This morning had been the first time he had looked at a woman with interest since the death of his wife and baby. The guilt he felt over the deaths had acted as an effective barrier to numb any attraction to the opposite sex for the last three years. His lacerated conscience forbade him to take the chance of loving a woman again.

David had dreamed of a house full of laughter and footsteps of children, his and Margaret's children. Margaret had been intent on fulfilling his dream, although he had not realized her attempt at completing it would be at the cost of her own life.

Margaret would certainly disapprove of this woman and her strange beliefs. David's wife had been a woman of deep religious faith. A faith he had unquestioningly shared. Precious little good it did her, or him. He had prayed in the hospital chapel all night after Margaret had been admitted in premature labor. Prayed . . . oh, yes, how he had prayed, pleaded, bargained, but nothing had helped. Margaret and the baby both died. From that moment, David's faith and trust in a higher power was shattered; cynicism and skepticism filled the void neatly.

This move to a new town, in a whole new part of the country, was to be a fresh start in his self-imposed therapy of healing. The state of Massachusetts was certainly a different world from the friendly suburb where he and Margaret had lived near Atlanta, Georgia.

His colleagues at the new Salem station were friendly enough, and plainly pleased at his competence and quiet personality. But as always, something was lacking in his life. Something, someone, who had been gone for three years now.

His curiosity was caught this morning and further whetted this evening, to see the graceful woman with the brilliant hair. He thought of those big frightened green eyes staring up at him from her car window.

This morning he had known she was upstairs. When he stepped into the downstairs hall he had seen clear impressions of a stranger's feet mingled with his own scuffed tracks. The dainty impressions were too big for a kid and too small for a man. As he followed them through the gritty dust on the floor, he knew they were too small to cause much alarm. He'd dealt with dangers much larger than these and was more curious than worried. The tracks led him upstairs to the room he planned to make the master bedroom.

When he reached the room, he had scented a hint of flowers coming through the crack in the door frame. Most punky vandals smelled of spray paint, not spicy expensive perfume. It was plain she was not out to harm anything, but why had she been so frightened? The sensation of being feared by a woman was a new one for him.

He spun the little red tag in his fingers and continued his train of thought. Her fright had probably been justified. After all, how could she have known he hadn't meant to harm her? It was best for a woman to be cautious.

She had fallen and skinned her knee. It looked painful. He would have liked to bandage it for her, patting the tape in place, and perhaps adding a kiss to speed it back to the perfection he had seen on the television screen. How tender her creamy skin must feel, satiny and so soft at the back of her knees. Her effect on him as he had watched her devastate the posing interviewer had been a surprise, a feeling of attraction he had not permitted himself in a long, long time.

His curiosity was no less than the cat's. He would call Lyric Solei in the morning. Fate—whatever that might be—had dropped this little metal calling card right in front of him with her address and phone number on it. *Let's just call it opportunity.* It would be good to make another friend in this new town, even if he would not, he resolved, make her a romantic interest.

He placed the cat's medal on the nightstand by his bed. Reaching down beside the bed, he touched his boots and canvas coveralls, his turnouts, ever ready for the call to come. Prepared; always prepared. He turned off the lamp and pulled the plain white cotton covers to his chest.

Almost immediately, his breathing slowed and deepened with the onset of sleep. He felt himself floating, slipping into the dream he'd been having since his wife died. It was the dream he'd had again and again, and it held a frightening intensity and reality. David could see every detail, smell every fragrance, hear every sound, taste everything that so much as brushed his lips. The same woman was there every time, but he could never see her face. Or perhaps his memory simply erased it when he awoke; he wasn't sure.

Most disturbing of all, he could feel each touch, every texture, and feel his body respond to any appeal to his senses.

It started the same as always, very shadowy and dark. Then the dream sharpened into a vivid picture. The small room, the packed dirt floor, the dark wooden walls. The door had crude wide black metal hinges, with a leather string above a bar latch. The furnishings were spare: a long wooden table, bench, small spinning wheel, narrow loom, almost hidden by the shadows. The only light came from the bright blaze within the mouth of the fireplace that spread across the back wall. A vast bearskin rug lay in front of the hearth, the fur dense and dark in the firelight. A cat blinked in the darkness to the side, almost invisible but for its eyes.

The fire appeared supernatural, a divine substance, not the horrific stuff he battled on a constant basis. This fire was beautiful, alluring, hypnotic. A woman emerged from the darkness to dance sinuously before the lit hearth. She swayed and hummed to herself.

Shadows licked and caressed her breasts, and her long ginger curls spiraled to end between the dimples on her lower back. Spring wildflowers twined to construct a fragrant crown. The intoxicating female fragrance of early blossoms mingled with the smoky male scent of the fire, filling David's senses.

Arms outstretched, she held up a small wide-mouthed bottle. One by one she added pungent-smelling drops to a crockery jar on the hearthstone and began a lyrical chant.

> "Belladonna . . . hellebore . . . hemlock . . .
> hemp flowers, I command your strength and
> charge ye with all powers. To aid in my astral
> flight, Amidst a witch's most potent hour."

With hands on her rounded knees, she bent to peer into a black iron cauldron. Her face was hidden by a sparkling veil of her ember-bright hair.

This was as far as he had ever dared let the dream take him. Always before he had willed himself into consciousness, waking before letting the action proceed. Tonight he let it continue. . . .

The door opened quickly and a man stepped in. He threw his flintlock musket upon the table impatiently and stretched out his arms to draw her in.

"Dante." The woman rushed to him like an ethereal creature. Unashamedly, she pressed her lush nude body against his rough woolen jacket. "At last you are home. Beltane is not a celebration one wants to spend alone," she said with a bold smile. She took his hand

and led him toward the warm hearth. He smiled an acknowledgment and followed, skirting her spinning wheel.

"I've missed you, Sarah." His husky deep voice vibrated as he drew her close within his arms. Sweeping her up on tiptoe, pressing his urgency against her, he buried his face in the slender arch of her neck. He drank in the sweet fragrance of his woman. His tender nuzzles turned into nipping and biting kisses as he ravished her creamy skin.

"Patience, my love." She slid from his grasp as liquid as mercury and pooled at his feet on the thick bear fur rug.

He sat on the raised hearth and allowed her to remove his black leather boots. "Patience be damned!" he exclaimed as he shrugged off his threadbare blue coat and tunic and tossed them across the crude wooden bench.

"Welcome back to the arms that shall always love you," she whispered, rising to her knees and running her hands up and along the inside of his long muscular legs and thighs.

The fire hissed and crackled, blazing behind them. Dante's tension mounted firmly in anticipation beneath the tightening laces of his trousers. A long low groan of welcome escaped his lips as the woman released his restrained masculinity.

"This is our moment to share ecstasy. The ancient rites demand this sweet, willing sacrifice," she said slowly and deliberately.

Cupping Sarah's face with his callused palms, he drew her lips to his eager mouth. His tongue sought depths deeper than her soul. With great tenderness his velvet kisses explored their way toward her firm ivory breasts. He languished over each nipple with a hard suckle. Roaring inside with desire, he laid her gently on the dark fur rug. His breath fanned burning coals into rapturous flames that licked her most secret places. Restraining his own pulsing needs, he continued his quest to drink from the secret chalice. Dante knew her arousal was approaching euphoria.

Dante reached for the jar of ointment which had warmed and softened beside the fire. He dipped into the pudgy crock, withdrawing a handful of oily warm lotion that dripped between his slender fingers. Slowly, sensuously, he began to draw a trail of the fragrant salve down the path he had just made with savoring delight.

"The perfect night for flying ointment," he said.

Sarah murmured her approval. Her flesh trembled with every stroke of his fingers. Reaching up, she slathered some of the mixture from her body across Dante's chest muscles and down to stroke his rigid interest. Their bodies glistened in the firelight.

"A celebration of sowing the seeds," he said, parting her thighs with his knee. As Sarah trembled, she gave off an erotic sparkle. Covered in the slippery concoction, she slithered beneath his powerful body.

"Of death . . . and of procreation. Spill your seed into the full richness of my womb, my lover, my husband," she purred.

"Damn!"

David bolted upright. The shrill alarm bell tore him from the warm arms of his dream. He looked down to confirm his feeling that his dream had crossed over into reality. Ten seconds to pull on his turnouts, slide down the brass pole, and rush away to the call of danger and the call of responsibility, forgetting the allure of a dream woman in a dreamland, long ago.

Chapter Six

A night sky of India ink black, spangled with stars flickering like white votive candles, spread its peaceful canopy over Lyric's garden. The white roses cast their rich scent on the warm air, faintly glowing masses of blossom in the starlight. Beautifully silent, nothing stirred or was heard except the mild summer breeze stirring the walnut tree branches to click and rustle.

Midnight exactly: the witching hour.

The thin white cotton robe Lyric wore swirled around her bare ankles as she stepped outside. The wooden porch floor was cool against her bare feet. Tonight called for the symbolic color of purity, innocence, and good. She paused, looking up at the crescent moon that hung low and large in the eastern sky, accompanied by its bright companion of the season, Venus.

Lyric touched her medallion and lifted it to rub

across her cheek. She stepped down into the garden, feeling the energy of the summer earth flow into her, up through the naked soles of her feet. As always, it was good to touch the earth, to feel the strength of life eternal pulsing against her, even in the air that pressed her gown lightly against her body. Nolan appeared by her side, as if he had materialized out of the dim moonlight.

"As is above, so also below." She addressed Nolan, and picked him up to drape her familiar over her shoulder. She stroked her cat from head to tail. "Would you like to join me tonight?" She stroked him again and placed him at her feet. He sat purring and blinked up at her in his wise way, patiently willing to participate, to add his animal innocence and energy to the power of her prayer.

Lyric stood before the ancient stone sundial that was placed at the very center of her garden. It had been there as long as she could remember, gray rough granite, strong as the cliffs surrounding the sea. The broad base seemed to grow from the earth itself. As a child Lyric had played ring-around-the-rosy here with her friends. Yes, it was a fitting place to memorialize and say good-bye to the child.

Tonight the sundial would serve as an altar for a ceremony, a prayer and ritual that would help Lyric close and free her emotions disturbed by the loss of the little girl in the city. The rite would restore the necessary harmony to Lyric's inner life.

She laid her ritual tools one by one on the stone, giving grave thought to the meaning of each, in order to center her energy and begin the ceremony with reverence. Her athame, the white-handled dagger, gleamed in the starlight. Next Lyric placed a chalice, engraved with twining vines and the waxing and waning faces of the moon, near the knife. The chalice was filled with dark red wine. She could smell the sweet fragrance of the grapes, rising keenly on the clear air. The reflection of a single star quivered in the flat mirror of the liquid.

A small earthenware bowl the size of a cupped hand held a mixture of seeds. Each seed was dry but held the symbolic and real promise of new life. The unglazed terra-cotta still wore the trace of the maker's fingers in its rhythmic ridges. A brass censer, shaped like a pomegranate, but pierced to let perfumed smoke escape, was next to crowd the stone top.

In the center of the circle, Lyric stood a perfect crystal bell with delicate traceries of silver filigree twined around the handle. Finally she balanced a faultless abalone shell near the brass censer. The iridescent shell held pure rainwater. On the ground at the foot of the stone column was a traditional black iron cauldron and a metal box of matches. The cauldron was half-filled with white sea sand to form a bed for pinecones and needles, and slivers of fragrant oak and applewood. It would provide the final ingredient, that of fire. All the necessary elements of earth and sky were represented.

Lyric was ready to begin. Taking a deep, cleansing breath, she covered her face with both hands. She released her breath, stretching her arms to the sides and down, and spread her fingers. Holding the athame and facing north, across the stone altar, she began to build a circle of imagination, of protective thought, a visualized incantation that would allow her to draw a barrier of protection around her as she performed the tasks that allowed her to touch the face of her deity. In her mind's eye, the knife left a trail of blue energy, flashing with purple sparks, flowing into an aurora borealis of invulnerability to ring the sacred space she was creating.

"Hail, guardians of the watchtowers of the north. Powers of earth be here." There was a great rush of wind as the energy of air and earth began to awake and course through Lyric's hand and down her dagger. Closing her fingers tighter on the haft of the blade, she walked clockwise to define the boundaries. At each quarter she repeated the invocation: east, south, west. With deep serenity she saluted the sky and earth with the raised dagger, then plunged the blade into the cauldron.

"The circle is cast."

Lyric withdrew the athame from the cauldron and laid it on the altar. She struck a match, the scratch sounding rough in the silence. Touching the tiny flame to the dry pine needles, she saw the blaze dance across the needles and lick up into the slivers of wood.

The scent was clean, almost that of water after a storm, and reminded Lyric of the reason for this ceremony. It was to be a release, a banishing of sorrow, and a reaffirmation of the power and immutable immortality of life. It would bring closure within her heart for the child she could not help.

For a heartbeat she stared into the fire, then continued with the words and actions needed. "The fire is lit. The ritual is begun.

"Goddess with wings of light, She who is the Mother of us all, my Mother, hear the prayer of your sorrowing daughter. I wish to bring peace and harmony into my heart." Lyric lifted the heavy crystal bell and struck one clear note. When the last shimmer of sound faded, she struck another. Then another.

"Three chimes are sounded for Jennifer Lee's spirit to ease its transition and release it from the heaviness of this world. Welcome her so that she may grow in peace and be happy in the light that is your arms. I plead for all those children who have found their way to the other side, to your side, too soon. Cradle them to your bosom and dispel the sorrows that they experienced on earth.

"I wish only love and happiness for these children. Let them know I will never forget them. They are always welcome to come to me."

Silently and deliberately, Lyric called the memory of Jennifer Lee before her, first the cold, dead, dirty face that made tears start in Lyric's eyes. She held this picture before her for a long minute, then replaced each ugly detail with a fresh, clean, warm memory that returned Jennifer Lee to the pink and golden child she had been, and would be again. The perfumed smoke from the tiny fire swayed in the breeze and swept in a feather's caress across Lyric's cheeks. She kept her eyes shut as the vision brightened and faded away.

Opening her eyes, Lyric looked down into the fire and smiled. The child would be happy and loved again. She picked up the pottery bowl. It fit her palm perfectly. With her index finger, she drew the sign of the circled star into the loose seeds, with each point invoking its properties. "For you Jennifer, so that you might one day experience all these things. Love." The first point. "Wisdom." The second. "Knowledge. Law. Power." The final three. Lyric stirred the seeds again, and sifted them in her hand, then began to walk along the freshly dug flower beds, trickling the seeds into the earth, where they, and the hopes they were charged with, would grow. Nolan wove in and out between Lyric's ankles, purring and trilling his approval. He sniffed the seeds as they fell and rubbed his whiskers on them.

"Wildflowers of blue and white to symbolize your freedom and beauty. May life thrive now and always in the element of earth." The bowl was empty. Lyric lifted the shell full of rainwater and held it in both hands. She retraced her steps, spilling the water gently onto the seeds. "May this element of water join and nourish the seeds to bring about their promise and fruition."

Again Lyric felt tears sting at her eyes, and a burning pain clutched at her throat. The negative feeling threatened once more to usurp the peace that the ritual was intended to bring. She forced her hands, her face, her throat to relax. *Oh, Goddess, how could such a young soul deserve such torture? So small, so alone.* "Bring justice to those who stole the lives of the children who touch my life." Her voice was strong now, strong with the resonance of entreaty and faith.

Kneeling at the foot of the stone, she traced the word into the dirt with the knife point. *Justice.* She scooped up the word in a handful of the dry earth and held her palm open, upward to the sky. "Spirits of the air, wing my prayers heavenward." As if responding to her plea, the wind plucked at Lyric in a sudden gust, breathing life into her hair, whipping it around her shoulders in a twisting embrace. The wind swept the soil from her fingers and lifted it away. "Ashes to ashes; dust to dust. So mote it be."

With both hands, she raised the silver goblet in a gesture of thanks, drank deeply, and spilled the rest to the earth in offering.

The embers of pine popped and a shower of sparks leapt over the cauldron's lip. Lyric sprinkled a packet of herbs over the coals. A puff of scented smoke, languid with the essences, floated upward. Rosemary and snapdragon for protection, juniper and basil for purification, cinnamon and sandalwood for second sight. The scant pinches of herbs sparkled on the embers. A second puff arose, and Lyric leaned her face into it, inhaling gently, eyes closed.

Lyric bowed her head in thanks. Her heart felt lighter now. The weight of sadness had been lifted. She felt her prayers had been answered. Lifting her athame from its rest on the altar, she began to walk again around the invisible circle. "Spirits of the north, I bid you thanks. Hail and farewell." She continued her path, opening the magic protection of the circle, the formal end to her ritual. What was this summer going to bring?

Chapter Seven

Lyric put the finishing touches on a generous tea tray full of breakfast treats as her childhood friend Jane watched. Little pots of strawberry and apricot jam crowded the fragile china teacups, old silver spoons, and crisp linen napkins. A chubby china teapot in the shape of a fat green dragon already sat on the kitchen table. His smiling mouth formed the pouring spout and his tail curled fancifully back to make the pot handle. A wisp of steam rose lazily from his toothy jaws.

The sunny kitchen was filled with the hot buttery smell of newly baked scones cooling on the stove top. A large basket of freshly cut white daisies, bright mixed zinnias, and blue cornflowers sat on the wooden counter, ready to be arranged into the collection of old vases Lyric kept on every table. Pink cabbage roses still wet with the morning's dew lay cushioned on a bed of ferns nestled in another basket on the floor nearby.

"Well, tell me all the news. Life is always more exciting with you around," Jane said brightly, surveying the enticing tray. Her straight blond hair was cut short, but still managed to swing into her eyes. She swept it behind her ear absently with one finger, while teasing a hot scone onto her saucer.

"Have you found any trouble to get into yet?" Jane seemed ready for some hot gossip with her hot tea.

Lyric filled the thin teacups. She had bought them last year in Ireland, and their translucent rims and saucers were painted with pale green shamrocks and gold ribbons. She knew the stay-at-home Jane considered her life extremely exotic and romantic. Jane kept an eye on the little white house when Lyric was gone, working in the city, or traveling. Before she came back to Salem she would call Jane, and Jane would use her key, let herself in, and open windows, fluff pillows, and turn the radio on softly, so the house would be filled with welcoming music when Lyric opened her door.

"Not much," Lyric answered, sipping her orange spiced tea. "Tell me what's new with you."

"Honestly, the same old thing. Weems is still the stingy old Scrooge he ever was . . . anyway I want to hear about your adventures first." Jane held her cup in both hands and turned it slowly, as if to admire the design while she talked.

"I drove out to the abandoned house on Stage Road yesterday." Lyric hesitated, still unsure of what had actually taken place at the house between her and the new owner. "I didn't realize ol' Spells-R-Us was listing that property." She knew her talkative friend wouldn't need much prompting to spill the details.

"Dreadful old place, never thought we'd get rid of

it. The Wolfton family finally decided to sell. What an evil man old Capt. Wolfton must have been for his family not to even consider living out there for generations. I heard there was actually some sort of curse on that house."

Jane loved to know all the intimate details of every transaction that ran through her office. Juicy gossip was the only perk of being W. Hayton Weems's personal secretary and single employee.

Lyric felt more interested. "Evil? What kind of evil do you mean?" Perhaps this was the source of the strange feeling of fear and unease that had almost smothered her in Wolfton House.

Jane leaned forward on her elbows. "You know, that basic heavy S and M kinda stuff. I heard he beat his wives to death; he had three of them. Funny how some rumors and gossip seem to never die. As far as I know, no one ever proved anything, but that old place looks spooky enough for anything to have happened way out there.

"What were you doing so far out? I thought you would have been catching up on your gardening or out shopping at that old bookstore you like."

"I suppose I was trying to confront any old spirits . . . or demons," Lyric said cryptically. "But I was certainly unprepared for what I found." She touched the bouquet of daisies and honeysuckle on the table. "What do you know of a curse?" she asked seriously.

"Oh, nothing really, just a rumor, not even a new one. I was just trying to tease you a little. Besides, you would be the one to know about something like that.

"Spirits? Did you see a ghost there? Does that old house have a poltergeist like in the movies?" Jane refilled her cup from the fat little dragon's snout spout. Her pretty round eyes sparkled with the mischievous interest of a child telling ghost stories. "Ooo, how cool!"

The previous day's encounter with the darkly handsome man had been almost like bumping into a ghost. Could he be a ghost from her past? Lyric doubted he haunted the house the same way he haunted her emotions. She hadn't been able to put him out of her mind since she'd first seen him. When he made physical contact, that had reestablished the bond immediately—whatever that bond was.

A shiver began at the base of her spine and danced electrically up to the back of her neck, just where he had touched her. She dropped her silver teaspoon with a clatter.

"Most houses in this town have ghosts, Janey, you know that." Lyric tried not to betray her thoughts on the subject. She picked up the spoon and stirred her tea slowly.

"Hmm." Jane narrowed her eyes. "Well, I have some interesting news about that house for you anyway, since you're so taken with it. You'd never guess who bought it. No questions asked, just signed a check and walked out."

Lyric merely had to look interested to keep Jane's flow of comment going. Jane folded her left leg under herself in the chair, a childhood habit she had never broken. She tucked her hair back again and leaned forward, preparing to add more spicy details. She might even make up a few, Lyric knew, if the story seemed to need it.

"His name is David Langston and he just moved up here from Atlanta. He has the most wonderful accent . . . when he talks, which isn't much." Jane took a sip of tea to let the suspense build a bit.

"He's absolutely gorgeous, if you know what I

mean; what a body. And that dark, moody-broody hero expression." She gave a deep sigh and leaned her chin on her fist. "He's a fireman and a paramedic. Well, he could certainly light my fire."

A frown creased Lyric's brow for an instant. The spasm of distaste gripping her stomach would take a little longer to pass. A fireman. A badge, a blue shirt, an attitude.

Jane smiled over the rim of the teacup and tilted her head. "What's the matter?"

"Nothing. Just a thought." Lyric waved in dismissal, then picked up her own cup. For a few moments they munched on the warm scones and licked strawberry jam off their fingers in companionable silence.

Jane took up the description of the new owner of Wolfton House. "He came to the office on the biggest motorcycle I think I've ever seen. It would be a thrill to ride something like that. I guess it goes with all that fireman-danger-macho stuff.

"He's about six foot four and his eyes are so beautiful. Long eyelashes any woman would kill for. Brown eyes and dark hair. Southern molasses, sweet and warm, I bet."

"Oh, Janey, you are incorrigible." Lyric had to laugh, but she shared Jane's assessment of David Langston's physical appeal, despite anything she might feel about his profession. Too bad he was a member of that bureaucracy she had sworn off.

Jane lowered her gaze as she buttered another scone. She scanned over the headlines of the week-old paper spread at the side of the table. "Missing Child Found Dead." Boston ferns and white tea roses lay strewn over the paper like a gesture to the dead child.

Sympathy came into Jane's eyes and she touched

Lyric's wrist with a gesture of comfort. "How are you feeling, really? I read in the New York papers about the investigation, and then that awful 'Invasive Eye' thing last night. I'm sorry, Lyric. I know how much these things mean to you."

Lyric tightened her lips. "I could have saved that baby if they would have believed me. That new chief detective hasn't much faith in psychics or anything he can't see. Even the parents didn't want to have anything to do with me. They acted like I was a vulture. It's really frustrating." She stood and gathered the flowers from the newspaper. Somehow the scent of the roses reminded her of the visions she had had of the child.

"Janey, I'm going to quit any police work. I've made my decision. Seeing that program last night brought it all back. It's just too painful.

"Losing this child has awakened something inside me. Since her death I have been more sensitive than ever. I'm not always sure where my own consciousness ends and my psychic vision begins."

Lyric stood the flowers in a tall blue vase by the sink. "I think there has been a change in me. Maybe I'm supposed to get a message from this." She turned and watched the steam from the copper kettle rise for a few seconds, then refreshed the brew inside the ceramic dragon with boiling water. She thought of her vision in the steamy bath.

There were no children in this warning vision, yet somehow she could not shake the impression of a child spirit with her, trying to tug at her, direct her in some purposeful way. Lyric shrugged her shoulders, trying to shake off the sensation that tickled the hairs at the back of her neck. She really did need a break. *I'm confusing events. Little Jennifer's story was overlapping with my other revelations.*

Would she ever get the strange vision of the captive and his tormentors out of her mind? She had never been given such an answer to a prayer without purpose. Somehow the vision and the new owner of Wolfton House were linked together.

The phone trilled as Lyric replaced the copper kettle on the stove. "Would you get that please, Jane? I'm not here, especially to any TV people after last night's Carwell Winston broadcast." She refolded the tea towel she had been using to lift the hot kettle lid and sat down at the table.

Jane leapt to her feet and snatched the phone off the hook. Lyric saw her eyes light with excited anticipation of who might be on the other end of the line. Lyric smiled at the thought of how Jane's occupation suited her nosy nature.

"Hello," she chirped in her most professional tones. "Solei residence . . . Oh! . . . What can I do for you, *Mr. Langston*?" She made a surprised face, stretching her eyes wide and rolling them ecstatically. Jane's voice rose to a schoolgirl pitch and she instinctively started to flutter her eyelashes.

"No, I'm sorry, she's not here at the moment, but . . . Yes, I'll give Miss Solei the message. . . . You found Nolan's tag on your driveway. . . . She can pick it up at your house this afternoon. . . . Yes, I'll tell her. Thank you." Jane replaced the receiver and quizzically confronted Lyric.

"You didn't tell me you ran into David Langston at the house. And you let me go on and on about him after you already knew what he looked like."

Jane seated herself at the table and picked up a daisy. She twirled it slowly between her fingers. "Now there's a man who seems to have as many secrets as the Wolfton place. You know, he bought the house alone. None of the paperwork shows that he's married or divorced, either." Her girlfriend gave a matchmaking wink and stroked the white flower along her cheek.

"I'm not interested in a summer fling, and you know it," Lyric scolded her romanticizing friend gently. "And especially not with a fireman."

Jane stuck out her lower lip and deepened her comically hurt look.

"I mean it. Not a policeman, doctor, lawyer, fireman, or Indian chief." Lyric wagged her index finger at Jane.

"Always keeping my eyes open for you, my friend." Jane turned on her motherly mode. She reached across the table and stuck the daisy behind Lyric's ear. "You're so beautiful inside and out, any man would die for you."

Several hours later, Lyric stood next to her car, gripping the door handle. She surveyed Wolfton House over the top of her car once again. Despite the state of shambles, it was her Pandora's box and it had whispered for years to be opened. Now the call had turned into a scream. The lure of the house was stronger than ever. Perhaps some critical point of urgency had been reached. Opening the door the day before had been her first step. Today was the next step into the maze, toward the secret heart.

Lyric left the car and walked to the doorstep of crumbling bricks. The overshadowing balcony loomed above her head. No picturesque garlands of roses or open blue morning glories hung from the rail or twined on the pillars. Only a few burnt, dry tendrils of what could have been poison ivy hung in crisp wisps, their parched roots still clinging tenaciously to the cracks in the wood.

She wore tight jeans that covered her ankles after

her last experience with the thorns and burrs that lined the walkway. A soft-sleeved white shirt covered her light skin. The golden chain of her medallion winked at the neck, shining in the morning sunbeams.

A snarling wolf's head fashioned of greenish brass made the door knocker. Lyric grasped it firmly by the wrinkled snout, her fingers curling under between the side fangs, and rapped the roughened wood. As she waited for a response, she scanned the facade of the building again, trying to pick up any clues to help deal with the strange feelings of melancholy menace. The only sound was the rustle of the dead vines in the faint morning breeze.

Lyric knocked again, then cautiously pressed her thumb down on the latch. The mechanism felt warm, almost alive. The latch opened smoothly, without a click. She pushed the door back slowly without stepping inside. The sunlight flung her shadow boldly ahead of her into the dusty hall.

"Hello . . . Mr. Langston?" she called. Lyric stepped inside, the one step she had been anticipating since childhood. Into the devil's den, into the maze, the house that Wolfton built. In the other day's chase after Nolan, she had not had time to ponder her actions, but today was a deliberate invasion into Wolfton House territory, and again she felt the aura of cold disapproval wrap around her.

She tried to calm herself by inspecting the faint hand-painted decorations of the hall walls. A hunt, with tiny mounted riders, scarlet coats, brown horses, cavorted across the faded green countryside.

She called again, "Hello . . . anybody here?" Langston had made the appointment to return the cat tag, after all, so he must be expecting her. An unshakable feeling of danger began to build inside her.

Why did she come out here alone? Jane would have come with her, if she had asked, or she should have had him mail the tag.

Still, she was intrigued, and her curiosity drew her further into the rooms to see the interiors no one but the new owner had seen for years, centuries. It was like a time capsule, she thought. She made her way quietly through the house, brushing aside a drape of cobwebs to look into a room of powder gray shelves and wainscoting. Only a few pieces of furniture remained, like small signatures as to the use of each room. A faint scurrying sound faded into the walls. Early ancestors of Nolan's prey had made a feast long ago of the leather-bound volumes that had lined these walls. A half-circle hunt table stood before the double window, the once-glossy oiled cherry wood now dry and white with age.

Lyric turned away and started quietly up the stairs, this time avoiding the telltale noisy treads. Any sound seemed to rip the fragile fabric of time that hung so thickly in the house. She felt as if the long-dead wives were around each corner, peeking and gossiping behind their fans, rustling their silken brocades, and waiting for her to appear, gauche and inarticulate. Had there ever been laughter in this house, fresh girls flirting, dinners with great hearty roasts and cold wine? Lyric felt not, and the bleakness touched her heart with a brush of ice.

Perhaps David Langston was not in the house at all. She paused at the first large room, where she had seen the chest with its fascinating treasures. She glanced into the room and saw the scattered clothing was gone, perhaps returned to the big trunk, which now stood closed by its companion, the faded blue chair. She moved down the wide hall, her steps quiet on the deep cushioning carpet of dust. It seemed to move under her feet, as if she were walking on a living organism, shifting in illusory waves and flowing over the toes of her shoes. Was it her imagination that her skin seemed to burn wherever the dust settled on her?

Through the doorway to the second room, she saw Langston kneeling at the window. She stepped into the room, a greeting on her lips that died soundlessly as she took in the entire scene.

The man's attention was keenly intent, focused on something outside. It was plain he had not heard her soft footsteps, as he snapped a rifle up to his shoulder and fired two quick shots. Lyric stuck to the spot, white with a wash of panic. She covered her mouth tightly with her hands, reflexively holding back a shriek of terror. Two more shots shattered the air.

"Hah! Got all three of you," his voice boomed in the small room as he triumphantly addressed his now-dead antagonists below.

He pulled himself to his full height and gripped the barrel of his rifle, leaning like a minuteman on the long gun. He was wearing the red coat Lyric had touched the day before and the image of a pre-Revolutionary soldier was uncanny. His bare, smoothly muscled chest stretched the unbuttoned front and dark black hair curled slightly beneath the lapels.

Lyric felt a curtain of dazzling light fall over her, crushing her back into a suffocating darkness. A terrible feeling of falling and strangulation gripped her. She clutched her throat and crumpled to the floor.

As clearly as if he were a single player spotlighted on a stage, she saw the man who had stood before her only seconds before. *But now he stood bloody, and within a noose, staring ahead. The gallows faced a wide heap of smoking ash and coals. Voices rang in her ears. One voice, louder, rougher, and dripping with crowing triumph, rang out above the others.*

"Dante Huels, you have been tried and convicted of treason and are sentenced to hang by the neck until dead. Your accomplice and wife Sarah Morgan already burns in the flames of hell for her sins of witchcraft and conspiracy with the Devil. She died for aiding in your protection. . . ."

Rough hands pulled Dante's arms behind his back and bound his wrists harshly. The noose was slipped tighter and the feeling of suffocation increased. Stones and mud were tossed from the crowd. A slimy ball of mud flew toward the gallows. It exploded across Dante's mouth. Lyric was jerked from her vision by the impact of something hot and wet across her own mouth.

Her mouth was covered by David Langston's lips. She slammed her fists into his broad chest and pushed hard. "What are you doing?" she exclaimed angrily. She pulled a huge breath into her starved lungs and sat up indignantly.

Still on his knees, David threw his hands up in a surrendering gesture. "I was just trying to give you mouth-to-mouth. You started to gag and turned blue. I thought you might be having a fit or something. I checked to see if you had swallowed your tongue and then loosened your clothes. It's my job to save lives. It's just instinct." He looked concerned, defending his right to have her awaken in his embrace. "Do you have these spells often?" he asked seriously.

"It wasn't a fit or a spell or whatever." Lyric pushed herself backward to lean against the wall and to be further away from his disturbing presence. The crush of his lips was still imprinted on her mouth. She rubbed across her face. His male scent lingered on her skin.

"I was looking for you and the gunfire startled me, that's all. I wasn't expecting it." She looked meaningfully at his still-warm gun.

"Oh, this." David touched the gun lying on the floor beside them. "I've been shooting rats . . . it's a losing battle. I put on this old coat to cushion my shoulder against the kick." Rolling his right shoulder, he winced a bit. He straightened his back and smoothed the front of the jacket. "I found it in an old trunk and it fits like it was made for me. I feel like a real militiaman." He shrugged and smiled.

"I thought I knew you . . . that you were someone else. It shocked me for a moment," Lyric stated, still on her guard. "Sometimes I see more than others might see."

"Really?" His deep voice had a curious but slightly sarcastic edge. The smile was gone. "I saw you on TV the other night. Interesting." His serious brown eyes swept downward from her eyes to her mouth and stopped at her breastbone.

"I noticed the charm around your neck," he said, trying to distract her. "Looks very old."

Lyric touched her blouse buttons, checking their security. What had he meant, "loosened her clothes," anyway? Sure enough, the very top button was undone. She fastened it discreetly.

"It's been passed down through my family for generations," she replied somewhat stiffly, still shaken by the vision, and the undone button.

A moment of silence stretched between them. His eyes traveled down her body and back up to the medallion.

"Beautiful."

"Thank you." Lyric thought he was commenting on the medallion, but perhaps not.

Langston sat back and crossed his long legs in front of him. He pulled the gun across his lap and rested his strong, tanned hands on the stock like an Indian scout. He gave off an air of rugged self-confidence and appeared to be preparing to make polite conversation. "Are those your initials? They look like little stick people."

Lyric grasped the medallion and leaned forward. She held it out toward him, to keep his troubling gaze fixed upon the protective inscription, rather than her body. "The marks are Celtic runic sigils," she explained. "Ancient symbols of magical protection."

David reached a finger as if to stroke the satiny metal. He looked vaguely amused at the idea of a magic amulet around the neck of a modern woman. "Magic?"

"When someone gives you a marked talisman, it bonds you together through lifetimes . . . if the love is pure." She pulled the small gold disk away before he could touch it. With a small move she dropped it back under her shirt to fall into its soft hiding place.

"Guess you need to believe in all that reincarnation stuff for a few squiggles to protect you," he stated. His tone became harsher. "I believe you get one chance in this world. If you mess up, you can never go back." He turned his head from her and spit the words out as if reading a punishment for himself. David stood abruptly and turned his back, raking his fingers through his wild hair, politeness exhausted. The mood of cautious exploration was broken.

Lyric stood slowly. Had she unwittingly touched a raw nerve? Silence hung in the air. A board popped hollowly above their heads, and dust sifted down from the ceiling like a slim feather of fine gray sand. Instinct urged her to comfort this man whose touch seared her flesh. Like a moth drawn to the flame, she needed to feel his heat close to her again. It would comfort both of them.

Lyric brushed the dust from her hair and reached toward David. She stopped the gesture and closed her fingers, suddenly unsure of herself. Another tendril of dust fell near her face, like a sheer veil between her and David.

With his breath, he had forced a part of his own soul into her in hopes of reviving her. Perhaps that was part of the riddle of these visions, she thought. Perhaps the purpose was to breathe life back into his soul and make him believe. She raised her hand again, but before she could complete the gesture he turned back to her and broke the silence.

"This is what you wanted, isn't it?" He pulled a red metal medallion from the deep front pocket of his jeans. It was Nolan's identification tag.

"Yes, thank you." Lyric scooped up the tag, her hand lingering for a moment in his rough palm. The tag was warm. She could feel an electric tingle from his body heat.

David smiled faintly. "I suppose it protects your cat throughout his nine lives, too?"

"I don't apologize for the way I believe, but I am sorry if I upset you." Her head was clear again. His manner irritated her, like the gritty dust that chafed her skin.

"So what life is your cat on?"

"Nolan's been with me throughout many lifetimes and, contrary to your opinion, will go through many more." She dusted her hands briskly together.

"Thank you for returning the tag. I can find my way out."

"Yeah, like you found your way in."

Lyric narrowed her eyes and did not smile. "Goodbye, Mr. Langston. Good luck with your rat hunting."

The dust on the floor thickened and rose like a malignant growth, covering the footprints of David and Lyric, for seconds each shallow depression becoming a purulence of boiling yellow and green before fading away, draining the last molecule of energy left in the imprints.

It was very good. They were together, and I drove them apart this time, and I will do it again. I am gaining strength but tonight, tonight I must hunt harder, harder. This dark man is driving the strong rats out of the house, the rats with the cunning blood and quarrelsome ways. The rats are no challenge to influence.

After all, it is the sport, the hunt, that is the challenge. Not always the kill. The kill, with its pathetic, cringing quarry, is not that interesting. But the game, there is the heart and heat of it all. And this game, this hunt, had the grandest reward of all . . . his freedom. Only once had he been beaten in his game, and it had been by these two. The biggest stakes of all and he, the master gamesman, had lost. Seldom had one the chance to play it over, and this time win. He was more than ready. He would win.

But first so amusing to watch this man and woman set apart, so amusing. And in the end, so rewarding. It will be my revenge, reward, and most of all, my release. The seed of distrust is planted—now I must nurture my intent.

Overall I must not, cannot, let them unite. If they

do, this time, for all time, I will remain the dust.

I need old blood, blood thick and potent with old sins. He would hunt first, and gather strength.

For all the risk, he couldn't resist toying with the two. *It would be worth it to make them suffer, like a cat teasing a mouse before the kill.* He had been wretched, humiliated throughout these dry centuries. *And kill them I will, but first I shall face the beautiful one and force her to release me from her words. The curse will be broken and I shall be free, and have power again. In their death, power and life.*

Chapter Eight

Lyric heard a loud knock at the front door. Seven twenty-five A.M.; awfully early for visitors, she thought. Glancing up at the little kitchen clock, she smothered a yawn. She was still wearing her short terry cloth robe and her hair was mussed and loose. Lyric frowned and slid the pan of bacon to the next burner. As she turned off the gas, the brass door knocker sent insistent metallic raps down the hall.

"I'm coming, I'm coming," she called. She wiped her hands on a linen tea towel, hurrying through the small house toward the front door. Lyric jerked the wooden door open. "Oh!"

A dark blue shirt. A uniform. A silver badge.

"Good morning!" the early visitor greeted her cheerily.

Dangerously desirable, the lean frame of David Langston filled her doorway. The lacy woodwork of the old screen door made an incongruous frilly outline for his hard, athletic male physique. He held a large crinkled brown paper bag clamped under one elbow. The bag crackled slightly as he gripped it.

Nolan placed his paws on David Langston's leg to stretch up and sniff at the interesting bag. He gave a meow and rubbed his whiskers on the man's jeans to mark his territory with a friendly feline gesture.

"Why, Mr. Langston, what a surprise." Suddenly Lyric felt her entire body flush in reaction to the most powerful aphrodisiac of all, the paradox of apprehension and desire. She looked down at her cat who was shamelessly winding around David's feet. Nolan was giving little cat trills of happiness. To cover her confusion, she opened the screen door a crack to coax the cat into the house.

It was too early for her heart to beat this wildly. Lyric was sure her scorching cheeks must be telegraphing her feelings to David. The sight of a uniform should be enough to start a little flame of anger. Although David Langston kindled a flame, it didn't feel like the anger she wanted to summon up.

She snatched Nolan up and held him close to hide her face. "What can I do for you, Mr. Langston?" she said through a mask of the cat's thick black fur.

"I wanted to explain about yesterday. I'm really sorry, ma'am, if I seemed abrupt." David shifted and peered repentantly through the screen. "I don't know what came over me. My mama didn't raise me to ever be so impolite." His big brown eyes pleaded, irresistibly apologetic as a puppy's. His softly blurred Southern vowels dripped like sweet wild honey.

Lyric hid her involuntary smile in Nolan's fur and composed herself for a dignified acceptance. "That's quite all right, Mr. Langston. I'm sure it was just . . . the dust and the heat."

David rocked back on his heels and lifted the brown paper bag he was holding. A flash of sunshine shot a spark off the silver badge pinned on his dark blue shirt pocket. "Actually, I have a puzzle that you might help me solve," he said with a confident smile, revealing even white teeth that contrasted pleasantly with his tan. "And please call me David."

"Well, it's a little early, but . . . come in . . . David." She eyed his mobile mouth, and the fleeting memory of his firm lips on hers caused another wave of heat to spread down to her stomach. But there was that badge.

She flattened her back to the door as he entered but didn't draw back far enough to avoid the brush of his shoulder in the crisp cotton shirt and the faint drift of his tantalizing masculine scent. As he passed, a painfully sharp flick of desire whipped across her body.

She certainly wasn't dressed to entertain him in the parlor. "Let's have a look at your puzzle in the kitchen. Straight down the hall, the last door on the left."

Lyric released Nolan and he skittered down the shiny wooden hall floor to the kitchen. Lyric padded barefoot behind David, taking in the lazy sensuality of David's walk.

"Please sit down. Would you like a cup of tea?" Lyric clung to the dignity of good manners despite her state of undress. She found herself gripping the warm handle of the teapot more tightly than was necessary. Why did he have to exude rugged male appeal? It wasn't fair, all this blatant virility this early in the morning.

"No, thanks." David's glance took in the friendly kitchen atmosphere. Breakfast preparations were scattered about the kitchen cabinet tops. The teapot was piping hot, and a red-and-gold tea mug waited to be filled next to a plate of buttered toast. He surveyed the sunny kitchen, a male lion taking in the territory. Lyric could almost see him shake his mane and cross his paws. She took a deep breath.

David set the battered sack on the table and pulled out a chair. He paused, gripping the chair back, before sitting down. His tantalizing dark eyes met hers, then boldly moved lower, much as they had done the day before.

Lyric felt his gaze as surely as a touch. It traveled down her body slowly, lingering where the loose robe barely concealed her breasts, then slipping lower, in a frankly approving appraisal. His smile deepened ever so slightly, crinkling around his lips and rising to light tiny gold sparks deep within his velvety eyes.

Lyric released the teapot and discreetly tugged the hem of her robe down in the back, only to feel it go embarrassingly shorter in the front.

"I wanted to check on how you were feeling today. You seemed a little shaky yesterday," he said. "That gravel took a pretty big chunk out of your knee."

Her scuffed knee was obvious, since her legs were bare from midthigh down to her toes. "Sorry," he said with sincerity, but seemed to appreciate the view. Apparently it was an effort to tear his gaze away from her thighs. He sat slowly, as if his body were receiving conflicting commands.

"Thanks; I'm fine." She swallowed. "It's kind of you to ask." Lyric hurriedly poured her mug full, grateful for the motion to draw her senses momentarily away from David's exciting appeal. The teapot lid chattered in protest at her hesitation.

David was rubbing the edge of the table with his thumbs as if he wished he had accepted the cup of tea so that his hands could be occupied. Suddenly she wanted to reach out and take his hands in hers and pull him around the table, to fling the robe away and find out if those long, strong, tanned fingers were as skilled as they appeared. *No, don't even think of it. The badge, the uniform.*

She took a firm grip around the hot mug. Taking a deep draft of the tea, she closed her eyes as she drew the warmth into her mouth. *Ahh, make a wish.* . . . Her eyes flew open in surprise at the eroticism of the wish that leapt full-blown into her mind.

Lyric knew she could resist temptation, even this one here in her kitchen. She schooled her expression to be as pleasant and as noncommittal as the one she used on that wretched television program. She forced her attention to David's lumpy mystery package.

The bulky parcel, their inanimate chaperon, squatted on the table between them with a demanding presence. Its rumpled paper concealed the contents completely. Lyric fairly burned to grab the sack and shred the paper to reveal its contents. *A secret, a secret. I've got a secret,* the package seemed to taunt her.

In a flash of her inner sight she knew, in all the sureness of her heart, that this day was special; this moment in time would change her life. This package and this man.

"I saw your name on the roster down at the station for the Fund-raiser Fair today . . . for the antique appraising booth." David picked up the conversation with little encouragement from the preoccupied Lyric. She was filled with an excitement that danced in her blood like champagne bubbles.

"I do that every summer. I don't even have to sign up; they just put my name down as a regular." Lyric topped her red mug with fresh hot tea. She took a seat at the table and lifted the steaming mug to her lips. The minty fragrance filled the air. With raised eyebrows, she regarded him with open inquisitiveness.

"I thought this might be an antique and since I'll be busy at the fair, well, I brought it. . . . " David's words trailed off, and he poked the bag with a forefinger. Despite her attraction, Lyric had a deep streak of practicality and wanted to get a better feel for what his intentions were. She knew he wasn't there simply for an appraisal. Making him sweat a moment more would confirm her suspicions.

"What will you be doing at the fair?" A little delay was good for the soul, she thought, even though she herself was about to burst with curiosity about the bag's contents.

"I'll be in the pumper team competition." David touched the bag again, tapping it with his fingertips.

"So you brought me something to appraise?" She enjoyed handling items that had been loved through the years and telling the history to the owner when she felt that it would only increase the affection and reverence for the object. When her appraisal was sought only for confirmation of monetary worth, her enjoyment was not as great. In the city her 300-dollar fee for an appraisal and written statement of authenticity sifted out the casually curious.

Lyric was accustomed to people asking for her opinions on any old piece of lace or cracked teapot, hoping it would be worth a lot of money. Most often these items had only sentimental value, but occasionally she would find a true gem, both spiritually and financially. David Langston did not strike her as the type of man who was looking for sentimental treasure. What could he have brought her?

He unrolled the top of the brown bag and lifted out the homespun red coat with black trim he had been wearing the day before. "I found this in my house," he said, with honest interest in his voice. "You saw it yesterday. Somehow it seemed important."

A cold shudder sparkled down Lyric's spine. It was the sensation she always felt when her spirit guides wanted to give her important information. No wonder her senses had been inflamed the moment she saw the bag . . . and the carrier.

David spread the coat flat on the wide table. Lyric pressed her palms to the tabletop and rose slowly. She could feel David's gaze caressing her face, but now absorbed and strengthened by her talent, his visual stroking did not unnerve her.

The dark crimson fabric radiated a message of importance to Lyric's psychic senses as clear as a magnesium signal flare. The coat was something that needed more than a cursory appraisal of age and worth. Silence in the room gathered like the last pregnant beat of stillness as the conductor raised his baton before the beginning of a great symphony.

Trembling slightly with excitement, Lyric ignored David's unsettling presence. She drew a deep breath to focus and clear her mind. She lightly smoothed her fingertips along the black lapel trim. Her fingers grew warmer, then hot, and every sense began to be magnified in intensity. The coat leapt to life, almost vibrating with urgency to speak to her. *You, only you! A message, a message for you!* whispered in her head.

Lyric flipped back the lapels and scanned the inside lining. She touched her medallion in surprise, then slowly lowered her hands to gently stroke the stitches in the seams.

There they were. The reasons that gave this coat a personal voice for her. On the hem and in the seams, the same protective sigils as were on her necklace; runic sticklike figures. They would pass as a beginner's unskilled stitches to the untrained eye. Lyric ran her forefinger along the message written there, plain to her eyes, but hidden to those of the uninitiated.

A talisman. The entire coat was a carefully wrought talisman to protect the maker and her lover. Lyric's hands bunched the fabric gently. *More,* the voices whispered, *and more! Betrayal* . . . a sad sigh. The soft sexless voices swirled in her head, so clear to her, unheard to anyone else.

Yes, betrayal. Their love had been betrayed. Lyric deepened her breathing and blanked her mind, willing the enormous sensory stimulation to turn within, to sharpen her perception and to enable the coat to pour out its story. The eager voices became stronger and the vision brightened. . . .

"It's beautiful, Sarah," the shadowed man said. He stood before a glowing fireplace, a sharp silhouette against the embers and flames.

"It will protect you from all the harshness of this world, so you will come back to me safe and unharmed. It is charmed." Sarah offered the coat with both hands.

The bare-chested man swirled the crimson blaze of wool around his powerfully muscular shoulders. The coat fit perfectly.

"But if it is to protect us it must never fall into a disbeliever's hands. Promise me you will destroy it before you let that happen," Sarah warned earnestly. She reached up to smooth the lapels over his chest and to gaze into his darkly shadowed eyes. "Promise. . . . "

"Well, have I found some pirate's treasure?" David's voice sliced harshly through the vision. His expression grew somewhat alarmed at Lyric's reaction to the old garment.

Only a minute or two had passed, yet it felt like a lifetime to Lyric. She had been motionless for minutes, embracing the fabric, eyes closed, seemingly unaware of his presence.

Blood pounded in Lyric's head as she was yanked back to the present. It was confusing and sometimes painful to be abruptly jerked back into today's world. She breathed in deeply, held her breath a moment, and exhaled slowly.

David shifted in his seat. He leaned up on his elbows as if to feign indifference and attempt to make light of his real interest. "Will it bring me fame and fortune?"

Lyric sat down, still gripping the coat. "It may have been worn by a pirate, but not the type of the high seas." She suppressed an annoyed glare at him for breaking her concentration. Yes, perhaps his fortune, his future, and even his past, was here, but would he ever believe her? "Give me a minute, please."

She glanced over the sigils again, noting the sign for fertility and children. There must have been a child between the lovers, she thought. Here were bonding symbols. There was also the sigil from her own amulet. The symbol of eternal love. *Love. Love never dies*, a faint whisper from her voices, *love*.

"Well, David," she began hesitantly, "your coat has a very interesting past." How could she tell him about the enchantment woven throughout the garment? It was literally a magical fabric that bound lives together. She was torn as to what knowledge to share with him. It was clear he was meant to learn of the coat's secret but with what effort on his part?

Would his skepticism be conquered to appreciate the wisdom and the story? Would he laugh at her like some and miss the lesson of life and death? His badge gleamed in the kitchen light. DAVID G. LANGSTON, the words were engraved there. *Will you be wise and listen, David G. Langston?*

Her father's voice rang out from the other inner voices. She heard him recite a snippet of ungrammatical doggerel that he would quote to her when she was too impatient to solve a life's-lesson problem.

Knowledge earned is a lesson learned.
Knowledge told is a lesson stole.

Langston was not ready to accept this gift of wisdom from the past. She could feel it. A puzzle, that was the very word David had used. He had said he had a puzzle to solve. Yes, he did, and apparently for both their sakes.

"In my professional opinion, all I can tell you is that this coat was made around the late 1600s, perhaps in the time of the French and Indian War. The fabric is wool, handwoven, very finely done.

"It's not the style of a highly ranked officer, but I . . . feel . . . it was last in the possession of a very powerful man, a man who was not the true owner of the coat. The last man to have the coat was not the man it was made for, of that I'm sure."

"What do you mean, 'you feel'? Are you going all psychic on me, Madam Solei? I don't believe in that stuff." He crossed his arms and raised his chin.

Lyric's jaw muscles twitched as she clenched her teeth at his sarcasm. "Listen. You asked for my professional opinion, and that's what you're getting." She held his gaze firmly. *Come on, David G. Lang-*

ston. Isn't your brain bigger than your badge?

"OK, OK. But I can't promise I'll buy all the extra color you're adding to the story."

"I wouldn't want to impose on your free will. May I continue?"

"Please. Sorry. I'll try to keep an open mind." He put on a contrite expression.

"Do you see these stitches here?" Lyric pointed along the hem. "There are those who believe them to be a type of very powerful magical symbols for bonding and protection. There was usually some sort of spell or incantation performed during the incorporation of the embroidery."

"So you're telling me this was made by a witch?" David started to touch the stitches, then thought better of it, and put his hands under the table.

"Most people in those times believed in powers greater than themselves and were respectful of what they did not understand," she said in a gentle warning tone.

"So do you think it's worth much?" David reached to casually finger the red sleeve, but avoided the stitching.

I think it's priceless, she thought. "I need a little time to do some research before I can give you an accurate appraisal," Lyric stalled. She knew already the value placed on this coat was life or death. Just whose, she wasn't sure.

"May I keep it for a few days? I'll get it back to you after the fair." She stood and began to fold the coat, signaling that the interview was at an end. She felt exhausted but exhilarated, much like a zingy after-sex buzz.

"Sure, no rush." He rose and started down the hall. The cat emerged from under the hall tree and twined himself around David's boots again.

Lyric had to smile inwardly; no rush, after he had appeared at her door at 7:25 A.M.? Maybe it wasn't the monetary value of the garment he was interested in. She melted a bit, thinking about this elaborate ploy to apologize and get in her good graces. Not too shabby a ruse. And it had been successful, she had to admit. At least partly.

Lyric followed David down the hall, her attention riveted by the ripple of his molded jeans. He turned to her at the door. "It's been in that old house forever; what's a few more days of mystery?"

Sure, no rush. Her spirit guides just loved to hear that. They had centuries. But she wanted an answer as soon as possible. She stooped and picked up Nolan to keep him from dashing out when she opened the door for David.

"So this is the tag loser. Mr. Nolan, is it?" David scratched slowly under Nolan's black-and-white chin. "I've met you before." His hand was scant inches away from Lyric's breasts. Nolan purred like a buzz saw, his deep, happy vibrations going clear through Lyric's chest as if she were purring herself. "I could use his help out at the house. Never saw so many field mice."

He balanced Nolan's little red tag on his fingertip. "Quite a few big, fat rats, too." His eyes met Lyric's. "Yesterday . . . I'm sorry we got off on the wrong foot. I guess the only rats around aren't four-footed."

"You're forgiven, believe me, Mr. Langston."

"David."

"David." She tilted her head. Somehow the badge didn't seem quite so much of an obstacle.

"Maybe I'll see you at the fair." David gave her a dazzling smile. It deepened the dimple on his left cheek and made her heart ache with desire. Involuntarily she tightened her grip on the cat. Nolan gave out a strangled squawk and struggled to escape her clutches.

"Yes, maybe you will." Lyric tried to sound in control of her emotions. "Oh, and call me Lyric. My mother was Madam Solei."

She watched David amble down her shaded front walk, brushing past the riotous red zinnias and white petunias. He turned for a casual good-bye wave at the white wooden gate. Her heart did another flip.

His gleaming motorcycle was parked at the curb like a great powerful stallion, waiting for its master. Lyric raised her hand as he put on his helmet; then she shut the door before he could kick his beast into life.

Trouble? What a tame word. More like chaos. From the first moment she'd encountered David Langston, her emotions were in chaos.

The throaty rumble of the motorcycle had hardly faded down the tree-lined street before she had rushed to the kitchen. Sweeping the red coat into her arms, she darted up the stairs. She could hardly contain her excitement, but for now there was no time to succumb to the coat's seduction. She was going to be late setting up the appraisal booth at the fair.

Chapter Nine

Lyric finished her fourth appraisal session of the morning. She folded the red-and-tan Irish chain quilt and slipped it carefully into its white cotton carrying bag.

"The quilt is in good condition, Mrs. Parsons. You should be very proud of it. Remember, don't let the sun shine directly on the fabric and your great-grandchildren can enjoy it, too."

"Thank you, Lyric. It's so nice to see you home for the summer." The tidily dressed woman held the wrapped quilt close to her body and stroked it affectionately as she talked. She laid a small envelope on the table. "Here's your check, and I added a little extra since it's for a good cause. Good-bye."

Lyric locked the check into the dented green metal box under the table. She shaded her eyes to search across the fair from the front of her canvas booth. The smell of popcorn and sweet cotton candy drifted by on the warm breeze. This year the Fund-raiser Fair for the local hospital's burn center seemed larger than ever. Small canvas tents dotted the edges of the commons, a broad rolling field once used to graze the community sheep and cows. Each stall would donate a share or all of its fees for the support of the burn center unit of the local hospital.

Every summer Lyric devoted fair day to using her skills as an appraiser to benefit the burn center. Her business was brisk, as true antique lovers knew her reputation. Often they would drive to the fair just to use her services. Faded quilts, worn rockers, dented silver teapots, and countless pieces of hand-painted china passed under her talented touch.

Thankfully there wasn't anyone waiting for her expertise at the moment. Grateful for the break, she placed her fists at the small of her back, stretched, and wiggled her shoulders.

Two teenage boys hurried by, untied tennis shoes flapping fashionably. "The pumper competition is in five minutes. I told you to hurry, dummy. Now we won't be able to get close enough."

"No sweat. There's plenty of time. Besides, Salem's team will win easy this year. There's a new guy from Atlanta that's supposed to be a real American Gladiator type. I heard my dad talking about it."

David Langston had said he would be in the competition. All those firemen, wet bodies, water everywhere. She stretched again and hummed to herself. It might be interesting just to stroll over and watch. Just for curiosity's sake. David was a newcomer. It was good to make a newcomer feel welcome. Lyric tapped her nails on the table.

She felt like an unpopular teenager left out of the fun. Everyone except her was leaving for the main event. After another moment's thought she grabbed the black marker from the tabletop. She ripped the end flap off a cardboard carton crammed haphazardly full of Blue Willow china.

The big box had been brought in this morning for her evaluation. Lyric flipped a chipped saucer over once and suppressed a grin. She told the thin young woman, "Sears, about 1974, Miss Atkins." The furious Miss Atkins promptly abandoned the box and stormed off to find the dealer who had assured her "it was old."

Before she could change her mind, Lyric scrawled a bold OUT TO LUNCH sign. She mashed a thumbtack through the cardboard and into the tent post. "There. I'm off to be a good neighbor," she muttered. Snatching up her wide-brimmed straw hat, she hurried across the field with the rest of the people.

Onlookers of all ages—friends and families—lined the edges of the field, ready to cheer on the teams of fire fighters. A bank of photographers had their cameras carefully positioned for the best action shots. Sunlight reflected from telescopic lenses that seemed to droop like long noses from the black camera bodies precariously balanced on spindly tripods. Photographers squinted through the viewfinders for final adjustments before the explosive action began. Lyric spotted Jane preparing her old Minolta, frowning over a complicated-looking lens, with a bag full of gray film canisters spilling over at her feet.

Spectators and participants had come from nearby towns and out of state for this special event, one of the real crowd pleasers. Lyric dodged and gently pushed her way through the crowd until she was near the Salem home team. She slipped past proud grandfathers in lawn chairs waving sweating cans of beer and shouting encouragement. Finally she was at the front where she could see the action.

The burnished brass water barrel of their antique hand pumper sent off flashes of sunlight. Shrieking red paint and bright gold pinstriping glittered excitingly. The tall wheels were spotless, and each wooden spoke was lacquered into a glasslike gloss. Instead of a team of snorting white firehorses, it would be pulled by a team of straining men.

Each team busied itself in last-minute preparations before the event. The men wore beautifully accurate replica period fire fighting uniforms. The Salem team wore classic bright red shirts with double rows of gleaming brass buttons, and skintight black trousers emphasizing their lean fitness.

Lyric noted with satisfaction David seemed to fill out his costume rather more dramatically than some of the other men. She pulled the brim of her straw hat down a little further to shade her eyes so she could watch him more closely. He moved in the garb of another time as easily as in the jeans he had worn that morning.

She saw him flash a brilliant smile and heard him laugh at a joke from his companions. Even in the flurry of activity, his form stood out to her as if he were painted in bolder, more vibrant brush strokes of life. Lyric could see the sparkle of alert tension in David's dark eyes. She felt a warmth of excited pleasure echo within her own body.

Her study of his confident motions and commanding energy was broken by the bell calling the teams to the starting line. A cheer swept through the crowd, and the 12 teams quickly readied their water-heavy pumpers. The object was to pull the wagonlike engines out to the center of the wide field, unfold the hoses, and get a steady stream of water going, all by smooth teamwork and sheer man-power.

The bell clanged . . . ready, set, go! The teams rushed out to the middle of the field. The groupies around Lyric shrieked their advice and support as the hoses began to unroll. Men on each side of the engines began the rhythmic up and down motion on the pumper bars that would pressure the water into the canvas hoses. The men who aimed the still-flaccid hoses tensed, supporting the long shiny brass nozzles, waiting the critical split seconds for the water to rush into the canvas, making the hoses buck with life as they filled to steel hardness.

A small stream started from one hose, and the crowd roared its approval. Another team quickly followed, but lost power and dribbled ineffectually. Suddenly a great gush of pressurized water shot from the Salem team's hose, arcing joyously up over the pumpers and almost into the crowd. Ten, then 20 feet high the water rose, a great plume turned up, then across the way to pelt the slower teams. Triumphant cascades of water rose and crossed to deluge the men until everyone on the field was soaked and laughing. It became a water fight, played with grown men's water pistols. The fresh smell of water swept across the fair, momentarily erasing the cloyingly sweet candy fragrance. Rainbows shone through the falling droplets, and a sprinkle of fat drops pattered over Lyric's hat and skirt, leaving a glistening trail.

It was plainly a victory for the town team. Good-natured laughter and applause finished off the event, as the participants pulled the empty pumpers noisily off the muddy field.

David's team parked the pumper engine. The fire fighters spread the canvas hoses neatly to drain and dry. Chattering boys swarmed around the men and the exciting engines, daring each other to touch the shining wheels. Mothers and wives took pictures of the smiling wet winners and losers alike. The clusters of people began to move off the field, toward family picnics spread in the nearby shade from the grove of old trees that circled the field.

David turned away from the group and walked slowly off the field alone, unbuttoning his sodden red shirt. He pulled it off and slung it over his shoulder. In the motion he glanced into the parting crowd to see Lyric. Their eyes met. He broke into a big smile, and playfully flicked water in her direction.

"Did you see? We won!" The ruby eye of his lifelike little snake tattoo winked knowingly at her from his glistening wet shoulder. "How about a beer with the victor?" He shook his dark hair as if he were a wet dog, and droplets spattered Lyric.

David shoved his hand into the waistband of his wet pants. Cut true to historical accuracy, they had no pockets and fastened in the front with a double row of buttons. For a man built as David was, it was intensely flattering. The black trousers as tight as melted chocolate flowed around his taut thighs and sealed themselves into the tops of his soft black leather boots. Lyric could see the outline of his fingers beneath the stretched saturated fabric.

She felt her pulse suddenly leap and kindle with the heat she had felt early that morning as he had come into her house. Her throat went dry. Lyric raised her gaze from his fingers to his face. The magnetism of his smile drew her to accept his invitation.

"I'd love one." Lyric fell into step with David as they strolled toward the beer and hot dog concession. His boots made a soft squishing sound at each step. "You're soaked."

"Well, there's an old saying where I come from. I'm not made of sugar or salt so I won't melt, you know." They stopped under a tree and David wrung out his shirt. He shook it briskly in the breeze and then slipped it on. The still-wet fabric clung tightly to his broad shoulders.

"It was certainly exciting; I wish I had brought my camera," Lyric said sincerely. The event, and David, were definitely the most photogenic things she had seen in quite a while.

"Yeah, I enjoy it, too. Our team in Atlanta was national champion five years ago." David rolled up the cuffs of his shirt and smiled. His thick dark hair was wet and tousled, begging to be touched.

They started strolling along the line of vendors. Greasy warm smells of hamburgers and hot dogs rose with the clouds of smoke over the grills in the concession tents. A foursquare display of tables crowded with potted plants caught Lyric's attention. David pointed to a flat of velvety purple and white blooms.

"What are those? They look like little faces."

"Pansies. They would look nice down your walkway."

"I'm not quite to the flower-planting stage." David inspected a group of potted herbs. "These smell good but don't look like much. Kind of weedy. Don't you have some of this in your yard?" He brushed his fingers through the silvery sage leaves and a delightful herbal odor rose. "Hmm, smells like Thanksgiving turkey."

He pinched a leaf of basil and held it to Lyric's nose. "I like this. It's good on tomatoes, I know." When he crushed another green leaf, the pungent fragrance of peppermint filled the air. "Mint . . . my mother put it in our iced tea."

"Yes, I have all of these. That's sage, and this is oregano. I love rosemary. Smell this." She plucked a tiny blue-green needle of rosemary and raised it to David's face. She felt a blush start when he lifted her wrist to hold the sprig closer to his nose.

"Smells like pine." He didn't release her. She could feel his breath on her skin.

"Yes, but it doesn't taste like pine." Her blush deepened when David bent his head and playfully nipped the green leaf from her grasp.

The owner of the plants drifted closer. She frowned when she saw the crushed leaves in David's fingers. Lyric caught her expression. "Hello, Susan. Remember me? Could you save me two flats of the yellow pansies and three flats of the white mums?"

The woman's strained face cleared at the prospect of a sale. "Of course, Lyric. Do you need any of the herbs to freshen your plantings this fall?"

"No, thanks. But maybe another flat of the mahogany and gold pansies would be good. What a gorgeous color." Lyric picked up a small plant and held the green plastic pot up critically. "They're nice and sturdy, aren't they?"

"I think they are some of the best I've grown. It's a new variety from the university. If you feed them properly the blooms will be as big as a butter plate." Susan slipped the tray of small chrysanthemum sprigs under the table. "I'll just keep these here. I can send Joey over with them tomorrow. You can pay him when he delivers them."

She scribbled a tag with Lyric's name and tucked it into the leaves. "If you are buying mums, you must be planning on staying here in town for the fall," Susan remarked casually. Fishing for a little gossip was always a fair game.

Lyric picked up a terra-cotta pot shaped like a

bunny and filled with trailing ivy geraniums. "This is so charming, Susan. Did you make the pot?"

Susan beamed. "Yes." Distracted from her quest for gossip, she pulled a newspaper-wrapped bundle from a wooden box nearby. "I do cats and ducks, too." She displayed a fat cat, sprawled on his back, his hollow belly ready for a planting or arrangement of flowers.

David hefted the pot, turning it this way and that. "I think it's Mr. Nolan." He tilted it in the sun. "Definitely. Could you fill this with . . . umm, those?" He pointed at a cascade of miniature red roses. "And that?" He indicated a lacy English ivy.

"Of course." The vendor took the pot from David. "I'll have it ready in about fifteen minutes."

"Just put it with Miss Solei's things. Here." He passed a 20-dollar bill to Susan.

"Why, thank you, David." Lyric tilted her head.

"Oh, it's not for you." David grinned. "It's for Nolan."

"I see. Well, Nolan thanks you, then."

"Perhaps Nolan might have the occasion to do that in person sometime." David raised an eyebrow.

"Perhaps he might."

The colorfully draped fortune-telling tent was close by a gnarled oak. Multicolored banners writhed lazily in the light breeze. Impulsively David grabbed her hand. "This should be right up your alley. Let's get Madam Fatima here to see what's in store for us."

An unbiased opinion might validate some of those unusual sensations she'd been feeling concerning David. He needn't know she actually knew the woman on a casual basis. A fellow Wiccan with an accurate and dependable reputation, Elizabeth Fatima Concordia Jackson always cheerfully participated in community events.

"I thought you didn't believe." She gave him a sideways glance, eyes narrowed. "Anything for charity, huh?" His palm was big and slightly rough, and very distracting.

"Something like that." He squeezed her fingers, and crackles of electricity raced up her arm and sent a chain reaction throughout her body. "Come on. It will be fun." He gently tugged her into the gypsy tent.

The inside of the pavilion was dim after the brightness outside. David and Lyric stood, still holding hands, blinking until their eyes adjusted to the gloom. There were no other clients waiting. Small threads of smoky incense slithered up silently into the still air. The sunshine falling on the outer walls made the colors of the tent luminescent, and a single candle was lit on a central table.

A corpulent woman, colorfully draped, sat behind the table. She fingered a long peacock plume as she studied the pair, then gestured expansively and laid the feather aside. "Hello, my friends," the obese woman spoke. "Sit, sit. I've been waiting for you." Silver, purple, and black fabric swathed and draped her arms from her shoulders down to her outstretched palms.

Lyric slipped her fingers free from David's to cover both of the woman's hands with her own. She took one of the two empty chairs at the small table and sat to face the seer.

"Blessed be," Lyric greeted her respectfully with the traditional greeting.

"Blessed be," came the dignified response.

"Now do we cross her palm with silver?" David began to button his shirt, not noticing the intense link between the women. "Isn't that what they always say?"

Madam Fatima broke her gaze with Lyric and reached to David. Her coal black eyes locked on his. The lightly mischievous expression drained from his face, and Lyric could see the sudden darkening of his expression. His lips tightened. He laid his strong tanned hands firmly atop Madam Fatima's pudgy soft fingers.

"It is as I thought. Your readings are intertwined. Therefore I must read you as a couple," she began.

David shifted uncomfortably in his seat, an unbeliever caught in the web of curiosity. Lyric bent forward slightly.

It had been years since someone other than her father had done a reading for her. Since his passing she had relied on her inner voices and her own intuition. But where this uncommon man was concerned, she seemed out of control. Her inner voices seemed to be encouraging her on one side and warning her on the other. Simply trusting her heart was beginning to scare her.

Rows of silver bracelets chimed softly as Madam Fatima released David and reached for a small magenta box. Her sharp red talons released the latch. She gave the box to Lyric.

Lyric smoothed her fingers over the cool marble lid. The weight of the box reminded Lyric of the small sarcophagus used to contain an ancient pharaoh's heart. She scooped the silk-wrapped pack of tarot cards from their tiny coffin. Lyric peeled the pink-and-gray scarf away, floating the silk lightly onto the table. It formed a sacred square on which to lay the reading.

Silently making her wish to know the secrets that linked her with David, she began to shuffle. The longer she handled the cards the more intensely she felt her aura merge with David's until both were totally engulfed by a shared pink glow of energy only she could see.

The 78 pieces of gold-trimmed painted paper slipped fluidly past one another. The flutter of air created by the arch of the shuffle made the deck appear to breathe with magical life. The jewel-colored cards flickered through Lyric's fingers. After seven shuffles she laid the cards on the silk square.

Layers of exotic fabrics rustled as Madam Fatima reached for the newly mixed deck. She offered the stack to David. "Mix them until you feel you should stop," she directed.

Lyric noted David's interest intensify as he began to reshuffle the cards. She knew he had entered the tent on an impulse, perhaps to show what he thought of her own abilities. But his cynicism seemed to have drained away, and betraying his own convictions, he seemed enraptured with the ritual process of contacting a higher plane. The large cards appeared dwarfed in the grasp of his long-fingered hands. Suddenly, purposefully, he stopped and laid the cards in the center of the silk.

Madam Fatima glanced at Lyric. "Please cut the deck," she instructed. "And again," she spoke to David. She pulled the three small stacks closer to her, one by one.

"I would first like to tell you," she spoke as she laid the cards out in the traditional crosslike formation, "that there is nothing to fear here. The information I will give to you should be used as a guide to better your life and . . . to avoid danger."

The intensity of the moment and the incense that swirled throughout the tent was making Lyric lightheaded. She wondered if it was having the same effect on David. He seemed entranced. He was falling deeply into the pool of cardboard pictures spread before them.

Madam Fatima contemplated the first card silently for several seconds, then inclined her head in a positive nod. "The first card you have chosen is the Tower card. I feel you have both gone through a trauma recently. Great sadness." David's eyes widened in shocked confirmation.

The woman's eyes were closed. She did not touch the cards, but waved her hands slightly above the layout, fingers fluttering slowly. Lyric saw David's gaze turn downward to the cards. "Yes, loss . . . the loss of someone very important to each of you. My spirit tells me neither of you is at fault. This present-day sorrow is connected to your past. Your past together."

Madam Fatima opened her eyes to slits and studied the next card briefly. "Yours is a karmic link. Your souls are bound to one another." She tapped a bloodred nail on the Lovers card. "To heal the sorrows of the present you must first solve the mystery of the past. Only then will you find true peace . . . and love again.

"The key lies within a physical object that is not what it appears to be." She trailed her index finger around a third card, splashed in fuchsia and bronze, with the words *The Hermit*. A bearded sage held a raised lantern and surveyed a mountaintop.

"Search beyond what you see. Your answer lies beneath the abuse of time. All the answers you seek are cloaked within this article. The Hermit is clothed in rags, yet the light of his knowledge illuminates the mountaintops. In the end, the disbelieving one will save the object from destruction."

Pulling a fourth card from the spread, the woman

knitted her brow as she concealed the image, pressing it between her palms. "The four of rods represents a structure, a house. This house possesses a connection with you both as well. It has a living interest in your lives and will make it difficult for you to manifest a new identity. You must find a way to release its control." She laid the card down with a snap.

Moving on to the next card she hesitated. She held the picture toward herself briefly, then laid it down gently. "Ah . . . the mystery concerns a child . . . both in the past and the future. The spirit of this little one knows the secret and will not return to you until you discover and understand it as well."

Madam Fatima laid her fingers on the final stack of cards. "This last card will reveal the outcome of your situation." She lifted the card dramatically and disclosed the depiction of a great golden chalice. It was spilling over with clear water. A large red heart nestled within. It was beautiful, instantly lifting the intense weight of the atmosphere. It promised a rainbow after the storm.

Madam Fatima clasped her hands happily under her trembling double chins. "Ah, so fortunate! The Ace of Cups. This card shows a love that is everlasting. A love that is both eternal and ever new." The old woman looked up at Lyric sharply. "It is also the promise of a faithful and fruitful union . . . an infant will seal this pledge."

Lyric lowered her eyes noncommittally, but the information caused another wave of provocative anticipation to ripple through her body. A baby with David? A mystery and promise indeed.

The rotund woman smiled and sat back to signal the end of the reading. "Any questions?" She was clearly pleased with the revelations of her cards.

Lyric was bursting with questions. She wanted confirmation that her most recent vibes were on track, but she didn't dare ask anything in front of David. He was sitting as if totally stunned.

"No more questions. You've given us quite enough for today," Lyric answered, with a genuinely appreciative smile. David sat silent, still apparently digesting the flood of information.

Lyric nudged him sharply, her elbow digging into his ribs. He yelped out, "Uh, yes! Thank you." He dredged out a crumpled and soggy 10-dollar bill from the tiny hidden waistband pocket and dropped it into a fishbowl of previous donations. He gave Madam Fatima a dazed smile and stumbled out of the tent.

"Thank you." Lyric touched Fatima's cool cheek with hers. "Merry meet again." She whispered the customary Wiccan farewell.

Madam Fatima winked wisely and whispered back, "Merry meet again, Lyric, darling. He's beautiful, but it's not going to be easy, love."

As Lyric slipped out the door, she turned to wave and deposited another five-dollar bill into the kitty.

Lyric ducked out of the curtains into the dazzling afternoon sunlight. David had his back to her, but she saw him shiver as if someone had walked across his grave. Something in the cards had struck a nerve.

"Are you all right?" She touched his elbow. He turned his head to her, but seemed to stare right through her. Was the prospect of being involved with her so alarming? For a self-professed disbeliever, he was certainly taking this to heart.

"I'm fine." He tersely defended his stance that the gypsy's revelations had no effect. His eyes cleared and he raised his chin, snapping back into the present.

Trying to lighten the mood, she said, "I think I really need that drink now." Lyric touched his wet sleeve. "They have a cauldron of good old Salem witches' brew just waiting for us over there." She gestured toward the beer counter with a pyramid of silver kegs stacked behind it.

"Are any of those witches named Budweiser?" David asked, playing along.

"Highly likely, Mr. Langston, highly likely." Lyric's hand felt just right when David folded it inside his. It was delightful to walk through the sun-spotted shade with him, and a totally different feel from the jarring clash of purpose they had endured at Wolfton House. Lyric walked slightly closer to his side, so that her skirt brushed his leg as they took each step.

They strolled past the other booths set along the sides of the commons. Artists' work hung displayed for purchase, and crafts were on exhibit, bright quilts, rag dolls, and wooden toys. Adults stopped to admire the handwork and chat casually with the artists. The lane was thronged with brightly summer-clad people. Children were attracted to the game area, and others clustered before the cotton candy machine. The silver tub whirled, spinning out great puffs of pink sugar, as airy as clouds.

A group of weary tourists trudged toward them. Several squealing youngsters raced ahead toward the stage for the Punch and Judy show. Small sticky mitts parted David and Lyric at the knees as the boys wormed through the crowd.

The last little one in the chase was a tiny girl of about three, having a hard time keeping up with her brothers through the forest of adult legs. Her large cloud of pink cotton candy fluff met its demise squarely on David's knees. There were two seconds of silence as she gathered enough wind to let the entire fair know she was out one pink cotton candy. Tears streamed from her huge blue eyes, and her bottom lip pouted to twice its size.

David scooped the dainty toddler into his arms and whispered something into her ear. Immediately she stopped crying. She gave only a sniffle or two for effect, then twisted away from David's arms and reached out for an exhausted-looking woman in wrinkled plaid shorts. "Mama carry!" The woman smiled a weak thank-you. She slung her tearstained offspring on her hip and plodded after the rest of her brood.

"What did you say to her?" Lyric asked, astonishment in her voice. Paternal qualities had not fit into her assessment of his personality.

"I told her not to be sad. God always makes more . . . when you stop crying." David's expression clouded. He flinched as if a knife had slipped between his ribs.

"Do you like children?" Lyric asked. Her innocent question seemed to twist the invisible knife deeper.

"Yes," he said softly. "Yes, I do." He closed his eyes briefly and then turned away to continue across the commons. Lyric thought she heard him mutter under his breath, "But I haven't stopped crying yet."

They walked silently for several steps. David's reactions to the tot and the fortune-teller seemed to drop him into introspection.

"So, was this your first reading?" Lyric asked cautiously, looking up from under her hat brim.

"Yeah. That gypsy woman put on a great show, didn't she? Can't take any of that stuff seriously, though. It's just all hot air. But she did have me going for a minute there." David's light tone seemed forced, as if to hide his true impression.

"I don't consider it a show. Didn't you find any of her comments interesting?" Lyric asked, trying to be patient with his disbelief. After all, it had been his idea to see Madam Fatima.

"It was funny how she knew about my house, but I didn't get the other stuff about the Hermit. What did she mean by the 'light of his knowledge illuminates'?

"I don't know any old man. In fact, I don't know many people here at all. Just the guys at the station." David touched the small of her back. "And you." Sparkles of beguilement spiraled around Lyric's body at his touch.

"She didn't mean it quite so literally. It sounded as if there may be something in your house that has answers for you," she said. And possibly me, she thought, with elation.

They reached the outskirts of the commons where the beer tent sat lonely and isolated among vacant picnic tables, almost abandoned after the lunchtime rush.

David stepped up to the counter. He held up two fingers—"Two, please"—and tossed three bills on the wet counter. He passed Lyric a brimming cup, and for a charged split second their fingers touched, hot on the beaded cold containers. A knowing current flowed between them, all but crackling in the summer air.

David released the cup abruptly. The shock of it made Lyric raise the beer and take a quick, ungraceful gulp, nearly choking. Her sputters broke the fragility of the moment. David chuckled and patted her back. "You OK?"

She waved breathlessly, cheeks pink with embarrassment and inner turmoil. "Went down the wrong way." She gasped. "None of that paramedic stuff, please."

They continued their slow amble between the trees, stopping at the re-creation of the old stocks, once a prominent feature in early village life. Lyric leaned against the hinged wood. "You know, not too long ago you could have been locked between these heavy boards just for drinking during the hours of church service." She touched the weathered wood and reflectively sipped her beer.

The cold, heady beer was refreshing, and she took a deeper swallow, sucking from under the frothy head. She was curious at the visible shadow that had fallen over David at the gypsy tent, and then again when he had comforted the distraught little girl.

Actually she was enjoying David's company, as opinionated as he sometimes appeared. Opinions came with the blue-uniform territory. There didn't seem to be the fearful apprehension between them that was there when they were in his house.

Lyric toyed with the green satin ribbons that held her straw sun hat. "I played with tarot cards when I was just a little girl. It was one of the first forms of divination my father taught me. Some things you learn and others you have inside you, just waiting to be developed. My talent for psychometry was inborn." There, she said it, if he hadn't figured it out yet. She glanced up with a hint of defiance in her eyes.

"You mean you believe in all this voodoo-hoodoo stuff? What's psychometry?"

"It's not voodoo-hoodoo stuff. Psychometry is being able to touch or feel something and understand everything about it. I can feel its past history and things about the person who owns the item. It helps me in my career, although I studied all the conventional methods as well. I'm especially good with clothing.

"That's why I am able to work with the Metro Police, locating missing people. But I won't be doing that anymore."

"Why would you want to stop? Aren't you successful?"

"Yes, I am successful, but it takes cooperation. The police have to believe me, believe *in* me." Lyric looked down and shrugged. "It hurts to lose when you know you are right. It especially hurts when someone dies and you feel it was your responsibility to have helped them."

"Hey! Hey, you, lady." A short man strode toward them. He was hampered by a large camera slung over his shoulder, two canvas bags, and a crumpled blue cloth hat that slipped over his sweaty forehead. He pushed the hat back impatiently and fumbled a small tape recorder out of one of the bags. "Hey, I want to talk to you." He thrust the recorder under Lyric's nose.

"I'm Patrick Peewasset from the *Rightly So Inquirer*. I'd like to ask you a few questions about the Jennifer Lee Jenkins case you left in New York. Please state your name for the recorder."

Lyric took a pace back to get the machine out of her face. "Mr. Peewasset, I have already made a statement about that. I'm not interested in talking to you."

The news hound closed in, reminding Lyric unpleasantly of Capt. Timmons. His pungent aura of cigarette smoke and city sweat reached toward her.

"Yeah, but I want to know what's the real deal

here. How come you scrammed out of town so quick after that case was over?"

David raised a muscular arm between Lyric and the obnoxious reporter. "She said she wasn't interested in talking to you." David slid in front of Lyric, making a wall between her and the pushy tabloid writer. Peewasset's shiny nose was level with David's chest. "You're interrupting something private here." David wasn't threatening, just large and immovable.

"Now listen, mister, you're obstructing the press." The disagreeable little man waved his recorder at David as if it would make him disappear. He unwisely poked his forefinger into David's shoulder. "It's my constitutional right—"

David took one step forward. His voice was low. "It's your constitutional right to buzz on outta here, buddy. Miss Solei said she didn't have anything to say to you."

The reporter curled his impetuous finger slowly, then retracted his hand as if he were pulling it away from a large, dangerous dog. Carefully. He pressed it to his chest and leaned around David to address one more plea to Lyric. "Please, Ms. Solei . . ." His tone was respectful.

"No." David's firm monosyllable cut off any more discussion. He crossed his arms.

"OK, OK." Peewasset cut off the recorder with a click and shoved it back in the bag. "How about a picture then?"

"No."

"Are you her bodyguard or what? Can Ms. Solei answer for herself?"

"Yes." David swiveled slightly to indicate Lyric.

Lyric peeked around from behind David's back. "No pictures." She added, "Go away."

The reporter frowned and mumbled, readjusting

his hat. He pulled out a gray handkerchief and mopped his red face. Shooting a frustrated glare toward the implacable David, he stuffed the rag back into his hip pocket. Finally he turned and plodded away, shoulders slumped, with his indignation written plainly in every gesture.

David turned to Lyric. "You have a lot of this to put up with, don't you?" He raised a sympathetic eyebrow, but at the same time seemed puzzled.

"Not usually this bad. When I succeed, there's always another excuse. When anyone fails, there's always me to fall back on. So you see, I serve a very useful function either way." A wry expression crossed her face. "Thanks for running interference for me."

"You know, I saw you on TV the other night." David seemed hesitant to bring it up. "I, I mean we, thought you were great. You managed that sleazy Carwell Winston like an absolute pro."

Lyric pressed her lips together. She wasn't too happy about that interview, even though she felt she hadn't done too badly. "Perhaps you can see why I am quitting that line of work."

They strolled away from the stocks and stood in the shade of the oak trees. The crowd had melted away to the other side of the commons. Faint sounds of the high school band drifted on the wind, flutes and brass trilling a Sousa march. There was a silence; then the music began again. A lilting waltz floated through the warm summer air. Lyric sipped her drink, leaving a slight ridge of foam on her upper lip.

Out of the corner of her eye, she saw David reach toward her. He touched her face lightly. Lifting up her chin, he smoothed his thumb gently across her mouth, wiping the moisture from her lips. He moved closer, within an electrified inch of her body.

He licked his thumb slowly. "The foam's one of my favorite parts." His eyes were half closed and dark, but never left hers. "Wherever there is foam, the ingredients had to have been . . . agitated . . . excited enough to whip up into a froth."

She could feel his breath on her cheek. Her knees felt as if they could not support the weight of her body. Every part of her was ready, ready for more, ready for him. Suddenly he pulled away.

"The froth is the subtle, most delicate flavor of all the ingredients combined." Trying to collect himself, he tapped the drink container against the tree in a nervous tattoo. What seemed to be anger came into his eyes. "It entices you to drink the whole thing, when sometimes you shouldn't."

He drained his drink in a rapid draft. He crushed the plastic cup in his fist and tossed it into a nearby trashbin. "I've got to get back," he said flatly. Turning away, he broke into a brisk trot across the commons. He disappeared quickly, retreating under his shield of detachment.

He had led her to the brink of a building passion. Why had he drawn back? She found herself trembling inexplicably, let down, deflated. He reminded her of obsidian. The cool black stone consisted of layers and layers of beautiful, subtly shimmering texture. Those layers were formed by intense heat followed by a fast hard cool. What had caused him to freeze over?

She lifted the cup unsteadily and took a long drink of the amber liquid. Not cool enough to quell the previous burning thirst he had created. Was that what he had intended to do? Whip her to a froth just to see what would come to the top?

She thought of her first impression when she saw

his badge and uniform shirt this very morning. A flick of anger at him, at herself, struck inside her head. A uniform, an attitude that seemed to be issued with the badge. He seemed guarded but interested at first. Then what? Had he considered and found her less than what he thought?

Lyric headed back to her booth. Just an afternoon of appraisal sessions. Then she could hide from her illogical attraction to this enigmatic man. She was only here for the summer. She couldn't risk any more heartache.

David walked briskly away from the commons and toward Pickerings Wharf, trying to escape prying eyes, but mostly to escape himself. He had to take a minute to regroup and sort out what had just happened. What had he let himself in for? He'd never felt so wholly enraptured by a woman before. Not even with his late wife had such depths of feeling brought themselves to the surface.

It was like the disturbing dream he had been having. In the dream, he was freely, wildly, dangerously in love, a strangely prophetic echo of what he felt stirring when he was around Lyric. When he touched her face, the rush of passion was unnerving.

The fortune-teller's spiel was too close to the mark for coincidence or comfort. How did they do that, anyway? Lyric seemed to believe. He had seen her inner animation, the way her breathing had quickened, her eyes sparkled. What did all this mean? David picked up a rock and threw it as far out into the river as he could.

Guilt and self-blame had wielded a heavy whip over his emotions for the last three years. How had he finally escaped their clutches for a moment?

Could this beautiful woman with such crazy notions and convictions be lifting the mourning veil from his heart?

When he reached the end of the pier, David sat down. He dangled his feet over the water and gazed intently into the cool green. The flush of heat he had felt when he had touched Lyric's lips was still pulsing and straining through his body, an uncomfortable reminder of what his emotions had started.

A breeze rippled the water's surface. The brilliant sunlight spangled over the wavelets, then faded as the sun went behind a cloud. The tidal pool spread beneath his swinging feet. He thought he saw a face there just beneath the surface. It was Margaret's face, contorted in the inescapable agony of the fatal childbirth.

One by one, David dropped a handful of pebbles into the water below him. The tragic image always had hovered near, except during each encounter he had had with this strange woman who seemed to thrive on ghosts of the past. Himself, he wanted to rid himself of the past, let it go.

He addressed the expanding circles, feeling the pain dissolve a little with each fading ring. "Maybe she's got a spell over me—for real."

Chapter Ten

Throughout the rest of the hot afternoon and evening Lyric didn't see a glimpse of the bewildering David Langston. She stayed until the end of the day, until the last flicker of fireworks faded over the water. Several of her appraisals had been slightly interesting, but nothing to compare to the appealing mystique radiated by the handsome young fireman. She left the gang of bantering young men that came to strike the tent and drove home in the cooling summer night.

Preoccupied by her thoughts, Lyric fed the vociferously demanding Nolan and locked the doors for the night. The cat followed her upstairs while muttering feline complaints about being left home alone all day.

She undressed rapidly without turning on a lamp and tossed her clothes over a chair. She lit a small white candle, lightly scented with jasmine, and stood it on her night table. The night was softly balmy. The faint sea breeze flowed in silently past the lace curtains. No gown tonight, just fresh air to stroke her body with its rejuvenating gentle force. Darkness had fallen, but bright moonlight cast a square on the bedroom floor like a glowing fairy pool.

Lyric dove for her bed. Her emotions had challenged her common sense all day and she was ready for some time alone. She sighed and rolled over onto her back, sinking into the friendly softness, stretching her arms to each side of her. Fingering the wool coat absently where she had placed it so long ago this morning, she thought of the strange vision.

So much had happened today, she had almost forgotten about the one thing she had been looking forward to.

She settled herself cross-legged in the middle of the four-poster bed, and spread the coat out in front of her. In the moonlit room the old crimson was blood black. Lyric touched the faintly rough wool, pressing and releasing the fabric, rolling it gently between her fingers.

She drank in its smells, holding the fabric crushed close to her face. Smoke, the sulfuric smell of gunpowder, and the personal scent of a man merged with the mustiness of age.

Nolan jumped on the bed and began to circle and snuggle himself in the spread of the heavy wool. Lyric knew animals were innately very psychic and perceptive. Instinctively they comprehended danger or love, their reactions so honest and unconditionally revealing.

How could this confusing man be the same tragic man she yearned to protect in her visions? She thought of how Nolan had wound himself around

David's boots that morning. The cat acted as if he had known David Langston all his life. Animals always correctly intuited and assessed the situation. Animals and children.

The coat, the house, the dream, but most of all the man were obviously parts of a personal riddle. All the clues were there if she could only put them together.

Magic surrounded this coat and she wanted to spend time with it alone. Her voices never lied and they had been emphatic about the coat this morning. Now was her time to learn what she could. She would have to return it soon enough.

She lifted Nolan off the garment and settled him to the side. Lyric slipped the coat around her slim shoulders to soak up some of the loving energy that still pulsed there.

Absorbed in the fascination, she lay back into the mass of fluffy down pillows and began to breathe deeply, controlling her breath, slower, slower. She quickly felt surrounded by white light and positive energy. It was a welcome comfort.

Recently the only clothing she had worked with had been from the "victim in question." Those vibrations had clawed at her senses with desperate talons of death. It had been a long time since she had been so passionate about delving into the secrets of an article without a total stomach-wrenching sense of dread. The dread was absent now, and a tingling feeling of anticipation swept through her with its own message.

A fleeting idea crossed her thoughts. She could get to know a bit more about Mr. Langston himself if she were a less scrupulous sort. He'd been the last one to wear it; traces of his vibrations still mingled within. She resisted the temptation to see what the past had held for David Langston. Today's revelations about the future had been confusing enough.

With another deep breath, her meditation drifted her backward in time. . . .

"Promise me," the naked woman spoke huskily. Lyric recognized the voice from the previous encounter with the coat that morning, even though she had yet to see the woman's face. *It was Sarah. The scene was that of a small, almost primitive room. The fireplace cast great waves of heat. The aroma of spicy herbal oils and early spring wildflowers filled the air.*

"That I promise with my very soul. We shall never be parted. You are my only love now and through eternity." Dante framed Sarah's face with his hands and looked into her eyes to make his eternal pledge. He spoke firmly. He released her face and pulled her closer.

"And tonight, my love?" Sarah rubbed her cheek against his bare chest with a sigh of pleasure and greedily inhaled the fragrance of him. His hot skin exuded a clean male essence of life itself. She hoarded the impressions of his scent, his taste, his every texture in her heart, to be taken out later and examined, her treasure. Her body moved against his slowly, swaying gently from side to side involuntarily, producing a feverish friction of senses.

"The plans are laid. Tonight I must slip into the cove. There is one who promised me a letter that will be proof. . . . Ask me no more." Dante checked his words. "You must not know more for your own safety. With luck I can send the Devil's wolfhound to lie at his evil master's feet. Wolfton must pay for all his abuse and traitorous dealings." Dante stroked Sarah's lustrous hair. He pulled a mass of the warm strands over her bare shoulder, and let them trickle

through his fingers like dark red wine.

"At least I know that the one thing he desires most he shall never have . . . you, my Sarah."

She knew this very night he would test the strength of her talisman. Sarah pulled Dante down to her mouth and bade him without words to stay a little longer.

The man became shamelessly aroused. He slipped out of his new red coat and pulled Sarah back down on the fur rug to lie with him. Their naked bodies side by side, he stroked the length of her inner thigh, stopping just below a crescent marking. With a shiver, Sarah tossed her rust curls back and offered Dante her long white throat. Lyric saw her own face looking up at Dante.

Lyric's eyes opened and looked down to find moonlight bathing and caressing her own inner thigh, her own crescent moon. Her face, her mark; the confirmation was there. There was no doubt. This was her life that was being revealed in these visions. She had lived this seventeenth-century life and it was David who had shared those burning times with her.

Sirens drifted in the distance. Instinct and custom made her say a quick prayer to protect those in danger. David would be surrounded by the sounds of the sirens and greedy lick of the flames. David. Dante. What should she tell him about the message of the coat?

A shadow cast by the branches of the big walnut tree flexed its claws across the sheets. Serene silver moonlight and charcoal dark shadow slid over her body as Lyric dragged the coat from her shoulders and gathered it tenderly in her arms.

* * *

Lyric pulled on her gardening clothes and skipped downstairs before the pink dawn light had begun to wake the robins. She propped open every window, upstairs and down, and threw the front door open wide, securing it with a large clump of Arkansas crystal rock. Fresh cool air swirled through the house, fluttering the curtains, sweeping out any lingering traces of staleness.

She stood on the front porch savoring the quiet. Nothing disturbed the peace except the swish of rubber bike wheels on pavement. "Morning, Lyric." The paper boy pedaled by and tossed the *Salem Torch* over her picket fence, squarely into the red zinnias.

The early morning sunshine was lighting the top of the old walnut tree as she piled her rake, shears, trowel, and cotton gloves into the blue wheelbarrow. She wheeled it out of the garage into the middle of the front yard. Nolan busied himself stalking late-sleeping lizards in the white petunias.

The morning hours passed in pleasant labor, until the sun was high enough to dapple the shade across the white picket fence. Lyric filled a large basket with clippings of dead blooms, a few rogue weeds, and remnants of the fall leaves that had eluded her last cleanup. A stray bit of paper had wrapped itself into the canes of the mauve rosebush. Lyric had to get on her knees to worry it loose from the thorns.

The bush was practically everblooming, tall and rugged. Lyric plucked a spent blossom and let the petals fall from her fingers. She rolled the round base of the bloom between her thumb and forefinger, inspecting it critically. By the fall there would be three crops of rose hips on the branches, for the birds and for rose hip tea. There was no chance in concrete and asphalt New York to work in the rich earth and let it give her the beautiful flowers she loved so.

"Excuse me, Miss Solei." A small boy's voice came hesitantly through the leaves and blossoms. "Is that you?"

Lyric backed away from the bush. "Good morning, Joey. Are those my new plants from your mother?"

Joey turned and waved awkwardly toward a careful stack of plastic flower flats in a little slat-sided wagon. He carried David's gift to Nolan gingerly with one arm. The terra-cotta cat planter was now stuffed with a rose plant bearing tiny perfect red blooms and lusty dark green ivy. "Yes, Mom said you would want them today." He wrinkled his freckled nose as he strained to remember the message. "She said something about the moon being in the right quarter to plant blooming things."

Nolan strolled over to inspect the visitor. "Nice cat, Miss Solei. He's sure pretty." He scratched Nolan's head and was rewarded with a regal paw placed on his knee.

Encouraged by the friendliness of Lyric and her cat, Joey looked up shyly. "Uh, are you really going to plant those flowers on the moon? I heard some kids say you were a witch. Is that so?" He patted Nolan again. "I think you're too pretty to be a witch. They're supposed to have warts and bad teeth and everything."

Lyric supressed a smile. "No, Joey, I'm going to plant them right here down the front walk. And guess what? Lots of witches are very pretty. You wait here and I'll get your money." She dropped her gloves and trowel into the wheelbarrow and went into the kitchen for the money she had slipped into an envelope for Joey's mother. Mrs. Bryson worked hard to support herself and her young son since the unfortunate death of her husband in a car accident five years ago. She pulled an extra dollar bill from her purse to reward Joey.

When she came back outside, Joey had arranged the flats neatly on the porch. "Here you are. Give this to your mother and thank her for the advice." She offered the envelope and Joey tucked it into his shirt pocket and carefully buttoned the flap. "And this is for you. Thank you for your help. Good-bye."

"Thanks." He stuck his own dollar bill far down into his jeans pocket and gave it a pat for good measure. He pulled his delivery wagon out of the yard at a trot, then stopped to wave back over his shoulder before he sped down the sidewalk.

Lyric looked at the fresh new plants with satisfaction. She placed the planter to one side of the front steps where there would be the proper amount of sun, and the white petunias would set a counterpoint for the tiny roses' deep crimson buds. Each bloom was perfectly shaped, but hardly as large as the tip of her thumb. The robust ivy trailed over the step. Roses meant love, and ivy, sacred to Cerridwen, was a protective plant. Appropriate, but she doubted if David was aware of the meaning of his instinctive choice.

Yardwork was pleasant to her at any time, but when she had things on her mind to sort out, it was doubly so. Making order from physical disarray usually helped her to mentally order her thoughts. Today its effect was not helping her to solve the complex feelings that were growing regarding the troubling Wolfton House and its equally troubling owner.

This morning every motion, every flower seemed to remind her of David and the revelations in the moonlight. The scents of the flowers and the fine sheen of sweat on her own skin called back the vision of Sarah and Dante embracing before the fireplace. It was hard to concentrate on her work.

She wiped her forearm across her face to discourage a persistent white butterfly, and caught the salt taste of her skin. She thought of David's thumb touching her lips and his breath brushing her face. Again his eyes haunted her. The eyes of the tortured man in the first dream, so sad. The eyes of Dante looking at his Sarah, full of passion and deep love. And David's eyes, the same eyes, wary and hurt. Why?

She got a flat basket from the back porch and started her favorite part of the outdoor work. Pulling off her gardening gloves, she fluttered her fingers gently over the tops of the plants. The aromas of basil, dill, oregano, and sage billowed into the air. Gently Lyric began to prune her herbs with tiny silver clippers. Small snippets of leaves and flowers fell into the wide basket.

Herbs of every use grew abundantly in the little wheel-shaped plot near the kitchen. In the center of the circle the crumbling stone sundial marked the hours. A small butterfly dried its dew-wet body there, slowly unfolding its golden velvet wings in the sunshine.

In her cultivation of these plants, Lyric felt a special connection to her ancestors who had long practiced skilled medicinal application of herbs. Through the shrewd observation of human nature, a desire to help, and knowledge of the folklore of healing plants, wise women had cured and mended and soothed generations.

Many of the women had shared another, greater gift of enhanced mental powers. For centuries they were honored as the healers and shamans they were, their ability to participate in both the spirit world and the physical world respected and revered. With the spread of religion other than those which celebrated nature and its power, the esteem for the woman healers was perverted into fear. Many had died, convicted of the crime of knowing how to help, to cure sickness, or to ease an injury.

Plants for flavor, plants for fever. A knowledge that had sent some to the stake, the rack, the drowning pool. All were encompassed in the tiny clips and snips and fragrances tumbling into Lyric's basket on a sunny summer morning. Yes, rosemary for remembrance.

"Plants for pleasure, too, right, Nolan?" Nolan sat expectantly at the border waiting for an offering of fresh catnip.

"Prrt," said Nolan, and winked both eyes slowly.

Lyric stripped a stalk and rolled the dark green leaves between her palms, scattering the crushed bracts on the grass. The cat sniffed decorously at first, then began to rub his face on the catnip. As the stimulation of the fresh herb spread, he rolled ecstatically. After several blissful turns and flips, he lay limply on his back, eyes half-open, exposing his black-and-white belly to the sun. "Cat nirvana," Lyric commented to herself and tickled his tummy to bring him back to reality.

"Hey, Lyric." Jane's happy voice came across the fence. Jane stood at the side gate with a sack of groceries. "You're certainly out early for someone on vacation."

Lyric rose and brushed the grass from her knees. "You know me; I love my plants."

"I can certainly see that. You definitely have the best flowers in town." Jane surveyed the tumbling blossoms, interspersed with flourishing vegetables. Lyric considered a shapely purple eggplant just as decorative as a zinnia, and so bright vegetables sprouted in unexpected places.

Lyric held her basket of herbs in her left hand and opened the gate for her friend. "Well, you might say it's in my blood. Come in and have a cup of tea. I'm ready for a break."

They clattered into the kitchen and Lyric set the copper kettle to boil. Jane rummaged in her grocery bag and came up with a thick red-and-yellow packet from the one-hour photo shop. "I had a great time at the fair. I've never seen so many good-looking men. Wait until you see these pictures. I dropped them off to be developed last night." As usual Jane's thoughts tumbled out of her mouth almost as quickly as they ran through her brain. "I have some of you, too."

A phantom of jasmine rose on the air as Lyric poured hot water over the tea leaves. "Yes, I saw you at the fair. Was that a new telephoto lens?"

"Yes, I think it's terrific. Worth every penny when you see these." Jane began to sort through the snapshots. A perfect photo of Lyric and David lay right in the center of the spread of pictures. "Look at this. You look great, and he looks simply incredible. What a body, and those pants and boots . . . wish men still dressed like that."

"I don't," Lyric said dryly. "Can you imagine your boss, old W. Hayton, in an outfit like that?" She set two hearty china mugs and a jar of clover honey on the table. She pulled a carved-back wooden chair up close and sat slowly, just where David had seated himself the day before.

"Oh gee, Lyric, you're right as usual. That would certainly take the romance out of it." Jane grimaced and flipped her hair out of her eyes. She continued to chatter as she spread the photos across the table like a fortune-teller dealing the tarot.

The events of the past day lay like tiny portraits. Several had caught her and David in the periphery, as they walked or watched. Three shots had framed them perfectly, every nuance of bodily motion intent on each other, David's head bent toward Lyric's face, Lyric's face raised to his in a glance or word. If pictures were worth a thousand words, these told a story plainly enough.

He was uncommonly attractive, with a dark feline grace evident even on paper. His interest in her showed plainly in their shared shots, his body turned slightly toward her, an incomplete gesture revealed, a reach to touch, but not quite.

"It seems like you had a certain target in mind here, Janey." One snap caught David perfectly during the pumper competition, grasping the handles of the long brass nozzle, a torrent of water rushing upward. "This looks like a calendar shot." In the shot, David looked more than spectacular; he looked noble, a hero from another time.

"Does, doesn't it?" Jane grinned over her tea. "Want them? I got doubles." Without waiting for an answer, Jane stacked the extra set and laid it aside.

She rolled the dregs in the bottom of the blue tankard. A few twisted flakes danced briefly and then settled. "Read my leaves, Lyric, please. Am I ever going to find a fireman . . . or any man of my own?" Jane leaned pensively, her chin in hand.

Lyric pulled the mug toward her. For a real reading, she should turn the tiny black bits out in a saucer, but this morning the bottom of the drinking vessel would do. She swirled the liquid slightly and looked in with a solemn face. "Let's see . . . tall, dark, and . . . no, sorry that's short, pale, and pudgy."

Jane howled, "Oooo, no, Lyric. Really, now. I need some hope. Don't tease."

Lyric looked more seriously. Suddenly she did see a configuration, one for danger and then a strong one for marriage, but not for Jane. "Stir it again." She pushed the container hurriedly back to Jane.

Jane swished the now-cold liquid, then let it settle. This time Lyric did not touch the cup, but looked down into the pale brown liquid.

The marriage sign was gone as well as the one for danger. Nothing of any momentous import was revealed, but then nothing of any unhappiness showed, either. "Happiness will come to you, Janey." After all, it was in how you interpreted it. *Harm none*; her powerful talent came with that single instruction attached.

Jane broke into a delighted smile. "That's what I like to hear." She gathered her grocery bag and dropped in her packet of photos. "Must go." Lyric saw her out of the door and waved a cheery goodbye.

Lyric returned to the table. She picked up Jane's blue mug and placed it slowly in the sink, trying to avoid looking into her own cup. Don't be silly, she thought. She rested her palms on either side of the red china and looked straight down. . . .

Chapter Eleven

David woke up with a mighty sneeze. He sat up, his sleeping bag tangled around him. He rubbed his gritty face, then sneezed twice more. Where did all this dust come from? The early sun was filtering in through the cracks of the shutters. David had made the biggest upstairs room his off-duty retreat with the addition of a sleeping bag, battery lantern, and cardboard box of clothes.

He ran his fingers through his hair and gave a satisfying, jaw-cracking yawn. Sleeping on the floor wasn't great, but sleeping in his own house was a thrill that overcame the discomfort. When he woke, he would stare straight up, tracing the faint lines of water stains in the plaster ceiling with his eyes as if they were a map.

At the sounds of his movements, a chorus of plaintive meows started in another cardboard box near the door. Clawing fiercely to climb over the edge, four scrawny kittens clambered over the top and scampered over the floor. They swarmed on David, pouncing on his toes and sinking in needle-sharp teeth.

"Ouch . . . hey, you cats, watch it." He picked up the leader of the bunch, a tiger-striped orange female, and held her to his chest. She continued to gnaw on his thumb as he carefully separated her brother from his big toe.

"I guess you're hungry again." He swept the rowdy group up and tumbled them into their box. He had padded it with one of his old uniform shirts. The blue cloth was much the worse for the wear and tear of the four lively cats. Nearby he had a large sack of cat food. Before he had finished pouring the dish full, all four were out of the box and devouring the food, making small growling noises deep in their throats. "Nothing but walking appetites covered in hair."

David relaxed on his sleeping bag again, stretching out his long legs and wadding up the thin pillow under his head. He watched the kittens eat. He had found them, weak from hunger, abandoned near his gate. They were hardly bigger than the robust mice he had seen, but maybe they would grow up and pay their rent in rats. What should he name them? Lyric would probably have some good ideas. He'd ask her.

He smiled, planning the next step to make the old place beautiful, feathering his nest as smugly as any proud male bird. When he was further along, he could show it to Lyric. Lyric would have to like it; the house was big, the view was spectacular, the kitchen would be beautiful.

The black-and-white kitten wandered over, licking his whiskers neatly. David scratched the cat's ears with a fingertip. Having the quartet of lively cats around made the house less empty. No wonder old ladies always had their cats. Lyric had the regal Nolan as her constant companion. She treated the black-and-white feline like a close friend, rather than an animal. In fact, if it wasn't for Nolan, he might not have even met Lyric. Nolan the matchmaker.

He was definitely getting the cart before the horse. There was lots to do here, and besides, he had no romantic plans. None. He would have to paint, and replace crumbly plaster with new wallboard, add plumbing, scrape woodwork, put in wiring. Lots of things to do. Lots of lists to make and check off, one by one.

He smiled, planning the next step to make the old place beautiful. Today he had relented slightly in his determination to do it all himself by accepting Ben's offer to deliver a load of Sheetrock panels, paint and plaster supplies, and an extension ladder. The four-foot-by-eight-foot sheets were too heavy and awkward to be handled by one person. The manager at the local building supply yard took one look at his address and decided the Wolfton house was too far out of the city limits for delivery. At least two dozen pieces were needed upstairs and as many downstairs. Ben had volunteered his help eagerly, burned up by curiosity to see his secretive friend's project.

David shoved his feet through the legs of his faded jeans, avoiding the holes in the knees. He picked up a tattered T-shirt and shook it vigorously. At least no uniform was needed for this kind of work. A cloud of dust rose from the shirt and the surrounding floor. He sneezed again and swore softly.

Three sharp beeps of an auto horn shattered the morning silence. Whining sounds of a four-wheel-drive pickup came closer and stopped under David's window. "Yo, Langston. Delivery man's here." It was Ben and the Sheetrock.

David loped down the stairs with his worn sneakers in his hands. He leaned in the open doorway and put on his shoes. "Yo yourself, Ben."

Ben got out of his green truck and stood. He pushed his blue baseball cap back and squinted into the sun, looking up at the severe gray walls. "Wow, it's really big." He came around the truck and kicked at the brittle mossy brick walkway. "And old," he added. "How old is it, anyway?"

David hopped on one foot as he tied his shoe. "I think it was built in the early 1700s. I'm still trying to find out everything about it."

"Brought us some coffee and doughnuts. Where's the fine-dining facilities?" Ben pulled two pink-and-white paper bags from the truck cab.

"In through here. I cleaned the bird's nests out of the chimney and I can use the fireplace to make a cookfire, but its pretty primitive. Kind of like camping indoors." David's voice echoed in the wide hall.

They entered the stone-floored kitchen. There was an ancient trestle table in the center of the room. David had spread a thick pad of old newspapers over the tabletop. Paint cans, hand tools, and nail cartons littered the top.

Ben shoved paint cans aside and plunked the bags next to a claw hammer and rasp. He rummaged into the paper bags. "Chocolate or regular?"

"Regular. Let's have that coffee."

The men pulled off the plastic lids of the steaming coffee. The fragrance of the brew spread into the kitchen. David's stomach woke with a healthy growl. He took a deep swig of coffee, then disposed of a doughnut in two bites. He fished in the bag for another one.

Ben strolled around the room, slurping his hot drink noisily and taking in the barren features of the cheerless early American kitchen. "I'll say; pretty primitive." He touched the iron crane that swung into the fireplace. It moved with a protesting creak. "I guess this is for a pot over the fire?"

He stepped into the fireplace, his head clearing the chimney space. He stretched his arms out to each side. "You could cook a whole cow in here.

"What's this?" He opened a small metal door set into the stone by the yawning fireplace.

"Some kind of an oven, I think."

"This is not a Betty Crocker–approved kitchen, that's for sure." Ben tapped one of the wavy windowpanes. The old stone sink and hand pump caught his eye. He made a dramatic jump backward, throwing his hands wide. "Look out . . . a modern improvement." He grabbed the handle and gave it a pull up and down. "Does it work?"

With a gurgle and splash, clear water spilled into the sink. "Clear as can be."

David stuck his hands under the flowing water, rubbing the sugar from his fingers. "I had it tested in town. It's supposed to be safe to drink. I've been brushing my teeth with it and I'm not dead yet."

Ben finished his coffee in a gulp and shoved the empty cup into the bag. "You've taken on quite a job, Langston." He picked up a hand plane and sandpaper block, and inspected them. "First thing I would do is get some electricity out here. Get one of those Honda gasoline-powered generators." He imitated pulling a starter cord. "Brrrrrrapppp! Doing all this by hand will take forever." He held up the plane and turned it from side to side to see the razor-sharp blade inside.

David shrugged. "I've got lots of time. And it's peaceful this way."

Ben warmed to the idea. He strode across the kitchen waving his arms expansively. "Yeah, that's it. A generator and an industrial shop-vac. That would take care of all this dust."

Stooping over a small black object lying in the corner, he poked it with his toe. "Gross . . . a dried-up bat."

David joined Ben in his examination. "I find them all over the place. Sometimes rats, too. I wonder if they die of excitement from having someone in the old place." He nudged the bat onto a piece of paper and tossed the body out the unscreened window. "But they're always all dried up like that. Hope it's not rabies."

Ben balled up the empty doughnut bags and pitched the debris into the fireplace. "Speaking of excitement, I saw you and the redheaded gypsy at the fair. Watch out, or you'll end up like that bat." He cackled suggestively and wrung his hands. "Sucked dry."

David raised his eyebrows innocently. "I have no interest whatsoever—" He ended with a whoosh as Ben poked him in the ribs with a hammer handle. They wrestled around the kitchen until David clinched Ben into a headlock. "OK, Ben Barker, you're paying for that." Ben's hat flew to the side.

David dragged Ben to the sink and primed the pump with the arm that wasn't clamping Ben to his side. He stuck Ben's brown head under the gushing cold water. Ben sputtered and laughed, struggling away from David's grip. Staggering dramatically around the room, he shook his wet hair, splashing water around the kitchen.

"OK! I surrender! Don't drown me. I sure wouldn't

want you to give me mouth-to-mouth."

David slung on his tool belt and and picked up his gloves. "That's enough fun. To work."

Out in the drive, David inspected the contents of the truck bed. "Glad to get that ladder. I had to climb up a tree to get on the roof and clear out the chimney." David lifted the aluminum ladder and propped it against the balcony. A shower of dead vine leaves drifted down. Ben unlatched the tailgate and dropped it with a crash.

"I got two gallon buckets of that Colonial Red you wanted. The box there has more turpentine, good brushes, and sandpaper. Here's a dozen number-one pine two-by-fours. The lumberyard manager and you must be on a first-name basis."

"Yeah, it's a pretty expensive project. But then I could be just spending it on beer like you, Barker, and build me a house out of aluminum beer cans."

Ben grinned. "I am shocked. Offended. Besides, my girlfriend would be happy, *dee*-lighted to live in my aluminum beer-can house just to be near my wonderful self."

"Oh, yeah?" David hefted the metal can of paint.

"Yeah." Ben picked up the box of brushes and turpentine cans. "Anyways, a beer-can house is lots more modern than this spooky old place."

They moved into the front parlor. David had spread canvas dropcloths across the floor and built a worktable of planks and sawhorses in the center. "It's not spooky. I don't know why everyone calls it spooky. It's just old." He pried up the tabs securing the metal lid to the bucket. "Here. Stir this while I go and get an empty can for the thinner."

Ben squatted next to the can and dipped a stirring stick carefully into the thick liquid. "What a color, Langston. Looks like cow blood."

"It's historically accurate. I looked it up. I scraped off some chips from a spot in the corner and had it matched." David reached out as he left the room and thumped Ben's cap with his finger. "Just stir; don't be an art critic."

Ben shoved the stick down and scraped the bottom and began to swirl the oily pigment. The paint coated the flat stick thickly, dripping in sluggish, sullen drops when he lifted the tool from the surface. Curls of unevenly mixed color, light and dark, formed with the motion.

Ben blinked. An eye formed in the paint. A nose, downward-curling lips. He dropped the stick and it sank soundlessly. Another eye was complete. The eyes opened, red eyes, red pupils set in a red oily face. They looked right at Ben. The lips moved, curved, opened to show red teeth, and a glistening, pointed red tongue extended, waggling obscenely. The tongue lengthened, grew, crept quivering over the rim of the can and reached toward Ben.

Ben screamed and scrambled up, kicking over the can. It toppled, releasing a gush of red paint over the drop cloth.

"Ben, what's the matter?" David ran back into the parlor, still clutching the paint thinner. "What a mess." Both of them grabbed the ends of the canvas and bundled the spread of wet crimson cloth outside.

"I'm sorry, Langston. I just . . . just thought I saw something and, shoot, I'm sorry. I'll go into town and get another bucket. I think something was wrong with this one, anyway."

"No, that's OK. Let's just use the other can." They walked back into the parlor. "Give me that screwdriver." David tipped the bucket a few times to mix the paint, then pried up the lid of the second container. "This time I'll stir it." He dipped in a fresh stirring stick and swept the paint around the can in an efficient figure-eight movement. "There. Looks good. Why don't you start in the corner, and I'll go get the ladder?"

Ben picked up a brush and approached the can. Turning his head to the left, he narrowed his eyes and stared into the can. He reached out and dipped the brush at arm's length.

"Ben, don't mess with this can. What's the problem?"

"Nothing." He slapped a generous brushful over the plaster. "Not a thing. Goes on nice and smooth."

David turned and left the room as Ben filled his brush and tapped the excess drops against the bucket rim. He stroked the paint horizontally away from the corner. Droplets ran down and skittered like water bugs, leaving an indelible trail. *Die*, they wrote. *Die for me.*

Ben slapped at the words, obliterating them with a thick layer. The droplets escaped and danced away. *She is mine. Death awaits*. He flailed at the words with the loaded brush, paint splattering wildly. *Die. Ben. Touch me and die.*

"Geez, Ben, now what? What a mess!" David strode back into the room and dropped the ladder with a crash.

"Look, David, look at this. It's crazy. It knows my name." He pointed at the wall and backed away unsteadily.

"What knows your name? The wall?" David frowned. "Are you sick or something? Ben, are you allergic to paint fumes? Do they make you hallucinate?" He looked at the haphazardly splattered wall and back at the pale-faced Ben.

"Let's go outside and get some fresh air. I think you need it."

Outside they leaned against the truck fender. Ben jerked off his cap, scrubbed at his hair violently, and jammed the cap back on. "Sorry, David, but this house has something weird going on. Really weird."

"I stay here every night I'm off duty and never see a thing. It's just old and dirty and shabby. Everything looks bad when it's not taken care of. What did you see, anyway? A rat? Come on, Ben, get a grip."

"OK, I didn't see anything. Just a rat."

David pulled his gloves out of his pocket and slapped them on his thigh. "Let's get the rock inside. It's starting to get cloudy."

"Where are we going with this stuff?" Ben pulled on his own gray leather work gloves and started to slip the sheets out of the truck bed.

"Upstairs."

"Well, naturally."

They took corners of the eight-foot-long panels and stood them up. David and Ben hefted the unwieldy sheets and balanced them easily, holding them upright lengthwise. They were used to working as a team, without direction.

Carrying the sheets up the stairs took some strength and agility. They jockeyed around the landing. "Next door down." David had decided one of the smaller bedrooms would be the supply room. They turned the corner, lowering the heavy gypsum board and supporting the weight by the corners of the panels.

"Easy . . . easy." It was awkward, but the men were strong and dexterous. They stood the boards against the wall. "Only twenty-one more to go." David slapped his gloves together and grinned. Ben was already sweating.

They straggled up and raced down the stairs; up and down. "Last load; aw'right!" Ben balanced at the bottom step and David started up the stairs. Something somehow caught his toe, then his heel, and his grip loosened on the big sheets of gypsum.

"Watch out." The sheets twisted out of Ben's hands to wobble and crash into the painted wall. They scraped across the painted scene and gouged the soft plaster in a broad swath. Flopping back against the banister, the panels cracked in the middle, then bounced down the stairs, tearing and breaking into ragged white fragments. Ben was sprawled on the bottom of a pile of chalky pieces.

"Ben, are you all right?" David scrambled over the broken Sheetrock and pawed chunks aside.

Ben sat up slowly. He raked shards of chalk out of his hair and blinked. "Yeah, no problem." A cloud of dust seemed to move with him. "Just bruised. Damn, that happened quick." He pulled his gloves off and rubbed his right arm. A large red welt showed angrily where one of the fragments had hit with some force.

"It was my fault. I stumbled. There's some loose treads on the stair I should have fixed, but . . ." David saw the damage that had been done to the mural. "Oh man, look at that."

Ben scrambled to his feet and slapped at himself with his gloves, knocking another cloud of chalk dust into the air. David stood with his hands on his hips and surveyed the damage to the wall. Reaching out, he ran his fingers lightly over the raw edges. The thin fresco plaster crumbled away in a peeling cascade pulled free by its own weight.

The lath was exposed in eerily obscene patches,

revealed like nasty bones and secrets that should be kept covered. Behind a patch of rotted slats was a desiccated corpse of what must have been a very large rat. Its yellow teeth and skull gleamed. Dust spilled in a stealthy trickle from the holes in the wall, hissing softly, making small cones of grains on the steps. A feeling of decay and uncleanliness seeped into the room.

"Let's get this cleaned up." David tugged Ben's sleeve. "Come on."

They hurried into the kitchen and out into the backyard. David had some buckets and shovels there. They brought them in and rapidly scooped up the debris of crumbled chalk and paint. Neither raised their eyes to the damaged painting. They worked furiously, as if they couldn't be away from the hallway quickly enough. Somehow a sense of heaviness, of another presence, hung in the air. Each man carried a full bucket outside and stood in the sun. Ben rubbed his abraded arm and shivered in the warmth.

"David, maybe . . ." Ben frowned. "Seriously, man, maybe you shouldn't stay out here." He gestured toward the open door.

David pressed his fingers to his eyes briefly, then lowered his hands. "I don't believe in ghosts." He met Ben's eyes. "Do you?"

Ben shoved his hands into his hip pockets. "Well, I'd say I didn't, but then I never came up on something that made me feel like that . . . that, whatever it is." He shook his head.

"These houses around here have strange secrets, David. I've lived here for a long time, and I wouldn't like to know what these old places have seen. Even the old-timers won't talk about some of it." All of Ben's banter and playful bluster had evaporated.

"Take my advice, buddy. Be careful."

David's lips twisted. "Of what? The boogeyman?"

"Do you have your beeper? If you need help—"

"Ben, I can't believe you've gone off the deep end like this."

"OK, OK. You're a big boy. You can take care of yourself." Ben didn't seem reassured. He scanned the front of the house and shook his head again, brow furrowed.

David stuck out his hand. "Thanks for the help, buddy. I'll see you on my shift." They clasped hands and Ben added a clap to David's shoulder.

"See you later."

David stood in the drive circle and watched the green pickup disappear down the weedy lane. To tell the truth, he didn't feel too confident about the house himself, now. But damn it, he didn't believe in ghosts or any of that, and having Ben get the heebie-jeebies in the parlor over the paint fumes wasn't going to scare him out of his house.

He walked slowly back into the hallway. He picked up the broom leaning by the parlor door. Looked like the only thing left was to tackle the attic, since the painting was clearly not going to happen and too much of the plasterboard had been destroyed. Carrying the broom and a trash-scooping shovel like rifles over one shoulder, with a bucket of paint dangling from his other hand, he marched upstairs and faced the small attic door. He had just found the door last week, hidden behind the rickety remains of a bookcase, but hadn't had the inclination to explore.

A tarnished brass key stuck out of the lock. "Lot of good that does," David muttered to himself.

He turned the key and swung the door open. Hot, musty air rolled out of the opening. He propped the door open with the heavy can of paint. Festoons of grimy cobwebs hung over the sill. David swept them down and stepped inside, ducking his head slightly to clear the doorjamb.

The room was much smaller than he had anticipated, but surprisingly still held furniture, arranged in a manner indicating the room had been used and abandoned. But for the filth, David could imagine the owner simply stepping away from the mahogany desk and closing the door.

A single small circular window made up of eight wedges of glass permitted a faint light to enter the still air. One glass wedge had been shattered, perhaps by a tapping branch, and the opening served as an entry and exit for the clusters of furry brown bats that hung around the edges of the steeply peaked attic ceiling.

As his eyes adjusted to the gloom, he began to make out a mural, a plaster fresco much like the one that had been destroyed this morning. Crossing his hands on the top of the broomstick, he studied the mural thoroughly.

Reading like a cartoonish picture scroll from left to right, apparently it depicted a number of events in the old settlement. It ran around the walls, filling in every available space. Although several events were highly detailed, others were sketched in roughly, emotion leaping from the angry brush strokes.

The main characters seemed to be the same. A short man with a black hat and buff coat, some kind of official. A taller man, with a red coat, furtively peeking from bushes, then in the company of soldiers, later standing on a gallows, head bowed. This house, Wolfton House. Two small ships in the cove behind it.

A small woman with bright hair was depicted variously in the nude, a drab Puritan dress, and rags and chains. A vignette showed her surrounded by angrily gesturing townsmen brandishing farm tools; then another exhibited her bound, within a circle of flames. The story did not seem to have a happy ending.

Worse than the events spread before his eyes was the way it made him feel. Ben had called it weird. David felt anger, despair, loss, and sadness. His eyes burned. He rubbed them, and scrubbed down his face and scratched his neck. Poor beggar, hung like that. And the woman burned. What a perverted thing to display, even hidden away up here, like a private gallery of pornography.

It felt too familiar, somehow, tugging at a buried memory like an old movie he half remembered. Maybe something on a late-night show?

He turned the broom in his hands, and a roil of dust stirred around his feet.

Historical value be damned. This had to go. David squatted and pried the top from the can of paint propping open the door. With a sweeping motion, he threw the gallon of dark paint in broad arcs, obscuring the fresco. The paint spread down the plaster, and dripped in long strings over the wainscoting.

Immediately David felt better. A puff of sea breeze rattled the dead leaves around the window and stirred the debris in the hall. He felt a weight lift from his mind, and he backed out of the door and turned the key in the lock.

All day David busied himself in the kitchen and the back of the house, avoiding the hall. In an uncharacteristic gesture, he turned on his battery-powered emergency radio, turned it to high volume, and hung it from the branches of the oak tree. Usually he worked to no noise but the soothing murmur of the sea wind through the lilacs. Rambunctious country western music bounced incongruously into the sedate gray rooms from the sunny backyard. It seemed to be the only station he could get in this remote area. It would do.

The family of gray squirrels that ordinarily chattered at him while he worked popped into their hole with disapproving flicks of their bushy tails and stayed hidden. Chickadees that nested in the lilacs fled in a protesting flurry. Even the bold robins wouldn't coast in and search for worms. A pair lit on the roof, then veered away when a snatch of the clatter and whine of Tammy Wynette drifted toward them.

Without seeming to, he avoided the hall. That night he strode rapidly up the stairs, two steps at a time, aiming his flashlight up the risers. The wall was black in the gloom when he flicked his gaze to the left.

The lantern chased the thick shadows away with its bright white light. David filled the kittens' bowl with food, then smoothed out his sleeping bag. He tugged off his dirty jeans and T-shirt and tossed them to the side. The orange kitten wandered over and curled up on his discarded shirt.

It had been a strange day's work . . . especially the disclosure of the disquieting mural. There would be some explanation of that, he was sure. He rolled onto his stomach and propped his chin on his fists.

Across the room, he had hung his antique fire fighter's costume, draped to dry out over a rickety chair frame. His pants and boots had been damp when he had come back from the fair. The fair had been fun . . . up to a point. The competition; winning was good. The fortune-teller and then the little girl; puzzling, disturbing. Lyric Solei; another kettle of fish entirely.

With his forefinger, he doodled her name in the dust near his head. *Lyric Solei. Lyric.* It made a pretty swirl. *Lyric.* He thought of her hair, with amber, gold, and cinnamon lights, shining in the sun. He drew her name again. *Lyric.* He wrote his name under it. *David.* Looked good. Now a big heart around both.

Stop it. He turned off the lantern. Flopping over on his back, he covered his eyes with his forearm. He could see the glowing afterimage of the lantern flame behind his eyelids. It turned into Lyric's bright hair and laughing face. He should apologize to her for the way he had acted at the fair. Seemed like he was always apologizing. That must mean something.

But he had been abrupt. And she had been friendly. David consciously squashed the little voice that pursued that line of thought. *Go to sleep.*

He slept almost immediately. He dreamed the erotic dream again, the one with the dancing, beautiful woman. The woman with the amber, gold, and cinnamon hair. Then he dreamed of the painting, and in the dream, the little people moved, fought, pleaded, and died.

Lyric written on my body. Her name, offensive, offensive. How can I make this unbeliever wake? In the substance of my very self, he has written the name of my enemy, my love. The dust rose and boiled near David's head in the night but dared not touch him. Protected by his serene unbelief, David slept on.

Wolfton's face of dust rose and peered at the

sleeping form. *David and Lyric. Sarah and Dante. Strong food. Not much longer, David and Lyric.* The dry lips twisted and sneered; then the tongue lapped across the signature, sweeping it up and away. *I eat your names tonight but soon you'll feed me, too, and then I'll have my revenge and be free.*

But tonight there is new life in the house. Four small creatures, but bigger than bats, and with the feline lust for warm flesh born in the blood. Hunters, strong hunters, not insect eaters like the despicable bats. Time is rushing, I will be strong, at last there will be an end to it all. Yes, soon, an end.

David awoke before dawn and went directly down the hall, still nude. He turned the key and stepped into the musty room. There it was. Every stroke of the obscene paintings had bled through the thick enamel he had splashed over the plaster.

Without hesitation, he grabbed a shovel he had left outside the door the day before. In broad, scraping strokes, he raked the plaster from the walls. It fell in a multicolored shower at his bare feet. He chipped and abraded until not a crumb remained on the wood laths. The dust boiled angrily around him, covering him in grit. Red flakes swirled and stuck to his sweaty shoulders and torso. He shoveled up the debris into the trash buckets and hauled it downstairs past the rat skeleton into the backyard.

There was a pile of dead branches and scraps of wood for disposal. He sprinkled the trash with paint thinner and threw the rags he had cleaned his hands with on the pile.

Lighting one of the wooden matches he used for his lantern, he tossed it on the fuel. The paint thinner and rags started with a sinister whoosh, and the dry wood began to smoke. Small bright flames leapt and licked within the tangle of branches.

David stood gazing into the flames for some moments. As the fire caught more steadily, he sprinkled the plaster and paint chips over the blaze. It sizzled and gave off a thick smoke as the enamel caught and fried; then orange flames danced irregularly over the mass. A stench arose like burning, rotten flesh, a cloying, putrid odor.

David stepped back from the smoke that reached for him. He was used to smoke, heat, and flames. It was just smoke. And fire was clean. He spread another bucketful of plaster shards over the flaming trash pile and waited for it to catch. When the fire was leaping, hungrily devouring the destroyed painting, he turned away. His head felt clear now.

Chapter Twelve

"Be there, be there, be there," David muttered to himself as he clutched the telephone receiver. Standing in the rec room at the fire station, he hoped no one would overhear him making an attempt at an apology.

Everything had been going so well at the fair until the little girl had bumped into him. That moment had slashed open the healing wound of guilt he'd been nursing for the past three years. Maybe it was the catharsis he needed. He was willing to consider it.

Oddly enough, the feelings of guilt weren't so strong when he was around the elegant Ms. Solei. They were hardly there at all. When he stopped to think about it—even half rationally—he could almost bring himself to overlook her involvement in whatever you would call it; the nefarious arts, her strange talents she claimed she had. How could he explain? And then, she was so, so . . . easy to talk to.

"Hello?" The light feminine voice on the other end of the line broke his stream of thought.

"Lyric, this is David Langston. Wanted to apologize about ducking out on you at the fair. I'd rather do it in person if you'd give me the chance to make it up to you." David shifted his position so he could see if any of his fellow firemen were close enough to hear his conversation.

"What did you have in mind?" Her voice seemed hesitant but with a hint of forgiveness.

"How would you like to spend a day on the high seas? I thought you might enjoy the Maritime Museum. You can pretend I'm a pirate and make me walk the plank if you like."

"The plank stuff sounds pretty good to me," she answered with a teasing tone in her voice. "When were you thinking of going? Keelhauling you sounds much more interesting than weeding my flower beds."

"I can pick you up in an hour." David tried to keep undisguised delight out of his voice.

"All right . . . in an hour. You remember your way here, I'm sure."

"Great. See you then."

David sprinted up the stairs, taking them two at a time. He rummaged in his locker and selected a fresh white shirt of soft cotton, and stuffed his shirttails roughly into the black button-fly jeans. He flipped up the shirt cuffs two turns, showing his tanned forearms. He pulled his black helmet down from the top of his locker, and then hesitated. He needed another helmet for Lyric to ride safely with him to the museum.

His friend Ben had a battered but serviceable helmet stored atop his locker. Ben wouldn't mind if his helmet came back smelling of perfume, although David might have to answer some embarrassing questions when he returned it.

On the wide side driveway, David slung a leg over his big Harley and balanced the powerful machine between his legs while he fastened his helmet strap. He sparked the motorcycle into purring life and then opened the throttle wide, to let it roar, banishing guilt for the day. The speed of the bike vibrated power throughout his body, making him feel immortal and in control of his destiny.

The short ride to Lyric's house was made shorter by the prospect of having her very desirable body pressed up against him on the outing. The bellow of his machine announced his arrival before he reached Lyric's gate. When he pulled up in front of her small white house, she was sitting on the porch swing, with that enormous black-and-white cat of hers. Cascades of pink roses hung from the porch roof and shaded the front of the house.

She was even more beautiful than he remembered. She was dressed in narrow white pants and an indigo blue silk blouse, cut low to show her very smooth shoulders. A thin golden chain drew a sharp vee pointing directly down between her breasts, where he remembered her medallion hid in tender seclusion.

All she needed was a delicate pair of wings and she would have been a perfect nymph, hiding among the roses. Her copper bright hair curled loosely on her shoulders. David resolved to give her his helmet instead of Ben's. If there was any perfume to be smelled, it would be in his own helmet.

David walked up the brick sidewalk, aware of her eyes on him from the shady porch. He paused on the steps to admire the enticing picture Lyric made.

The soft fabric of the shirt clung slightly to her arms and breasts, almost begging to be stroked. "Good morning," David said, knowing it would be if he spent it with her.

"Yes, it is, isn't it?" Lyric pushed the porch floor with one toe of her white leather sneaker to make the swing sway gently. David felt the warmth of her smile wash over his body. Did her smiles always make little seductive sparks dance in her eyes?

David crossed the porch and turned his back to the porch swing. He looked over his shoulder to match the rhythm of the swing and, at the right moment, dropped quickly into the seat.

Lyric gave a little laugh. "Nicely done. Did you have a porch swing when you were a little boy?" The cat blinked up at David, then rolled his head against David's knee and purred loudly.

David laid his arm casually along the back of the swing, the better to be close to the silk and cream of her shoulders. "Yes, we did. My mother would put a quilt on the seat and I'd swing and read in the hot afternoons when everyone else was taking a nap."

Lyric turned slightly to face him. "Were you a town child or a country boy? We traveled so much, I never quite knew what I was, even though I knew Salem was home."

He felt a current of excitement flow through his skin as her heavy shiny hair slid across his forearm. He nonchalantly moved his arm a little closer to the back of her neck. He was near enough to feel the delightful glow of her body heat. "My father had a farm." Lyric looked at him and frowned slightly, as if she were imagining him driving a tractor or milking a cow. The motion of her head caused another stomach-swooping emotion as her hair brushed across the bare skin of his arm.

David reached to stroke the cat at the same instant Lyric reached to do the same. Their hands tangled like a hawk and sparrow above the soft fur. Lyric laughed softly and the cat stood and jumped off the swing from his position between them, leaving room for their thighs to touch ever so slightly.

"How is the house restoration going? It takes a lot of time to get those things done, doesn't it?"

David glanced down at the contrast of well shaped short pink nails and smooth skin captured in his generous grasp. Lyric left her very soft hand in his for a second before returning it to her lap. David replied, "Yes, it's very slow, but I'm not in a hurry. Things that you have to wait for are usually better than things that come too easily." He glanced around the porch and front wall of Lyric's tidy house. "Is this house very old? It looks in great shape."

"Parts of it are very old, perhaps as old as your house, although it was never so grand as Wolfton House. Other parts have been added on here and there, over time. I like to think each person who has lived here has put a part of their personality into it. It's been in the family for a long time. Now it's mine."

A wish passed through David's mind that someday his house could be filled with the love and peace this little house seemed to radiate. He knew it was not just the walls and windows that created this atmosphere but the energy and vitality of the serenely sexy woman who sat by his side.

"Would you like to see the parlor? I think it's the best part of the house." Lyric rose and David followed in unconscious harmony with her body.

"Sounds good. Maybe I can get some ideas for my place." David held the door open for Lyric. The cat made a deft move between their feet and scooted into the hall. "Any skeletons in your closets?"

"No. Just my kind of everyday magic," Lyric answered.

David paused in the hallway to admire the big Victorian hall tree. He ran his fingers over the deep carvings of twining ivy that ran up the sides and surrounded the oval beveled mirror at the back. At the top of the mirror, a mischievously sensual faun's face watched with half-closed eyes from under the leaves to see the motion in his mirror. The broad seat was littered with Lyric's house keys, purse, and mail. The arms on each side were fitted to hold umbrellas or walking canes.

"My grandmother bought this in Ireland before my mother was born. It's solid walnut. It's not the right period for your house, though." An ornate, frivolous Victorian piece would never fit in the severe Wolfton House.

"I like it." In the faded old mirror, David could see Lyric standing behind him. He smiled into the glass and saw her eyes light in return. Their faces were reflected below the faun's cunning stare. "It has personality."

"I think you'll like this room," Lyric said as she turned to the parlor, the first room on her left.

The sound of David's boots were muffled as he stepped from the polished wood floor of the hall to the strangely patterned rug in the parlor. The wide carpet was deep bloodred, faded black, and mellow brownish cream. It seemed to have animals, flowers, and tiny people all mixed up. He stepped quickly back to the wooden floorboards.

"Don't worry . . . you can't hurt that rug. But it is very old." Lyric moved over to a side table and snapped on a lamp shaped like a drooping lily flower. It cast a small pool of soft light on the richly colored carpet. "When I was a child I would sit on this rug and pretend it was my magical flying carpet. It took me to so many wonderful places. Maybe it was magic after all."

David walked on the exotic rug, but kept his step purposefully light. He squatted and ran his palms over the designs. Touching the nap forming the rich patterns was irresistible. "I see these in the decorating books I've been studying. For my house, you know. But I've never touched one. Feels like wool, but softer."

Lyric knelt at his side. "It is wool. It's called a Tabriz. It took a desert woman years to weave it. Every tiny knot was tied by hand. When she finished, she was almost blind and she would never make another.

"This little design represents lightning. This is clouds. Mountains. This one, water." She moved her finger from one stylized design to another, each dark on the old wool. "Here, prosperity.

"When her man sold the rug, he bought two camels and ten sheep. It gave their second daughter a proper dowry so she could marry well. It was the mother's sacrifice for the life of her daughter. Without a dowry, a second daughter would have been a slave."

"How can you know all that? Did the rug come with a document?"

Lyric stroked over the rug's smooth weave a final time and stood. "No document . . . but it can tell its own story to me. It's my profession to know these things. This carpet is spun of love to make happiness."

A small crease of a frown showed between David's eyes. "But the mother was blind when she finished."

"It was her choice. Sometimes that's what love is. Choice and sacrifice."

"No philosophy this morning, all right?" David held up a hand and rose from the floor. Lyric nodded.

David moved slowly around the room, surveying the vases of fresh, lushly fragrant roses that were complimented by clusters of natural stones and crystals. Sparkling clumps of amethyst and rose quartz glittered on the low windowsills.

Pristinely white, a marble mantel and hearth framed the small fireplace. A tidy stack of fragrant apple wood waited on the grate, and a basket of pine needles and cones sat in reach for quick kindling. A small, heavily carved and painted wooden chest sat to one side. A massive split geode filled with radiant purple jewels lay on the hearth. Well-worn chairs almost asked a visitor to take a seat nearby.

A spindly pianolike device stood between two tall windows. It had two short keyboards, and the sunlight reflected from its dim gold finish. It seemed impossibly fragile and old.

"This is my harpsichord." Lyric struck one key, making a bell-like note. The silver tone hung suspended between them like a soap bubble.

David gently touched the gold leafing on the delicate lid. "Where did you learn to play?" he asked. He had never seen such unusual and mystical furnishings and decorations in a private home, or anywhere else for that matter. He felt as if he were on a stage set. But for all her peculiar surroundings and strange attitudes, Lyric's home was gracious and friendly, and did not give off the eerie feeling he often felt at his new house. Lyric's house was enchanting. He could feel the spell falling over him.

"My father was a master musician, an accomplished violinist." Lyric struck a soft chord on the keyboard. "He would play his violin outside beneath the trees on summer evenings. He played for me every night, no matter where we were." She struck another chord, slim fingers pressing yellowed ivory keys tenderly as a caress. "Father could charm the birds themselves to make music for him."

If he was anything like you, I'm sure he could, David thought happily. He could almost hear the mellow tones of her father's violin floating above the walnut trees as the sleepy birds twittered softly in harmony.

"When my mother was alive, she would play the harpsichord and he would accompany her on the violin. I remember it a little." Lyric struck a third chiming chord.

"Have they been gone long?" David asked sympathetically.

"My mother died when I was a very small child. I hardly remember her, but my father passed over just last year. They are with me always." She closed her eyes briefly and seemed to be thinking of her parents, as a soft shadow of a smile crossed her lips. "Love transcends time, you know."

"It sounds like you and your father were very close. He must have encouraged you into your profession. My dad never understood why I had to be a fireman." David let his guard down somewhat in the presence of this beguiling woman.

Her cool green eyes filled with genuine compassion. "Is there a special reason?" she asked, tilting her head.

"Always wanted to be one. I've felt compelled to fight, really fight, fire. It's like personal revenge to drown one out, to crush it. I've never really understood it myself, just something deep inside." David wondered if Lyric was sensitive to the emotions rocketing inside his head.

"Perhaps someday you will know." Lyric turned slightly away from him. He couldn't see her face as she spoke. "I believe reasons from long ago sometimes make us act in the present. There's nothing without a purpose, you know."

David saw that books were everywhere. Shelves were filled neatly and the overflow was stacked on tables here and there. Piles of books leaned like amiable old dogs against the ample wing chairs near the fireplace. "You must be the bookstore's best customer." He picked up a brightly covered best-seller and riffled the pages.

"Several bookstores, actually. If you see anything you might like, I'll be glad to lend it to you." She gestured with a rueful shrug and a grin toward the floor around the chairs and fireplace. "I'm sure I have some I can spare. It's my addiction, I suppose."

Glossy new paperbacks curled with an air of insincerity, with insolent little tongues of ribbon and paper sticking out from their pages. "That is one thing I do like about New York; lots of wonderful bookstores." Lyric tapped seven slick-covered romances into a straighter pile, and sat them atop a tattered leather volume that looked to weigh ten pounds. The faded tip of a pheasant feather marked a page halfway through the old album.

"My father said no one in this family has ever discarded a book. If you look in here, you'll believe it."

An omnivorous reader himself, David could not resist scanning the book backs. The titles ranged across the spectrum. There was the newest spy novel just off the press, a ragged old book in what may have been Russian, and many small thin volumes of poetry. An oversize portfolio of botanical drawings filled one small tabletop. The thicker volumes looked as if Merlin himself had thumbed the gold-tipped pages. A wide desk with pigeonholes stuffed with letters and papers held a clutter of leather-bound tomes leaning on either side of a competent-looking small computer.

The bindings were heavily impressed with elaborate tooling stained with deep dyes. Golden engraving outlined the title lettering. "These are beautiful." David carefully lifted the top volume, holding it nearer his face to inspect the intricate ornamentation more closely.

A spark leapt through his fingers as he held the book. There was his wise serpent, subtle red eyes and all. He rubbed across the image slowly, feeling the slight ripple of the raised scales under his palm. He flipped open the cover to read the inscription on the title page, but it was in a foreign language, written in a flowing script. He couldn't begin to decipher it. Maybe Latin, if he remembered correctly.

"Yes, whenever I find a really old book in a shop, I have to buy it and bring it home. My little rescues. I think each book is grateful to be here with friends." Lyric touched an open book, tucked a yellow ribbon back inside, and closed the covers, pressing on the leather. "I guess I'm being silly, but I love them all."

David rubbed the serpent again. "A diary?"

Lyric took the book from him with an air of respect. She glanced across the parchment and closed the deep red leather covers, holding the book like a prayer between her palms. "Something like that." Holding the book to her face, she tapped her mouth with the corners. It hid her curving lips, but her eyes danced above the edges, captivating David. "A family tradition." Her index finger slid down over the serpent's head as if she were caressing it.

David touched the fabric that cloaked his own serpentine mark. His flesh tingled beneath the indelible imprint.

He turned away from the desk and peered at a large crystal ball carefully balanced on a stand of three smiling dolphins. He could see the room—and himself—reflected in it upside down. Just the way he felt right now.

"Maybe we ought to be going." The past; Lyric was comfortable with it. He wanted to forget it. Sadness had started to creep up the back of his neck and he didn't want to lose the happy mood they had been enjoying so far.

"Hope you don't mind riding a motorcycle."

"Can't wait; it looks exciting. Besides, we can finish the tour some other time." Lyric picked up her house key from the hall tree bench.

David held the door open for her and as she brushed past him; she looked up into his face briefly. Could she have caught a hint of his feelings in his unguarded eyes?

David offered his helmet to Lyric and pulled Ben's over his own head. Lyric leaned far forward to shake her hair over her head and grasped the cascade of silky curls, twisting it into a thick rope in order to stuff it into the confines of the helmet.

David stood speechless at the temptingly lovely neck revealed in her casual gesture. He was unprepared for the rush of desire and longing the actions provoked. Hormones, just hormones, he told himself. Seemed to be a lot of those going around these days. He swallowed and forced himself to turn away and mount the motorcycle.

With the bike purring obediently, he turned to steady Lyric. "Just grab my shoulder and step on the peg right there." She stepped on the left peg above the hot chrome exhaust pipe and swung her right leg wide to straddle the bike. Settling behind him, she rolled her hips under to meet his. The machine let out a feral growl and lurched forward, causing Lyric to clutch David's waist tight. David smiled. He was going to enjoy the ride.

Chapter Thirteen

The Maritime Museum was only a short distance from Lyric's house down the coastline highway, but long enough for David to savor the soft feel of her breasts pressed against his back. She rode with her arms around him, circling him in a grip that locked just above his belt buckle. Fantasy washed over him. He envisioned her hips, her flat stomach, and those soft sweet breasts pressed to his front against him, flesh to flesh.

It had been such a long time since anything had felt so naturally wonderful. Nothing in the supernatural world seemed to frighten her, but he felt the urge to protect the part of her that was mortal and clinging to his back. She was safe in his skilled hands, even if she didn't know it. David looked into the rearview mirror. He could barely see her. One tendril of flame-colored hair had escaped her helmet and whipped like a living ribbon, dancing in and out of his vision.

As he leaned into a final curve Lyric squeezed her thighs tighter to maintain her balance. He closed his eyes for a split second and hoped she could not see in the mirror the erotic effect she was having on him. He opened the throttle wider and roared down the final half mile to the docks.

David brought the bike to a showily commanding halt. The cloud of dust that had been chasing them caught up and then swept past, peppering them with grit. Lyric's arms were still clamped around his waist.

"Did you enjoy the ride?" Perhaps he would have to peel her arms from his stomach; not that he wanted to. She seemed a bit unsure about this mode of transportation. "You first." He twisted around to steady her as she dismounted.

"It certainly seems . . . powerful." Lyric tilted her head to the side to unfasten the unfamiliar helmet.

"Wait, let me help with that." David swung off the motorcycle and flipped down the kickstand. He stepped close enough to see how her thick lashes cast a shadow against her wind-pinked cheeks. She didn't seem shaken now that she was off the bike.

"It's really lots of fun once you relax and just sort of embrace the danger of it all."

Lyric bent her head back so David could work the double-ringed helmet fastener. He fumbled with the chin strap, brushing her velvety skin as if by accident. As he slid the nylon from the metal rings, he stole a closer look at her captive face in the helmet's frame. It was the face of an angel, a classic oval shape with pale perfect skin and soft moist lips that glistened slightly, as if she had just licked them, ready to be kissed. Her big eyes were sparkling with animation from the exciting ride.

David slipped the helmet up and freed Lyric's hair. He was right: his helmet was gonna smell great.

"Hi. Two, please." He shoved a five-dollar bill across the counter at the admission booth. The big wooden sign read SALEM COUNTY MARITIME MUSEUM and featured a ship's figurehead of an Indian chief. The teenage girl selling tickets smacked her gum with a loud pop and appraised David with a near-sighted stare. She hurriedly ripped off her glasses and thrust them and her algebra book under the counter.

"Could we leave our helmets here while we visit the museum?"

The girl fluffed her hair and bestowed her most dazzling braces-filled smile on David. "Sure. I can keep them under the counter." She managed to touch his cuff as she took the helmet straps. "I'll be here when you want them."

David gave Lyric her ticket and tucked his in his jeans pocket. When his back was turned, the girl fumbled on her glasses and leaned over the counter, propping her chin. To David's chagrin, her sigh was audible as they pushed through the turnstile.

He shot a glance at Lyric to see if she had noticed his admirer. She seemed to be restraining a look of amusement, and gestured toward the water. "I love the sound of the waves, don't you? I always feel more peaceful when I'm near the water."

"I've never lived this close to the sea, but I know I'll enjoy it. I can hear the waves at night below my house."

Noisy gulls mewed and cackled overhead. The greedy birds jostled each other in the air as they watched closely for any sign of a cracker or bread crust. A sharp breeze came in over the bay, carrying with it the clean salt smell of the ocean, spiced with a tang of seaweed and a drift of exhaust fumes from puttering oyster boats working in and out of the channel.

The museum was broader in scope than just a traditional building full of old articles. There were ship chandlers' sheds carefully recreated with all the fascinating and obscure articles necessary for a long voyage at sea. Small boats were displayed firmly dry-docked on the lawn where children and curious adults could clamber inside, work the wheels, and peer into the tiny cabins.

David climbed into a small fishing boat and turned to Lyric. He lifted her over the edge, surprised to find that his handspan almost met around her narrow waist. A jolt of male primal instincts flashed through his body, much like the adrenaline-pumping, heart-pounding sensation that seized him when he saw a blaze he would have to enter.

He willed himself calm, and concentrated on the sights around him. The small craft was a curiosity for David, as he had grown up far from the sea. "I've never been in a boat like this before. Just bass boats, all aluminium." He stroked the brass-ringed instruments and wooden rails. His concentration was diluted by Lyric's closeness, so close he could see the tiny blue strokes in her extraordinary green eyes.

He stood behind her at the wheel of the little boat and covered her hands on the wheel with his, steering their craft on an imaginary sea. She pressed back into his chest slightly. Her head came just below his chin and the wonderful aura of her body made him almost dizzy with its nearness. Her faintly spicy perfume drifted around him, reminding him of red flowers.

"What are you thinking?" Lyric turned her face up to ask the question. The motion made her head rub ever so pleasantly against his chest. He wondered if she could hear his heart beating.

"A poem my high school English teacher made us memorize. It didn't make much sense in Georgia but now I'm getting the idea."

"What poem?"

> " '*I must go down to the sea again,*
> *The lonely sea and the sky.*
> *All I need is a tall, tall ship,*
> *And a star to steer her by.*' "

A mob of noisy children wearing identical yellow T-shirts and herded by a team of harassed teachers invaded the little boat. "Ahoy there, matey, I think we've been boarded. Abandon ship." David and Lyric laughingly gave up command of the wheel to a seven-year-old wearing a baseball hat that bent his sizable ears down like small wings. "Here you go, Captain. Take the helm."

David jumped over the side of the boat, then turned to swing Lyric down to the grass. She was light, but her vibrant energy left David's skin tingling.

The focal point of the museum grounds was at dockside. It was an original, beautiful example of the famous Yankee clipper ships; her sleek lines and almost feminine beauty drew every eye. The incoming tide made her tug like a well-mannered horse at the restraining lines that kept her tethered to the land.

"Here's your tall ship. She's a beauty. She'll make you understand what that poem is about."

David and Lyric walked up the gently bobbing

gangplank and stepped onto the smooth wooden deck. She walked in front of him and he couldn't take his eyes away from her rounded hips as she climbed the inclined boards. They stood a moment to get the feel of the motion, like lifelike breathing under their feet. The breeze sung gently in the rigging and the cries of the sea gulls came from over the water.

David touched Lyric's waist and guided her toward the rail. They rested on their elbows, shoulders together, watching the lapping green water. Close to the surface tiny silver fish nibbled at the hull of the ship, then darted away. Lyric rubbed the wooden rail, polished to a satin gloss from years of sailors and tourists touching the dark mahogany.

"I wonder what it was like to do battle on the high seas centuries ago?" Lyric turned toward David and lounged back against the rail. For a second the posture thrust her full breasts temptingly forward and pulled the blue silk tight. Her glittering hair drifted in slow rhythm with the slack pennants hanging from the mast.

"Sometimes dangerous, but mostly boring. Lots of time out to sea in between battles. Bad food, hard work, and nowhere to spend your pay, if you ever got paid." David flashed a wicked grin. "But lots of excitement, now and then." He hoped he looked rather like a sailor of old himself, with his open-necked white shirt setting off his deep tan.

"Sounds to me like being a fireman in Salem," Lyric joked. They shared a laugh, and strolled easily down the deck together.

David was pleased the morning was going so well. The light talk was coming easily, and there was not the feeling of strange opposition he had felt with Lyric when they had spoken in his house. He liked her house and wondered what her bedroom upstairs was like. He pictured her in a huge four-poster bed, surrounded by fluffy down pillows. . . .

"I like your house. It seems very comfortable."

The leather key ring had been showing at the edge of Lyric's pocket. David saw her shove the ring down and turn the heavy brass key beneath the white fabric. "Yes, I love my home. I'm really ready to quit the city and stay here forever. That would certainly make Nolan happy."

"Your books . . . there were some very old ones there. The one with a snake on the cover; I could swear the emblem was the same as mine." He saw Lyric's eyes sweep across his shoulder where the mark was hidden. He was gratified to see she had remembered.

Lyric answered calmly, "That was my private journal. My grandmother had it made for me when I was born and my mother gave it to me when I was old enough to read and write. It's a family tradition.

"The symbol is a very ancient one. It stands for eternity, rebirth." She waited for a reproach, but David only blinked with genuine interest. "Some say it stands for the magic that is within us all."

"Magic within me, too?" He met her eyes.

"More than you know." He saw her serene smile again, and she reached for him, slipping her cool fingers trustingly within his. He drew her a willing step closer. They were interrupted by a cackling flurry of sea gulls overhead quarreling over a crust.

The avaricious birds dropped the bread and it fell to the deck in front of Lyric's toes. She stooped to pick it up, then held it high over her head. David was amazed to see the bold bird hover, scarcely two feet away, balancing on its broad white wings. The gull cocked a fearless black eye shiny as a bead at

David, then plucked the crust neatly from Lyric's grasp. Lyric flicked away the clinging crumbs. They laughed at the selfish bird, gobbling the crust as he flew and fended off his disappointed brothers.

"How do you like living in a town with so much history? Everyone's house has an intriguing past. Even your house must have a story." Lyric bent to inspect an interlaced cloverleaf of stout tarred rope.

"Well, the history of the town doesn't interest me as much as the history of the house. You seem to be interested in Wolfton House, as well."

Lyric looked up into David's eyes briefly, as if to see if that was meant as a reproach for her earlier trespassing. She saw nothing of the sort in his expression. Only honest curiosity was displayed there.

"Yes, I've been interested in the house for a long time. It seems to have a personality of its own, and not always a friendly one. It makes me uneasy to be inside, but I still feel a connection with it. I think there's lots of secrets to be learned about Wolfton House."

He was silent and they started to walk slowly back to the stern. Their sleeves touched; then Lyric's soft hand was in David's warm palm. Their fingers laced as if by habit. "Why did you buy that house?" she asked with her head down, it seemed before her courage ran out.

"I wanted something I could pour my heart and soul into." David stopped beside the great wooden mast. "But lately my heart has been distracted," he added softly.

Lyric's cheeks turned a peachy pink as she blushed at his sudden confession. David was intrigued to see the color spread down her neck and disappear under her shirt. He wondered if she would blush all the way down to her toes.

Lyric stepped forward quickly and spontaneously flung her arms around the single thick timber that soared up and up. Laying her cheek against the sun-hot wood, she pressed her body to the pine as if it were a lover. Her eyes were closed and David thought she must be hearing the timeless voice of the ship, the motion of the water, and the thrumming of the wind against the mast.

David circled to the other side and reached to Lyric, joining so that they embraced the ship's heart. They tilted their heads back and gazed up the length of the mast, traced by lines dark as penned ink against the bright sky, and crossed by the yards bulky with tightly furled sails.

Far above them the clouds raced by the slender topmast, and the slight rocking motion of the ship gave a feeling of speed, of rushing toward a waiting goal.

It was as if they could see the whirling motion of the planet itself speeding past the thrusting tip of the mast. Lyric staggered slightly, clinging to David as to a lifeline. He felt her waver and stepped around the mast to pull her toward him in a circle of safety. She buried her face to his chest and he felt her moment of dizziness pass.

David slid his palm up the nape of her neck. Her hair slid over his wrist like a warm silk banner. He wove his fingers gently through the curls to tilt her head back and reveal her face.

How small she seemed, standing enveloped in his shadow. Now she waited for him to cross the threshold she had been cautiously revealing. He closed his eyes and bent down to taste the velvet darkness of her mouth. She hesitated but a second and then he felt her answer, the slick sensual skin of her tongue, like molten lava, soft then firm.

Lyric lightly dragged her nails down his tense back, then rested her touch on his hips. She pulled him closer. Even through the thin cotton shirt it was as if she were touching all the most sensitive places at once, creating furrows revealing deeply buried emotion. He felt his heart showered with a kaleidoscope of a thousand colors. Colors sparked behind his closed eyelids.

A riptide of emotion swept through his mind and body. A passion for life he thought forgotten burst through, and he knew they were changing in this instant, this blink of time that would be an eternity. They were reforming, melting, recast into one entity.

The feeling could have gone on forever, but suddenly they were engulfed by a wave of running, laughing children, tumbling past their legs and shouting. The school trip and the weary teachers had reached the clipper ship.

David looked down at her face. He stepped back slowly, sliding his hands down her slender arms. He held her fast in his strong grasp, waiting for her verdict.

Lyric stood very still, her eyes closed. Then he saw a slow smile begin on her lips. Yes, the smile seemed to say, it was good. It was right. She opened her eyes and gave a firm nod. It was right.

He returned the smile and tightened his grip. His heart gave a sudden jump. His heart wasn't distracted; it was attracted, like the magic lodestone of the compass drawn to true north.

He bent and kissed her irresistible mouth, the soft, smiling lips. Once was not enough. He knew once would never be enough, as a happy turmoil swirled throughout his body.

Chapter Fourteen

At the edge of the gently rolling lawns of the Salem County Maritime Museum sat a small Colonial house that held exhibits of life in an old Salem village. The museum and its grounds had been built recently, hardly five years ago, and Lyric had never had occasion to visit it. Working so often in museums as she did, she hadn't found the need to visit one in her hometown. But today it seemed the thing to do, with David at her side, asking questions in his slow sweet drawl about life in the East, so different from his former life in the South.

Near the house a cluster of tourists stood under a large tree. They watched a sweating museum guide in period garb toiling over a black washpot. A small fire smoked under the iron cauldron. The wind shifted and the visitors stepped back from the smoke. The laundress persevered, poking into the bubbling wash water with a worn stick.

"Looks like wash day." Lyric pointed to the costumed woman laboriously pulling a steaming garment out of the boiling water. "What a chore. They say the Pilgrims landed on Monday and the first thing they did was wash all the laundry. That's why Monday is traditionally a wash day."

She and David strolled hand in hand from the dock area to the museum building, passing in and out of the pools of deep shade thrown by the old walnut trees. His large hand folded her small one inside as neatly as a love note in a pocket.

David teased, "I'll take a nice automatic washer and dryer any day, thank you. Now there's some real magic—electricity." They paused in the shelter of the trees. He ran his thumb slowly over the tops of her fingers, in and out of the hollows between her knuckles, then pressed a quick, soft kiss in the palm. A jolt of their own electricity passed between them.

David drew Lyric close and brushed her hair lightly back from her face, letting his touch rest on her cheek for a moment as he smiled down at her. Lyric felt tiny tingling hot footprints of desire run up into her scalp and around her ears. Spreading her fingers against his strong warm chest, she felt his intense heartbeat jump against her palm. She raised her face, hoping, inviting, asking for another kiss. David slowly lowered his face to hers. He laid a kiss over her willing lips as tender and teasing as the erotic stroke of a feather. His touch made her feel light-headed enough to float away on the sea breeze.

Lyric pressed her head into the hollow of David's shoulder, basking in the discovery of the heated response his slightest touch could awaken. She stepped back, but could not relinquish her contact with him. Swallowing unsteadily, she said huskily,

"Perhaps we should go inside."

They walked into the cool hall. The hushed museum atmosphere was a familiar one to Lyric, one that she often encountered in her work with antique clothing. Their footsteps echoed hollowly in the deep silence. No one seemed to be inside this afternoon. The lights were low to avoid fading the costumes and artifacts displayed in the rooms off the wide hall. Here and there a mannequin stood dressed in antique costume. Their frozen postures and glass eyes under lids that seemed to be lowered secretively gave a ghostly, faintly sinister air to the silent rooms.

In one corner were a number of tablelike display cases clustered around some comfortable tables and benches. Lyric knew they would be map tables. Dark paintings hung on the walls nearby in an alcove shielded from the light.

"Look, David. These maps go back to before the 1600s. They should show the earliest land grants and farms. Let's see if we can find your house." Lyric pulled at David and tugged him over to a large display case. Beneath the finger-smudged glass lay examples of antique cartography depicting seventeenth- and eighteenth-century Salem.

The central chart was titled SALEM VILLAGE: 1692, the lettering scribed in the erratic penmanship of an ancestor on the land. The edges of the document were curled and brown with age. Houses, docks, and farms were depicted in realistic miniature sketches across the vellum. Tiny houses, little cows, clumps of trees, and winding paths illustrated the early settlement. Anything considered of economic importance was carefully penned in.

Toward the lower left corner, fronted by its early possessions of fields and backed by the sea, was a tiny illustration of Wolfton House, once dominating and proudly aristocratic. The house was gray; the shutters dull blue. A carriage house and several small outbuildings were to the side of the manor house. The curving drive was a tiny petal-sized circle on the paper.

"There it is," David exclaimed. "It must have been an important house to have been marked like this on the map." They leaned over the case, their heads touching. Lyric could feel David's breath stir over her cheek and hair. She took in his scent happily, inhaling deeply. He smelled like fresh green grass, pine trees, and wind and sunshine; all the beautiful natural things. Her shoulder nestled against his, and she pressed against his solid body, perhaps a little more heavily than necessary.

David reached over the glass and tapped it sharply with his forefinger. He squinted at the almost microscopic writing. "It has a notation to the side. Can you read it?"

Lyric bent closer to decipher the tiny script, a spider trail of faded sepia ink. "It says: 'Last witch . . . burned in Salem . . . executed here for treason against the Crown.' " Her voice faded. Lyric felt a wrench of pain in her stomach like a snakebite of remembered malice. Even the heat of David's nearness could not keep a frigid wash of fear from shuddering through her body. She gasped and spun away from the case.

"Lyric, what's the matter? You shook like someone walked over your grave." A crease of concern appeared on David's face. He reached for her and touched her forehead and cheeks. "You're pale and cold. Are you feeling faint?" He slipped his forefinger and thumb around her wrist as if to take her pulse.

Lyric retreated another step and pulled David with her. "I told you sometimes I can feel things from objects."

David hugged Lyric to him and patted her shoulder rather awkwardly. "Oh, just bad vibes, huh? I understand. Why don't you not stand so close or something."

"Bad vibes, yes, that's what it is."

David walked around the cases and stared into each case with interest. "Looks like we're on the right trail. Do you think there might be more information here on old Wolfton himself? I mean, besides the things I heard at the station house. No one seems to have details on the history of my house, or maybe they're just not telling. I wonder if he had anything to do with the shipping trade." David glanced about the room and peered at the gloomy landscapes.

Lyric's apprehension grew. "Maybe they still have the tax rolls. We might find out what trade he was in," she responded faintly. She tried to shake the sensation she picked up from the map. Hugging her arms around herself, she looked out the windows, trying to settle her feelings. Sometimes her talents could be a problem in situations like this. She remembered being unable to cross the threshold of the White Tower in London. That place was steeped in too many memories, too many sad, sad memories.

David walked behind her to scan the portraits more closely. "Listen to this. 'Capt. Quinton H. Wolfton was appointed to the colony as a land governor to assess and collect taxes for His Majesty William III,' " David read from a small framed plaque, his back to Lyric. " 'A greedy and tyrannical man, he soon realized the power assigned to him would not be monitored. He governed the village of Salem with an iron fist, and was particularly noted for his enjoyment of sadistic treatment of those who were delinquent in their taxes, traitorous in speaking against the Crown, or religiously deviant to the customs of the time.'

"I'll be darned; here he is. Old Capt. Wolfton himself. I'm impressed. I'm probably sleeping in his bedroom."

Lyric whirled and almost cried out at the sight. She covered her mouth, pressing her lips against her teeth, as a nauseous wave of horrified recognition swept through her. There above the small plaque was a life-size image of the haughty man who lurked so loathsomely in her visions. It was the man who sent Dante to his death.

The artist had done his job well, and the pale man stood realistically as if he were behind a gilded window frame. The glittering wicked eyes on the canvas met Lyric's living, stricken stare. Wolfton was posed holding a brown leather-bound book close to his green brocade waistcoat. One finger was stuck into the volume, as if to keep his place. His left arm stretched slightly back with an open gesture, negligently indicating the sea view from the window behind him . . . and David's red homespun coat, arranged prominently over a chair.

Lyric moved closer to David for protection from the evil intent evident even in the painting. David draped a strong arm around her shoulders and pulled her closer without looking at her face. Lyric's mind fought the emotions of horror the picture evoked as David's comforting, vital touch safeguarded her.

"What do you think, Lyric? No wonder none of the locals wanted to live there. Sounds like he burned witches in his front yard. Nasty character." David was scanning the time-darkened oils with deep interest. He looked down at her in concern when she didn't reply. "Are you all right? You're shivering. More bad vibes?"

"It's the coat," Lyric said. "It's your coat." She gathered her wits. The red garment was draped across a chair; the artist's skilled strokes had recorded the silver buttons, and tiny crosshatched black lines danced down the lapels where the magic runes marked the stitching. The singular piece of clothing had plainly been regarded as a significant trophy in Wolfton's career, to be memorialized in such a manner.

"My coat? Are you sure? How can you tell? It might just be some other red coat." David hugged Lyric tight to his side in his excitement and moved nearer for a closer look. "I think you're right. This is exciting. Look at that; my coat."

"Excuse me." David and Lyric turned to find an elderly lady in a demure blue dress smiling at them. She had approached silently on her crepe-soled shoes. A docent's tag was pinned to her immaculate white linen collar. "Are you interested in Capt. Wolfton?

"They called him the Devil Chaser, you know." The museum guide raised her eyebrows wisely. She sat down on a bench near the exhibit. Assessing the interest of her audience, she continued. "Sometimes he was called Hell's Wolfhound, but I suppose that was before he put on weight and lost his hair." She gave a genteel smile and bobbed her head toward the painting. She patted the bench seat beside her. "Come sit, dear, you look a bit pale."

Shakily Lyric sat, but David remained standing politely. "I'm David Langston, from Atlanta, and this is my friend, Lyric Solei. We've been trying to find out something about the house I bought here in Salem. I bought his house, Wolfton House."

The woman placed her slender, white-gloved fingers lightly on David's palm. "Yes, young man, I know you're not from around here. You're with the fire department, am I correct?"

"Yes, ma'am. I'm a paramedic, too."

She folded both hands in her lap and turned to Lyric. "Southern men are always so polite, don't you think? Such fine gentlemen."

Without waiting for an answer she continued. "I remember you as a child at the town library. I couldn't mistake that lovely hair. You're Prof. Solei's daughter, aren't you? I was so sorry to hear of your father's passing last year; such a kind and talented man."

David took a seat on the bench so that the fragile docent was between him and Lyric. The woman paused for a moment to remove a small flowered handkerchief from her pocket. "I'm sure you don't remember me, but I am Mrs. William Hubert Smythe-Turner, of the Upper Walscott Smythe-Turners. After Mr. Smythe-Turner passed on, I had time to devote myself to studying the local history and architecture, always a passion, if I may use such a strong word. Now I work here as a volunteer once a week."

David and Lyric hardly had time to exchange a glance over the docent's head before the torrent of words began again.

"Now, the Wolfton house was important for a number of things, but you would probably like more of the personal details, I'm sure, and the personal details of the man can hardly be separated from those of the house.

"Capt. Wolfton was a man whom power corrupted, to put it in a nutshell. He started as a fairly good administrator for the times, but seemed to be unable to keep a rein on his baser impulses." Mrs. Smythe-Turner fanned herself gently with the small linen square and looked up reproachfully at the somber features. She shook her head sadly as if the man had been a personal acquaintance.

"You won't find all the details in the local history society pamphlets, but my husband's family had dealings with the captain's family very early on, the Mayflower and all that . . . so I happen to know a little more about this particular case. Letters, you know, and diaries. They were wonderful about keeping diaries.

"Wolfton himself supposedly kept a diary in which he listed all his . . . thoughts. That's the book he is holding in this portrait. But it has never been found." David and Lyric looked up at the small book in its protective clasp.

"This was at the end of the ghastly witchcraft trials that racked this part of the country. It was very sad, and as they say now on television, umm, sick." Mrs. Smythe-Turner looked down for a moment as if distressed at using the distasteful word and neatly refolded her hankie. She patted it into a square and continued with renewed energy.

"Wolfton's young English wife, his third, by the way, died scarcely a year after she arrived from London. He had a way of . . . losing . . . his wives, but in those days that was not too unusual. There were rumors about his personal habits, but of course he was an important man, and powerful."

Mrs. Smythe-Turner touched Lyric's knee and leaned slightly toward her, as if she were gossiping about her next-door neighbors. "Now this comes from one of our own family diaries, and I have read it myself, so I know it's true." Her old eyes sparkled in delight to have a rapt audience for her tale of corrupted power, lost love, and betrayal.

"There was a beautiful young seamstress and weaver in the village named Sarah."

Lyric caught her breath in surprise. She saw David's eyes widen, and then he frowned slightly, as if in recognition at the name. "Wolfton developed a desire for this woman that began to consume him. Believing that he was assured of success due to his status and breeding, he pursued her unmercifully. She repeatedly repulsed his advances. It was humiliating to be rebuffed by a common village seamstress. At last, enraged that Sarah would continue to resist him, he charged her with witchcraft. It was, of course, a death sentence.

"It was the time of one of the earlier French and Indian wars, always something like that going on, you know, in those days. Sarah was deeply in love with a young militiaman who desperately wanted to save her from her fate.

"Somehow Sarah's lover uncovered the fact that Wolfton was trading with the enemy, meeting ships down in that sheltered cove below his house. I'm sure you've noticed, Mr. Langston, the excellent view of the sea that your house provides. There, behind the captain."

David nodded in acknowledgment, absorbed in the story unfolding before him.

"The militiaman, Dante Huels, secured several letters from the captain of one of the ships. They were signed by Wolfton and proved without a doubt Wolfton's own traitorous actions. The letters would be Huels's desperate key to save his wife, but instead they became his own death warrant. The papers proving Wolfton's guilty actions were confiscated when he captured Huels. Historians have assumed that the red coat depicted here is a symbol of the capture.

"The documents were an extra benefit for the captain to twist the story to his personal gratification, swearing himself, uncontradicted, that the treason was Dante's. He would be rid of two troublesome influences in the village. The letters were said to have been used to light the fire that consumed Sarah. The militiaman Huels was hanged the next day, branded with the crime Wolfton himself had committed." The docent sighed.

"The gallows were erected in front of the still-smoking pyre. Huels was denied a hood, in order that the coals would be his final sight. It was a touch that would certainly characterize the captain."

Lyric felt as if her skull were being squeezed by invisible steel bands. A great weight sat on her chest, crushing sorrow for the cruel end of a great passion. Her eyes filled with tears at the story of doomed love put together so coolly in the dusty museum room. Her last vision with the telltale scarlet jacket had shown the link between her and David, Sarah and Dante. So this was the whole story. All her suspicions and visions had been stitched into a whole by the age-dry voice in the quiet room.

"It was a particular pleasure of the captain's to have executions or floggings done at the front of his house, where he could watch them in comfort. The balcony over the entryway of your house is not a usual feature in this period house, Mr. Langston. It is a special detail Wolfton added."

David's attention was completely on the narrator of the sad tale. "Burned her in my front yard? My God, maybe that's why the grass won't grow there!"

"Yes, Mr. Langston, it is a common folk belief that grass won't grow on a place where a violent crime was committed." Mrs. Smythe-Turner was obviously pleased at the effect the story was having. Perhaps she had never had such responsive listeners. "Even nature can express its outrage at such a crime as the captain's." She offered her handkerchief to Lyric, whose eyes brimmed with tears.

"But the nefarious captain was not to escape the consequences of his actions. Before the fire was lit, Wolfton taunted Sarah from his balcony. Sarah presumed her lover was already dead." Mrs. Smythe-Turner closed her eyes briefly for effect, and then opened them to look straight at David for the most exciting part of the story.

"A terrible storm, filled with thunder and lightning, but strangely no rain, materialized as Sarah was tied to the stake. She cursed Wolfton most effectively as the flames began to lick her body. It seems that the charge of witchcraft, though misguided, in this case was true. She bound his soul to earth forever." The docent spoke slowly and clearly. "In that house specifically, Mr. Langston."

David jumped to his feet in agitated excitement. "A curse? My house is cursed? I knew that sleazy real estate agent wasn't telling me something!" Outraged, he ruffled his hair wildly. "No wonder it was so cheap."

Lyric interceded. "No, David, the house itself is not cursed. Wolfton's soul was bound within that house, to never reach a possibility of redeeming himself. I understand what Sarah did. Wolfton was condemned for eternity to a damnation of emptiness, earthbound without recourse."

"Great, just great. There's a ghost in my house and he's spending purgatory on my property." David stood with his fists on his hips, glaring indignantly at the captain. "I suppose that blows any resale value."

"You've got to admit, David, there is a certain feeling to that place. Ghostly souls can only wreak havoc and survive by sucking the life energies from living beings to which they can bond and attach themselves. Otherwise they eventually lose their strength and slowly diminish until they are powerless and harmless," Lyric tried to explain. "You should consider this more seriously."

"Maybe I should call the local chapter of Ghostbusters." David grinned wryly.

Mrs. Smythe-Turner raised a finger in mild admonition. "Mr. Langston, Lord knows, I'm a good Methodist and I'm not superstitious, but that house is supposed to hold Capt. Wolfton's soul. He was certainly not a pleasant person. Perhaps you should exercise some caution."

David responded confidently, "Thank you, ma'am, but I don't believe in ghosts so I guess he can't hurt me. A couple of new coats of paint and everything will be fine."

Lyric rose. "You've been very kind. Thank you so much for your story. It has certainly been a discovery for us." Too much of a discovery; she couldn't wait to get outdoors and away from the unnerving gaze of the painted figure.

The elderly woman inclined her head graciously. "It was a pleasure, my dear. I'm here every Monday afternoon, if you have any more questions. And Mr. Langston, do take care."

Lyric and David thanked the gentle old lady again and left the museum. David slipped his arm around Lyric's waist and pulled her close so they walked hip to hip, in rhythm. The feeling of his strong, long legs striding in nonchalant grace close to hers gave her a sense of security welcome after the chill of the shadowy museum.

"Pretty exciting. What a story, and it all happened right there in my front yard. But it's all over with now. Wonder if I could get a copy of that painting. It would be pretty impressive in the parlor."

Lyric supressed a shiver. "Let's not talk about that."

"Don't take it so seriously, Lyric. It happened a long time ago. It was sad, but what's done is done."

Lyric was silent, deep in thought, comforted by David's presence, but vastly unsettled by the revelations of the docent. She had had her suspicions, but now she realized why Wolfton House emitted such dark vibrations.

Like cloyingly sweet perfume, the thick atmosphere of malignancy had overwhelmed her each time she was near. It was Wolfton, calling her, to claim what he lusted for long ago and was denied. The threatening feeling of opposition between her and David was created by Wolfton's still living malice. *If love is everlasting, can hate be everlasting, too?* Yes, Lyric thought, both she and David should take care in Wolfton House.

Chapter Fifteen

Two horse chestnut trees, older than the house, grew near the cliffside. The thick trunks leaned away from the constant sea wind and were placed perfectly for a hammock to be slung between them. David had purchased a wide-knotted rope hammock and suspended it from the trunks. It was an inviting spot, swaying in the dappled shade of the afternoon.

David rolled into the laced ropes and set it swinging. He let one leg trail over the edge to keep the relaxing sway in motion with the barest push of his toes. The hammock swung, as tranquilizing as a rocking cradle, and lulled David into a trance. He yawned and shaded his eyes with his forearm, squinting at the sea gulls balancing on the updraft sweeping up the cliff. The dazzling sun forced afternoon sleep upon him. The cool breeze off the sea left traces of salt on his mouth. He licked his lips, and the weight of his eyelids won the battle between conscious thinking and unconscious memories.

"I've grown very fond of you, mistress, whilst on this voyage."

"And I of thee."

By the light of the second full moon that they had shared on this ship, he gazed into her shadowed face. With the moon behind her in that silver bath of light, she seemed powerful, a queen from another world. He had seen her power.

Food and water had run dangerously low as the little vessel floated becalmed, a painted ship on a motionless, painted ocean. The wind dropped to nothing, not a whisper to stir the pennons hanging atop the mast. Dark clouds drifted on the farthermost horizon, dragging tantalizing streamers of rain, but none came near them. Sails were slack, water barrels nearly empty, and tempers short, until dry mouths checked even the angry words.

Soon the weakest would begin to perish, either on their own, or at the selective discretion of the captain. Less mouths to share would mean more of the meager rations for those who survived.

The tall young seaman had been the one to stand the lonely night watches, scanning the still water. Unseen, he observed the quiet woman from Plymouth standing by the rail in the moonlight. Suffering with all of them, silently, her round smooth cheeks had become thinner as the dry, idle days passed. Night after night she leaned against the rail, hugging her thin shawl to her shoulders. The moon waxed to fullness under her watch.

The watchman heard her sigh. She paced once, twice, three times around the deck as the full moon rose. It slid along the spangled sky, standing above the deck like the noonday sun, bright enough that the woman stood on her shadow like a black pedestal.

He saw her slip off the cap that covered her rich hair. Head bowed, she folded the kerchief slowly, creasing and recreasing the fabric. She tucked it in her apron pocket. Pulling her fingers through her hair, she loosened her braid and let the silken tresses lie free on her shoulders. The seaman heard faint snatches of a low, soft song as she stretched her arms out and tilted her face upward. Standing in the moonglow, she whistled three times, trilling as softly as a sleepy bird, then stepped into the shadow of the cabin.

For a long moment all was silent as the watchman thought of what he had observed. Then as furtively as a creeping mouse, there was a faint tap and creak, small sounds of the long halyards rustling, touching the thick wooden mast. Gently as spring leaves in a shower, the lines began to sway against the yards, teased by the smallest of breezes. The seaman heard the movement in the canvas, then felt the zephyr dance across his face and move his hair. The pennon at the mast tip shook, then rolled out in a languid swirl. The sails ruffled and luffed, then filled lazily, fuller and fuller.

Elated, the watch called, "All hands on deck! All hands!" The mainsail bulged like the belly of a white cat and the ship shuddered and awoke, coming alive in the rising gale. The canvas cracked like a shot as it stretched to accommodate the freshening wind. The crew, weak from hunger and thirst, dragged themselves aloft, knowing every gust brought salvation from the deadly calm where they had lingered.

The seaman at watch had seen the secret of the wind and kept it to his heart, watching the woman move among the passengers with her graceful carriage and silent ways. Every day it seemed his heart was more touched by her soft words and gentle manner. When he understood she had been watching him as closely, he could feel his emotions fill like the sails in a booming gale.

Tonight a scarf covered her head and hid her face in the cool night air. Only her eyes were revealed. In the darkness, the pupils expanded to their dark fullness, hinting of the black of a magic mirror, glittering with secret knowledge within.

"If ever I should wear velvet, I pray that it holds me as warmly as your embrace, my love."

"If I should ever touch such fine a cloth as velvet, I know that it would feel as smooth as your skin." He inclined his face to touch her cheek with his and stroked the front of her throat, feeling the quick beat of blood so close to the surface there. He lifted her fingers to his lips and murmured, "And as warm as your mouth upon my own."

"You taste of the sea, my lady, and all the mysteries therein. It makes me thirst for a draft of you as well."

"Nay, I am no lady. I am but a spinner, a weaver; one who works with her hands." She held her small hands up between them, rubbing the faint calluses where the harsh threads of the loom and wheel had roughened her fingers. "When we reach the port, I must work. Yes, seven years I must work to pay my passage. I shall be tied to the land, while you can roam this sea."

The seaman drew her closer. "There will be a way." He gathered her to his body, feeling the soft pressure of her breasts against his chest. "We shall be together. My duty as a seaman will be up; I can join the militia. The army is always hungry for men.

"Since the night I saw you conjure the winds to save the ship, I have known you are my life's mate. There will be a way." How fitting the term bewitched, *for*

that was what he was, and by his own choosing.

"Do not worry, my love. We shall always return to each other. There will be sacrifices we each must make. I know there is a beautiful life that awaits us in this new land. No harm shall come to me or thee. Trust in thy heart. My magic shall protect us now and always. As long as you believe."

"Wouldst thou seal your promise with a kiss?"

"Now and forever."

Again David tasted the sweet familiar lips in his dream, yet could not see her face in the shadows. So sweet, too sweet to forget, and yet faintly he knew he would awake and the memory of her face would hover near, but tantalizingly unclear. *The woman broke the kiss, and nuzzled beneath his chin. He rested his chin on her head, feeling the crinkle of her starched cap, and smelling the fragrance of her hair. As he looked toward the bow, he stiffened as he saw a familiar silhouette on the bridge. Someone watched their embrace. Pray God he had not heard their words. The night winds peeled back the clouds that drifted to cover the full moon. What was Capt. Wolfton doing so late on deck?*

Splash! "No peace for the wicked!" Ben boisterously emptied a bucketful of cold water over his dozing friend. It was too tempting an opportunity to miss.

"What the . . ." Yanked so rudely back from his daydream, David thrashed and struggled in the shifting hammock, shaking water out of his eyes and hair. The hammock twisted as his weight came too close to the edge. Momentum and gravity took the advantage, dumping him unceremoniously onto the hard ground. David looked up from his sprawl on the grass at Ben, who was holding an empty bucket and grinning widely.

"Wake up, lover boy! Man, from the expression on your face you musta been having one doozy of a dream. Thought you told me to be here at ten A.M., anyway." Ben checked his watch.

David shook his head and groaned. He was used to Ben's antics. "I can't begin to tell you what you interrupted." He stretched and turned the hammock to rights, untangling the ropes.

Ben stepped beside him and dropped into the hammock, setting it swinging. "Sorry 'bout that, old man. Just couldn't resist." Lacing his fingers behind his head, he lounged back comfortably, feet crossed at the ankles. He raised an eyebrow to encourage David to go on and tell exactly what he did interrupt. "This is neat. No wonder you spend so much time out here." He dangled out a leg and gave a shove to keep the motion going. "Tell me a story, Daddy."

David sat on the grass near Ben. "Have you ever felt like you've done something or been somewhere before?" He pulled a long-stemmed primrose and chewed the stem.

"Probably just dreamed it before. Something you saw on TV." He set the hammock to swinging again. "Sounds like some wishful thinking to me, especially if it concerns your date yesterday."

"No, come on. For real. Haven't you ever felt that way?"

"Well." Ben pushed his cap back with a thumb and gave a deep thoughtful look up into the leaves where the chickadees chirped and fluttered. "My aunt Nellie used to say that was called deja vu or something like that. She says it feels like you are having the same feeling or experience over again."

"That's right. Exactly." David flicked the pink flower away. He rested his elbows on his knees and scrubbed through his wet hair.

Ben experimented with rocking the hammock while hanging both feet over opposite sides. "So? What is it that you think you're experiencing for the second time?"

"You know, I don't go for all this reincarnation stuff—"

"Here we go again. . . ."

"Not funny, Ben. I'm serious. When I'm with her . . ."

"Doc Solei's daughter?"

"Yeah. Lyric." He paused. An involuntary smile had come to his lips when he said her name. "Lyric."

"Yes?" Ben primed the conversation.

"I swear, when I'm with her, it always seems like somehow we've done it all before, that we're repeating ourselves." David laid back on the grass, staring up into the green lace of chestnut branches. "It's confusing; we're doing the same things but somehow just a little bit different, like maybe there is supposed to be a different outcome or ending this time. I don't know what it should be, though."

Ben rolled his eyes and gave a theatrical shudder that threatened to send him careening from the hammock. "Oh yeah, Lyric. She's scary all right." He sat up and planted both booted feet firmly on the ground. "Sounds like you got yourself a good case of plain ol' lovesickness. And if I can remember what else my aunt Nellie said, I can prescribe the cure."

David looked at his lighthearted friend.

"She said always follow your heart." Ben stood and stretched. "I personally say trust your gut, but I think she meant the same thing."

David scrambled to his feet and grabbed Ben's shoulders. "You're right. Your aunt Nellie's right, too. It's time I did listen to my heart and my gut." He flipped the bill of Ben's red cap. "Sorry for dragging you all the way out here on your day off, but I've got to make a little magic of my own."

Ben straightened his cap and put on an aggrieved expression. "But I thought we were going to fix that hole in the hall wall. We sure can't fix that hole in your head."

David was already straddling his motorcycle and fastening the buckle on his helmet. He just grinned.

Ben shook his head. "Yeah, I guess I'd pick pretty red hair and big green eyes over you in a pinch, too. Go on, Langston, we'll finish some other time. I'll just lie here and watch the birds for a while."

It was early evening. Nolan sprawled drowsily on the chintz cushion on the old green wicker chair and watched Lyric finish washing her hair. She gathered up the length of tangled wet curls and wrapped her head in a towel. She stepped into the fragrant bubble-covered bathwater, and slipped down to recline with her head cushioned by the towel. The spicy carnation-scented bubbles fizzed and popped around her face as she sank deeply into the sweetly soothing sensation.

Lyric relaxed, closed her eyes, and began to turn the previous day's events over in her mind. The kiss on the ship, their first kiss, filled her senses. She wanted to examine every second, every touch. The wavelets of bathwater became the lapping of the water around the tall ship. The heat of the water became the heat of David's body pressed eagerly and firmly to hers. The scent of the water was his scent. The gentle touch of the bubbles was the brush of his breath against her cheek. His face, his smile, his touch. The way the very corners of his mouth turned up, even when he was not smiling.

She ran her palm slowly up her stomach, where she could feel the heat he had built start again. Lyric drew a slow, deep breath, and the feeling of buoyancy the water gave her was the floating feeling of happiness David had given her on the ship.

Light as a feather, swept off her feet. Yes, that was what she felt. Her good sense told her to go slowly and cautiously, but her instincts were more than ready to go with the flow and tug of her physical sensations. Anyway, not a single one of her guardian voices had made a peep to the contrary. It was as if they had presented her with a wonderful book, all hers, and let her page into the story, leaf by leaf, but no faster.

The story of the lovers, Sarah and Dante, just made her more confident. Reconciling the threat of Wolfton House would be difficult if David continued to refuse to believe. It wouldn't be easy, this love, but it would be real love, she knew, because it had been love before. Lyric raised a double palmful of water and let it dribble gently over her face. Time was the river, soft and ever flowing, inexorable as water, and as powerful. Time. How easy life was when you believed in eternity.

The bedroom phone trilled. Lyric jerked upright, rudely startled out of her reverie. A tidal wave washed over the edge of the tub and splattered Nolan. He spit and dashed out of the room, slipping and sliding in the spreading puddle. He leapt up on the bed, leaving a row of wet paw prints across the lace-trimmed linen coverlet. The towel fell from Lyric's hair into the bathwater, sinking soddenly to the bottom.

The phone rang again before Lyric could stride

drippily into the bedroom and grab the offending receiver. "Hello." This had better be important.

"Lyric?" A warm masculine voice sounded taken aback by her abrupt answer. "This is David."

David! His soft accent made her suddenly feel as liquid as the bathwater. Her inner temperature climbed as the feeling of heat that had been beginning in the bathtub spread down her thighs.

"David." Lyric's voiced softened. "I'm sorry; the phone just . . . startled me, that's all." It was erotic mental telepathy to hear his voice just as she had been thinking of the sensuous effect he had on her body. Lyric pictured David's supple fingers wrapped around the phone and thought of them spread over her hips, the way they had been on the ship at the museum. She sank onto the bed and stretched out on her stomach luxuriously, letting the linen coverlet dry her body. Nolan sniffed with disgust and jumped down to find a drier spot without a wet human to crowd him.

"I have a little surprise for you and I thought I might come over. That is, if you're not busy." He added temptingly, "It's such a beautiful evening."

Lyric sat up in delight mixed with dismay. Her hair was a mess, and what would she wear? "That would be fine." She tried to sound calm, and not too eager, but her breath caught in anticipation. "I'm just . . . doing some paperwork. I can put that away until later."

"All right. I'll be by in an hour."

"Wait, David. How about a hint? Please, just a little one?" Lyric hated to hang up and break the connection with his silky voice.

"You might want to dress for dinner; we won't be on the motorcycle. And that's all the hint you'll get."

"See you then. 'Bye!" Lyric hung up the phone and

bounced off the bed. What to do? First the hair dryer. She began to brush her hair and fluff the warm air through her curls as the problem of what to wear ran through her head. Of course she must look her most romantic. A dress, definitely. She finished her hair and ran to the walk-in closet.

Lyric frantically shuffled the neatly hung clothes and slid the squealing hangers back and forth on the long racks, grabbing and discarding as she went. The mauve velvet? Too hot, too old. The leather miniskirt? Definitely not; too slick, too new. Where was the slinky black silk, the one Jane had lent to her? No, tonight she couldn't wear something borrowed.

Romantic, romantic: what could she wear? She tapped her fingers against her mouth and scanned the colors and textures. It had to be perfect. It had to be . . . blue.

The second she touched the garment she knew it was the right one. Blue, almost silver, a diamond blue that made her eyes the greenest of greens. The day she had bought it, she had known it was one of those special dresses, made for a future occasion that would be made even more wonderful by that dress. It was soft sueded silk that clung in the most unexpected places; it was psychological warfare and it was perfect.

Lyric fairly flew around the room, opening and shutting drawers. Lingerie, hose, shoes. What could be the surprise?

She held earrings up to her ears, turning her head before the mirror. The pearls, definitely.

Breathing rapidly from anticipation of seeing David, she made the final check of her clothes, twirling before the long glass. Done and ten minutes to spare.

As she began to pin up her hair, she became aware of a new sound on the quiet evening air. Lyric rested her wrist on the dressing table and turned her head toward the window. A slow clop-clop of hoofbeats could be heard clearly. They were coming down her street, stopping in front of her house.

Carrying her satin pumps, Lyric tried to check her speed as she ran eagerly down the stairs. She had slowed only a little before she was at the front door. There at her curb was a horse and carriage. The horse glowed a fairy-tale silver in the early twilight.

Lyric was speechless with amazement. David was wearing a full-sleeved white shirt, open provocatively at the collar, and a rich dark brocade waistcoat. The waistcoat somehow made his broad shoulders look even more invitingly wide. With his tall black boots and tight trousers, he looked quite the dashing highwayman, come to sweep his princess away.

He looked unbearably sexy. Such looks should be illegal, Lyric thought; they should come with a disclaimer: Not for the underage or faint of heart.

"Cinderella, your carriage is waiting." David opened the door with a flourish, and drew her out of the house. She fought the childish impulse to laugh and clap in captivation. Where was her city sophistication to be swept off her feet so completely by this unexpectedly imaginative and tender gesture?

David knelt in front of her and took her shoes out of her hands. She lifted her foot as he wrapped his fingers gently around her ankle and heel, then slipped her shoe over her toes. At his touch, Lyric felt her pulse waver and then jump strongly.

"A perfect fit." He looked up, with dark mischief in his eyes, then took up her other foot, so that she had to lean slightly and balance on his shoulders, giving him an unobstructed view of her cleavage. Her skirt swung sinuously forward and brushed his shoulders. He rubbed his thumb thoughtfully over the top of her foot as his smile broadened lazily; then he stood.

"We have dinner reservations at the castle, your majesty," he said, offering his arm as gallantly as any cavalier to escort her down the walk to the shiny black carriage. David picked her up without apparent effort and swung her up to the red leather seat. He hopped up and took the reins, pausing and turning toward her as if to see her reaction.

"I don't know what to say." Lyric finally regained her speech. She had seen the carriages around town, pulling tourists on a slow amble past the historic houses. There were carriages in New York, too, for newlyweds and special dates, but she had never had an occasion to indulge in the old-fashioned pleasure of low-speed and slightly aimless transportation.

"Well, I'd say 'Giddup!' " David seemed pleased at the effect his surprise was having.

"Oh, giddup, then." Lyric laughed and laid her head happily on David's shoulder. David clucked to the horse. The carriage wheels began to roll, making a hollow metallic rattle on the asphalt. They progressed slowly along the street. Behind their screens of shrubs and trees the small lighted windows of the houses they passed glowed like a doll village under a Christmas tree.

The gentle evening breeze caught Lyric's skirt and rippled back the light silk in a sudden billow, revealing her lace stocking tops. Lyric smoothed the thin fabric down, but not before David caught a glimpse of lace and thigh.

"That's a beautiful dress." David ran two fingertips

lightly down her thigh to underscore his compliment. "My favorite color."

"Where did you learn to drive a buggy?" She watched the long reins threaded through his competent fingers. David had that elusively erotic scent that gave Lyric a persistent blush of arousal. How would that aroma blend with hers to make the salty smell of love? She snuggled contentedly closer and took a deep breath, filling herself with the essence of wonderful male.

"It's the first thing we learn in fire fighter school, you know," he teased as he put his arm around her and pulled her tighter to his side. He rubbed the backs of his fingers gently on her cheek. "Really, I learned from my grandfather on the farm. I can even plow with a mule, if I have to, but I sure wouldn't want to."

The full white moon rose silently over the ink-black treetops. Soon the carriage wheels rolled off the asphalt and crunched on a small dirt road. The soft slow thud of the hoofbeats had the rhythm of a heartbeat. Their progress was slow enough for them to hear the crickets fiddling in the tall grass. Time slipped away as easily as a silk scarf from a beautiful woman's shoulders. It could have been any time, any century, with a man and a woman in the summer moonlight.

The horse slowed and, sensing the inattentiveness of his driver, stopped. David let the reins go slack, and in a gently possessive motion, pulled Lyric to him. She raised her face to him and let the imagination of her emotions color her kiss. The response of her body was so quick it was frightening. They broke the kiss with a sigh and David pressed her head to his chest. She felt her pulse gallop and hammer, and realized it was not just her desire she could feel and hear; it was his also.

Reluctantly David picked up the reins and woke up the horse. Tall grasses with pale plumes swayed and murmured in the evening breeze. Tiny marsh frogs riding the gently dipping leaves trilled like nocturnal birds. The freshening light wind carried the clean salt smell of the sea.

"Where are we going? It feels like we're near the sea."

"We are. It's a special old place; I understand Samuel Adams himself stopped here. Most people come here on their boats. Look." David pointed down the slope to a small two-story stone building near the water. "I heard it was a smuggler's hideout in Revolutionary times."

A long pier stretched away into the water with a small number of pleasure craft anchored there, docked for the night. Their tiny running lights twinkled red and green on the gently swelling water. Out in the bay a single radiant sailboat cut a great silent vee across the moon's reflection.

David stopped the carriage in front of the dimly illuminated front entrance. Two antique lanterns hung at the door. The candles inside the lanterns were lit, protected from the night wind by the lovingly cleaned glass.

A young man slipped out of the darkness and took hold of the horse's harness. "I'll park 'im for you, sir. He'll be just fine." He slapped the horse on the neck and ruffled under its mane. The horse rubbed his head against the boy and nickered gently.

"Thanks." David lifted Lyric down from the carriage seat. He held her hand tightly and they went into the front door. The front hall was broad, and to either side were large common rooms, with white draped tables, gently candlelit. The smell of old woodsmoke, roast venison, roses, and ripe apricots mingled to make a sumptous welcoming odor. Other guests dined quietly, with the sound of violins in the background. A hostess in a soft rose-colored gown with an ecru lace kerchief appeared with a rustle, looking like a demure portrait of Dolly Madison herself.

"Good evening. Welcome to Old Hawthorne Inn." The hostess sketched a gracious bow and turned to lead them away. To Lyric's surprise, they did not turn into either of the common rooms, but started up the staircase. She turned half around to look a question at David, but he waved her on to follow the trailing rose brocade skirt. At the landing tall portraits of portly men in red coats and tight white pants stood on either side of a polished walnut door. The hostess unlocked the door with an ornate brass key, then silently passed the key to David.

"Thank you, Mrs. Miggins." David smiled as their hostess withdrew with a conspiratorial wink.

"Close your eyes," he commanded. Lyric heard the quiet click of the opening door. David pulled her inside, touching her shoulders lightly to turn her around twice. "Now . . . open them."

A round mahogany table was laid for two with starched white linen. Tall crystal champagne flutes caught a flash of candlelight. A dark green champagne bottle chilled in a sweating bucket of ice. Heavy pewter service plates supported thin china. The fireplace was filled with old-fashioned pink and white cabbage roses. The leaded pane windows were open, and a soft sea scent flowed over the broad stone sills, stirring the flowers.

Lyric stood with her hands raised slightly in amazement. David stood very still, observing her reaction with satisfaction, then shut the door quietly.

He crossed the room and carefully spun the champagne bottle in its bucket. He pulled the bottle from the rattling ice and pressed his thumbs to the cork, pressing and teasing it upward with the heat from his palms.

The bottle gave the expected festive pop, and a faint sparkle of the smoke of old grapes rose from its mouth. David held the bottle and swept Lyric with a look that went from head to toe and back again. She stepped forward and lifted a champagne flute toward him. The anxious pounding in her chest lightened as he extended the bottle and filled the thin crystal with the effervescent wine.

They walked to the window and looked out over the bay, washed sequin-white in the moonlight. "David, this is lovely. How did you ever find such a wonderful spot?"

"Instinct, I guess. Sometimes I'm lucky about finding extra-special things." He looked into her eyes and she felt her heart fill with something that was feeling more and more like love.

Lyric lifted her champagne and asked, "What shall we toast to?"

"How about magic?" He waved toward a huge luna moth poised on the windowsill. It spread its great luminescent pale wings and skimmed into the night as they raised their glasses in salute. They sipped and Lyric dipped a fingertip into the golden liquid. She ran her finger gently around the rim until the excited crystal began to sing, a long humming tone.

They sipped again, then leaned into an inevitable kiss. Warm mouths met, with the cold tingle of champagne for added spice. The fizz in Lyric's brain was not just from the champagne.

They sipped from their glasses. David leaned toward Lyric again, and gave her the most tantalizing kind of kiss. He touched only her lips with his, softly, teasingly, keeping his body well away from hers, holding his hands away from his sides. It was tender, it was charming, and it was the most maddeningly seductive kiss imaginable. Every inch of her skin longed to be pressed, yet only that hot mobile mouth touched her. She stepped forward; he stepped back in a mischievously teasing erotic waltz.

They sipped once more. David refilled their crystal flutes, and raised his in salute. "To you, Ms. Solei." They met glasses with a clink. Lyric knew the gods always heard a toast made with a clink. David embraced her, and feeling the hard wall of his chest pressed against her, she made her own secret toast and touched her glass to his again.

She brought the thin lip of the elegant glass to her mouth and took a long, slow swallow, to cool her senses briefly. She sat on the windowsill and savored the bouquet of the old wine, the bubbles bursting on her tongue and sending sparkles of feeling down her throat and through her veins. Streams of bubbles leapt to the top of the glass, tickling her nose as she sipped.

From below in the darkness, the old-world harmony of notes squeezed from an accordion floated up, accompanied by a bow on strings, hauntingly nostalgic. The flickering, mellow candlelight flowed over David's face, making him more painfully handsome than she could bear.

He sat facing her on the window seat and took the glass from her grasp. He looked into her eyes, and every part of her melted. He stroked down her neck, pressing the soft silk off her shoulder, and lowered his head to kiss the hollow there at the curve of her throat. She gave a murmur of invitation and touched his hair, gently as a butterfly. There was a discreet knock at the door.

David raised his head and Lyric straightened her dress.

"Come in," David called. He rose and pulled Lyric to the table. "And now, Act Two. Your chair, my lady." He pulled out the mahogany Chippendale chair.

"Thank you, kind sir," Lyric said. The gentlemanly gesture brought a smile. Pulling her skirt out to the side, she gave a graceful curtsy and sat with regally exaggerated femininity. David really was all Southern, the gentleman never far under the rugged surface.

A serving maid in dove blue Colonial garb brought in the first course—a baker's dozen of fresh oysters on the half-shell, garlanded with vivid yellow lemon slices. The plump oysters were followed by dish after dish, each more exquisite than the last. At last the silent maid cleared the table completely and freshened the linen for the final treat.

Mrs. Miggins, the hostess herself, brought in a huge tray of dessert. With a smile at David, and a flourish, she laid the tray on the table. Bright red strawberries, brilliant green kiwi slices, and plump yellow-gold apricots glowed in an opulent mosaic of fruit. Some were striped with chocolate, white and dark layers of the creamy, addictive aphrodisiac. Naked blueberries and dark raspberries were strewn across the top for contrast to the vivid display of colors.

Lyric surveyed the array with interest. "Strawberries dipped in chocolate. My favorite."

"I hoped you liked chocolate. Somehow I thought you might."

"This is so beautiful . . . like a stained-glass window." She took a sip of her champagne, then selected an artfully striped apricot.

"I think it's time for some entertainment." David rose to pull out Lyric's chair, and bent to kiss the nape of her neck. She inhaled sharply, too late to mask the quick color of feelings that spread over her body. As she turned her head, he captured her mouth. Slow, tender kisses parted her lips. Leaving her flushed and trembling, he turned away.

"Come sit closer to the window, where we can hear the music." He pulled a wing chair from the corner and patted the seat. Lyric heard the soft sounds of music from the courtyard below as she settled into the chair. David leaned down to nuzzle her hair, but straightened quickly at a sound at the door. Lyric caught a glimpse of color in David's face as she whirled to see Mrs. Miggins and two serving maids peeking in. The three looked the way Lyric was feeling. Moony eyed, they hurried in to clear the table, stealing glances at the couple and sighing.

"Looks like it's time to go." They left the room with the maids' romantic adoration following them. The carriage waited at the front door, and as they left they turned to wave at the two serving girls hanging admiringly from the windowsill above.

Lyric hummed the tune of the last song David had sung. David pulled her to his side. She laid her head back on his shoulder and looked up at the stars, so close tonight. Suddenly a bright streak brushed across the sky. "Look, David. It's a falling star."

"Make a wish." They followed the path of the dying star, faces raised. When they looked into each other's eyes they found they had been granted their wishes.

Chapter Sixteen

The shriek of the firehouse alarm ripped through the station, shredding sleep into a ragged edge of memory. Urgency flushed into David's system. He kicked his feet out over the edge of his cot and shoved them into his waiting boots and turnouts.

Ten seconds.

He was not jaded or blase about his vocation. That initial rush had never gone away in the seven years he had been a fire fighter. There was always the thrill of combating danger and treachery. He was determined to win. Someone needed him and he could help. St. George slaying the dragon.

David was the first to the shiny pole, wrapping his arms and legs around the polished brass and sliding down with gusto. He landed with a spring beside his position on the massive hook and ladder truck. His yellow protective coat and helmet awaited him.

Hastily donning his gear with a slap over each fastener of his coat, he slammed on his helmet. It fit so tightly it bit into his forehead, but the discomfort would be forgotten. He was always grateful for the indestructible lightweight Cycolac, not the heavy iron armor of knights or even the old-fashioned helmets made of heavy leather.

He bounded onto the shiny silver steps and up to the steering wheel into the tillerman's position at the tail end of the truck.

Thirty seconds.

Actions meshing like precision machinery, the rest of the crew fell into their respective places: laddermen, pumpmen, and engineer, hosemen and salvagemen. They were a unit; a team. Red lights flashing, sirens screaming, they rolled out to protect their right to be called heroes.

Each blaze was always different, each with its own personality and agenda. It was a living, breathing creature with an attitude. It was always the black knight and David in his own shining armor. No matter the guise, always good versus evil.

The air was already heavy with the scent of carbonized wood. Still blocks away, David could see the sky illuminated. These were not the clouds one gazed at on a lazy afternoon and picked out bunny shapes or bears. These clouds were glowing, reflecting hell. It seemed the clouds themselves were taking the shape of demons, evil black matter sculpted by the dark master's will.

As the engine drew nearer, David imagined he saw the reflection of the Prince of Darkness himself, watching his handiwork and sitting on a throne of the poisonous smoke to taunt and thwart David personally in his quest. To David, fire was hell on earth. The beast itself. It was eternity.

The clouds glowed with crimson pyrotechnics.

This was going to be a big one. An ominous smell of danger tainted the summer night air. He felt his heart pound against his rib cage like a prisoner railing a cup against the bars. With one hand he pulled his helmet chin strap snug. Only three blocks away.

The oily smoke belching into the sky was a dreadful signal. The color and texture gave a sign that would bring a terrorizing chill into each fire fighter's heart. The tint was the signature of gasoline and lots of it. This fire was not straightforward; it would not fight fair, or play by the rules. This fire was deliberate. It was arson.

There was no telling what lay in wait for David and the rest of his team.

Arson was guerrilla warfare and made the job that much more perilous. Doors might be blocked or deadfall traps laid to hinder rescuers.

A similar trick had trapped David during a rescue attempt in Atlanta. It was an antiquated factory, with a maze of halls. The building was worthless except to the slumlord owner and the arsonist who contracted to torch it for a percentage of the insurance money.

Massive oak timbers had closed about him, stunning him and trapping his legs as if they were in the mouth of a hungry creature. Luckily his team had been tightly behind him. They had pulled him from the throat of death, but it had been close that time. Too close. He had learned his lesson.

The crackling embers spoke a secret language, but David understood. *Sticks and stones may break my bones, but my flames will always hurt you.* David heard the sinister whisper in his ear, followed by a cackle of laughter.

David clutched the steering wheel tighter and maneuvered the huge Kodiak in sync with the front driver. The 30-foot-long emergency vehicle whipped around the last corner, and the flame-engulfed building came into view. The fire was spreading rapidly, but it was obviously burning more intensely in two separate places. It didn't take a fire chief to see that.

"Someone was pretty sloppy." Ben tossed his comment at David and jumped off the back of the truck before it quit rolling. He clipped a flashlight to his belt, shrugged on his air tank harness, and grabbed an ax.

"Or maybe too cheap to have the job done properly." David secured the wheels and quickly manned the ladder at the center of the truck. "Scan the crowd."

"Done."

David's vision swept the crowd as well, in hopes of spotting someone who appeared to be getting more than the usual thrill from watching the fire. A torch, the professional arsonist, would be long gone by now, but the amateur pyromaniac would cast suspicion on himself by hanging around, wearing an expression of ecstatic absorption.

Pink curlers peeked from beneath the flowered hair net of a middle-aged woman. She clutched at the throat of her chenille bathrobe, gawking upward. Scuffing her sloppy slippers in the direction of the fire, she bumped into Ben.

"Oh my! You're . . . tall." The woman touched her hairnet.

"Do you know if anyone is still in the building, ma'am?" David called out from his position above.

"That building was condemned. Just a rat trap." She squinted upward, shading her eyes from the glare of the flames and emergency lights in order to focus on David. "No one lives there 'cept a couple of vagrants now and then, but I haven't seen any of them lately."

"Yes, ma'am, I'm sure, but do you know where in the building the vagrants usually stay?" Ben persisted.

"Sometimes I see smoke come from those corner windows." She pointed to the third-floor window where the fire was already devouring the brittle wood with ravenous speed. "I guess they cook or try to keep warm."

She lowered her voice and poked Ben with a stiff forefinger. "Sometimes kids go up there to smoke dope." She poked him again, her eyes bright. "Serves 'em right if they burn up. Roast like a chicken. Go straight to hell."

She dogged Ben's steps, chattering happily at his side. "I called nine-one-one, you know." She looked prideful. "I have it written right on my phone. Big numbers."

The woman turned to Ben and gripped him by the elbow. "This is as exciting as a ringside seat to watch the Bone-Crusher and Snake-Man at the Wrestledome." She released him and clasped her hands together enthuastically. "Do you think anybody's dead?"

David cast a glance toward them and turned his head in disgust at the overheard conversation. Why were people such vultures? What drew them so? This was his job, his calling, and that was why he was here. They all seemed to be hoping something awful would happen, that someone would die. He was there to see that it didn't.

"I wouldn't know, ma'am. You'll have to please step away from the fire engine and behind the barriers." Ben hastily but firmly escorted the woman toward the police barriers, then skipped away from her.

"I'll tell the captain we've got potential victims." Ben called over his shoulder to David and broke into a trot.

"I'm readying the ladder to go in," David shouted after him. He flipped the hydraulics into place and four giant braces unfolded from their pockets on the unit and lowered smoothly. They settled their pads onto the ground like shuffling elephant feet. They would secure and stabilize the unit so the men could climb up and down the ladder safely. David maneuvered the ladder to reach the third floor and locked it in position. They were doing well for time so far, but there was never a second to waste. A bright-eyed rookie named Marvin popped his head up over the side of the truck.

"You ready for me, Lieutenant?"

"You can take her from here, Marv. I've got every faith in you." David gave him a reassuring slap on the back as he relinquished the controls.

The young man beamed. He would man the ladder from here. The ladder would have to be moved and adjusted periodically, a responsibility for alert eyes and quick reflexes. David himself had started at this position as a rookie. David was too experienced a fire fighter to be left on the ground. He was a team leader and his team needed to be on that third floor ASAP.

The ladder team had gathered about the right side of the engine and readied to attack the building, axes in hand, hose lines over shoulders, and rescue equipment in place.

"Ready to go?" David addressed his team as he pulled on his own breathing apparatus. He let the mask hang loose as he scanned everyone's equipment. "This could be arson, so be on your toes. There's no telling what kind of boobytraps might be up there. I don't have to tell you to be careful." A silent understanding rippled through the five men. They nodded and saluted their readiness to David as they adjusted their masks and tanks. "Marv, watch those windows. Ladder up, Marv!" David shouted to the rookie and was the first up the ladder.

"Let's go, let's go!" Ben responded and started up behind David.

They clamored up the ladder, booted feet clattering on either side of the canvas hose stretched up the rungs. Dense smoke was already belching out of almost every window. David reached the window, where the heat had already crumbled the ancient limestone sill. Fire Company 12 hit the third floor.

Marvin watched the ladder, the men, and the windowsill, judging the intensity and position of the fire, trying to second-guess when the team might appear at a different opening, requiring a quick shift in the positioning of the ladder that would be the bridge to safety. It was a heavy responsibility, and Marvin took it seriously.

An inferno slapped David in the face as he jumped into the room from the ladder. The temperature was already hotter than it should be, another sign this was no accident.

Fire was cascading down the far wall like a boiling red waterfall. In an instant, it reversed and swept upward, crawling across the ceiling. It would advance aggressively and then just as quickly retreat to gain strength, hungrily seeking oxygen, life.

"Fire in the walls, Lieutenant!" Hanson called out as flames burst through a charring portion of plasterboard.

One neophyte's eyes widened with hyped tension and fear. He was paralyzed, mesmerized by the scintillations of the flaming arms, the blaze beckoning a deadly embrace. Fire rained down from the ceiling, showering him with embers and caustic-hot liquid metal. Molten lead pattered onto his helmet, as fluid as silver mercury.

"Jackson." David grabbed his young teammate by the shoulders and rattled him roughly. "We'll make it. Just stay calm and follow my lead."

"Right, sir." The young man gave a determined nod and mustered up his courage, taking a tighter grip on his ax.

"Hoses!" David barked into his walkie-talkie to the engineer below. The flat tubes burst into life, writhing like pythons, filled with power. "Let's dance with the Devil, boys," David called.

"Hoses, let's go," he shouted to the team. "I like to lead." David affixed his oxygen mask and uncapped his hose, turning the water full-force on the sheet of flames that covered the wall, clawing toward them.

They crossed the room, spraying the walls as they went, and moved into the hallway. Small licks of flames stood in puddles of water. The water was spreading the flames—unbelievable, but a definite sign of the presence of gasoline.

A trail of blazing debris led them like a map. It was following a track of high octane, scattered broadly the length of the hall. David touched the edges of the first closed door, feeling for heat. With one good swing of the ax he broke it open. Nothing but smoke waiting here, but flames already licked out of the heater grates. They sprayed the walls and floors, and proceeded down the hall.

A room was doorless, and flames slithered and teased in the opening like a fan dancer. Ben stepped forward and aimed the full force of his hose into the room. Suddenly, boards and plaster fell in a horrible flaming cascade from above. The wood grazed Ben's right shoulder, knocking him to his knees and setting the heavy canvas jacket ablaze.

David turned his hose on his friend, squelching the fire before it could eat through the thick padding and into Ben's arm. He capped the hose, knelt by Ben, and snatched his mask up. "You all right?"

Ben shrugged and patted out a spot on his smoldering jacket that the water had missed. "Yeah, yeah, just a scratch." He grinned and stood unsteadily, picking up his ax. "Don't drown me."

"Been wanting to do that for a while now, anyway." David smiled in relief. They stood, shoulders touching.

"Help!" It wasn't clear but definitely the sound of a human in distress. A weak scream was almost covered by the cracking and crashing of timber.

"Help . . . someone, help!"

"Hanson, take over my hose. Ben, come with me." David tightened his mask. The smoke was getting thicker, malignantly dense and sooty. The two started cautiously down the hall. David could feel beads of fresh perspiration mingle with the sweat of fortitude, stinging salt at the corners of his eyes. Someone here in this hellish place, not protected, not trained like him. Someone terribly vulnerable.

Another closed door, smoke seeping from beneath. The fire was waiting inside. The door heaved and breathed as if it were the chest of an animal, the heart of the beast. David heard another faint cry. Behind this door, a lion of fire held its prey.

The door could explode or they could open it. Either way the backdraft was waiting inside for them and would sweep out and over them for a gulp of fresh air, and perhaps their lives with it.

"Help," the voice of a woman pleaded again. She coughed twice. Her voice was getting thin.

David motioned to Ben and spoke inside his mask. "On three." He held up one finger, two fingers, then swung his ax from the side. David and Ben pressed themselves to the walls and shielded their faces, instinctively holding their breaths. The fire washed out and over them, down the hall, and into the backup team, to be quenched by their spray of watery death.

The fire fighters stepped through a conflagration into the room and found a disheveled young woman huddled in the corner. Ben swung his ax, breaking out the rotten window frame in one blow. He leaned out, waving to Marv, waiting tensely below. Marvin spotted him and began to rotate the ladder controls. As the ladder began to swing slowly toward the window, Ben went back to kneel by David and the woman.

"Is there anyone else with you?" David pointed the flashlight beam toward the corners of the bare room. The high beam of light cut through the smoke to reveal a still body on a ratty mattress against the far wall.

"My boyfriend was with me, but I'm afraid . . . I'm afraid . . ." She started to cry, and then broke into a racking cough.

David lifted her in his arms and headed for the window. "Don't worry, lady, if he's here, we'll take care of it. Just relax now."

He jerked his head toward the mattress. "Hanson, check out that corner and let's get the hell outta Dodge." David ducked his head out the window and searched for the ladder. It was firmly in position under the sill. With one smooth move, David hoisted the woman across his right shoulder and got a good grip around her knees. He stepped out onto the ladder and walked down each rung as if it were a stair.

"You'll be fine, miss." David handed her down from the ladder unit to a waiting paramedic.

"Anyone else?"

"Ben's coming down with the boyfriend." He shook his head. "Doesn't look too good."

Ben climbed down from the fire engine with the second body over his shoulder. "Sorry, guys, I'm afraid you can't help this one." He laid the lifeless body on the ground near the paramedic unit. He shoved his hat back and went down on one knee beside the body of the young man. "I really hate to lose one."

The paramedic spread a light cover over the charred corpse. "You do the best you can, and that's all you can do."

"Ben, I'm going back up," David shouted as he stepped on the first rung of the ladder. A fireman's order of priority was rescue, containment, attack. Rescue was all he could think of.

"Are you crazy, Langston? This place is ready to blow. It's all clear; we got everyone out. The girl says there was no one else in the building. She's sure."

"I'm sure I saw something move from that window. It was small . . . maybe a child." David's voice faded; he was almost up to the third-floor window.

At the window David adjusted his mask and took deep breaths of the cooler air before he stepped in. He knew he had seen something else up here. The room before him was almost completely obscured by swirling smoke. Bloodred and tarnished gold flames twined and leapt in a macabre pas de deux advancing across the floor. Nothing could be alive here now. He was grateful for his oxygen. Turning from side to side, he flashed his light into every corner.

He must have been wrong; it happened. The roiling smoke often seemed to take on a life of its own, forming shapes and teasing the inexperienced into situations that turned deadly.

As he was satisfied that no one was there, he put his hand on the window frame to exit the room. A motion from the far corner, not black smoke, not orange flame. It was a little girl, maybe five years old, curly red hair braided back and covered with a white cap. An old-fashioned white pinafore covered her long dark dress. How did she get in here? She held her hand out to David, palm up.

"I'm waiting for you." Her voice was scolding, as if she had been waiting for him to join her in play and he were tardy. David heard no sounds, no sirens from below, no roar of the fire or even the crashing surf of his own blood in his ears. Only the sweet voice of the girl-child hung in his mind. They stood in the center of the maelstrom, a tornado of heat whirling around the tall young man looking down at the small trusting girl. Seconds passed and David heard the crash of a nearby beam, falling, taking part of the wall. He must protect the child, rescue her. It was his life, his duty.

"These are for you." She reached up a small hand, delicate white skin unsmudged. There were three acorns in her palm. "Now will you take me home?"

He reached to her hand, compelled to take her gift, perhaps her fare to safety. He swept the acorns from her palm and at the touch felt the surge of awareness that meant danger, bringing him back to his purpose. Smoke, danger, rescue.

He stuffed the acorns into his jacket pocket, at the same time pulling out the silver flameproof rescue blanket from its pouch. It crackled and sparkled as he wrapped it around the girl. "Don't be afraid, honey, I'll take care of you. I have to carry you down. This will protect you."

As he lifted the girl across his shoulder, he thought he heard her say, "I knew you'd come back if you knew I was here."

Somewhere down the hall, another beam crashed. The fire was almost into this room. No time.

He sprinted to the window and out over the sill just in time to feel the backdraft explode into the room. A blowtorch of flame billowed toward them. David clattered down the ladder, feeling the weight of the youngster secure on his shoulder. Ben and Marv watched anxiously from the foot of the aluminum ladder. Ben stood and waved a signal to hurry, hurry, then turned away to help the paramedics on the ground. Marv hunched over the ladder controls ready to pull away as soon as David was clear.

A feeling of triumph began to fill David's heart. It was the elation that came when he had dealt the dragon a losing hand. He gripped the little girl tightly as he came down the last steps.

He clambered down from the big red engine. "Here we are."

Hanson trotted up. "She's all clear now, Lieutenant. The boys have got her under control."

"Hey, you were right, Langston." Ben appeared from the paramedic van, eager to assist with the last victim. His face was smudged, eyes ringed in weariness like a racoon's. He carried a red paramedic kit in one hand. "Let's see."

"Thought I saw something." David gently brought the blanket off his shoulder, cradled it in his arms, and passed the heavy child to Ben. He turned back a corner of the blanket to reveal the child's face and smiled into her trusting eyes.

Ben received the limp blanket. He held it up and patted the thin fabric in amazement. It was empty; nothing there. He stared at his friend and then back at the blanket.

"Langston, sit down over here. I need to give you a check-over."

David touched the blanket dangling emptily from Ben's hands. "She was there. A little girl. I talked to her." His expression was a mixture of amazement and pleading. "She was there."

Ben dropped the blanket. "Come on, David. Sit here. Breathe this." Ben forced David down to the running board and held a mask to his face. "Take a deep breath. Breathe."

Marv looked down from his controls in concern. Ben met his eyes briefly. "It's going to be OK; just take a deep breath."

"Damn it, Ben, I don't need anything." He wrenched away from Ben angrily. "She was there. I talked to her. I carried her."

Jumping up, he snatched the silver blanket and flapped it to and fro. "Not a hallucination; I could feel her on my shoulder."

"You got a good whiff of those gas fumes. You know it happens sometimes. . . ."

"Not to me." David threw the blanket to the ground and stared up at the window, where great plumes of flame gushed into the night air. The building, and everything in it, was a total loss. "It doesn't happen to me."

Ben stepped closer. "I won't mention this to anyone, but maybe you need some time off, David."

"I don't need anything." David cut him off. "I

know what I saw. Besides, no blanket full of smoke weighs sixty pounds. I felt the weight on my shoulder, Ben."

"Sometimes the fire plays tricks on us all. You know that. She's got a wicked sense of humor."

"What's the point here?" David glared at Ben. "I don't get it."

"All I'm saying is that sometimes some strange stuff can go on in your head. I've seen some bad business." Ben compressed his lips and took off his hat. He swept his sweaty hair back from his eyes. "No problem about the blanket. It's forgotten, but . . . take it easy. Not so intense for a while, agreed? That's an official diagnosis."

Chapter Seventeen

W. Hayton Weems frowned at the ledger book spread over his dusty desk. The real accounts, not the books that dried-up Jane Ivy woman kept on her computer in the little front office. He ground out a cigarette butt, thinking about the foreclosure coming up on the Compton farm.

Market was slow. Should have made a lot more money on that sale to the fireman. He was ripe for the picking. Thought I'd just get rid of that millstone, and screwed myself. It was a good profit, what he paid, considering there hadn't been a tenant or an offer in something like 200 years, but Weems liked to squeeze every penny he could out of each transaction. Had to, to keep both sets of books healthy. Helped it along a little now and then, too. It was a game; it was better than sex, what he remembered of it.

The game paid for the secret condo down in West

Palm Beach, and the white Lincoln parked in the garage there. Told Hilda it was real estate conventions in Minnesota. Minnesota in January. What a laugh. He scratched his ample stomach idly. God, she was stupid. He could tell that woman anything.

Two weeks in Cancun already booked, coming up this January. He smiled and laced his fingers behind his head, rocking back in the creaking chair. And this weekend, a nice long three-day one he had planned for himself, alone. Fly down to Key West, cruise a bit, fish, whatever. No pressure; it was great to be alone. He owed himself. No phone calls, no Hilda. Maybe he should think of a new alibi, but the old one, an important client meeting in the city, worked so well, why bother?

A muted roar rattled the loose panes of the dirty window over his desk. Speak of the Devil. There was that fireman Langston swanning around like some kind of stud on his motorcycle. Going out to his country estate, no doubt. Maybe over to visit his sweetie, the Solei woman.

There was a fancy one, but too snooty for his kind, she let him know right off. Just a friendly little invitation to dinner to get to be neighborly. Turned him down flat, with some mighty smart words, too. Hoity-toity. Just because she knew his wife from that Firemen's Burn Center fair business.

Weems stuffed the ledger into a crushed brown paper sack and then under a pile of yellowed newspapers on his desk. He yanked open a drawer and pawed through the envelopes and letters there. "Jane!"

Jane hit the save button on her computer console and watched the screen clear. She took a last sip of tea from her cup and set the cup down neatly on its coaster, then rose from her desk, smoothing her flowered cotton skirt as she went. Jane opened the old-fashioned glass-and-wood door between her orderly front office and his grimy inner sanctum. "Mr. Weems?"

"I need the paperwork on the Compton farm. Has that got back from the county offices yet?"

"I have it all in the file up front, Mr. Weems. Just a minute." She shut the door.

Jane paused to test the moisture in the begonia plant with a forefinger before she slid open the file drawer. She pulled the crisp manila folder from the file cabinet.

"Jane!"

"Yes, sir. I'm coming." She tapped the papers into order. She hummed softly. The Compton foreclosure. Weems would be in a good mood—for him—today. He loved a foreclosure, especially if it meant making someone really miserable. Jane's pace was deliberate; her personal blow against Weems's daily unjust reprimands. If he knew she was looking for a new job, he'd fire her on the spot and somehow manage for her to owe him money. Jane had come to the realization that Weems's shady practices were not something she wished to be involved with even peripherally. She closed the file drawer so slowly the click had two separate sounds.

"Bring me a cold soda while you're at it."

Jane formulated an angry reply but only shouted it mentally as she pulled a bottle from the small office refrigerator in the corner.

"And none of that canned diet junk, either."

Jane carried the folder in one hand and the bottle in the other. She dropped the papers on the small open space on Weems's stained blotter and placed the drink near the litter of sticky empties half-full of cigarette butts. "Shall I take these away?"

"No, leave that be. I've told you before to leave my stuff alone in here. Don't you have enough to keep you busy up front?" Weems drained the bottle in a single draft and let out a resounding belch. "Get out. I'll let you know if I need any housekeeping done."

Nosy old maid. Keep out of his office. If he didn't need her to keep up the public books, he'd get rid of her. Slow as molasses. Sure didn't add much to the decor, thin as a stick, and hair always in her eyes. One of those aerobic-hoppy-jumpy figures; no meat on her anywhere. Got all huffy when he asked her to wear some nicer clothes, miniskirts, some good tall heels, maybe a sweater, to work. Damn women's-libber bullshit. Customers seemed to like her, though.

He pawed his shirtfront pocket for a cigarette. He flipped open a book of matches and tucked the cover closed, bent, and lit a single match all in one motion, with one hand. It was a manly gesture he had see his uncles practice when he was a teenager.

Blowing out a satisfyingly long stream of smoke, he spread the papers over his desk. Signed deed, survey, sheriff's warrant for foreclosure, this and that. He ran an index finger down the neatly typed documents. *Oh yeah, foreclosures, love 'em.* He tapped the papers again. *Should turn a pretty penny on this one.* He might have to give Dixon, his old lawyer friend, a call, but it would be worth it.

He stuffed the papers roughly into the folder. "Jane," he shouted through the door. "I'm going out to look at some property." He pulled on his rumpled gray suit coat.

In the outer office he dropped the disordered folder on Jane's desk. "I won't be back in this afternoon. And I'm taking Saturday and Monday off, so you can open the office yourself. Got a meeting." He yanked his tie straight. "And no goin' home early, either, just because I'm not here."

Weems's ancient Cadillac wallowed up the unpaved road to the Compton farm. Marsh elder mixed with ragweed taller than the fenders slapped the car doors. Giant yellow and brown grasshoppers whirred off from sunflower leaves as the Caddy bumped along at 10 miles an hour. There was a small track beaten down the center of the lane, wide enough for old man Compton's tractor, but hardly enough for the lumbering dinosaur of a vehicle the penurious Weems favored.

It had been years since he had been up that driveway. Last time was homecoming night, with Merle Ann Wallyburton, her with the incredible—Wham! An unseen rock took a bite out of the Cadillac's oil pan. Weems swore with great imagination as he fought with the steering wheel, his attention rudely pulled away from Merle Ann's teenage assets.

The oil indicator gauge flashed red, then showed the needle dropping rapidly to "0." The dash lights started popping on one by one as the engine's lifeblood poured out into the weeds. Weems's profane vocabulary got another workout. He switched off the engine and sat in the dead car, the odor of burning oil and hot engine mixing with the smell of crushed weeds. A grasshopper landed on the windshield and began to crawl across, its antenna twiddling alertly.

The Compton farmhouse was another two miles down this hellish lane. Now what? Weems pounded the steering wheel with his palms.

The Compton property adjoined the Wolfton estate lands. Weems knew the property surveys in the county as intimately as the top of his desk. At least he wasn't lost. As the crow flies, he'd be a 15-minute walk from Wolfton House.

He let out a heavy sigh and sat back in the cracked leather seat. He hated to walk. Hated it especially in the country; fresh air clogged his sinuses and who could tell what disgusting, dangerous creatures were lurking in the weeds? Look at the size of that bug on the windshield; probably poisonous. Ought to pave it all.

However, he didn't have a mobile phone, and the nearest house would be Wolfton House. Langston was supposed to be making lots of improvements; maybe he'd have a phone. If he was there, Weems could wheedle a ride back into town.

Weems hauled himself out of the seat and slammed the door. The startled grasshopper left a large, runny brown spot on the windshield and sprang away with a dry flutter. Weems jumped at the motion and swatted defensively with both hands. Damn bugs.

Which way was west? He glanced up at the sky and squinted at the sun. That way, yeah, he could see the stone fence that marked the property line. He trudged off, slapping the weeds aside.

At last, to his relief, he saw the gray shingle roof above the trees. He pushed through the lilacs and stepped out onto the driveway. Didn't see the fireman's motorcycle; must not be around. *Well, let's just give it a look anyway. Maybe there's a phone inside somewhere. Doesn't a fireman have to be in touch with the station all the time?*

He stopped some feet away from the door, mopping his sweaty face with his handkerchief and staring at the faded wooden balcony. His grandmother's scratchy voice seemed to speak right by his ear.

"Cursed . . . haunted . . . Capt. Wolfton, your namesake, boy, his house. Blood kin, you are. Bad stock, all of them. They say beware the bats, but beware more if there are no bats." Then she would thump his head with her ever-present wooden spoon.

What did that mean? Beware if there were no bats? Who was "they"? Granny was nuttier than a tree full of squirrels, like most of his family. He rubbed his head absently on the spot Granny had thumped so often.

Langston had been spending lots of time out here. So where were the improvements? Three shutters were off; two windows were propped open on the upper floor. The tall dead grass had been hacked away from the granite foundation, exposing the dressed stones. Several fascia boards had been replaced with new pine. If it were him, he would have had the aluminum siding people out here in a heartbeat.

He pulled out a cigarette and lit it with his one-handed trick, then flicked the spent match away, heedless of the dry grass. Nobody around; he could just take his time and give it a real close look. He strolled nonchalantly up the brick walkway, and inspected the door knocker closely. A wolf's head. Pretty clever. He thought he would have liked Capt. Wolfton. Wolfton was a crafty old bird; probably had gold stashed all over this dump.

There was a rustle and flutter in the dead vines above the doorway and Weems ducked warily. Wouldn't be a bat in broad daylight, would it? What was that bats–no bats thing? He picked up a sturdy stick and swung it to and fro. Still had a pretty good swing. He could bunt a bat about 50 yards if he tried. He snorted out a chuckle.

He grabbed the knocker and rapped the door

sharply. Nobody home for sure. He tried the latch and the door swung open easily. He looked up the stairs from the threshold. The house was quiet, just the sound of wind sighing upstairs, singing through the open windows. The smell of paint thinner and fresh enamel hung lightly in the air. Weems stepped in, hearing his footsteps loud in the emptiness.

Part of the hall wall had been knocked away, leaving a gaping hole between the stairway and the adjoining parlor. Only small splintered pieces of lath projected here and there.

Dust everywhere. He swiped his fingers over the banister. Felt like ashes. Gritty. He rubbed his thumb and forefinger together, feeling a slight tingling in his fingertips. Just a quick walk-through; satisfy his curiosity. Wonder where the captain's bedroom was, upstairs probably. He started up the stairs.

The dust rippled and laid quiescent, but aware. Something was approaching. Something large, full of latent evil, an entity with a delicious aura, almost . . . familial, kin. Did he know it? Had he met this person before?

It was a man, a large one, and one that was vulnerable to the power of the dust because he, too, was evil, vile, and concerned only with his own needs. The dark man who perplexed and crippled the dust so much was strong in his goodness, protected by a shield of his unknowing virtue.

What made this human so familiar? Oh, he was a tempting one, one that pulled the dust to the edge of frenzied hunger, more than anything had done for years, centuries.

The blood of the young cats had given him strength, more than that of the bats. One had escaped, wiser than the others, protected by its habits of sleeping out of his reach in the lilacs or huddled close to the dark man.

The feline feral instinct had fed his own hunger, always there, always waiting. *This man has something special for me, but what?* The dust swirled, a tiny whirlpool crossing the upstairs hallway.

Weems hesitated and then continued down the hall. Had he seen movement there? Probably just the wind blowing around some of the dust. What a mess. Dust piled up against the junction of the floorboards and riffled against the wall in little dunes. The place needed a good sweeping. Weems peeked into the big room. A sleeping bag was rolled up neatly and lay by a cardboard carton and Coleman lantern. Must be Langston's little hideaway.

A puff of wind swept down the hall, making the windows chorus discordantly. Somewhere above his head, a branch scraped and tapped against the roof. Weems gave a nervous flinch, then gripped his stick tightly and whacked the doorjamb, unleashing a shower of grime. Just wind and dust. What could happen on a bright sunshiny day like this? Sure no bats around in this light.

The breeze lifted drifts of dust and sprinkled it thickly over Weems's shoes. A tendril hung on the air like a genie, then sunk slowly as a ghost to the floor. A cold snake of a shiver wriggled down Weems's back. He heard his granny again. *Maybe it is a cursed place; sure doesn't seem like any phone around here, anyway.*

He pulled out his handkerchief and scrubbed over his face. The heavy grit of house dust ground into his skin. He slapped at the dust on his shoes with the hankie, and only succeeded in spreading the substance higher over his legs, up to his knees. It looked as though he had been wading in ashes. He brushed at his pant legs, and puffs rose to settle on his arms and chest. He sneezed, inhaled a great lungful of dirt, and sneezed again, dropping his stick in a whooping spasm of coughing. Unthinking, he wiped at his nose with his soiled handkerchief. The grit clung to his skin, searing, biting, crawling like a thousand ants.

Lungs burning where he had inhaled so deeply, he thumped his chest with his fist, and continued to cough. His eyes stung as if acid had been poured into them.

Something here . . . must be allergic to something in the air. Have to get out of here quick. Itching all over. He scratched at his scalp with a violent motion and was horrified to see blood, bits of skin, and hair sticking to his nails. An eddy of dust flowed up and over his shoes, lapping like a wavelet at the beach. He shuffled back, appalled, backward away from the small gray ripples moving across the floor.

Dancing on tiptoe, he tried to avoid contact with the motion and grabbed the banister. He went down the first few stairs as fast as his fat legs could carry him; then one step creaked, and another, and he fell with a terrible cry, clutching at the newel post ineffectually.

He hit his head, bit his lip almost through, and cracked his back. Worst of all, when the feeling of faintness cleared, he could see his leg, bent at a sickening unnatural angle. He couldn't feel the pain yet, but he knew it would hit soon in a shock wave. He tried to move and agony washed over him like a tide of black thorns, stabbing and ripping.

A pool of blood seeped away from his mangled leg, slowly spreading on the dusty chestnut boards.

Panting, he struggled to pull himself into a sitting position, but the pain was too much and he stopped his motion and lay still, pressing his cheek to the cool floor, feeling his heart laboring in his chest.

No phone, no one near. Langston might not show up for days. Hilda and Jane were not expecting him back in town until Tuesday. What would he do? He groaned and raised his miserable gaze from his throbbing leg to the stair risers.

Down the stairs the dust spilled, silently, like evil gray water, a languid cascade flowing toward him.

"Help, somebody, help!" Energized by terror, he scrabbled backward, pulling himself with his hands. Pain was forgotten as he saw the dust reach the dark, spreading puddle of warm blood. As he watched, the pulsing gray haze hesitated, then flowed into the red spill, absorbing it greedily. He heard a small humming sound, almost as if the dust were talking to itself, happily. He screamed again.

The powder touched his leg, the injured one, and the burning sensation intensified and became a coldness of such magnitude he began to sob. It spread upward, toward his groin, and then into his stomach.

"Please, what are you . . . listen, listen to me. I'm sorry, I'm sorry . . . only stop a moment, I'll tell you. . . . " The fabric of his trousers billowed briefly, then sank away, flat as if his flesh were turning to paper under the cloth. He shrieked again and again, and the burning climbed still upward into his chest, his lungs, his throat. He dug his fingers against the wooden floor, trying to move, to run with no legs, to flee with no means of flight.

"Are you the Devil? Are you? Are you?" He moaned and shrieked again. His mind brightened, seeking desperately for a last defense. "Can't we make a bargain? Oh God, I'm sorry. I did it, you know I did it. The fire . . . I'm sorry. Yes, I set the fire, but I'm sorry."

The burning dust reached tendrils across his face almost tenderly. It touched his eyes and lips, gentle as a lover. "Please, I did it, but . . . the first time . . . no, it was just once, really. And it was Dixon's idea. Twice. Only twice. It was just for the insurance; I didn't know anyone was in there. No more! I'll never do it again, never. . . . "

The dust stroked across his tongue and his speech turned into a bubbling cough. His sight clouded, went red, then black.

He screamed, but he knew no one would hear. No one but Wolfton House, the house that had heard many screams, and kept them in its heart.

How good to hear the screams, and so much blood, so much. It was wonderful, how much blood one human could hold. He had almost forgotten. As he covered the writhing and babbling Weems, he knew what had attracted him so. He was family. It was his own blood. How strong he would be, power, power in the blood.

First the blood, then the flesh, and filled with strength, to suck the marrow from the bones. The fleshy body of Weems fed the dust, until it, too became dust, the dust it fed.

For a moment, a moment only, he drew himself together into the form of his family, a human form, for old times' sake. He stood, tottering, a nebulous, dirty gray shade. Weems's clothes lay in a heap on the floor, unsustained by the animation of the dust. Wolfton took a step and turned, raised hazy arms in a remembered triumphal gesture. Feeling for an instant the shape of a phantom hand, the heaviness of humanity repulsed him. Perhaps it was better to be the fluid dust he was. With a sigh of the summer wind, he swirled away, jubilantly filled with the strongest energy he could ever possess.

The wind rolled Weems's clothes into a ball and out the door. A gust moved them further along the drive, and then a sudden sweep snatched them aloft, above the hedge of lilacs that swayed gently, and over the cliff into the sea.

Chapter Eighteen

The trilling of the phone ripped the last shreds of dreams from Lyric's brain. "Hello." Lyric's voice was groggy with sleep.

"Have you seen the headlines this morning?" Jane dispensed with the formalities.

"Janey?" Lyric groped for the alarm clock and squinted at the numbers. Seven o'clock. "What's up?" She rubbed the sleep from her eyes and listened with concerned patience. What could possibly have happened in Salem that would warrant Jane waking her so early?

"There was a big fire last night. *The Salem Torch* says someone was found dead in the Manson building, a street person or something, the paper wasn't specific. Lyric, that was one of our properties! Now I'm going to have to go and help old creepy Weems inspect the damage . . . ooh! This kind of stuff is right up his alley. I think he just drags me along to torture me.

"Anyway, didn't you hear all those sirens last night? I heard at least five trucks leave from the station. The article also mentioned something about one fireman injured . . . but they're withholding the name."

David. Lyric came fully awake as fear lurched into her throat. She sat bolt upright in the bed, clutching the sheets. Jane charged on, hardly taking a breath.

"I'll tell you, we need to get over there and make sure your man is alive and kicking."

Lyric tried to disguise the apprehension in her voice. "He's not my man, but I guess we could go over and check on things." She was already at her closet, pinching the phone between cheek and shoulder as she fumbled through the hangers to drag off a shirt. "We are friends, that's all." Lyric hopped on one foot, then the other, squirming into her jeans.

"Whatever. I'll be over in, umm, about thirty minutes. I'm taking the morning off." Jane paused. "As long as we're there, maybe you can introduce to me to a few of Mr. Langston's buddies?"

Aha. The real reason. "Make it fifteen minutes."

Lyric dropped the cordless phone into its receiver and snapped her jeans. *Please.* She paused to light a votive candle on her nightstand. *Not David. Let him be safe.*

"Hello? Anybody here?" Lyric called into the recreation room. She caught a glimpse of the kitchen as three young men looked up from stacking plates and wiping counters. The rich fragrance of fresh-brewed coffee rose from the glass and chrome double-sized pot near the stove.

Two of the firemen gave welcoming grins as the third man, the tallest, approached Lyric and Jane. "Good morning, ladies. What can we do for you?" He slung a dish towel rakishly over one shoulder. "We're just cleaning up breakfast."

"I'm Ben Barker." The left sleeve of his uniform shirt was rolled up neatly above a stark white bandage. The fact that it set off his tan was not lost on Jane's appreciative eyes.

The other men shut the cabinet doors, pulled the plug from the sink, and left the room quietly.

"I'm Lyric Solei, and this is my friend, Jane Ivy. We heard about last night's fire." Lyric extended her hand for a polite shake. Ben took it briefly, then turned to clasp Jane's hand much more warmly.

"Was anyone injured?"

Ben and Jane still grasped hands. "Injured?" Ben appeared to be concentrating on projecting his most manly aura for Jane. "Just me, ma'am. But that's all in the job, you know."

"What happened to you? Looks like that arm's not up to KP duty." Jane looked pointedly at the bandage.

"No, but this one is just fine." He released Jane's hand and flexed his biceps, making the shirt material tighten across his right arm. The rooster in him took the opportunity to strut while there was no one in the kitchen but him and his captive audience. "Better to answer the phone with, Doc Tucker says, at least for a while."

"So are you the one the paper was talking about getting hurt?" Jane widened her eyes and gazed up with an adoring expression.

Thank goodness Jane had voiced the exact question stuck somewhere on Lyric's lips.

"That's me." Ben poked himself in the chest with

his thumb. "But if it hadn't been for Langston, I'd probably have a lot more injuries than just a busted wing."

Ben pulled his attention away from Jane. "I guess you mean Langston, though. Nope, he's about as fit as he can get. Outside washing the Kodiak."

"What's that about me?" David sauntered in, wiping his hands on a tattered towel. His face lit up when he saw Lyric standing by Ben.

Lyric's heart begin a wild tattoo against her ribs. How dare he be all right? How dare he worry her so? How dare he make her care so much? She laced her fingers together tightly to stop the sudden tremble and forced down the constriction in her throat.

"I was just telling these two ladies how you saved my life . . . among others'."

"Maybe I should have just let that beam squash you." David swung the towel between his hands and made it give a resounding crack. "What else might you be telling them?" He twirled the cloth again and aimed it at Ben. Ben skipped to the left but still caught a stinging pop to the thigh.

"Ow, hey, I'm an injured man." Ben stepped behind Jane, grabbing her shoulders and using her as a laughing shield.

"Hey, gorgeous." David whipped the towel around Lyric's waist and pulled her close. He nuzzled her hair roughly. "You smell good."

Lyric felt the wonderful hard living flesh of his body tight against her, comforting and assuring her in the immediate warmth that he was fine. She wanted to drown in the flood of relief that washed over her, to sob into his chest and have him reassure her that her fears were just that, only fears. She wanted to pound with both fists and scream at him in helpless frustration, How could he have risked everything they had? But instead she blushed at his intimate gesture and twisted away.

You always had to have a cause. She heard the statement in her head. It was her voice speaking to him.

She hadn't realized how anxious she had been until she saw him step into the room, relaxed and self-confident. The binding of tension she had carried wound around her emotions started to come unraveled like an old rubber-band ball, spewing bits and pieces.

"This is my friend, Jane." She would give him a piece of her mind later. "I think you met her when you bought your house. She works at the real estate agency."

"Yes, I remember. I bet you know lots of its secrets." David drew Lyric back to his side firmly and kept his arm around her waist to keep her there. "Every time I get one thing figured out, I just find some other puzzle."

"There are lots of secrets in that house. Too many for me. All I know is that it's always been one of the scariest places around. But Lyric is the one that is good with secrets. She always knows a little more than the rest of us, one way or another."

"Now you tell me," David said with a rueful laugh.

"Hey, every building in Salem has a ghost story. Even this station." Ben picked up on his lead for getting further with Jane. Ghost stories always made teenagers snuggle closer. Maybe it would work with Jane. "How would you like to see a real fire station? A haunted one."

"Cool! Do we get to slide down the pole?"

"Sure. Anything you want." Ben put his good hand at Jane's waist and guided her out the door into the hall. "They say the ghost of old Fire Chief O'Brien still haunts this station. That's his fire helmet right there in the display case. Sometimes after a big fire, you can see fresh smoke marks on it. On cold winter nights . . ." Ben's voice faded as he and Jane meandered down the hall past the glass shelves full of mementos and trophies.

"Are all firemen so full of . . . blarney?"

"He's harmless, really." David gathered Lyric close, now that they were alone. "Not so sure about me, though." His voice lowered as he buried his face in the curve of her neck. "What's the matter?"

A lump of emotion in her throat made it hard to speak. "I was scared, David, when I heard . . . I was scared it might be you." Lyric didn't want to reveal the panic that had struck when she heard Jane's words this morning. The slight tremble in her voice was undeniable.

David pulled away for a moment and looked into her eyes. "It goes with the territory." He touched her cheek with his and then nibbled soft kisses up her neck. "It's sweet of you to care." Warm breath in her ear. "Don't worry about me. I'm good." Another gentle kiss. "I'm the best."

"It's only that . . . I've just found you. . . . "

David captured her mouth with a possessiveness that made her body sag into the curve of his own. Lyric's mind sparkled and they were timelessly together again, spinning and whirling. They were no longer in the fire station. They were in the past. They were in the future. They were always.

"I can't lose you this time," she whispered, almost to herself, as she lowered her head and pressed her face into the hollow of his throat.

She took a deep, deliberate breath, and opened her eyes. She needed oxygen. Oxygen gave strength, power. David had captured her breath, her soul, and she had willingly let him.

David stroked her hair. "I've missed you. My dreams haven't been the same since the other night."

"Mmmm. You know what they say about dreams."

"What?" David gathered her hair in both his hands and playfully piled it on top of her head like an amber silk turban. He held it in place and looked admiring. "You have the most beautiful hair."

Lyric tossed her head and made her hair fall down around her shoulders and face. "A dream is a wish your heart makes."

David brushed the curls back from her forehead. "Perhaps it is." They stood silently, wrapped in their thoughts and the nearness of an unspoken word. David pulled away and yanked open a drawer.

"Come on. You need the peanut tour. Little kids love it. Big ones, too." He rummaged in the drawer and pulled out a red-and-gold plastic firefighter badge.

"Now, the first thing you must do is put on the badge." He slipped one hand under the collar of her shirt to pin on the emblem. The backs of his fingers brushed the skin along her collarbone. Could he feel the rapid beat of her pulse? Surely he must.

"This tells us all that you are now a junior fireman. As such, you are entitled to inspect this station with a senior member of the squad. Are you ready, Jr. Fireman Solei?"

"Yes, sir."

"Let's start out then. You already saw our kitchen." They started down the hallway.

"Are these all awards?" Lyric peered into the glass case burgeoning with framed photos and sparkling trophies. Gold-plated plaques and miniature silver fire trucks gleamed on the shelves. "What's this?" She pressed her nose to the glass in order to see a small plaque that had a bronze water faucet at the center. A large hanging drop of bronze "water" hung at the lip in middrip. THE LAST DROP AWARD was engraved under the faucet.

"That's the award you receive if have the dubious honor of being last in the pumper competition. Since we've never been last, that's just a joke award the captain had made to wind us up." David pointed to the small brass plate under the "drip." "See. All our names are engraved."

Lyric's mind flashed to the pumper competition and how exciting the day had been. They pushed through the double doors into the open bay area where the fire engines, emergency vehicles, and hook and ladder unit were parked. The bay smelled like rubber tires and oil. The big vehicles were fiercely shiny, aggressively red and chrome. It was all orderly, hoses coiled, ropes looped and tied, emergency kits stacked and stowed.

"So, how'd you like to see my equipment?" David gave a boyish grin.

"Great." Big boys, big toys. Lyric stood in front of the massive chrome grill of the hook and ladder unit. The hood emblem was far over her head. She leaned forward to see her elongated reflection in the red fender. "All the engines are so clean and shiny. Didn't you just use these last night?"

"Yep, but every one of them gets washed every day. And waxed once a month." David stepped up onto the running board and reached in for his boots, turnouts, and jacket. "These are kept on the engine during the day and then at night they are ready next to your bed." He settled the yellow helmet on Lyric's head. "There. Now you need your protective jacket."

He held the heavy canvas jacket by its collar so Lyric could slip her arms into the sleeves. The sleeve ends came far over her hands, and the weight of the padded material pulled at her shoulders. The stiff cloth carried a faint odor of smoke. Sooty spots smudged across the lettering on the chest.

The coat swallowed her, but also wrapped her with a sense of immense protection. She could feel each moment David had spent in the jacket. The events, each emergency, overlapped and yet they were all the same, that feeling of urgency, the feeling you must complete your mission. Lives to be saved; nothing else was important. The elation of triumph.

A burning sensation began in her left thigh. Something in the coat was seeking her attention. Now was not the time or place for a vision. Lyric smoothed her hand over the canvas to rub the pain away. The pain sharpened as her palm crossed the pocket of the jacket. She slipped her hand into the deep pocket and wiggled her fingers. Something small, hard and not quite round jiggled around under her touch. She captured the objects and withdrew her hand. The pain ceased instantly. So this was what was speaking to her.

She unfolded her fingers and three brown acorns lay on her palm. "Where did these come from? Are they your lucky charms?"

David's voice was alarmed. "Where did you find them?"

"Here in your pocket. I'm sorry; I'll put them back if they are special."

"No, no. I . . . she really was there." His voice was barely audible. He took the nuts from Lyric and rolled them between his fingers. "These are real. She had to be real."

"What are you talking about?"

"Last night, there was a child. I found her in the fire. She spoke to me and gave me those acorns." David sat on the running board and stared at the ground between his boots. "I carried her down the ladder." He looked up at Lyric. "When I got down to Ben, she wasn't there. Not there. I could feel her on my shoulder, but then she wasn't there."

Lyric took the acorns back into her hand and rubbed them thoughtfully. "Acorns."

"Three acorns. I told you before I don't believe in this spooky stuff, but this was so real. Ben thinks I just got a whiff of fumes. It happens, you know. But the acorns, here in my pocket, after all." He shook his head. "I don't know."

Lyric sat beside him, shoulder nestled against his side. She folded the nuts tightly in her fist, then held them by her cheek.

"I haven't told anybody. They'd all think I was crazy. Ben's probably forgotten the whole thing by now. I hope so."

"Shh." Lyric's head swam, swirling with colors. The nuts seemed to whirl in a vortex of hues flowing like a glowing ribbon. Each seed was like a tiny message in a bottle.

"What's going on? Are you getting some kind of vibes? Do you see something?"

Lyric lowered her hand and the colors paled and disappeared. "What did you see when you got these?"

David took a deep breath and looked across the bay as if he would see the little girl there. "There wasn't a lot of time for me to see anything. Just a little girl." He frowned and shook his head again. "Maybe her dress was old-fashioned. White apron, you know. She was very clean, and calm. She seemed . . . to know me.

"You believe me, don't you? You think there really was someone. Who was it?"

"I don't know who it was. I think the important part is what she had to tell you." Lyric rattled the acorns loosely in her fist.

David picked up one nut and held it between his thumb and forefinger. "Seemed like these were the message somehow. But I don't know what to make of it."

"Acorns represent longevity and immortality." She dropped the other two brown nuts into David's hand. "And fertility.

"The oak is traditionally a magic tree. The Druids worshiped under the oak." Lyric put her hand over David's, wrapping his fingers around the acorns. "No matter how you feel now, keep these in a safe place and guard them as if they were your own children. They are a promise."

"Longevity, fertility. What's that got to do with me?"

"I think that these were sent to you as messages of comfort and hope." She paused, too near a very private memory. "I don't know your past, David. I could look, but it's like a breach of privacy, unless you want me to. Call it professional ethics."

David quirked a corner of his lips. It was not quite the cocky grin he could usually summon up when he talked about her talents. "OK, just for the sake of professional ethics. Don't look at my past. Tell me about the future." He seemed to remember what the fortune-teller at the fair had said. "Everyone seems interested in my future."

"Your future is what you will make it, but somewhere there is a child waiting for you. Three children. The first one will be a girl, but she is waiting for the right time to come to you through the one you are meant to love."

David stood up and smiled the dazzling smile Lyric had grown to crave. He dropped the nuts into the pocket of his shirt and buttoned the flap over them. "Not a bad future. I'll have to get busy to find the right woman, I suppose. Three children." He patted his pocket. "When you put it like that, it doesn't feel spooky at all." He stretched out both hands to Lyric and pulled her up to him.

Chapter Nineteen

"David?" Lyric called down the hall of Wolfton House. "David?" His shiny motorcycle was outside, so he must be somewhere near. She carried a large wicker picnic basket and made her way in and through to the back of the house.

More than a week had passed since the revealing trip to the Maritime Museum. She had no chance to discuss the findings with David. Certainly she hadn't wanted to mar the romance of the candle-light fairy-tale dinner, and frankly, the thought of evil curses and death was not on her mind at the time.

Since that evening, David had been on 24-hour duty. A hard week it had been, indeed, in the dry summer days. There had been the Manson building fire and after that Lyric heard the big red trucks roll out every night but one. After she and Jane had visited the firehouse, David had made a point to call her, but his voice was blurry with fatigue, the hours for sleep eaten up by the responsibility of his profession. Today was the first of his four days off. She had planned a treat to distract and reward him.

"David?" Lyric called again. Here and there she could see signs of his progress with the renovation. Part of the staircase wall had been knocked out, leaving a gaping hole into the parlor behind it. Odd; she didn't think David had planned structural changes. Several doors and shutters had been removed, cleaned, and stacked neatly to the side. One door had been painted deep crimson, the very paint she had mistaken for blood the first time she saw David. She tapped lightly on the mirror-smooth panels, thinking of that mixture of fear and anticipation she had felt at that strange first meeting.

The same apprehensive feeling was creeping up her spine and prickling the hairs on her neck. This house would never be her house, she knew. Wolfton, cursed to be within these walls, would not allow it. His vileness lurked here, waiting for her, still coveting what it could never have.

How could David not feel the malice that swirled to engulf her, even on this sunny summer day? David, the sturdy pragmatic nonbeliever, protected by his refusal to acknowledge anything but what he could see and feel. Would this be the wedge that Wolfton could drive between them to separate them again?

Sanding, plaster repair, and stripping woodwork had added several more layers of dust and grime to the floor. In some places David had laid thick carpets of old newspapers to avoid scratching the mellow walnut floor planks. She could see he was a meticulous and patient craftsman with a plan in mind to turn this empty shell into a beautiful home.

"David?" Lyric called again, as she wandered down the hall. At the very end of the hall she found the kitchen. The window was propped open with a stick, and the floor had been swept clean. A fresh new broom leaned by the open back door. Iron pot-hooks waited for eternally absent pots in a vast blackened stone fireplace, yawning emptily at the end of the room. A large soapstone sink, the height of luxury for its time, boasted a water pump.

Lyric could not resist the temptation to prime the wobbly handle a few times and force up whatever might be below. With one, two, three pumps she began to feel the pressure ascending. Tingling started in her fingertips, spread into her palm, then rapidly up her arm and across her chest. *No.* A vision was coming. *No. No. Not here, not now.* Her pleas seemed to give it perverse momentum, and it came even stronger. She could not release the pump handle. She tried frantically to throw up her mental blocks, but it was too late. As she squeezed her eyes shut in a desperate hope of dissolving the feeling, she heard a bell, and instantly she was there.

"What does it say? What news? What news?" the growing mob shouted, surrounding the town crier. The crowd jostled the crier so closely he dropped the tarnished brass bell he was clanging to announce his presence in the town square.

"Oy, there . . . give the man a chance, mates." A short man braced his sturdy body and spread his arms in front of the harassed crier. He picked up the bell, rubbed it on his shirt, and gave it back to its owner. "'Ere, sir. Gits a grip and let us know the latest."

Sarah stood at the well coping, where she drew water daily. She had made many wishes on this spot, as the crystal drops of cool water fell back into the mother-spring deep below. Trembling, tight as one of her weaving wefts, she stood straining to hear what the crier would read from his parchment roll. A group of men swept by her, close enough to brush her brown skirt, and she shrank closer to the stones.

The crier stepped atop a granite mounting block and cleared his throat, letting his moment of drama build as he fiddled with the strings and seals wrapping the parchment. He unknotted the last strand of red ribbon and unrolled the scroll slowly, squinting as he focused his nearsighted eyes on the florid writing.

He drew a deep breath and with as much self-importance as he could muster, began to read. "On the thirteenth day of December in the year of our Lord 1693 . . ." He swept the citizens with his gaze and interjected, "Night before last, that is."

"We know the date, John, get on wi' it," an impatient voice came from the citizens. The men around John the crier nodded in agreement and shifted from foot to foot.

Sarah held her breath. Her knuckles were white on the wooden bucket.

"Dante Huels was tried and found guilty of high treason against the Commonwealth. He is to be executed before dawn on the day of our Lord, December the sixteenth, by Capt. Wolfton personally." He paused and cleared his throat again. "Hanged by the neck until dead."

"Hanged . . . hanged . . . hanged . . ." The murmur swept from mouth to mouth, an evil echo. "Hanged tomorrow."

The blood drained from Sarah's face. The pail slipped from her grasp, tumbling down, down in slow motion to hit the surface of the water with a hollow splash. Rage, mixed with a smothering terror, seized her heart with rough talons. Her faith and protection had failed him somehow. "My love, my faith. It was my pride that made him feel so confident. He was careless because of me." Forgetting danger, she covered her face in despair.

The mutter stilled briefly as the crier's voice raised. "And furthermore, there is evidence . . ." Another dramatic pause as he darted his glance from face to face. ". . . there is someone in league with Dante Huels. . . ."

Women in the gathering drew their children close into their skirts. John the crier continued his revelations. "There is a witch among us." The audience burst into bedlam. A woman screamed and men began to curse, hands curling like claws around rake handles and shovels. In a doorway nearby, three old ladies bent their heads together, white caps touching and withered mouths working as they stared toward Lyric. One raised her gnarled fist in the old sign against evil.

Lyric clutched her cloak at the throat and pulled the hood further over her head, futilely hoping no one would notice her presence. It was as if her breath were thunder, each intake echoing for miles. Her heartbeat was a drum, signaling "Here, here, here I am." Her heart hammered on as she whirled and blindly pushed her way through the people. She shoved her way past the women at the fringes of the throng and heard her own death sentence.

"She was named. Sarah Morgan, the town seamstress, wife of Dante Huels." A terrible rolling moan swept from every throat, the sound of a beast hungry for blood, arousing, ready to kill.

"Witch!" A woman's voice, edged in hysteria.

"Witch." The commanding tones of a man.

"Stone her. Thou shalt not suffer a witch to live." The deep voice of Rev. Mather.

"No, she must burn to cleanse our town. Only fire

will clean her vileness away. Burn her . . . remove the evil . . . burn, burn!"

"Torches, get torches!"

Sarah's cloak fell unheeded to the ground as she lifted her skirts and darted away. Home, safety. No, that is the first place they will be waiting. The stables. *If she could mount quickly enough she might escape. She would rather take her chances with the beasts of the woods than the ones that screamed for her life in Salem town.*

Panting with terror, she flung a glance over her shoulder. The shouts of the mob reached a crescendo, then broke into the ragged baying of a pack on the hunt.

"Burn her. Burn the witch!"

Sarah flung open the side door of the stable. Please let there be a horse . . . any horse. *She clucked to a bay horse and jerked the reins from the iron ring in the wall. The horse shied and danced, scenting her fright. She struggled with her tangling skirt, fighting to get her toes into the stirrup. She swung up, astride like a man, and gathered the reins for a desperate flight.*

The side doors crashed open. Two beefy men, ropes coiled round their shoulders, stood there. Close behind, more of the village males hurried toward the stable. Sarah swung the stamping horse around. The other, smaller door was blocked by yet another man.

The mare pranced and snorted, eyes rolling, whites flashing in the gloom of the barn. With a shout, Sarah dug her heels into the mare's ribs, hoping to burst through by sheer force. The chance was slim but the horse had no heart for the turmoil that surrounded it and hesitated. The largest man grabbed the bridle firmly and gave it a rough shake.

"None of that, now, missy. You'll not ride any hobbyhorse out of my barn."

From the height of the saddle, Sarah could see what surrounded her. A mob. Those who had been helpful neighbors and confiding friends had become strangers, strangers with every intent of killing her. There was no need for a trial, and if there was one it would only postpone for the briefest of times the surety of her death. The scent of blood was on the air. They had heard the word witch, *reason enough for seeking immediate justice. It would not be a clean death.*

"Nor any broomstick, either." A man wearing the blue jerkin of a worker at the Wolfton estate grabbed for her, clamping her arm in a grip like a vise of bone. He dragged her from the saddle and dropped her in a tumble at the horse's feet. Her skirt and petticoats bunched at her waist, revealing her long legs.

"Except maybe the one I got here." The hot gleam of desire sparked his usual slack expression.

Sarah shoved her skirt down and struggled to rise. Another worker from the Wolfton estate, a gardener, Sarah remembered irrelevantly, stepped forward. He swung a thin rope and narrowed his eyes, sweeping the length of her body with a lustful glance.

"Such a high and mighty wench she's been, don't ya know." He drew the rope through his palms. "Too good to marry the captain, too good for any of us'n, just her precious Dante. Turned down the cap'n himself for a common sailor. Makes you wonder, don't it? Not too good to be the Devil's whore, though." He snatched the cap from her head and dug his fingers into her hair. Shoving his face into hers, he sprayed spittle as he whispered lewdly, "How was it, witch? Is it true, is the Devil better than any mortal man?"

Sarah twisted her head away from his rancid breath. His teeth were as green as the plants he tended.

"Is he hot like a poker? Or is it cold, cold like an icicle?"

Sarah clawed at his eyes and pounded her fists against his chest. He pulled his head back, laughing at her distress, and then slapped her so hard her nose started to bleed.

The mob was gathering, filling the stable. Hysterical religious fervor bubbled like hot tar, stoked with a fearful forbidden sexual flavor. Sarah could see men normally spineless and meek made bold by the frenzy. Later they would be ashamed but now they would leap forward eagerly to participate in her torment.

The pig-eyed gardener yanked her to her tiptoes with his hold on her hair and shook her like a dog shakes a rat. "Looks like you won't be doin' any more fancy stitchin'." Lascivious snickers met his attempt at humor as gave her another fierce shake and released her.

She stumbled dizzily. The cold flat back of a wooden shovel hit her lower back with stunning force. The blow took her breath, and she crumpled to the straw-covered floor. Blackness and flashes of red light danced before her eyes. Pain radiated from her spine like a spider's web of knife slashes. For the moment she lay stunned, unable to move or think, feeling nothing but agony.

Instantly, Pig-eyes was on top of her. Pinning her shoulders with his knees, he straddled her waist. " 'Tis a waste to let only the flames lick such tasty lips."

An encouraging murmur rose from the audience surrounding her as he trailed a filthy finger down her cheek to rest on her lips. Cruelly, he rubbed over the cut where she had bitten her lip and dabbled his finger in the blood, a captor teasing a trapped animal. "A waste . . ."

She gathered all her strength and struck at his appendage like a snapping turtle. She bit down hard as she could and felt teeth grate against bone as she wrenched her head from side to side.

He leapt up, shrieking with pain, shaking his wounded finger and spraying the onlookers with blood. "I've been marked by a demon!" he howled, pushing through the ring of men to escape, clutching his streaming finger. "A demon!"

Still in agony from the shovel's blow, Sarah could not stagger to her feet quick enough to avoid more abuse. Three more of the bloodthirsty gang were upon her. One of the men—Steadfast Hopkins—yes, it was Steadfast. She remembered because she had finished a length of fine linen for his daughter's trousseau last month and he had complained bitterly about the cost. He kicked her roundly in the left kidney.

Stunned, she lay on her stomach. The men pulled her hands behind her back, trussing her like a chicken to be roasted. They yanked her upright and slammed her against the splintered stall boards. A male voice jeered, making some rough joke, and Sarah concentrated on the rotten wood. It was grating away the flesh from her cheek, but the pain was small, absorbed into the infinity of hurt that consumed her entire body.

The smell of blood mingled with a warm, familiar smell, oddly comforting. Fresh horse manure clung to her face and hair. Her captors tugged her along, and she began to turn within, preparing to leave her body. She must not feel anything when the time came.

Her rag-doll knees buckled once more with the weight of her life, but the men tightened their grip on her elbows and dragged her on. Her toes raked a trail in the dirt as she was dragged like broken prey to the hastily assembled pyre. Sarah felt a warm trickle begin from her womb.

A child. This was the child, Willow, that only

Sarah knew about. Things were beginning to make sense to Lyric now. The weight of Lyric's arm forced the pump handle down. With the metallic click, her eyes opened.

A burst of blood-thick dark red liquid trickled out onto the stone as if it had been wounded. Lyric released the handle with a gasp and swiped at the tears that still rolled down her cheeks. Yes, there had been too much blood spilled into this ground.

"David!" Where was he? She snatched up the basket and made for the backyard. She'd rather not spend much time alone in this house. As she hurried out the propped open door, she saw David working intently on a peeling shutter laid across supports under the gnarled tree.

David wore a pair of cutoff jeans that hung wonderfully low on his hips and a scuffed pair of very worn boots. The casual outfit left lots of handsome flesh exposed to the morning sun. Unseen, Lyric paused and admired his motions, the muscles in his arms bunching and relaxing as he stroked the wood with energetic passion. His back was a glistening tawny triangle, like living sculpture, tapering to an apex at his narrow waist. His shirt hung on a nearby bush.

An orange-and-white kitten chased a leaf nearby. Sawdust and wood chips littered the ground liberally, and old hinges from the shutter were soaking in cans of chemical stripper. Since there had been no improvements made to the house in centuries, there had never been electricity run to the old mansion, and all the carpentry had to be done without the aid of any power tools.

David looked up with surprise. He broke into a delighted smile. "Lyric! Hi," he greeted her. "What are you doing way out here?" His voice was velvety mellow. The welcome in his voice replaced any chill she had felt inside the house.

"I thought you might enjoy sharing a picnic basket with me." Lyric cast an edgy look over her shoulder. "Outdoors." She left the basket on the steps and came to where he was working.

"Sounds great. I just need to wash up." David tossed a paintbrush into a waiting coffee can full of turpentine.

"Where? You don't have any plumbing yet, do you?" In order to gain her composure, Lyric bent to inspect the newly stripped shutter, careful not to let her full white skirt fall against the still-wet wood.

"No, but the old pump in the kitchen still works. Pumps up clear as a bell. I'll be back in just a minute." David disappeared cheerfully into the house.

"The pump?" Lyric felt her face go white. "Does it?" she said faintly. Could Wolfton's soul be strong enough in its ill wishes to cause the gush of blood from the pump?

"Clean as a whistle." Reappearing, David held his hands up and flipped them front to back for her inspection. Hands were one of her favorite parts of a man's body. For Lyric, they held secretly coded lines in each palm, a map of all journeys past and journeys to come. Seductively long fingers, hard sinewy power, delightful dexterity. David's hands held music, she knew, and skill. Then there was the more basic appreciation. As hands went, she knew David's would feel just perfect around her waist or even lower.

She stooped and picked up the kitten, who was inspecting the picnic basket closely. "Hello, sweetie. What's your name?"

"I was hoping you'd name her for me. I had three others, but one by one, they've wandered off, I guess. This one stays close to me as glue. Won't go inside without being right under my feet." He scratched under the kitten's chin. "Don't you, fuzz-ball? On my days off, she goes to the station with me."

"A cat's name has to be special, you know." She put the kitten down gently. "I think you have a name already." The kitten rubbed around her ankles and gave a loud purr. Lyric laughed. "See, David, she says she does. She says her name is Embers." Embers meowed and bounded off into the hedges after a sparrow.

"Embers. That's a good name for a fire fighter's cat." David plucked his shirt from the branches of the old shrub, gave it a shake, and slipped it on quickly. He grabbed Lyric and swung her up into his arms as easily as he would swing up a child. David cradled her much as she had seen him hold her confident cat the first day they had met. She felt like purring, protected and secure in the circle of his strength.

"We call this a fireman's carry. What do you think about it?" He hugged her close enough that she could feel the steady heartbeat beneath his sweat-damp chest. Her own heart gave an alarming jump. "You should feel very safe," he said in a mockingly serious tone.

Lyric slid her arms around his neck and kissed him behind the ear, nuzzling under his dark tousled hair. She could taste the salt of his morning's work, and finished the kiss with a soft lick and a nibble. He tasted good; salt was the taste of life and talismanic protection. Lyric always had preferred salty food over sweet.

"Oh yes, I feel very safe," she assured him softly. She did feel safe. The feeling of his sinewy arms lifting her easily, holding her close to the pulse of life in his chest, was enough to dispel the unclean fright the vision at the pump had wrapped around her.

He turned his head to cover her mouth with his own. A delightful flood of sensations skittered and raced all over her body. She could feel his heartbeat even more clearly, but now it was pounding as if he had just answered the alarm of the firebell in the night. After a too-short eternity, he let her down, sliding her slowly against the length of his body, out of the perfect cradle of his arms.

"Ready?" David took up the laden basket easily. "I've got a surprise for you."

"A good surprise?" Lyric asked, still a bit breathless from David's embrace.

"Remember the cove where Wolfton met his traitor friends? I found the secret trail and the cave. The tide should be out now. We can have our picnic in the cave." David seemed as pleased as a little boy who had just found a new playhouse.

They crossed the weedy yard and parted the hugely overgrown lilac bushes. The fragrant purple blossom heads hung heavily and drooped, releasing a ripely sweet shower of tiny spent flowers when they were touched. David held back the branches so Lyric could step through and have a clear view of the sea below.

They stood at the edge of a precipice. David sat the basket on the grass and pulled Lyric in front of him. He wrapped his arms protectively around her shoulders. She leaned back against his straight body, bracing against the sea wind that swept up and swirled violently. Their bodies fit together so well. Lyric bowed her head and laid her cheek against the powerful muscled arms that encircled her, and brushed her face against the silky soft hair on his forearms. She closed her eyes briefly and pushed down a feeling of vertigo that plucked at her senses. The combination of the proximity of David's masculine magnetism and the cliff's dizzying height made her feel as if she could step over the edge and fly.

She felt the wind tug and flutter the pale blue ribbon that she had braided into her hair. The sea spray teased tendrils of her curls out of their confinement to dance temptingly on her shoulders. The soft low ruffle that made the neckline of the dress fell loosely over the top of her breasts. She felt David's bold eyes on her skin, not the ocean view.

David rubbed his cheek against her forehead and touched his lips to her cheek, a deliciously disturbing sensation. She raised her head to press more firmly against his mouth.

The cliff dropped off steeply into the surf, exposing a forbidding but breathtaking panorama. The cove opened into the Atlantic, and the horizon of silver water swept away endlessly. Black and gray boulders with patches of slick green algae tumbled and jutted into the surging water. Clumps of barnacles bristled on the rocks. Revealed by the low tide, they presented their razor-sharp edges for defense.

They stood for a moment surveying the dramatic view. The rushing current of air whipped Lyric's thin cotton dress close to her legs, then swirled it high to wrap around her hips and David's legs, pressed so disturbingly close behind hers.

David whispered in her ear, "Afraid?" His breath had quickened and felt hot on her wind-cooled skin.

"No," she answered and turned in his arms to meet his lips eagerly. How could she ever be afraid with him so near? A spinning feeling of euphoric rapture swept her up as he kissed her softly once, then twice before parting her lips wide, seeking entrance. Lost in the dizzying flood of sensation, they embraced as the wind swept past.

At last they turned to look across the water. Lyric's heart was pounding louder than the surf below her.

"It looks like you can't possibly get down the cliff, but I found the trail." David stepped confidently down into what looked to be thin air. Lyric followed closely and they picked their way down the cliff on a perfectly accessible, and perfectly hidden, narrow path.

"Watch your step here; it's slippery." David offered Lyric firm assistance as she stepped over the last few feet of wet rocks. Sheltering rocks deflected the fierce updraft and turned the wind into a pleasant breeze. The sun warmed the private little beach in front of a small cave. "When the tide comes in, this is underwater."

"David, this is beautiful!" Lyric surveyed the charming area floored by pockets of sand, gray pebbles, and shells. Several feet below the cave's ledge was another narrow sand beach. Small pools of water were trapped in the crevices of the granite boulders. Lyric flicked a finger of water at a tiny hermit crab clinging to his stolen shell house and scurrying to escape her shadow.

"This should make a wonderful dining room, don't you think, Ms. Solei?" David smiled. "Maybe afterward we can do some exploring."

Lyric turned in a circle to survey the area. She selected a plot of smooth clean sand to spread the old picnic quilts she had brought to serve as a banquet table.

She slipped off her sandals at the edge of the quilt

and knelt with the basket in front of her. "I packed this full of my favorite things. I hope you'll like them, too."

David pulled off his boots and set them neatly side by side, as if he were in the firehouse, then sat on the quilt expectantly. "Can't think of anything of yours I haven't liked so far," he said, with a slowly raised eyebrow, looking straight into her eyes.

Lyric felt her inner fever deepen, like a fire fed slow-burning coal. She pulled a slim amber bottle from the basket. "This is my own apple cider . . . home brewed. I'm sure you'll like it; it has a special kick to it." She watched David's eyes follow the motion as she circled the long neck, stroking the elongated dark glass in a languid, up-and-down gesture. She passed the decanter and the silver corkscrew to David. "Would you do the honors, please?"

As David opened the bottle carefully, Lyric unwrapped two sturdy wine goblets. Emerald green stems and brilliant purple glass cups made them wink like jewels in the sunlight.

David filled both goblets and corked the cider. "I think we should toast such a beautiful day." Lyric held the sparkling goblet extended in salute.

"And to such beautiful company," David added. "Here's to new beginnings and leaving the past behind."

"Here's to new beginnings and learning from the past," Lyric amended. The solid clink from their glasses sealed their wishes. Lyric closed her eyes and took a slow, thoughtful sip of the fermented apple juice, making a special wish with the first swallow of the new wine. She opened her eyes and watched David's face as he raised the goblet to his lips.

Looking into her eyes, David seemed to be thinking of the message sent by her gesture on the neck of the wine bottle. He took a hearty gulp and gasped, "Whoa! What a kick. What's in this?" He took a deep breath and shook his head appreciatively.

"Only apples and spring water . . . and maybe just a little magic," Lyric warned with laughter in her voice. "It's a special brew I make up for the summer solstice."

David took a long, respectful swallow. "It's good." He took another sip and blinked rapidly. "Why for summer solstice?" he asked over the rim of the glass. He kept the goblet near his face and inhaled the heavy, sensual essence of the long-ago apples.

"I like to celebrate the seasons," Lyric answered. She balanced her goblet on a flat rock nearby and continued to arrange the food.

"Do you know what something called Beltane is, then?" David asked.

Now where did that come from? she thought. "Beltane is a witches' celebration of May Day and the rites of spring. Actually, it's an ancient ritual that celebrates fertility . . . fertility and fire. That's why the Maypole is decorated. Why do you ask?" Lyric picked up her goblet and spun it between her palms, watching the sunlight shoot emerald green and amethyst sparks over David's thighs. His curiosity seemed a good sign.

"I heard about it somewhere and thought you might know." David took a swallow of the fragrant golden wine. "Seemed to be something in your line of work."

"I suppose you could call it that. The celebration of the seasons . . . it's important to keep the power of nature in mind, and to remember the grand cycle of life." She gestured toward the sea, alive with the motion of wind and waves above, of unseen fish and mammals below. "Our lives, all lives, are part of the rhythm of the universe. Most religions try to teach something like that." With a sweep of her goblet, Lyric outlined a circle in the air. "A circle, never ending. The present, the past."

David made no comment and looked thoughtfully into his wine, swirling it and sniffing the rising vapors. "This area seems to be caught in a time warp. Everyone is as familiar with the past as the present."

"You can't escape from your past, you know. It makes you what you are." Lyric pulled a covered dish from her basket. "What about your past? I know you are from Atlanta, and you grew up on a farm. What else?"

"Nothing interesting. I came here for a future, not a past." David looked away.

"A dark man of mystery? Sounds like something a fortune-teller would say." Lyric rolled her eyes.

"No more serious stuff. I want to see your surprise. I showed you mine; now you show me yours."

"Yes, sir. And here is our menu for today. Shall we start with . . . Persian peaches?" She plucked a velvety golden peach from a bright blue bowl. Cocking her head, she rubbed the soft fuzzed skin to her cheek. Looking directly into David's eyes, she took a large, seductive bite, her lips trailing over the torn flesh. The overripe fruit's juice burst out and ran down her slender wrist.

With one gentle move, David cradled her wrist in his palm and brought it to his mouth. Slowly as a cat enjoying cream, he licked away the nectar. He kissed the faint blue thread of fluttering life just below the thin skin of her wrist. David pulled her nearer and took a great, slow bite from her ripe fruit, then released Lyric's wrist.

"Would you like one of your own?" she asked innocently, gesturing toward the blushing golden peaches.

David leaned on one elbow to recline regally, like an emperor on his couch. "Actually, I want yours," he said with a flashing smile. His shirt blew open to reveal his firm, tanned chest, a triangle of soft curls trembling in the breeze.

She ignored his request and his tan and continued to search the ample basket, revealing more plates and bowls of delicacies. David's eyes grew wide at the spread of food appearing. The appetites that had been awakened were in conflict.

David plucked a large green olive from a tray and offered it to Lyric. "And you? What about your past? Boyfriends?" Her pursed lips met the fruit's opening. She sucked the red pimento filling in with a pop, and tilted her chin up to let the olive roll in. She saw David watching her neck as she chewed. His eyes traced down her throat as she swallowed.

"No boyfriends." She shook her head.

"I'm sure."

"Really." Lyric popped an olive into David's mouth. "There was one, but it didn't work out."

"May I ask why?"

"No, but I'll tell you anyway." Lyric paused and drained the last drop from her goblet. She looked David squarely in the eyes. "Religious differences."

"I see." He filled her goblet and recorked the bottle. "You know, such a beautiful neck really should be adorned." David leaned closer to Lyric, brushed the hollow of her neck up to her chin with his finger. His full lips pressed a light kiss to hers, keeping her interest piqued. Lyric was feeling much warmer than the weather merited. "I'll show you another talent of mine. Perhaps I can paint you just the accessory. This looks perfect." David dipped his finger into a small silver bowl and sucked sticky red puree from his finger.

"Um, yes. Raspberries and honey." Using one finger as a brush, David draped Lyric with a sparkling garnet chain from collarbone to collarbone. Each trembling, vivid drop stood like a cold bloodred jewel on her flesh. He freed her from her bondage by softly licking away the chain, link by link. The softness of his hot, slick tongue erased each jewel, leaving her skin glowing with the effects of the intimate brushwork.

Lyric selected a satiny red apple from a small basket. She veiled it by draping a white linen napkin over it like a magician. "The forbidden fruit," Lyric announced dramatically, holding it toward David, balanced on her palm. She whisked the napkin off with a flourish. "The size of the heart . . ." She drew the crimson orb close to her bosom and nestled it between her breasts, with a melodramatic extravagance of gesture. "The color of love and passion . . ."

She took a small ivory-handled knife and cut the apple crosswise. "Within is knowledge, the promise of new life." She showed him the tiny star made up of the seeds within the core. They leaned close together, Titian red hair and sable dark mixing in the breeze.

David took a crunchy bite of the offered apple and licked his sticky lips slowly. "Thank you, Eve." He looked as if couldn't tear his eyes from her figure. The sea breeze had dampened the gauze of her dress to near transparency. "This must be Eden," he said huskily.

Lyric leaned forward, watching David's eyes turn darker still. The soft white fabric of her blouse dipped away from her body to momentarily reveal a glimpse of her breasts. The color of his eyes were deepening with every bite, deepening to a midnight black.

She mischievously shoved the slippery oval of a deviled egg into his mouth. Her fingertip lingered on the tip of his tongue and dragged slowly, firmly, out and over his lips. "What do you think of my appetizers so far?"

David swallowed the tidbit almost whole. "What's the main course?" He picked up a crisp asparagus spear and dipped it into a creamy herb-speckled dip. He dangled it in front of Lyric's nose like a carrot on a string. She tilted her head back and waited. David let the stalk dive into her hungry mouth.

Lyric snapped the dripping bulbous tip off with a sharp click of her teeth, and took the remaining portion from David. She spread a coating of dip up and down the length of the stalk. Placing it slightly within her mouth, Lyric held the vegetable spear with her teeth. Her eyes sparkled with a challenge as she leaned closer, offering him the remaining portion.

David understood her lead and leaned forward to bite down on the other end. Their hungry tongues balanced, licked, and urged the stalk inward to be devoured. Their lips met, but they did not move away from each other. Lyric slowly licked the creamy dip from David's lower lip. Her eyes held an I-dare-you look.

"Can't say I've ever enjoyed my vegetables so much." His dimples deepened as he met her invitation.

David leaned forward to kiss the smile on her lips, their hungry tongues finally meeting each other and entwining with true desire.

David stood and swept her up into his arms. Lifting her around the waist and beneath the knees, he crushed her to his hard body. He carried her to the water's edge, where the incoming tide lapped thinly. Lyric nuzzled soft kisses into his shoulder and chest with a soft noise of anticipation.

David walked into the waves shin-deep and stood her on her feet. Cool water swirled around her calves and knees. She hastily bunched up her full white skirt from the reach of the waves and held it high, exposing her thighs for his pleased inspection. An errant wave lapped higher than the others, splashing under her skirt, its sudden cold sting making her nipples stand up harder against the fabric of her blouse.

Lyric admired the classic, clean lines of David's robust body as he splashed his face and ran his tongue over his lips, as if anticipating new flavors. She watched him splash through the cleansing salt water, and her breath began to come faster.

David stepped closer to Lyric. His eyes were as depthless as the sea as he began to lift handfuls of the cool water up to her. He dribbled droplets of water onto her shoulders and began to massage her damp skin gently.

Lyric took David's hand and laid her mouth against his palm, then kissed and pulled at each finger, tasting the salt of the sea. She tilted her head to the side and gave a shiver of delight as David dragged a wet finger from behind her ear to the hollow of her throat. She felt her grip go slack, relaxing out of her control, and soon the edges of her skirt were floating with the rhythm of the waves.

David's touch felt like warm ribbons of sensuous honey trailing over her throat and chest, moving down to her breasts, beneath the damp ruffle of the transparent wet white cotton. He loosened the ribbons at the front of her blouse and tugged at the fabric, exposing her breasts. David stroked and teased, spreading a warmth that started at the base of her spine and radiated a trembling eagerness throughout her body. Lyric murmured her approval. Like the petals of a rosebud, she felt herself loosen, unfold, and bloom, becoming in full flower, layer upon layer of silken red petals. As his palm cupped the seam to her very soul, swollen plump in acceptance, a satin moisture of joy burst through.

His passion stirred and hardened, rising and straining against the rough denim of his shorts as he gave her a deep, fulfilling kiss, the real sustenance she had been craving.

Running her hands down his lean back, she slipped them under the waistband of his cutoffs. She paused, savoring the athletic narrowness of his sleek waist and hips under her palms. The skin there was silken soft, and she wondered fleetingly if he would have a tan line. She slid her hands forward, feeling his stomach tighten with anticipation of her next move. She paused the barest fraction of a second before releasing the top snap, and then the first button came undone easily, and the next button even easier. The next two took no urging, and the final didn't matter.

David's powerful arms encircled Lyric and pulled her against the length of his body. He led her two steps up the sand and gently laid her down. He buried his face in the curve of her neck, his eyes closed, inhaling the essence of her. The little waves foamed and lapped at their interlocked limbs.

"Margaret," he whispered.

Chapter Twenty

"Margaret!" The name exploded from Lyric's mouth. She felt as if a bucketful of ice water had hit her square in the heart. Shoving David off her body with one abrupt turn of her knee, she dumped him into the surf and scrambled to her feet. She grabbed her dripping skirt around her and splashed up to the cave in furious humiliation.

"Lyric! Let me explain." David jumped to his feet, buttoning his cutoffs with haste, and followed her toward the picnic spread.

Clutching the wet ruffles at her cleavage in an attempt to regain some lost dignity, she recklessly gathered their lovers' banquet and slung the remains haphazardly into the picnic basket. China clinked and fruit flew.

David dropped to his knees on the quilt facing Lyric. "There's something I need to tell you." His anxious eyes pleaded with her to understand. He took the plate of disheveled sandwiches out of her grip, setting it aside, and captured her free hand in both of his.

"Obviously!" Lyric eyed him angrily and continued to worry her neckline in hopes of reestablishing some sort of boundary between then. All the tender kisses and caresses had been for another woman. Lyric's pride was stung with the feeling he hadn't been with her at all.

"She is . . . was my wife." David's eyes suddenly filled with deep pain and sadness. "She died three years ago. I haven't been with another woman since, or even before. We were childhood sweethearts." David's grip went slack.

"Dead?" she said in a faint voice. "I'm sure she is in a much happier place." The stock polite phrase came to her lips instinctively. Three years. The bitterness of his grief was apparent, as well as his distress at offending her.

He released Lyric and stood, turning away from her, facing pensively toward the gray ocean. The rising wind ruffled his dark hair. "I have to tell you. It's not fair to you, or to me. That's why I moved here. I wanted a new start, without memories." He echoed their toast wryly. "A new beginning to leave the past behind."

He hitched up his wet cutoffs and leaned against a boulder. "Margaret died in childbirth. I lost her and the baby." He scrubbed across his face with a rough gesture and slapped the rock angrily. "Some hero, big macho fireman saving lives. Couldn't even keep my own wife from dying."

Lyric's outrage melted at the sight of his sorrow. A wash of soothing understanding calmed her. His explanation was perfectly valid. Relief filled her; surely if this romance had been wrong her voices, her instincts, would have warned her long ago. Was this the child that was between them, David's lost child?

"It was your fault that she died? Was it an accident?"

"It wasn't an accident, but it was my fault. She wanted to please me, to give me a son. The doctor knew she had a heart problem, but she had sworn him not to tell. She thought . . . who knows what she thought . . . that her love would overcome it, I suppose." He compressed his lips in a harsh line. "It didn't."

"David, what I said about the past and present being a circle. I believe it. It's true. Everything has a reason, a lesson." She touched his arm. "You have to believe that. It wasn't your fault, or hers, or the doctor's. Think about it."

"Think about it? That's all I have thought about for three years." He jerked away from her touch. "I don't want to think about it. I want to forget it." David rubbed over his face again. "Learn from it; not forget it," he amended. "I can't take another chance."

"It takes time, David."

"I'm sorry. Maybe that's what I need . . . more time." David's shoulders slumped with sadness. "I'm sorry, really, really sorry. I rushed you, and . . . myself. Another time, another place, maybe, but not now. I wanted it to be right, but it's not."

There was something that Lyric had to tell David as well, but she could not. She ached to make him understand that she could heal all his pain, that her love was what he'd been waiting for, but in order for his destiny to be fulfilled in this lifetime, he must make his own decision, free of her willful influence. The power of fate was strong, but it, too, took time.

"I understand time, if that's what you think will help." Lyric knew that time had bound them together, yet something was trying to hold them apart. She must be strong enough to confront that obstacle. All the signs pointed to it. Her visions with the coat, the feelings near the painting at the museum, the horrible incident with the kitchen pump. It was Wolfton, her old nemesis. How would she resolve it all?

"When I'm with you, it seems I can put everything else aside. But I guess I can't. I just can't risk hurting you." David turned to her and stared into her eyes. For a split second he seemed to forget he was trying to sever their newfound attraction. He stroked her cheek and drew her face toward his. Lyric closed her eyes and didn't pull away as he gently pressed his mouth to hers. A good-bye kiss.

Her eyes flew open as she felt a cold wash of wetness surround her legs and knees.

"My God, the tide. Quick, we've got to get out of here before the water rises any higher." Taking command, David grabbed the basket and his boots, urging Lyric to hurry. She snatched the quilts into her arms and ran for the path, only to find her way blocked by water surging powerfully into the tidal inlet.

David extended his hand. "Hold my wrist and don't let go. We can make it." David gripped Lyric's wrist firmly, and she clung to him in a lock of safety. He plunged into the water covering the hidden path and pulled her along.

The clutch of the water dragged at her skirt and sucked at their legs as the incoming tide swept into the cove. Barefooted, Lyric slipped on the harsh wet rocks. As she stumbled, the quilts were sucked out of her grasp and swept into green oblivion. The backwash of waves pulled her down hungrily. An involuntary scream ripped from Lyric's lips.

David dropped the basket and boots. He grabbed her other wrist and jerked her upright. "Don't let go." Only David's implacably steady hold on her wrist kept her from the sea's jealous embrace. "We can make it," he repeated. He drew her along past the boulders where the water dragged and rushed in the crevices.

"Not much further. The path's higher here." David's strength and calm in the face of danger was impressive. A few struggling steps more and they were above the wave's covetous reach.

They stood at the cliff's edge, hearts pounding, still tightly holding to one another. The water had filled the cave and obscured the little beach completely in the few minutes it took for them to clamber up the slippery path. The little cave kept its secrets well. Its benign charm could turn into a death trap within seconds.

"I can't swim." Lyric shivered from the tension of the moment and wished he would take her in his arms where she knew she was safe. "I can't swim." She shuddered again at the thought of the foaming water pulling like tentacles at her ankles.

"Thank you, David." Her voice shook slightly as she expressed her gratitude for his coolness in the face of nature's fury. She dropped his wrist, but he clung to her for a second longer.

"You're welcome," David said, his tone bitter. "It's my job; saving people." It seemed as if he would say more, and perhaps melt in his fierce sadness, but then he stepped away from her. She looked out toward the ocean one more time before walking back to her car in silence, alone.

* * *

Almost lost! Out of my reach, they had almost slipped away from my grasp forever. So close, the woman of fire had drawn the man so close and only by chance had the water broken her hold. Dust roiled in agitation in the lifeless rooms. *Their energy is too strong; I cannot leave more to chance. I must not tarry. They must be driven apart.*

But, oh how I love the frustration, the beautiful hostility between them. What strong anger. How delicious it will be, at last, when I finish this.

In the attic, a small fat bat squealed and clung to a rafter before falling to the floor, already drying to a dusty shell.

David sat on the back steps of his house halfheartedly cleaning dismantled door hinges. He looked up and out over the choppy water. A storm was building on the horizon and the leaden sea looked as dark as he felt. He couldn't shake the empty feeling that seemed to be gnawing away his heart. David had felt the new joy Lyric brought ripped from his body. With each step she took away from him, happiness drained from his soul, leaving only this desolate feeling of dullness, of lifelessness.

Two days had passed since the damning slip of his tongue. Why was it that he couldn't forgive himself, or at the very least forget? David scrubbed listlessly with a small brush at the engraved brass of an old hinge. Three years was plenty of time for the guilt to have dissipated.

He rubbed the plate with a clean rag and looked at the elaborate design without interest; it meant nothing. Nothing meant anything anymore. It was like all the juice had drained out of life; his batteries were dead.

Now he was jeopardizing the most appealing

thing that had ever come into his life. Could it be that by not being prepared to share this wonderful woman's affections, he risked losing the true love of his life? He dropped the hardware into the can of stripper with a dismal plop.

Lyric touched things in him that he had only felt in dreams. She was enchanting, whether it be real magic or not. He was about ready to believe anything simply to be with her; to look into those mischievous green eyes was to adore her. But calling her Margaret was cruel to both himself and her. He could never make up for this.

David lethargically picked up a second hinge and then replaced it in the cardboard box. He folded his arms across his knees and rested his head on his forearms. He could see Lyric's face in the blood-darkness behind his eyelids. When Lyric had appeared on his doorstep he had forgotten the sadness, the loneliness since his wife had been gone. In fact, at that moment, Margaret was the farthest thing from his mind.

He had loved Margaret, but it was an innocent love. They had grown up together. Marriage just seemed like the right thing to do at the time. But they were young, so very young, and she was eager to fulfill his every wish to the point of death, never realizing that a child was not all that was needed to complete their marriage.

He meant no disrespect to Margaret; he loved her then in the best way he knew how. But people continue to grow, and he was ready to get on with his life. So why couldn't he? That was the whole idea in coming to Salem, buying such a demanding house, and even for pursuing the complex Lyric Solei.

What was it he was to do? A lesson from the past. Lyric kept saying that. She might be all mixed up in her crazy gypsy psychic ideas, but this time she was correct. He kept going around in circles, all right.

A cool breeze from the ocean washed over him. David raised his head and welcomed its shy caresses. Those were all the caresses he would feel for a while. Embers scampered over and rubbed against his knees. That was all the affection he deserved, even more than he should receive.

He rose slowly and slouched into the kitchen, his hands stuck into his hip pockets, head hanging. He felt like he had the worst hangover in the Western world, headache and all. Even his usually boundless energy seemed to be beyond his reach today. Work had taken away his tension and soothed his mind before; it would have to do the same now.

The house was emptier than ever. Embers refused to enter the house, muttering and meowing plaintively on the step when David stepped inside.

He took the new broom with him to start the task of sweeping out the pervasive dust that seemed to grow from the very walls of the house. Damn dust. Already the kitchen floor was covered again. Wasn't it just yesterday he had shoveled out a bucketful? It made sense to start from upstairs and work down. He trudged up the stairs, so deep into his thoughts he hardly heard the routine protests from the two noisy treads.

He went into the smaller side bedroom and struggled to open the window. It resisted his efforts and he fought the bad-tempered impulse to smash the panes with his fist. So stay down, he thought, the flash of anger telegraphing red through his brain.

David began to sweep. The vigor of his motion increased as his thoughts began to gallop in time with his rising temper. *Unreasonable, that's what it is. An unreasonable attraction; she isn't my type at all. Eternity, protective talismans, witches, curses—what a bunch of crap.* Dust swirled around him in the hot, close room.

The dream he had had was just that—an erotic dream, dredged up from being without a regular love life for three years. Lyric's silken red hair was just coincidence. And all that magic stuff in her house. Just what he needed, some kind of religious weirdo nut.

A thick coat of dust covered his dark hair. *Forget her. There are other women in Salem. Ben has a pretty sister. Forget this strange witchy woman. She has spells, alright. A spell on me and enough is enough. Forget her.* He scrubbed the back of his wrist across his forehead in an impatient gesture. The grit and sweat made a maddening itch all over his body, like a terrible incurable disease.

David continued to sweep, heaping dirt and tiny dry insect bodies in the center of the room. After making a methodical pile, he realized he had no way of scooping it up; the shovel and bucket were still downstairs. He stood for seconds, knuckles white on the handle, then threw the broom down atop the pile of debris. *To hell with it.*

He turned and stomped out into the hall. He needed a beer. Lots of good cold beer to forget this millstone of a house, to forget everything. *To forget everybody.*

David stormed down the steps, two at a time, making a satisfying clatter on the hollow wood.

With a crash and a windmilling fall, he slipped and skidded, banging his shins and landing in a heap on the hallway floor. He was going to be black and blue. Coughing out a mouthful of dust, David slowly pulled himself up to rest on his knees. He turned to look at the very step that had caused his spill. The third step.

Giving an involuntary yelp of pain, he cursed as he stumbled to his toolbox in the kitchen. "I'll fix you." It would feel good to really bang something. His shins throbbed and he could feel the angry bruises rising. He rummaged for a hammer and grimly stuck a fistful of nails between his tight lips. Hammer in hand, he limped back to the offensive step to do battle.

It took three tries with the clawed end of the hammer to pry up the wobbly top plank of the step. There, in the secret box formed by the structure of the stair, was what appeared to be a stick, cushioned in a nest of spider-silk, dust, and wood fragments. David ran his forefinger around the edge of the time-worn wood, skimming away the thick sticky webbing.

He lifted the batonlike rod from its hiding place to discover it was not a stick at all, but rather a dried, cracked leather riding crop. It was about 20 inches long with an 18-inch lash curled around its tip. The crop was hard but the lash leather was fragile as paper, black with the stain of age and what looked to him like old blood. It could no longer give the supple slap to flesh for which it was originally intended.

A silver grip was tarnished from the atmosphere of neglect. David rubbed his thumb over the blackened metal, bearing down on the tarnish, and a tracing of a wolf sinking its fangs into the neck of a doe was revealed. The rough handle felt uncomfortably twisted in his palm. It had conformed long ago to the hand and uses of its former owner.

David laid the scourge beside his knee and squinted to see into the dark compartment. Spider work lay thick as spun glass in the secret cavity. He saw a slight movement and a fierce bright stare unwinkingly held his eyes. He leaned in cautiously for a closer look. Fangs flexed in a defensive gesture. A black spider that looked as big as a fuzzy Volkswagen raised on tiptoes, then made an aggressive rush toward him.

Its movement and quickness caught David off guard. Reflexively, he scrambled backward away from the attack. He missed a step and lost his balance, crumpling down the next two steps, nails flying. He landed with a thud, squarely on his behind, a nailhead digging into his lip. He spat it out and sat in a heap at the foot of the stairs.

"Damn, I hate spiders," he muttered and reached up to a splintery banister spindle. He pulled himself to his feet, leaning on the newel post. He rubbed his bruised backside and dusted his knees.

Taking one step up, he turned and sat sideways on the second step, in order to be braced for what came next.

David picked up the antique crop and poked cautiously, hoping to avoid any of the spider's relatives. Years of matted gray spider's web coated the heavy silver handle as he dug deeper into the time capsule.

There, sharing the spider's nest, was a small brown leather book. David made one last check for anything aggressive, then snatched out the book.

He rubbed the book across his jeans to remove the sticky grime and opened the brittle cover gently. On the fly leaf an inscription was penned in a flowery feminine script:

To Quinton Harrel Wolfton
January 13, 1686
Upon the occasion of our betrothal.
Emily Gillian Adams

Chapter Twenty-one

Wolfton! My God, Capt. Wolfton's lost diary. David licked the blood from his split lip, the pain forgotten in the excitement of his discovery. He carefully turned the first crumbling page. A ledger filled with accounts and amounts for the construction of Wolfton House were logged in neat columns on the first several pages. There was a sketch of the floor plans and a detail of the moldings that capped the parlor walls. The artist was a talented one. The style was similar to the strange fresco David had felt compelled to chip away from the stair wall.

David turned the brittle pages slowly. The writing was clear, small, and angular, not too hard to decipher despite the variable seventeenth-century spellings. The ink was a faded sepia on the ivory-colored pages. The first entry of prose concerned the moral instruction of his servants and wife.

It appeared Wolfton believed in a firm hand, quite

literally. David drew in his breath through his teeth as he read excruciatingly precise details of extreme whippings and beatings, the number of strokes laid on, and subsequent deaths apparently recorded with pious satisfaction. Justified satisfaction for salvaging the eternal souls of the erring from the clutches of the ever-lurking Devil. The sinner's death was indisputable proof of guilt.

The blackened whip had been God's tool of instruction wielded by the earthly hand of Capt. Wolfton. A short list of appropriate biblical injunctions to be read before and after chastisements was jotted along the margin for easy reference.

Repulsed yet fascinated, David read on. He paged through several more registries of financial activities. A lengthy entry concerned what appeared to be military shipping maneuvers. Dates, places, times, cargo . . . and several ships' bills of lading. Sums of money given in pounds and livres. Looked like the little lady at the museum was on to something. She said Wolfton had been involved with some sort of shady ship trade in the cove.

A rustling sound in the wainscoting startled David. He glanced up in the action of turning a page. When he looked back down his eyes were drawn to a bold intentional mark at the bottom of the page. A crisp thumbprint, the indelible burgundy black of old blood, was pressed firmly as a seal. Above the macabre signature was a charming sketch of a Puritan woman standing with her hand on a spinning wheel, dressed in a modest bonnet and neat apron.

David looked closer at the detail of the face. Looking solemnly from under the humble turned-back bonnet brim was a face as familiar to him as his own. The eyes of the ink-and-paper woman stared back frankly with bright intelligence and a distinct wariness of her artist. Under the portrait was the name "Mistress Sarah Morgan, spinster and weaver of the village." But the face and the voluptuous figure under the homespun was undoubtedly that of Lyric Solei.

David slammed the book shut. *No, this couldn't be.* He snapped the book open. Page followed page of her image, here a smiling face, there a hand lovingly detailed, another place a full figure turned, carrying a pail, again her face in profile, hair disheveled, the laughing look David recognized caught in her eyes, the mouth, just so.

He banged the covers shut. *No. No, no, no.* He pressed the small brown book to his forehead and closed his eyes. "This . . . cannot . . . be," he said out loud. Pictures flickered behind his closed eyelids. His dream. The story of his coat. It was the story told by the mild gray-haired docent. It was the story on the salacious hidden fresco.

Sparkling-haired Sarah, dancing Sarah, the woman named in his dreams. The ripely luscious Sarah joyously offering herself to her lover by the fire. The erotic Sarah glistening with sweat and magic lotions, every hollow and curve glowing in the heat, but her face ever shadowed. Now her face was revealed as the tragic Sarah burned not 10 yards from where he sat. Yes, Sarah revealed as Lyric.

David flipped the covers open again and inspected the pages more closely. As the narrow pages laid out their mute but eloquent tale, the horrid progression of mad ardor in Wolfton's swelling obsession became clearer. The tiny pictures began to crowd the pages, overlapping, frenzied scratchings of the quill pen cutting the paper. Covetous Wolfton's increasingly lascivious sketches became more warped and almost unrecognizable as the woman David knew.

Sarah laughing became Sarah weeping, howling, horribly twisted, starkly nude, caged like an animal, whipped, bleeding. Sarah bound spread-eagled, naked, the traces of the lash making an evil lace over her back and body. And finally, Sarah with her fanned hair making hungry tongues of flames, eager Devil's faces formed by the tangled curls.

A single loose page drifted to the floor as David sat shocked, the book loose in his hands. He stood slowly and picked the paper from the dirty floor. It had been ripped and crumpled, but then smoothed and replaced in the book. A detailed depiction of a gallows with a single victim was cut deeply into the page, ink pressed so hard in places as to slash the paper. At the bottom of the page, two brief paragraphs tersely described the disastrous end of an obsessive passion.

Sarah Morgan, spinster, weaver, known witch, for the sin of consorting with the Devil sentenced to death by fire in order to cleanse her immortal soul for judgment. Sentence carried out December 15, 1692.

Dante Huels, militiaman, former sailor, guiltly of crime of treason and fornication with known witch, his wife Sarah Morgan, sentenced to death by hanging after having his soul improved by the observation of his devilish consort's death by fire. Sentence carried out December 16, 1692.

Signed this day of our Lord December 16, 1692.

The Right Honorable Judge, Capt. Quinton H. Wolfton

David held the book quietly, despite a rising sickness he felt deep in his stomach. The metallic taste of bile grew in his mouth as he read the sentences again and again. Then he tucked the detached page back into the volume and closed the book. He pressed the volume between his hands as if to wring the truth from its dry covers.

The past, too close. The circle, too close. Here was the connection Lyric had felt for this house. Had she already known when she heard the story at the Maritime Museum? She, Lyric, had died here. Died.

Wait a minute, he was thinking as if it all were true. The anger he had felt upstairs in the hot little room cunningly reasserted itself. *Unreasonable. Reincarnation, the love-lasts-forever stuff, the talisman that failed to protect a lover, Sarah the witch-weaver.*

No, I don't believe. I don't believe.

Lyric the psychic lover, touching the red coat with rapture, and all the time did she know? And what did she know?

I do not believe. I believe in what I can see, not dreams. Circles, circles. Past, present, future.

In the portrait, Wolfton held this volume of his triumphs. A memento of his great lust for Sarah or a trophy, like his red coat inexplicably painted into the background? Sarah died proudly defiant, with a curse for Wolfton's soul on her lips.

The depravity of the man seemed a distant tale at the museum, told by the dry old voice. Here in the gloomy house, shadows lay heavily across the bare dusty floors. The silence was like a stealthy breath. Suddenly David felt watched. Invisible corpse-cold fingers stroked his hair, touched his eyelids, caressed his arms. The dust seemed to shift on the floorboards as if aimless, weightless footsteps pressed and scuffed.

The final question burst into his brain like an explosion. *If Sarah was Lyric, who was Dante, the luckless man sentenced to watch his beloved burn? Dante, dream-Sarah's powerful partner before the hearth. Dante, whose charmed coat fit David as if it were made for him. Dante, who loved the long-ago Sarah.*

Who loved the present-day Lyric.

David leapt to his feet, stuffing the book into his shirt, leaving the crop wrapped in its trailing spiderwebs forgotten on the step. He ran from the house to his motorcycle. He must see the sun; see Lyric now.

The sunlight shone through the wavy panes of glass, stretching across the floor, warming the dust. On the stairs, dust trickled silently, sinously as a snake, step to step, grains as smooth as those in the waist of an hourglass.

Just then, upstairs, the man had been totally in my power, his thoughts directed now here, now there as easily as a lathered, beaten horse.

It is good to feel the old power again, to feed on the fear and confusion and become strong. Fear is food stronger than blood.

I am stronger, growing always stronger from the fear and confusion, and I am patient. I can wait. I will triumph.

The dust spread and thickened over the floor, the walls. Ripples, tiny tides of grains. Soon he would be free.

David roared into Lyric's driveway and slammed down the kickstand. He bypassed the fence gate and vaulted one-handed over the low barrier, brushing through the flowers. He startled a fat white cat, snoozing on the porch swing. It hissed and dashed away, leaving the swing to sway and jerk emptily.

Where could she be? It was late afternoon; her car was in the drive. David ran up the porch steps and into her front hall without a thought of knocking. "Lyric!" His voice rocketed through the hallway.

Lyric came hurriedly down the stairs, barefoot, carrying a stack of freshly folded laundry. "David, what is it? Are you all right?"

Laundry tumbled around her feet as David crushed her vibrant body into a breathtaking embrace. "You're real. You're alive."

Lyric disengaged herself reluctantly. "Well, yes, I have been for a while," she said, looking puzzled over his sudden appearance and frantic concern.

David pulled her toward him again and wrapped his arms around her tightly in sheer relief. He rested his chin on top of her head and rubbed his face in her beautiful crown of hair. He inhaled the living fragrance of her body, the clean sunshine smell of her. Alive, she was alive, not the beaten, tortured creature drawn in the book.

The resemblance had to be only a coincidence. His grimy hands and grubby shirt left unheeded smudges on her white blouse. He touched her soft cheek with his dusty fingers, leaving a smear of dirt like a charcoal tear, then pulled her tighter against his body.

"David . . ." Lyric's voice was muffled by being mashed into his chest. "David. I can't breathe."

He loosened his grip and stepped backward enough to fumble with one hand in his shirt to fish out the brown book. "I found something exciting at the house."

If the face in the book was not hers, his mind would be free. He didn't believe; not in reincarnation or anything like it. One life, one chance, that was it. Finding it was not her face would prove the other things to be mere coincidences of time and place, and the question of who was Dante would not be a question at all.

David riffled rapidly through the pages of the book, quickly locating the illustrations of Sarah. "It's the book in the portrait, Lyric. I found it today hidden in the staircase. It proves the story about Sarah and her lover, and Wolfton's treason in the cove." He held the pages open at the first loving portrait of Sarah. His fingers covered the blood mark at the bottom of the paper.

"Look. It's her. It's Sarah Morgan." He thrust the book toward Lyric.

To his surprise, she put her hands behind her back and refused to take the volume. "No. I don't want to touch it." She was looking at his face, not at the sketch.

"But Lyric, look at the picture." David shoved the book toward her urgently. He held the page near her face and compared the eyes, the mouth. "Sarah is you; you have to see it."

Lyric closed her eyes briefly and then opened them to look directly into David's face. "No, David, I don't have to see it."

The excitement drained out of David, to be replaced by an ache as dull and empty as the one he had felt this morning. His voice was filled with a sick apprehension as he asked "What do you mean? What do you know?"

Lyric smiled a sad-around-the-edges smile. She touched David's wrist with one finger and pushed the hand holding the book away gently. "What do you think I know, David? I know who I am, certainly."

David stood angrily. He tossed the book on the

floor in a gesture of fierce frustration and grabbed her shoulders. "Oh, you know who you are, do you? Well, answer me this, Miss Mind Reader, psychic person, just who the hell am I then?"

Lyric's calm eyes met his burning ones. "I can't answer that for you. You must find the answers for yourself. I think you know."

David resisted the impulse to shake her until her teeth rattled. Everything he had ever believed was falling in shreds around him. "How can I find out anything if no one will help me?" He tightened his fingers, feeling her firm shoulders beneath his tense grip. He saw sympathy flicker in her eyes. "Please, Lyric, help me!"

Lyric laid her hands lightly on his chest and looked seriously into his face. The warmth of her palms made two glowing spots on his skin through the cloth of his shirt. "Believe me, David, I wish I could. But this is something you must do yourself. I can tell you that the answer is there, if you look within."

Overcome with frustration, David balled his fists furiously, and strode from one side of the hall to the other in tense agitation. "More riddles." With an abrupt gesture, he seized Lyric roughly, spinning her into his arms.

"No, no more riddles." Without a pause he vented the ferocity of his unanswered questions in a blazing kiss. He would not be denied in this, and his mouth did not become softer. There was none of the tender playfulness from the picnic, or the wonder of new exploration that he felt near the ship's mast.

He kissed her with the rage of passion that had not died when Dante's body had been buried and the winter wind had blown the ashes of Sarah's funeral pyre into the cold sea. He kissed her and she returned his ardor and he knew.

He knew who he was. Who he had been.

But he could not be.

He pushed Lyric away harshly and held her at arm's length, his fingers digging into her shoulders. He stared into her face again. "Will you tell me?"

David saw her eyes fill with tears, and she shook her head slowly, *No*.

He stormed down the hall and away from her house, away from her, away from what he knew in his heart.

Chapter Twenty-two

The savage roar of David's motorcycle faded down the street. Lyric's heart was pounding from emotion and the fierceness of David's kiss. The battered little book lay at the bottom of the stairs. Lyric avoided touching it, and gave the volume a sideways glance when she picked up a shirt that had landed on the tread above it. Her fingers trembled as she began to slowly gather the scattered laundry. The tears finally tumbled silently down her cheeks.

With an armful of disordered towels and clothes, she strode into her bedroom and dumped the articles willy-nilly on the wide bed. A white linen shirt flopped on top of Nolan. He poked his black-and-white head out and shook his ears with an annoyed expression. He looked up and wrinkled his nose when Lyric gave a loud sniff.

Crying wouldn't solve a thing. She began to make order of the tangled clothing. The calming motions of the everyday task would soothe her as she thought. Her hands smoothed over the soft cotton of a bathtowel, folding it into neat quarters.

What should she tell him? She wiped her eyes on the folded towel with a fierce, angry swipe and plopped it to one side. *Nothing. He must figure this out on his own.*

She popped the wrinkles from the next towel. *Don't interfere. This is his karma. It is his destiny.* Pop, pop! Fold. Wipe the tears again.

The next towel met the same fate, along with vigorous yanking to straighten the seams. *It will be meaningless if he doesn't discover it on his own. All the pain and heartache for nothing if he doesn't figure it out and accept it on his own.* Pop, yank, fold!

It wasn't a matter of life and death, this time. No one would be hanged, burned at the stake, or die in childbirth, but the attitude was the same. That I-gotta-see-it-to-believe-it, comes-with-the-uniform attitude. This was just like New York, just like the hardheaded policeman that couldn't believe, wouldn't believe until it was too late.

No, this time no one would die. But they had died already, and died for love. The love that still lived and could live and could not be denied in the great wheel of time that turned inexorably.

Lyric threw the hapless towel on the bed with an exasperated sigh. Tears were gone but her chest felt empty where her heart should be. Work wasn't going to make her feel better. Nothing would make her feel better right now except to see David again, and see him happy.

She sat in her rocker by the bed and pulled the red wool coat into her lap. Stroking the fabric lightly, she hugged its bulk to her and rocked slowly. She must think her way through this. Nolan came to the chair and placed a paw on her knee. He jumped up and snuggled against her.

Yes, it was like the policeman. Disbelief had caused disaster. She could not interfere, but somehow she must. She rubbed her cheek to the faded wool. Give fate a little helping hand, a push, a hint, something. Surely she had the power to keep this man that she had loved in past lifetimes from sorrow in this one.

She must try, to be at peace with herself. Tomorrow she would drive to Wolfton House and return the coat and the book. David would be calmer and somehow she would be led to do and say the right thing. It was the least she could do.

The morning had dawned leaden and cloudy. Humidity hung in the air so heavily that the birds stayed hidden in the trees. Even the brazen sea gulls were staying low today. Sound seemed magnified on the air. People around town were starting to bring in lawn chairs and potted plants, taping their windows, and preparing for a real blow. Wal-Mart on South Main Street had sheets of plywood nailed over the plate-glass windows, but was doing a brisk business in batteries and candles.

David walked to the front bay of the fire station and looked out across the street. Embers followed close behind him and parked herself on the toes of his boots when he stopped moving. Ben was already standing on the drive, squinting at the sky. "It's going to be a bad one, Langston. National Weather Service has already put everyone on alert. We're going to be busy." He jerked his head toward the grocery store where cars were crowded. "Sometimes these things last for days. Never been through one of our eastern coastal storms, have you?"

"No." David crossed his arms over his chest. He was in no mood for small talk about the weather.

"Oh man, it can get wicked. Flooded roads, downed power lines, people trying to drive in water over the tops of their wheels." Ben shook his head. "You can't believe the dumb things people do, sometimes."

David grunted. "I can believe it."

Ben shot a concerned look at his partner. "Trouble, amigo?"

"No. Nothing I can't handle." The friends turned and walked by the shiny trucks, automatically checking gear and counting supplies. Embers jumped on the leather seat and curled up to sleep.

"Listen, Ben, I have to get away for a while. I'm going out to the house."

"What about the storm?"

"You're not my mother, Ben," David snapped. His face flushed. He didn't need to be clucked over by his buddy. "I'll take my beeper, and when it gets bad I'll head back in." Ordinarily he would stay around the station on such a threatening day, but today he had to be alone, and in action.

"Watch the cat for me, will you?"

"Whatever you say, D. L., just watch the sky. Don't want to have to rescue you."

There was no electricity to chase away the gloom at Wolfton House. David considered lighting his camp lantern, but then dismissed the thought as dangerous with so much dust and fumes from the chemical stripper. *Fine. Just fine.* The melancholy dimness suited his mood.

David gathered his forces for a renewed attack on the never-ending problem of the shutters. Maybe he could forget his troubles with enough sweat. That had certainly been the original plan, what seemed so long ago.

Wrestling off the heavy old shutters was a real man's job. The eight-foot-tall balcony doors were bulky and caked with grime. Decades of salt air had corroded and swelled the joints into immobility. After struggling and swearing for some time, he decided to leave the doors in place and work on them as best he could. Nothing seemed to be cooperating lately.

David slapped a haphazard layer of paint stripper on the slats of the louvered doors. The violent chemical ate away the flesh of old paint.

Just weeks before he had heard for the first time of this past life, reincarnation stuff on that stupid "Invasive Eye" program. Now it was here today, affecting his life, causing him to reevaluate his own deepest convictions, and there was no 900 line with the answers he needed.

He really did need answers, and his own personal psychic wasn't going to help him. No, she said he must find the answers from within. Well, what did that mean?

He squatted on the toes of his boots with his hands hanging loosely between his knees. The thick gel bubbled and burned the ancient pigment away as he watched. A flicker of something moving below caught his eye through the shutters. David leapt to his feet and looked out the open window, resting his hands on the sill and leaning far out to look to both sides. There was a low kettledrum roll of thunder in the distance.

Only a bird, I guess. His nerves were playing tricks on him. Nothing was dependable and concrete in his mind anymore. He glanced out the hall and down the stairs; nothing there.

"I'm really fed up with this!" he shouted out loud to the walls. He heard a faint scurry of tiny clawed feet rustle behind the walls. "The hell with it," he muttered. David knelt in front of his work and began to wipe away the dissolved paint and grime. "This house is my only fate." He spoke to the echoing walls.

David scraped at the slats with a vengeance and caught another glimpse of movement through the louvres. Again he heard the low rumble of the impending storm.

He saw the faintest wisp of smoke curling upward, like a tiny evil snake sliding silently away from a sickened animal.

Lightning crackled and chained across the sky. Still looking through the cracks of the weathered door, David gasped as his gaze was drawn down to the once barren spot in his front yard.

It was teeming with people surrounding a tumbled stack of wood. Branches and small logs were crowded around a tall pole; a stake with a woman bound against it. Broken furniture and a wicker cage with two cats were thrown haphazardly upon the fuel. Shocked by the sight of what lay below, he dared not move.

A man in a bright officer's uniform tossed a handful of flaming papers on the pyre, then curtly signaled the torch-bearers to do their duty. Three men thrust bright torches at the bundled wood and dry kindling, then flipped them to land by the prisoner's skirts. Flames caught quickly, greedily leapt and licked at the victim's body.

Smoke billowed sullenly upward to mingle with the heavy storm clouds rolling and boiling, thickening and blackening them into an almost physical poison. The familiar smell of burning possessions alerted

David's trained nostrils and heightened his senses. It was the smell of death.

Heaped around the woman's feet were a spinning wheel and a smashed loom with its carefully threaded warp and weft tangled and ripped, precious thread floating in the currents of heat. The cats lay still in their cage, already overwhelmed by the smoke.

The victim's face was concealed by a mat of long auburn hair. Her head hung bowed as if she were preparing for her transition to the next world. The small woman had not once cried out in pain or fear. Suddenly she tossed her hair back and stared up directly at David. Her eyes were filled with inner power and a great sorrow.

It was Sarah.

David clapped his hand to his mouth and felt as if he might retch, yet he continued to stare from behind the door. Why did he feel he had seen all of this before, felt all these painful feelings of helplessness and responsibility before? How could he be kneeling here and watching another century below?

Suddenly David felt a presence by his side. His eyes remained transfixed below.

A hand clapped his shoulder roughly. "Enjoy this, Huels. She's dying for you." Unmistakably Wolfton's roughened voice, his malevolent chuckle.

"Sarah!" David's scream of anguish filled the room. He struck out at the shutters, splintering them in blind, impotent grief.

"David, David!" Lyric frantically shook his shoulder.

Lyric? How did she get here? "Lyric, get out. We've got to get out of here." He grabbed her and hauled her out of the room in a stumbling run. He pulled her down the stairs like a rag doll and flung the door open. They ran out into the darkening day.

Thunder growled and the clouds seemed almost to touch the top of the dark house.

"What's happened?" Lyric's words were jostled as he pulled her farther from the house. "David, what has happened?" They came to an abrupt halt in the great barren circle. The cold wind sweeping before the storm clouds tore at Lyric's hair and whipped it about her face. David's eyes were wild in the strange storm light.

David looked around the circle frantically. "They're gone. The fire, it's all gone." He clutched Lyric in a rough embrace of assurance, then shoved her away to arm's length. She was holding the red military coat in one hand, forgotten in the tumult.

"Did you see it? A fire here, and Sarah . . . I saw Sarah, saw you, Lyric." David paused and came to his senses as the cold wind tore around them. He released his grip on Lyric and touched her face. "It was you, I swear it."

He rubbed his eyes, then massaged his temples. "No, wait. Seems like the strangest things . . . the fortune-teller, that business at the museum, that damn diary and whip, and . . . now this." David could hardly take a breath between words.

"I've just had the strangest experience in there." He shook his head, then looked up at the shuttered door where he had stood. "Right up there," he pointed to the gray doors for emphasis. "I saw it all happen from right up there."

The wind was making a hollow tormented sound, sweeping over the cold chimneys of the mansion. Gusts of air were picking up tiny dust devils that whirled and cavorted around David and Lyric as they stood in the scorched circle. The crackling smell of ozone increased as the squall approached from the sea.

Lyric could see the near panic in his eyes. "Tell me what happened, David. You look like you saw a ghost." She reached out toward him but he drew back sharply.

"I can't believe in this ghost stuff. I can't. But just then, I saw you, I mean Sarah, I think," David continued, visibly shaken. Now he reached for her and grasped a huge fistful of her wild hair, looking intently into her face. When her hair blew like that, it looked like the last hideous portrait in the diary, that of Sarah with a crown of flames.

"You were standing on this very spot and an angry mob was tormenting and torturing you. It was Sarah, but it was you, Lyric." He shook his head, having trouble separating the two. "They dragged you to the stake and burned you right here." He pointed down to the ashy gray dust around their feet.

Lyric held his gaze silently, then looked down to the red coat she held. She still wished to hold back her explanations of the visions, holding to her rule that David must come to his revelations on his own. But it was difficult, more than difficult, to see him so tormented. She looked up to catch his troubled glance with compassion, then reached to press a cupped palm to his face with a tender gesture.

David caught her wrist and brought her palm to his mouth, planting a grateful kiss in the softness of its solace. "All that stuff about curses the museum woman told us. I saw it happen. I saw it all right before my eyes. The woman they dragged to that fire is a woman I've been dreaming about since, since . . ." David's voice faded away. "Then, when she looked up to the balcony, I finally saw her face. Plain as day, it was your face, Lyric." A patter of raindrops peppered the dust in a whirl of clawing air.

The door to the house banged back and forth in the wind, as if it were frantically calling them inside. The daylight had gone flat and green. The gale twisted and pulled at their clothes. Lyric clutched the red coat to her chest in both hands, to keep it from the greedy talons of the wind.

David's voice was firm again. "I'm sorry; I can't believe it. All this is just too much to take." He held her shoulders as if to anchor him in the maelstrom of wind and emotion. "I owe you an explanation. I can't bear the responsibility of causing one woman's death in this life, much less in a past life."

His voice rose over the howling of the wind. "My wife died because of me. That's a hard fact I can believe. I couldn't save or protect her." The wrenching sadness of his admission brought tears to Lyric's eyes. "Lyric, you've got to understand. If I am Dante, I killed Sarah, killed you, too.

"It's too much, too much." David stepped closer to Lyric and looked deep into her darkly sad eyes. "Can't you see that?" He embraced her with all the desperate longing that all his guilt and logic could not disguise. Heart to heart, the length of his body molded to hers. Droplets of rain sprinkled down, driven by the wind, stinging like icy bees. The drops speckled her blue blouse and soaked into her hair as if to quench its life-flame color.

David's fingers slid beneath the back of her blouse and the flat of his hands pressed the warm skin at the small of her back. Her vibrant life trembled and burned into his palms. He threaded his fingers into her wildly blowing hair. With a great handful, he pulled her head back to look into her eyes, so enlarged with passion and sorrow they seemed black as his. Lyric's hands held the woolen coat between them, unheeded in the chaos. Lightning crashed with a roar, and Lyric flinched tighter into his embrace.

David leaned down to press his lips upon hers. His whole body began to tingle. Lights sparkled before his eyes. He squeezed his eyes shut tighter and breathed in with a deep shudder. . . .

He opened his eyes, and saw the sweet face he was looking down on was the face of Sarah, warm, alive, and in love with him. He smelled the flowers in her hair, the smoke in the room. She was looking back at him, about to speak.

The light was warm, flame lit, not a stormy day, but a night scene. "Welcome back to the arms that shall always love you." She stretched up to kiss him. He tasted the sweetness of time on her lips. "And when mine are not there, this will protect you from all the harshness of this world, so you will come back to me safe and unharmed." Sarah offered a beautiful new red coat with both hands. "It is charmed."

"It's beautiful, Sarah," he heard his voice say and felt the wool on his fingers.

"Promise me that you shall always come back to me." Sarah's voice trembled. "Promise me."

"That I promise with my very soul. We shall never be parted. You are my only love now, and throughout eternity."

"And I, I promise also, Dante," Sarah affirmed, looking into his eyes.

A blinding flash of lightning and crescendo of thunder ripped David from his vision of discovery. One of the mast-tall pines near the cliff fell smoking into the sea, its length shattered and charred. David released Lyric and staggered backward. Away from the coat, away from all the images that were fitting the last pieces into the puzzle.

"That's it. I don't want any more to do with this mystical, magical reincarnation bull." David stormed over to Lyric's car and yanked the door open.

"Oh, no!" Lyric's voice rose. A note of panic edged her voice. "You had a vision from touching the coat. There's nothing to be afraid of. Let me explain." She took a step toward him and reached out to touch his arm. Lightning flashed again, and again; then a deathly green calm fell. The rain grew heavier. They were in the eye of the storm.

"Sometimes dreams explain our destiny."

David spoke firmly. "I'm not afraid of anything. There's no way; there's just no way. I'm not Dante. I am not the person in my dreams and neither are you. I wasn't the cause of this woman's death."

Lyric pleaded with David for understanding. "I'm so sorry I couldn't explain this before. This was something you had to figure out for yourself. It's all part of your karma. The law of lessons. If you learn from these lessons you'll never have to repeat them."

"At this moment, I know all I need to know and want to know. Right now I need some serious space. I've had enough of all this curse and ghost stuff." David stooped to snatch the diary from the drive where it had slipped from Lyric's fingers during their embrace.

He was determined to exorcise any phantoms or shadowy spirits left over in his life. "Take the coat. Take the diary." He threw the articles into Lyric's backseat. "As far as I'm concerned, I never want to see them again. Take them back to your museum. Burn them. I don't care."

David's voice softened only slightly, "Good-bye, Lyric."

Lyric was rain-soaked. She looked so fragile and sad that for one moment he wanted to take her in his arms and beg her to stay. Forget everything he had just said. He really had fallen in love with Lyric . . . and Sarah. Maybe he could learn to live with all that weird stuff. Maybe . . . no.

"I'm really sorry . . . but good-bye." David stood and waited for Lyric to get into the driver's seat. He hated to see her go, but they came from two different worlds that could not be bridged or mixed. David thought he saw tears on her cheeks as she brushed past him getting into the car. He could not let her femininity melt his heart. He must be firm and stick to his convictions. Maybe they were only raindrops, teardrops by a goddess.

The trees writhed and whipped, and leaves flew like flocks of frightened birds. As Lyric's car disappeared down the drive into the tunnel of trees, the storm broke anew in all its fury.

How the dust swirled and danced in the great house, the fine house, Wolfton House. The electricity of the storm charged it, made it fly with joy. It was joyful, so joyful. It remembered the feeling, joy. The strong man was losing his strength, again sucked dry by the woman, that evil woman. But he, the dust, Wolfton, could feed on the fear and confusion of the man. The fear-feelings of strong things made him strong.

If the man stays longer, I will grow stronger, even without the blood of the little things. I can feed and make my prey fear more, a wonderful, horrible cycle of energy.

I will live, live forever, even as dust. They will not unite, I can feel it. The dark man was weak now and would not unite with the woman.

The exultant dust devil whipped through the house. The bats in the attic wriggled in unknowing fear. Today many would fall to the floor, strange little husks, soon to turn to black powder, even finer than the dust on the wind.

Chapter Twenty-three

Lyric drove home in a blur; a blur of teardrops, raindrops, and a shattering feeling her destiny was beyond her control. The storm was settling into a fierce, pounding rain. Gusts of wind rocked the car. Grateful to finally arrive in her own driveway, she was hardly aware of the details of making the trip. She sat at the steering wheel watching the knifelike windshield wiper blades slice away at the cascading raindrops, then clicked them off.

The stormy weather matched her emotions. She was battering her chance at love in this lifetime against the unyielding rocks of David's doubt.

Lyric pulled the keys from the ignition. She wrapped the red coat around the small leather book and hugged the bundle close to her chest as she fought the wind to shove open the car door. The door was slammed out of her grasp, and she dropped her keys. The brass-and-silver ring disappeared into a deep muddy puddle.

She stooped to feel around in the icy water with her fingertips, probing for a feel of metal. She felt the keys connect with her fingers at last. She scooped them up, dripping muddy water, and turned to make her way to the house, head bent away from the gale. Her hair whipped wildly, lashing her forehead and cheeks.

The wind had smashed her fence gate back with such force that the gate dangled precariously from one hinge. Her beautiful proud flowers were bent and broken, almost completely flat in crumpled disarray. Nolan's pot of roses and ivy was nowhere to be seen, swept from its place on the steps.

Lyric battled her way up the steps of the porch, through torrents of wind and water. Large twigs and debris whirlpooled in the air and around her body. She felt so empty it would have been no effort for the wind to swirl her away into the black sky as well. Riddled with raindrops like buckshot pellets, the only pain she felt was a gaping emptiness, as though her heart had been torn from her body.

The wind jerked the screen door out of her fingers and flung it back against the wall with a violent crash. The upper hinge snapped and exposed the old screws to the downpour. Lyric fumbled with the slippery keys, at last managing to find the correct match. She tumbled into the hall on a great gust of wind, bringing in a shower of water and litter of leaves. She fought the oak door closed, and pressed her cheek against its security, the storm thrashing and howling like a cheated maniac on the other side.

Lyric was soaked to the bone with a chill of numbing sadness that steeped her soul. David Langston was undoubtedly the other half to her self. Was her soul mate really about to slip through her fingers?

Would the gods really allow that to happen?

David's gaze had dropped when he said good-bye, as if his eyes couldn't dare meet hers, couldn't dare take just one last chance on loving her. Devastated with heartsickness, Lyric felt completely void of any life force. She had aided David as far as she could without overstepping the boundaries of karma.

Now and forever. I am yours, as you are mine. The words echoed in her mind. Both Sarah and Dante had spoken the binding spell freely. Lyric knew a love that strong and pure could never die. For that love, they had suffered and died so many centuries ago.

Tears welled up again in her eyes as she recalled the ancient truth of the law that David must acknowledge who he was and come to her freely. There must be no pressure, no force. They had come so close, yet he had made his choice and now she must comfort herself. With time, she would heal as best she could. She would never be whole again without him, nor he without her. The sum of their union would be greater than the individual parts.

Shivering with a cold deeper than the iciness of the wet cloth that clung to her body, she stood in the hall and looked around her. She felt the familiar sanctuary she had created take her in. Here things welcomed her with no challenges. She was secure within these walls, accepted for who and what she was. If only she could leave the cruelty of the world behind as easily as she had slammed the door.

Leaning heavily on the door, she slid down despondently to the floor. Her restrained sobs finally burst through, racking her body with overwhelming spasms of grief. She buried her face in the rolled-up coat she still hugged tightly to her body.

She had been rejected on the most hurtful level.

This wounded more profoundly than anything that could come from a skeptical public.

A flash of lightning revealed Nolan galloping down the hall to offer his comfort. He took a two-foot lead and leaped heavily into her lap. Planting his forepaws on her collarbones, he let a loud meow of protest at her sorrow. Nolan sniffed her cheeks and rubbed his whiskers in her tears as if to take away her pain. Lyric knew he was aware of how thoroughly depleted and vanquished she felt.

It was good to feel the comforting vitality of his living energy. "I'm glad *you* still love me," Lyric whispered through her sobs, dropping the coat to wrap her arms around her familiar cat.

Nolan squirmed and freed himself of her soggy embrace. He pushed off her body and with three springs he was up on the stair steps, poking his head through the banister spindles. "Meow!"

Lyric looked up and sniffled, rubbing her wet face and dragging clinging strands of hair away from her cheeks. "What is it?" The charged atmosphere was obviously enlivening Nolan's supernatural awareness as well as imposing on her own. There were the first stirrings of the vertigo that announced a visit from her guardian voices. The top of her head felt light. For the first time in her life, she ignored the feeling, overwhelmed with the despair of David's rejection.

She wiped her face again with the back of her wrist and then spied a small towel lying askew on the broad seat of the hall tree. It must have been overlooked from the explosion of laundry the last time David burst into her life. She pressed the dry towel hard over her eyes with both hands.

David. Lyric felt a wrenching yearning for his searing touch. Only his heat would ever make her warm again. She remembered how he had held her to his body and mercilessly kissed her on the steps where Nolan was now beckoning her.

Nolan let out another plea that sounded as if someone had hit the wrong note on the bagpipes. He jumped two more steps upward and turned slightly to see if she was following.

"All right, I'm coming." Lyric followed Nolan up to the top step of the landing and into her bedroom. With one big leap he gained the top of the television and pawed downward at the controls.

"Honestly Nolan, I'm really not in the mood to watch a movie." She tossed the used towel down and tugged her waterlogged blouse over her head. It was as dank as a dead fish, clinging to her arms.

Nolan pawed the dial, claws scraping the plastic. His gold eyes were dilated and round as an owl's.

Not having the strength to deal with his insistence, Lyric reached to the remote control and clicked the set on to calm him. "There. Satisfied?" Local news flashed on the screen, with the fierce weather the lead story.

The clamminess of her clothes intensified her fatigue and sapped the heat from her body. She peeled off her saturated jeans and struggled with her clinging underwear, as the voice of the newscaster mumbled in the background. Nolan added a squalled comment now and then. Pulling her warmest robe from the closet, she wrapped herself like a cocoon from head to toe. Turning the down-filled collar up around her ears, she tied the belt tightly at the waist, trapping in whatever body heat she had.

Nolan continued to mutter and pace on top of the television set. Lyric got a big towel from the bathroom and swathed her hair, blotting the rainwater from its tangled length, then covered her head until nothing but her face showed. Still shivering, she was beginning to regain her composure.

The cat pounced on the foot of the bed and continued his restless prowling, tail lashing. "Calm down, Nolan." She caressed him briefly.

Piece by piece, she gathered her wet clothes and dropped them into the bathtub in a sodden lump. Every movement was an effort. A cup of tea would be so good right now, but she was too fatigued to go downstairs. Finally she crawled into the middle of the bed and pulled the agitated Nolan into her lap for additional comfort and consolation. "Come here, dear. Come be a good kitty."

Nolan yowled and wriggled, pressing on her thigh with his paws and butting her in the shoulder with his round head. "Poor baby. It's a bad storm, isn't it? Don't be afraid; we've got each other." She pulled him close.

The movement on the TV screen caught her distracted attention. Shots of rising water, floating cars, and downed trees were accompanied by excited narrative. Lyric clicked the sounds up enough to discern the newsperson's warnings.

"Electricity is likely to go off at any time. Everyone should take emergency precautions."

She heard the sirens in the background of the television, and heard them pass down her street again. The sirens. She knew David must be out in this ominous weather. Eyes closed, Lyric prayed, "Gracious Mother, protect this brave man. Wrap him in Your wings of light." She fervently envisioned David, his body wrapped and protected by a gleaming coat of protective white light.

"Highways are closed and only emergency vehicles are moving," the newscaster continued. The scene on the TV screen swept to the local marina, showing boats bobbing and tearing at their moorings. Many had been flipped and swept ashore. Upturned white hulls gleamed like dead tuna bellies under the brilliant glare of the TV lights.

"The speed and fury of this monster storm caught many off guard in the Salem area. A family camping in the nearby National Forest was separated by the confusion of the hurried evacuation of the park. All but one of the members of the family have been rescued and reunited. However, eight-year-old Deborah Maxime is missing in the storm. The weather is so violent the search and rescue units are unable to continue their efforts." The picture flicked black and shrunk to a pinpoint, then popped back into focus with a frying sound. The last thing shown before the power weakened was a close-up of the distraught mother weeping in the schoolroom used as a storm shelter.

The lamp dimmed and brightened, then dimmed again as the storm's power sliced through the atmosphere. Lyric just had time to roll off the bed and find the candle and matches she kept on her dresser before the house was plunged into darkness. It should have been a sunny afternoon, but instead was as dark as midnight and cold as October. The dark was emphasized by the repeated flashes of lightning that burned across the sky. In a pause between crashes, Lyric heard the sirens; the weather-warning sirens and the sirens of the rescue trucks trying to move in this fierce weather.

These East Coast storms had to be respected, but she had been through them before. She reached beneath her bed for the large flashlight and battery-powered emergency radio. No need to use the flashlight yet; better to save the batteries and continue by candlelight.

Lyric took the candle near the closet so she could find a sturdy pair of jeans and a thick sweater. She dressed quickly, feeling more ready to meet an emergency with clothes on. Rummaging across the top closet shelf, she felt the large red canvas backpack she was looking for. A touch to the outer pockets assured her the Swiss army knife was still there, as well as a small first-aid kit and a waterproof container of matches.

"Sorry, Nolan, but you just might have to take a ride in here," she addressed her reliable companion. Nolan sniffed at the canvas. The backpack would easily accommodate a few emergency articles, with Nolan snuggled on top, although it would not be his preferred mode of transport. She heard the sirens again, as if an ambulance had passed down her street; then the sound faded into the drumming of the rain.

"Downstairs; come on." She motioned for Nolan to follow her, turned, and quickly made her way down the stairs, backpack over her shoulder, flashlight and radio gathered under one arm, and candle held aloft. Nolan squeezed through the stair spindles to leap down and scamper down the dark hall to the kitchen. Lyric caught up with him at the sink cabinet.

To her dismay, there were no additional candles to be found. She scolded herself for not remembering to replenish her supply since her return home. The only candles that were left in the house would be her ritual supplies in the parlor. The little taper she had been holding chose this moment to gutter and die. Thunder crashed again and the rain hit the windows like fistfuls of gravel.

Nolan butted her and leaned on her legs, then bolted back down the hall, ducking into the parlor.

The dark meant nothing to his navigational skills.

"Please, Nolan, what is it? Stick close to me. This weather is too dangerous for me to go looking for you if we have to leave," Lyric called as she followed down the hall slowly, trailing her touch along the wall, still reluctant to use the flashlight. As she reached the doorway, a bolt of lightning and simultaneous crash of thunder rocked the house. Reflexively she fell to her knees, covering both ears, dropping her burdens with a clatter, gasping in surprised shock. The ozone smell from a near miss filled the air. Close, too close.

Gathering her things, she snapped on the flashlight switch and hurried into the parlor. This room was on the side of the house most sheltered from the wind, but the way the gale swirled and tore tonight, it hardly seemed to matter. Lyric dropped her pack and radio next to the biggest armchair. She found her raincoat and waterproof hat on the hall tree and brought them into the parlor, placing them on top of her emergency items. She curled into her big chair and stood the flashlight on the nearby table, then took the radio into her lap. As she adjusted the dial a few words could be made out of the hisses and static cracks on the emergency band. ". . . continued rain and high winds . . ." *Hiss, pop, crackle, pop* ". . . citizens should take cover if possible. High seas and rising . . ." *Buzz, pop* ". . . Park evacuation . . . child . . . search to be abandoned. Rescuers unable . . ." *Hiss, buzz.*

Lyric covered her eyes briefly in dismay and sadness; to be unable to help a lost child. Was David out there tonight, searching? She remembered the look on his face when he picked up the little girl who had cried, and knew the answer would be yes.

Aiming the puddle of light, she moved carefully

into the hall and picked up the damp red coat. The diary she had wrapped inside fell out with a small thump. Draping the coat across the chair opposite her at the hearth, she placed the book, still unopened, on the nearby small table. It would give her a focus for her jangling thoughts, a beacon for the dizzy swarm of voices that clamored in her head. It was a talisman for love and safety once; perhaps it would be again.

She huddled back into the comforting chair. She pulled her medallion out from under her sweater and pressed it to her lips, then to her forehead. First she felt cold, then feverish. She looked across at the coat and the book. It seemed as if Dante and Sarah were there in the darkness behind the chair, pleading with her. They wanted her to do something, but what?

She took this storm very personally, as if it held a message and purpose for her. Perhaps the storm was setting the mood for enlightenment concerning her and David. Weren't the lessons over for one lifetime? Hadn't she learned she couldn't force what wasn't meant to be? Wasn't that the lesson?

Energy crackled through the air, and her paranormal awareness heightened to an almost painful level. Power awakened within her, surrounding her. She felt a familiar humming that pulsed through her body, preparing her to receive powerful and important knowledge. Gooseflesh waved over her arms and legs in an eerie response to the atmosphere. No matter how exhausted she was, the feeling was a command to listen to her sixth sense. It could not be ignored. Connection to a higher plane was in order. It was demanded.

What was the lesson? She stared again at the coat, so dark in the dimly lit room. Not so long ago she had gathered it tenderly to her breast, eager for its messages. What was the lesson? She touched her medallion to her lips again. She needed to find out for certain. If David truly wished to be free of her, she must do her part to release the binding spell held within the coat, the talisman.

Lyric heard the hollow sound of wood toppling and creaking as it shifted and fell from its tidy stack in the mouth of the fireplace. Nolan put a paw on her knee and looked up at her, his great golden eyes luminescent in the flashlight's small beam.

"You're right." She stroked her fuzzy guide's sooty head. "A fire ritual." She knelt before the fireplace in the near-dark and stacked the dry splits of apple wood, using her sense of touch as guidance. Thick bunches of dry pine needles and pinecones would be kindling beneath the seasoned wood. It took some expertise to adjust the damper, with the wind whistling in the chimney, first sucking up and then blowing down. If the damper wasn't perfect, the smoke would be pushed right back into the room. But Lyric had dealt with this chimney and its idiosyncracies for years, in storms and in fair weather.

The metal box of long fireplace matches was in its accustomed place on the stone hearth. She struck a single match and carefully touched the pine needles here, there, here again. Tiny flames danced, then caught, giving a dimly flaring light in the room. Lyric snapped the flashlight off and let her eyes adjust to the friendly firelight. Its glow seemed to push the force of the storm away from the windows. The sweet clean smell of the pine needles and softly fragrant fruit wood soothed her senses as the fire licked rapidly into a small blaze. Lyric reached toward the heat, then pressed her palms to her face. Faintly,

faintly through the roar of the storm, she heard the sirens again.

Yes, this was a ritual for both her and David. He might never know or understand her intentions. Her protectiveness for him was deep and fierce.

Lyric pulled the small old chest she kept by the fireplace toward her. She flipped open the wooden top and began to remove her sacred supplies, used for her year-round rituals. Clearing a space on the central hearthstone, she pulled out the chunky, pure white beeswax candles, setting aside the special oils and incenses. She told herself to work faster, filled with a sense of desperate haste.

Yes, the sooner this was over the sooner she could get on with her life, and David with his. Her trembling fingers settled each thick candle on the sharp points in the middle of a flat silver holder. She arranged them in a triangular configuration on the white marble mantel. Impromptu articles would suffice to symbolize and pay homage to the different elements of nature, the basis of her worship. Sulfur stung her eyes and burned her nose as she struck a match on the rough gray strip at the back of the matchbox.

She lit the first candle and whispered with reverence, "For knowledge of the past."

The flame trembled, as if at first feeling her uncertainty; then it stretched up, leaping and doubling its winking light in the carved mirror tilted above the mantel. Lyric saw herself in the mirror, her face drained of color and her eyes strangely lit by the wavering flames. She pursed her lips to blow out the match, and glimpsed her face again in the silver pool of light reflected by the mirror. Tonight there was no time for mirror magic, no time for indulging in reflection. There was something waiting for her ahead and she must know what it was.

Wick to wick she lit the second candle from the first, saying, "For courage and strength in the present." The flame caught quickly and strongly. Lighting the final candle from the second, the last request was spoken in a voice stronger and more throaty. "For guidance in the future." Her voice resonated with her full, deep power. The flame crackled and popped, giving off tiny sparks as it caught, then flared brilliantly.

Lyric was taut with a sense of apprehension mingled with anticipation. There were answers to be revealed about David Langston, and she would know tonight; she could feel it in the energies in the air about her. One way or the other she would know if this man would be allowed to fit into her life.

The storm had become even more intense and whipped frantically at the windowpanes. The ravening wolves of wind howled at her doors, her windows, clawed at the cracks and made them sing in terror. Unchanneled rivers of raw energy surrounded her, pleaded to seduce her, called for her to surrender to their will.

Lyric ran her hands through her damp, tangled hair, pushing its disheveled weight away from her face. Her nerves hummed like the power wires in the gale outside. *Focus, focus*. Surveying her makeshift altar, she knew it would do.

Candles to represent the element of fire. The cascades of rain for water. A piece of petrified rock for earth. A mourning dove's discarded feather trembled in the drafts of the room, representing the element of air.

Lyric stood before her magic fire, no longer afraid of the power the storm unleashed on the rest of the world. She was ready to command its knowledge, to dominate its energy in order to understand the powerful link between David and herself.

Lyric raised her arms slowly and began to entreat the Goddess to hear her prayers. "Aradnia, goddess of the stars, help me understand the mystery, the link between David Langston and myself, between Sarah Morgan and Dante Huels. My heart is true and sure that David is my one true soul partner. Will he accept this truth in this lifetime? Are we meant to be separated for yet untold centuries, lifetimes to come?"

A moment of silence suddenly fell in the fury of the storm. For one brief moment, the wind drew breath and the rain paused. Lyric dropped to her knees before the fire and waited for her answer. The guidance of a higher power was crossing over to help her understand. Would it be too late? David had made himself clear; he wanted no more connection. To him it was over. But Fate was not satisfied with the choice. There must be a different outcome.

It began to rain again, heavier and heavier, a steady pounding on every exterior surface of the house. The small fire fluttered and brightened. Lyric's face became calm; she could feel the hands of her Mother, her Goddess, stroke her cheeks and hair. She bowed her head and closed her eyes. The sounds, the cares of life fell away to silence in the bliss of communion.

The beautiful voice that was no voice, soft and powerful in her mind, began the litany, the charge she had learned as a young woman.

Mine is the ecstasy of the spirit and mine is also joy on earth. My law is love unto all beings. Keep pure your highest ideals, strive ever toward them. Let none stop you or turn you aside. Mine is the secret that opens upon the door of youth and mine is the cup of the wine of life, the holy grail of immortality.

Let my worship be in the heart. Rejoice, for all acts of love and pleasure are my rituals; therefore, let there be beauty and strength; power and compassion; honor and humility; mirth and reverence within you.

You who think to seek Me, know that the mystery which you seek, if not found within yourself, you will never find it without. For behold, I have been with you from the beginning, and I am that which is attained at the end of desire.

Tears slipped from Lyric's eyes unheeded, tears of joy. A great peace fell upon her. It was as if her body were being stroked by a thousand soothing feathers of unselfish love. She felt the blessed vision begin to withdraw, and then the presence became stronger again.

Lyric, faithful daughter, a final word. You know now that what you seek will be given to you. But beware—

The vision shattered into a thousand, thousand shards as the front door burst open. Wind swept into every room of the house in a victorious burst. The candles went out in an instant, and the tiny fire scattered in a poof of ashes and sparks. Papers swirled around the room, and the mirror on the mantel rocked. Dark surrounded Lyric as if a heavy black blanket had been dropped over her.

The lightning flashed and thunder roared, revealing a tall figure in the doorway.

"Lyric!"

Chapter Twenty-four

"Lyric!" A whirling wind rioted through the parlor. Had the Goddess herself manifested David's form or was he really here?

"David," Lyric cried, scarcely aware of her voice. It was no illusion. He was standing just inside her doorway. The erratic flashes of lightning illuminated the reflective stripes on his rain gear, giving off a bizarre yellow glow. He looked powerful, wet, and wild. She rushed to him, wanting desperately to fall into his arms, to feel the hard reality of his flesh and bone pressed against her. He was real. Anxiety and frustration spurted through her. Electric energy of their own crackled between them.

"Lyric, I need you." David voice was hoarse and strained. Tension siezed her body like a hand.

Her heart lurched into her throat. She wanted to scream: Yes, she needed him, too. "Have you changed your mind about me?"

"No . . . no, Lyric." David shook his head, raindrops flying from his hair. "There's a child," he spoke in rasping gasps. He was dripping on her floor, clutching a yellow canvas raincoat like the one he was wearing. "We have to find her. She will die in this storm."

The sharp bold lines of his jaw and the contours of his cheekbones were cleanly drawn in deep contrasts of light and dark. The wind swept and circled around both of them as if they were two statues unable to move from nature's fury. The lightning flashed and his eyes gleamed in the unnatural light. Lyric was aware that anything boyish about him had disappeared. The movement of his full lips broke the illusion of a statue.

Lyric looked up into his eyes, searching for a meaning for his desperate appearance.

"The search has been called off, but I can't quit. You can tell me where she is. I know it. Will you help me find her? Please, Lyric, for the child's sake. Put aside the way you feel toward me and think about her. You are my last hope. I have to . . ." A strike of lightning and roll of thunder muffled his words. "I must find this child. I can't let go."

He had looked within and found a spark of the truth, she thought. He was reaching across that boundary and asking to link with her for a purpose. The uncontrollable wind swirled in her parlor with a supernatural life, trying to point her in the right direction to do what she must with David Langston.

She took a step toward him and held out her hand. She could not shirk her purpose in this lifetime, her responsibility to use her talent. "Do you have anything of the child's? Clothing? A toy?"

David nodded, and his dark, soaked hair fell across his forehead. Lyric wanted to brush the hair back from his cold, slick skin and soothe the obvious torment that was racking his body. He pulled a ragged shred of orange knit fabric from his coat pocket. She reached out, and his palm covered her hand, his wet firm fingers encircling hers for a moment with such a tightness she connected with all the sadness and responsibility he was feeling. Her heart filled her throat. She knew he had to save this child, for his sake and theirs. It was the component she had not figured into this equation of fate; the lost child. David's lost child; Sarah and Dante's lost child. This and this alone would redress the karmic balance for them.

As David released her hand she could barely stand to be set free. He was her lifeline and she refused to slip into that bottomless desperate black hole of loss. Lyric balled the fabric within her fist and brought it to her breast with a thud. She could feel the trembling commitment and fear of David's own soul within the fabric. He had held it so tightly in his palm, refusing to give up his search.

Lyric spread her fingers over the fabric, pressing it to her breast. The tattered scrap of the child's shirt was permeated with an intoxicating mixture of vibrations. The child's own aura mingled with the moisture from the storm.

Lyric's senses pounded in her head. She closed her eyes, concentrating, trying to visualize the child by using her third eye, her psychic eye. Suddenly the panic streak of fear she had felt when they were almost sucked away by the tide washed over her again. There was darkness, a feeling of falling, and fear, great fear. She heard whimpers, then sobs. What seemed a mile away was a ragged opening, lit by lightning, dazzling white, then black again. The sound of the sea was everywhere, roaring, pounding. A picture of a small frightened girl huddled in the back of a cave came into her vision.

"She's in our cave! She's not hurt, but her foot is stuck in a crevice." Lyric opened her eyes and saw David paralyzed in delayed reaction. He shut his eyes briefly, then opened them in relief.

"We hadn't thought to look there. Nobody knows about that cave but you and me." He shook his head.

"David, you must believe me. We must hurry!" She grabbed his arm urgently with both hands. "The tide, remember the tide. The water is pouring in; I can feel it." She shouted and shook his arm. "I know she is there."

"I'm in the rescue truck. We can make it."

Lyric ran back into the parlor and tugged the brass grate over the fireplace, hurriedly checking for any stray sparks that might have escaped in the blast of wind that had entered with David. "Hurry, hurry. . . ."

David took a few steps into the parlor and met Lyric in the middle of the room. "Lyric, I . . ." Words seemed to fail him. He held the oversize slicker up mutely.

"Save the talking for later." Lyric slipped her arms into the large coat, feeling his hands rest briefly on her shoulders. In the midst of this perilous time, it seemed natural for him to wrap her in his protection. No time to savor his touch; she grabbed her abandoned backpack. "Nolan! Let's go."

Nolan trotted to her feet obediently and looked up trustingly. "Hop in, sweetheart." Lyric held the big flap open, and the cat hopped in without delay. The flap fell loosely across the top of the pack. Lyric hoisted the heavy pack over her shoulder and glanced up at David. "You don't mind, do you? I can't leave him."

David's eyebrows knit in surprise at her question. He raised a shoulder and shook his head. Lyric heard the low growl her coat fabric made rubbing against David's coatfront as she brushed past him. The same noise could have willingly, easily come from her own throat under different circumstances. She hurried into the hall and grabbed her house keys from the hall tree ledge. Nolan popped his head out from under the loose flap, bobbing with her hurried steps. "I'm ready," Lyric said.

They rushed out into the full force of the storm. Lyric felt Nolan hurriedly retract his head and wriggle deeper into his snug sack as the rain hit them. David tugged the wooden door shut. The screen door had already ripped from its hinges and disappeared.

The powerful yellow rescue unit waited on the street, the brightness of the warning-light bar damped by gray curtains of rain. David grabbed her hand and they sprinted to the truck. Lyric gasped as sheets of cold water pounded her body.

Lyric clambered into the front seat and shrugged off the backpack. She tucked pack and cat behind her seat in a safe cubbyhole, then fastened her safety belt. "Your house. The cave." She looked at David and nodded, her whole body rocking with tension. "Hurry."

David crashed the truck into low gear, and they roared down the street, throwing rolling waves of water on each side of the truck. They passed blocks of darkened houses, and then were into the country. David snatched the radio and keyed the switch.

"Base, this is Rescue Unit Two." A burst of static sizzled on the speaker. "Come on, Base."

"Geez, Langston is that you?" Ben's concerned voice crackled in reply. "Listen, everybody's been called in. Nobody's on the street, nobody. Can you get to the station? It's too dangerous; come on in."

"Ben, I'm going out to Wolfton House, to the rocks behind it. Can you be ready with some backup?" David dropped the handset briefly as he wrestled the vehicle up and over a hidden curb to avoid a felled tree. Its branches covered a small car. Lyric caught the bouncing handset and pressed it back into David's hand as they regained the road.

"Wolfton House? Are you nuts? Get your butt in here!"

"Listen Ben, I can make it. I think I know where the child is. I've got to beat the tide. Can you give me some backup or not?"

Static spit and fried on the speaker again. Lyric heard snatches of excited crosstalk in the background before Ben's voice came back. "Yeah, we'll be right behind you, buddy. This better be a damn good hunch. Out."

"It is. Thanks, Ben. Out." David slammed the handset back into its place.

The drive into the country had never seemed so long before. The water already covered the road deeply in several places, and downed trees almost blocked the way as they neared the turnoff to Wolfton House. No houses were visible along the countryside, the storm having extinguished their usually cheerily glowing windows. The darkness enveloped the truck as if it were a tiny insect caught in a great hand.

When they reached the turnoff to Wolfton House, David paused. He raced the engine and peered down the drive. The tunnel of trees covering the driveway looked like a black, writhing wall, towering before the headlights of the truck. He swept his hand over his face and turned to look into Lyric's eyes. "You're sure?"

She wrung the scrap of cloth between her fingers. "Yes. Hurry, David, the water's rising. She's so scared."

David raced the engine again, and behind them Lyric could see the lights of the second rescue van blinking red and blue through the storm flashes.

"Can we make it?" Lyric leaned anxiously forward, bracing her hands on the dash. She could barely see past the windshield.

"We have to." David dropped the truck into a lower gear. The tires spun and whined as they lurched and lumbered down the sodden drive. They would trust the robust four-wheel drive and David's skilled driving to push them through. The headlights swept dully over the front of the old house, glinting off the windows briefly. David swung past the house and parked as close as possible to the lilac hedge that masked the cliff's edge. The old lilacs whipped and bent, their branches stripped almost bare by the gale. The booming of the waves and the rush of wind blended into the storm's fury, making a horrible cacophony of sound.

David and Lyric spilled out of the truck. Lyric followed his lead to the rear doors, uncertain of what she could do. David pulled the climbing safety harness from its storage place and strapped it on. The tough yellow polyvinyl climbing rope was in a neat ready-to-use coil. He splashed to the front of the truck and knelt by the front bumper, fastening the rope to the anchor of the truck's weight. He looked up at Lyric. The rain streamed from his face, flattening his hair, almost blinding him. He slapped on a helmet and snapped on the light fixed in the front.

"She's there." She held the scrap of knit twisted around her fingers.

David backed away from the truck, playing out the yellow rope as he went. In three steps he was through the battered hedges and poised on the brink of the cliff itself. He met Lyric's eyes and then dropped out of sight below the lip of the cliff.

Could she be wrong? He couldn't think about it. All he could do now was let the rope out slowly, feeling his way with his feet. The path wasn't there anymore; just a boiling, tumbling sea, sweeping up and in and out again as the tide rushed in like galloping, foamy horses. A wave slapped him, and for a heartstopping moment he felt his feet tread water, not rock. His eyes were full of water, and the feeble spear of light cast by the helmet light flickered out. He gripped the lifeline and felt his hands slide, slide down the rope in a sickening uncontrolled whirl.

Dangling, kicking, praying, he used every tactic his training had taught him to hold on and pull up and away from the tearing force of the wind and sea. The waves slapped him from side to side like a ball on a string. He fought, and managed to take a wrap around one palm, but then lost his hold completely. He flailed, gasping for breath, feeling himself falling away from the rocks and into deeper water. He choked and struggled for breath. *Please, one more breath. One* . . . The green water closed over his head, and with great calm, David realized he was going to die.

Then he felt . . . what, a hand? Warmth surrounded him, and strength poured back into his aching shoulders and arms. Lungs filled with air, not water. His hands were on the rope and feet firmly on the path as if he were walking down on a fine summer day. "Walk, David," a soft voice whispered, clear over the roar of the wind. "Walk in the light." Right, left, right, wade waist-deep over the little beach were he had made the ghastly slip of the tongue.

He ducked to get into the cave. Water already swirled on the cave floor. Far to the rear he saw a figure. As he came closer he recognized his wife, Margaret.

She raised a hand. "Now it's done, David. My chapter is finished. Let yourself be loved." She smiled, that innocent, young smile David remembered. It would erase forever the picture of her tortured death. "Good-bye."

From the back of the small area came a whimper. "Help me, Mr. Fireman, please?"

Seconds stretched into days as Lyric waited on the clifftop, watching the yellow rope slither into nothingness. She clutched the coat collar up around her face in a white-knuckled grip. How long would it take to reach the cave? Twenty seconds? Thirty?

Lyric couldn't tell if the tide had come completely up or not. The day they had almost been caught, it had streamed in as if from an open spillway. The water had ripped the quilts from her like a mad dog. Today the sea was so rough and waves so high in the storm, perhaps the cave would be filled even if the tide had not yet risen. But the spark still trembled in the cloth she held, an ember of life in the storm.

There were shouts behind her, and she whirled to see another rescue truck behind David's. Its light bar blazed, the red and blue lights soaking into the surrounding raindrops and mist.

Men rushed past her, the reflective bands on their

coats glowing from the headlight beams. A tall man in foul-weather gear—David's friend from the fire-house—grabbed Lyric by the shoulders and demanded, "Where is he?"

Lyric just had time to gesture toward the cliff, when she saw the man's face clear in relief. He pushed her away to hurry to help as David appeared at the edge, burdened by the limp form of a small child.

"Thanks, Ben. I knew you'd make it." David let his friend take the exhausted child from his arms. "She'll be OK." Ben rushed away to wrap the child in blankets and warm her. David was forgotten for now.

David remained kneeling, head bowed, panting with the exertion of the climb. He looked up to find Lyric standing frozen by the truck. He stood and slowly walked toward her. The red lights continued to flash and glare off the clouds like fresh blood billowing in water, until the sky glowed an eerie red.

Lyric looked at David through the still-pounding rain. The lightning flashed and thunder shook the clifftop where they stood as he took her face between his hands. His palms cupped each side of her face as he looked down, half shouting to her and to himself.

"I believe!" The vow still on his lips, he sealed his mouth on hers. Kissing her hard and deep he reached for her soul, tasting her tears of joy and release in her eager lips. Her body ached for more and leaned into his as he pulled her close, a shelter against the storm. He kissed her with the passion of the hurricane that raged around them and she felt a remembered heat such as she had never felt in this lifetime. It spread from the heart, moving like an avalanche through her veins, devouring and banishing the numbing cold she had felt so long and thought she would never escape.

"Yes, I believe!" He held her close, one hand spread across her wet hair, pressing her head beneath his chin. "How could I not?"

With a crash like a whistling cannonball, a brilliant flash of light fell from the clouds to smite Wolfton House. The lightning danced over the ridge of the roof and down the corners, outlining the great house for one last time. The house burst into flame in an explosion of dazzling glare against the darkness. Glass flew outward in sparkling diamond shards. Another strike and a branch from a heavenly tree of light ignited the life-sucking brittle entity that enprisoned and embodied the evil Wolfton himself.

Rolling puffs of flame erupted through the shattered windows. Whining shrieks like faraway sirens rose from the house, loud enough to be heard where David, Lyric, and the fire fighters stood. The fire fighters stood in awe of the sudden, powerful display. Even they had never seen anything like it. It burned like tinder. Even in the rain, how it burned. David kept his arms around Lyric and they watched the flames, as Wolfton, perverse to the end, burned in the wetness like St. Elmo's fire.

The malignant house had been like the sirens of old, luring Lyric and David to the rocks in hopes of taking their lives and souls forever. The black waters of the abyss lost this time. Ageless, timeless love had protected them both. Love woven, freely given. As they held each other tightly, David and Lyric watched Wolfton House and all its evil cleansed by fire.

"Langston, I'm sorry but we can't do anything about the house. It's too far gone." Ben stood at their side, watching the flames consume the skeleton of the mansion, which blazed like a funeral pyre despite the rain. "God, I've never seen anything go up so fast." The roof collapsed, taking down the hated balcony in a cascade of sparks.

"It's OK, Ben. Let it go. I want it to."

As they watched the cremation of Wolfton's crumbling existence, Lyric felt the malevolent influence dissolve. The remains of Wolfton's obsessive love and hate decomposed in the cleansing combustion of the flames. A final gnarled finger of electricity touched one of the still-standing chimneys, shattering it into dust and sparks quickly quenched and swept away by the rain. The bolt left a lingering, charged smell of divine intervention in the air.

"Destroyed!" The voice shrieked above the roar of the flames.

"I am undone, it is true. Foiled. Vanquished by love stronger than me, stronger than evil itself." For a trembling moment, the bitter shade of Wolfton stood in the fire storm of his blazing house. He raised his fists with a scream of anguished defeat, and then faded, faded to ash that scattered away, never to come together again.

A final pitiful cry rode the wind, piercing their ears, and then sharply dwindled away. Wolfton's trapped soul was at last free, released from Sarah Morgan's binding. It faded, alchemized, neutralized, and dispersed with the smoke into the endless damnation of nothingness, oblivion.

As Wolfton was damned to eternal loneliness, David and Lyric could find the blessing of reunion, as the souls of Dante and Sarah were able to fulfill the promise of eternal love. Enveloped within David's embrace Lyric felt that she had truly, finally come home.

Chapter Twenty-five

Finally home.

David kissed her at every pause along the way. He seemed loath to break the connection with Lyric. As he wrestled the truck through the rapidly dying storm, he restlessly alternated from gripping the steering wheel to pressing her hand tightly. He reached to stroke her thigh throughout the journey back, as possessive evidence she was his. With each touch, heat raised under his palm and surged through her body. There was only one way this tension could be, would be, vented.

David pulled the truck behind Lyric's car, creating a great tidal wave of muddy rainwater. Lyric snatched Nolan's carrier from its storage place. The house was dark, as was every house they had passed on the street. The electricity was still out, darkening and silencing the town. The furious lightning and thunder no longer flashed and rolled so often, but the rain poured steadily. They splashed up to the porch and flung open the door. As soon as the backpack hit the floor, Nolan struggled out and streaked for his hiding place under the bed upstairs.

They shucked out of their wet slickers and dropped them on the foyer floor, unheeded. Seconds were textured with urgency. The smell of fear, blood, and evil was replaced by the potently sweet smell of desire.

They stood panting, their eyes locked, awareness flowing between them. David swept his fingers through his wet hair. His eyes smoldered with the intensity of the experience on the cliff. Lyric could hear the primitive drumbeat of her blood pounding in her ears. She would not deny her heart any longer. She felt her senses spin a glittering web of captivating tension as his eyes swept her body and rested at her mouth.

David took her face in both hands and stepped close. He smoothed his thumbs across the contours of her lips, then ran his forefingers across her cheeks. Her lips parted and she caught his finger with her teeth. Running her tongue around his fingertip, she tasted the salt of his skin and gave a quick tug of suction, then release. He was real, no longer a dream. She saw the dark stirring of passion in his eyes. As he melded his body to hers, Lyric yielded to the bold intrusion of his tongue and felt his blatant signal of desire. Hungrily, she savaged his mouth with relentless craving. He was hers and she was his, and she must anchor herself to him now. Rough, bruising kisses filled her mouth as he connected deeper and deeper with her soul. As she welcomed and met each kiss, she had never felt so whole or unbelievably free. She felt unshackled and ready to love him with rampant fierceness, to become part of him, to be one with him. His kiss was timeless, endless, as if she were falling into a great black hole. Eyes closed, she saw sparkles like diamonds spread loose across blue velvet as he kissed her again and again. Raw passion was all that would sate the hunger Lyric felt prowling throughout her body.

David yanked her sweater over her head, tossing it into the darkness of the hall. Her bra followed. Slippery rain-cold fingers fumbled with unfamiliar buttons.

"Are you as quick getting out of your clothes as you are getting into them?" Lyric asked in a throaty whisper, trying not to tear his shirt off his body.

He gave her a wry smile and showed her. His clothes followed hers into the oblivion of darkness down the hall. Her eyes widened and she cried out at his beauty. Lightning splashed his naked body with dangerous illumination. Light spilled around the sculpted muscles of his torso, hips, and aroused masculinity. He looked like cast metal, shimmering silver and dark bronze. His shaft stood thick and tall, powerful. Magnificent.

She kneeled down and took him greedily into her mouth while he shivered and gave a whispered gasp of pleasure. Her fingers explored him with a deft, sensuous touch, cupping the weight of him in her palms. A groan of approval escaped his throat. His musky, compelling male scent hit her nostrils. Even his smell was familiar.

"Not yet." His voice rasped as he straightened her up, forcing her to wait. Anxiety plucked at her taut inner strings. "I need to taste you."

The sharp edges of David's teeth nipped at her earlobe, then bit at the tender skin of her neck. The restrained pressure balanced rapture and pain, causing her to squirm in exquisite torture. The wet denim of her jeans dug with maddening precision into the plumped layers of flesh between her legs.

His wet mouth continued its downward path. Her nipples ripened to hard nubs, attentive beneath his suckle. The day's growth of beard prickled and scratched the tender skin of her breasts. He grazed his cheek across her delicate flesh and sent a twinge of painful pleasure across each beaded nipple.

Blood soared unbidden and beat an insistent tattoo of impatience within her sex. She felt the familiar twinge of release, of slippery welcome as her body prepared for his fulfilling entrance.

The adrenaline rush of crisis she had felt throughout the emergency was overlapped by another wave of a much more tumultuous kind of excitement, the kind that made rough and frenzied coupling necessary.

He lifted her up onto the seat of the hall tree, raining kisses on her stomach, and bent to peel off her wet jeans. The warmth of his ragged, moist breath washed her with feverish anticipation.

"Every inch of you," he murmured. He seemed so very in control and aware of his effect on her, but his need was reined in only for the moment. How much longer could he stand it? Lyric shifted from foot to foot, steadying herself on his shoulders as she kicked free of the last bit of restricting clothes.

His fingers combed through her auburn down and across the crescent birthmark. The massaging pressure from the heel of his palm brought a Cheshire cat smile to her lips. Fantasies of him touching her, tasting her, loving her had never been this good. This was vivid and this was real. She cried out as he slid two fingers deep into her. She rocked against him and let out a long hum of pleasure. Slowly,

slowly, then faster in circles until she was poised on the threshold of euphoria.

He turned her around so she saw her own face in the dark mirror. She caught her breath sharply as the softness of his mouth pressed moist kisses to the sensitive back of her knee, up her thigh, and over the curve of her bottom. His kneading fingertips plowed deeply, so pleasurably, into her skin.

Contrasts of pressure, between front and back, inside and out, made her deepest muscles ripple involuntarily. Spasming waves unfurled the tension he had built inside her. David turned her again and worked his way around the swell of her hip and back to the smooth patch beneath her navel.

His hair brushed her stomach as his head descended and the tip of his hot tongue flicked against her. She shuddered and convulsively clutched his wet, thick hair. He licked again, slower. Running his rough palms up her thighs, he cupped the tight orbs of her buttocks and lifted her from behind. Burning inside, Lyric wrapped her legs about his powerful hips to draw him closer. She was desperate for him, ready to race and ride with him to the peaks of oblivion.

"Every inch of you." She acknowledged her desire. Need broke through his dam of restraint. Clearly he could wait no longer. With a lift and quick turn to the right, David settled her with breathtaking force upon his rigid length, pinning her against the front door.

Thrusting deep and hard to quench her heat, he seemed to touch her backbone. Curling tremors of ecstasy spiraled through muscles awakened by his filling her. Hammering strokes pounded out the frustration of centuries of separation. David shimmered with unharnessed wild energy. It was as if their passion had erupted into flames, flames of rapture. As the wood grated into Lyric's back she felt only ferocious, barbaric satisfaction. Mindlessly, she raked her nails into David's back, as feral noises came deep and thick from both of their throats.

They were at the invisible point of completion where the circle ends and begins, seamlessly, again. The next level of the spiral began, tightening and drawing them upward and together into the next level of consciousness. She tightened around him as she rushed into her climax like a high diver cleaving water from a great distance. He followed her instantly with his own explosive release. She heard herself call his name before feeling the last of the sparkle bounce from the walls of her deepest channel.

"Lyric," David purred with the resonance of a lion satisfied by its mate. He rubbed his face against her neck, sighing deeply.

Still clinging to his hips, she ran her palm down between their bodies to feel their point of union. She laid her head on his shoulder as he turned and carried her effortlessly into the parlor.

Lyric felt a lazy, involuntary smile spread over her face. Reluctant to let go, she let her legs slip down across his hips and shakily placed her feet back on the floor. He gave a crooked smile and she felt his long lashes brush her cheek before he kissed her lips softly.

She sank down, pulling him to the floor with her. David crouched before the hearth, raking through the ashes to find a few dim coals still alive. Carefully he coaxed the remains of Lyric's prayerful little fire into new life. Tiny crackling flames cast an amber light into the dark room, making the shadows dance away into the corners.

The rain fell softly now, a purling hum against the windows. The fury of the storm had been abated and the hushed, healing rain smoothed over the ripped branches and crushed flowers outside. The storm had made its point, and Lyric had served its purpose, her purpose. The lightning had ended, at least outside.

As she lay back and watched David, she remembered. The heavy smell of smoke, the sweet taste of love; she knew they had done this all before. The comfortable feeling of deja vu washed over her, welcomed her home.

The wood hissed and popped. The room smelled of fragrant apple wood and clean rainwater. A log shifted and settled with a softly hollow clatter, shooting sparks onto the hearthstone. David lit the three white candles she had left by the fireside when she rushed away to help him. The room was awash with softly intimate light that flowed over him, highlighting his chiseled features. Lyric wet her lips and drank in the silhouette of his face against the flickering glow. Yes, David was the one. Dante.

As she ran her eyes down the curve of his back, her attention fell on the red wool laid over the arm of the nearby chair. She took a deep, thoughtful breath, rose to her knees, and picked up the bundled coat reverently.

David shifted his weight on the balls of his feet and turned fully toward her.

"David, you've shown me that I should never doubt my talents or destiny. You've proved that you believe in me." Still loosely hugging the coat, she looked at the flames, then at him. "I can prove to you I never had a spell or hold on you." She raised the charmed clothing and prepared to offer it to the fire. "I never manipulated your free will."

"No!" David cried out and caught her wrists. "No one, Lyric, could have been more careful in this. You tried and tried to show me, without influencing me." He shook her gently to make her comprehend. "It was me. I had built such a wall of guilt and superstition around me. It is my choice to be with you, the same as it was then." He took the coat away and laid it aside. He pressed her hands to his lips, then held them closely to his chest. "I believe, Lyric." Leaning forward, he kissed her gently again, "I'll always believe."

His eyes fell on Wolfton's diary, the little book of sins and scores. "Lyric, the coat stood for everything Dante and Sarah loved. The book is the symbol of Wolfton's hate. This is the last evil influence that stands between us."

He opened the leather book and crumpled a fistful of pages, ripping them from the binding with a vengeance. He threw the damning memoirs into the hungrily crackling fire and offered her the book to do the same. Lyric tore pages from the ledger of death and let them dance in the flames.

Smoke rose as the pages browned and turned to ashes. Together they each held an edge of Wolfton's book of shadows and tossed in the remains of the captain's obsessive love and hate. David and Lyric watched all the evil that had touched them or stood between them decompose in the flames, neutralize into nothingness.

"His evil will never harm us again. This coat is a symbol of how everlasting our love is." David picked up the coat and spread it before the fire.

Lyric's hair had dried around her face, making an auburn halo. David wound one of the small ringlets of curls around his little finger to make a love lock. "You're so beautiful," he whispered. He nipped at her lower lip, pulling it gently, then kissed her fully. "Tonight I come to you in perfect love and perfect trust, with my heart, body, and soul." He spoke the words he remembered so well.

"This is my token to you." She took the gold chain from her neck and slipped it and the medallion over David's head. Touched beyond words, he pressed the still-warm medallion to his chest, then reached toward her.

He ran his fingers down the inside of her arm with a feathery touch. He tugged her downward onto the red blanket of timeless love. They lay intertwined, stretched before the soft warmth of the fire. "For the past three years—"

"Since your wife's death?" Lyric interrupted softly.

"Yes, since my wife's death, I seem to remember a poem. I only now realize what it means."

"What is the poem?"

"At first I thought it was something corny that I'd probably read somewhere like vacation Bible school when I was a kid. My guilt helped me dredge up those old feelings. But now I understand." He drew her closer to his body and grazed his lips across her forehead.

"What did the poem say, David?" Lyric asked curiously.

"'*If I do not have a spark of love within me,*
Then I will never find it outside me.
Love is the law and Love is the bond.' "

"What do you think it means?"

"That I have been bonded to you all along. Since before time began. You are my love of past, now and forever. I had to look within myself to find my other half. You." David sealed his pledge with a kiss. "I love you."

"I love you."

In fluid harmony, their bodies cast dancing shadows about the walls in a ballet of love made upon a coat woven with deathless devotion.

Epilogue

Lyric tiptoed her way through the sea of flowers to the center of the rioting plants. Where once not even the most thorny of weeds would grow, purple and yellow velvet pansy faces now crowded and beamed up at her. She glanced back toward the cliff and saw David napping peacefully in his hammock. Up and working since dawn, he had earned a break from the intense construction of their new home. It was as if he had a deadline he could not miss.

Nolan and Embers stretched in the shade beneath the slowly swaying hammock. Three kittens, one orange, one black, and one tricolored calico, pounced and prowled in the weeds, earnestly practicing their newfound hunting skills on the agile grasshoppers.

"Sweet dreams, my love." She blew a kiss on the wind toward David. Turning her attention back to the bed of flowers, she kneeled gingerly, mindful not to crush any leaves or delicate shoots. Her bare knees sank into the fluffy earth. She gently waved a buzzing bumblebee away from her ear before the clumsy insect became tangled in her hair. She drank in the tangy smell of the rose geraniums and sweet star lilies mingling on the breeze. To Lyric, this was the beautiful smell of spring, of new beginnings.

As they turned and prepared the dirt for planting, the soil appeared dark and lush, full of nutrients, alive with wriggly fat earthworms. David and she had intentionally planted the acorns in the center of the once-burned circle, challenging the earth to bring the nuts to fruition.

They ringed the seed with rounds and rounds of purple pansies for friendship and thoughtfulness, bright yellow marigolds and vivid scarlet geraniums for protection, elegant purple irises for hope, gaily striped fuchsia and white star lilies for purity and joy, and broad-strewn wildflowers of every color to fill in the gaps. The charred dead spot was transformed into a fountain of color and fragrance, pulsing with the vibrancy of life. Butterflies and hummingbirds fluttered and drifted across the banquet of blossoms.

The silky petal of a star lily stroked across Lyric's cheek as she crouched close to a single wobbly green sprig. Like a triumphant arrow quivering in a target, it clung to its position of victory. It had taken weeks for the tender young sprout she had been nurturing to make itself known and push its way up and out into the light.

Not three inches off the ground it was. Lyric crouched, eye to leaf. "You've fulfilled your promise, little acorn," she whispered. The delicate leaves, tinier and softer than a fairy's ear, trembled at the touch of her breath. Lyric smiled and tears welled in her eyes. As the seedling's roots reached out and took anchor, grasping and claiming life, she felt her own womb quicken.

"Thank you, Blessed Mother," she addressed the clear blue sky. She had not dared to hope or believe it was true, but now she was sure. The flowers bloomed and flourished, the sign the harm and evil done there was really purged. The land was cleansed and life could thrive again, filling the void death had created.

But this, this was the last sign she needed. The child had brought them acorns and now the acorns had brought them a child.

"You will grow into a strong and mighty majestic oak, a brother to our daughters." Lyric patted the earth about the base of the tiny sapling. The gritty soil felt warm and alive beneath her palms. "Where else could life begin except from where it ended? This is the circle where we shall begin."

Lyric stood and brushed the brown dirt from her knees. A butterfly landed on her wrist, flicked its golden wings, and took back to flight. Smoothing her palm over her tummy, she looked back at David.

"Let's go tell Daddy he needs to finish the nursery first."

Dear readers,

I hope you enjoyed *Flames Of Rapture*. I would like to take a moment to say thank you for choosing my first book to spend magical time with. I am very excited to be offering a romance with a New Age slant.

Reincarnation fascinates me; we live and relive our mistakes and triumphs in order to learn the lessons of life. The ultimate lesson is building the perfect love.

I know, deep in my heart, that love truly never dies. The love of Lyric and David was reborn in the embers of *Flames Of Rapture* to become a blaze once again.

If you are enthusiastic about seeing more romance with metaphysical and paranormal elements, please let me know how you feel, or even what you would like to see more of.

Your opinion and thoughts are very valuable to me. Write me at P.O. Box 17191, Memphis, TN 38187 (SASE, please, for reply and autographed bookmark.)

Sincerely,
Lark Eden